Empires: Infiltration

GAVIN DEAS

To Simon Spanton, for giving me a chance

Copyright © Gavin Smith & Stephen Deas 2014

The right of Gavin Smith and Stephen Deas to be identified as
the authors of this work has been asserted by them in accordance
with the Copyright, Designs and Patents Act 1988.

First published in Great Britain in 2014
by Gollancz
An imprint of the Orion Publishing Group
Carmelite House, 50 Victoria Embankment,
London EC4Y 0DZ
An Hachette UK Company

This edition published in Great Britain in 2016
by Gollancz

1 3 5 7 9 10 8 6 4 2

A CIP catalogue record for this book is available
from the British Library

ISBN 978 1 473 21674 7

Printed in Great Britain by Clays Ltd, St Ives plc

www.gavingsmith.com
www.stephendeas.com
www.orionbooks.co.uk
www.gollancz.co.uk

Chapter One

Weft Prime, Mid-Fifteenth Century

The Pleasure Mindship just appeared in Weft space. It was less than five light minutes from the planet. The Weft name for the planet was a complex excretion of fermions. The Pleasure knew it, simply, as Weft Prime.

The Mindship was already reconfiguring as it returned to normal space-time. It went from looking not unlike an iridescent conch shell to a shape that suggested insects and drills. It was an altogether more war-like shape. They had arrived this far out because they had detected the presence of a significantly-sized nickel-iron-cored asteroid family that could provide them with the raw materials they required. It had the secondary benefit of giving Weft Prime at least twenty minutes warning. Twenty minutes to contemplate the error and futility of resistance. Twenty minutes to live in fear and wonder at their punishment.

The main asteroid in the trinary family was a monster, a little over five hundred kilometres in diameter. The Mindship mated itself to the asteroid. It began to infuse the basalt crust with picotech; the atom-sized machines permeated the olivine mantle all the way to the core and began to rework the structure of the matter at atomic and molecular levels. The Mindship sank into the rapidly transforming asteroid.

Missile-shaped growths sprouted from the rapidly transforming matter and launched themselves at the two 'moons' that made up the remaining bodies of the asteroid family. The other rocks were significantly smaller, the largest having a diameter of no more than twelve kilometres. The missiles disintegrated as they impacted, seeding the two smaller asteroids with uncountable picotech machines. The machines immediately began to transform the matter of the 'moons' as well, fuelled by mining the latent background energy of the universe. It was the same fuel that powered all Pleasure technology.

Massive sub-light engines grew from the rocks and burst into life as they began their rapid acceleration to .5 light speed. Meanwhile, the main-body asteroid continued its transformation to a massive modular capital ship, growing weapon arrays and batteries, drone craft and autonomous intelligent missile systems. The Pleasure was capable of much more advanced technology but the thing about punitive expeditions was that the victims had to understand what was happening to them. In terms of technology, there had to be a common reference point.

*

2

The sub-light engines had continued growing out of the transformed war craft on nacelles. At the end of the nacelles the engines turned at one hundred and eighty degrees, reversing their thrust, bringing the massive capital ship down to a manageable combat speed. Or rather, a combat speed manageable for the main body of the Weft Prime main system fleet that was accelerating towards them. They were currently one light minute from the planet.

Transmit the inevitable destruction of their fleet to the planet? the Face wondered, aiming the question at the Enforcer.

There were only the two of them; there were only ever two of them. Their transformations had been complete moments after the ship had finished riding the wave of contracting and expanding space and emerged from the protective warp bubble generated by the ship's monstrous mind. They had shifted from their protean form, required for their previous expedition, and into the form of primal Weft. Their new forms, like all their forms, had been designed to engender awe in the subjugated aliens. They could never, however, mimic the complex exotic matter and entangled quantum states of the Weft's shadow-selves. Some races the Weft had encountered had come to think of the shadow part of the aliens as their 'souls', though the Weft themselves scoffed at such mysticism. Their only god was cold hard maths. It was, however, this shadow-self, this somehow natural link to the universe itself, that was causing the problem – from the Pleasure's perspective, anyway. The narcotics that the Pleasure had introduced and then dealt to the Weft resulted in the addict being separated from, and the eventual death of, their shadow-selves. Soul destruction. The Weft had fought back.

The Weft were a tall, almost spindly, humanoid race with leathery skin. They made some of the other races they had encountered, in their explorations of the surrounding star systems, nervous. Mostly because of the way that the air behind them seemed to shift of its own accord. Their fixed rictus grins, a peculiarity of the physical composition of their cadaverous faces, didn't help either. When a Weft communicated verbally, they did so through gritted teeth.

The Enforcer nodded in answer to the Face's enquiry. He looked like one of the Weft, only larger and much more powerfully built: a warlike proto-Weft from a semi-mythic past. In as much as the Weft had a mythic past. They would prefer to think of it as a not yet-fully-understood past.

I still think that planetary destruction will send a message to any other recalcitrant systems, the Enforcer thought.

The Face mused that Enforcers always thought that planetary destruction was the way forward. A physical form had been more difficult for the Face. Faces normally chose to look like the idealised form of beauty for any given race they were in contact with. The closest the Weft had to a concept of beauty was a mathematic ideal of proportion and distribution of facial features. The Face, however, couldn't see it. To his mind he looked the same as every other Weft.

What recalcitrant systems? the Face enquired. *Everyone loves us, we give them what they want. That's the whole point.*

***

From the Weft Fleet's perspective it must have looked like the three transformed asteroid warships had just exploded as they launched drone crafts and missiles. Each craft or weapon was a tiny pinprick of light against the backdrop of space and the distant pale light of the K-type main-sequence star.

A few moments later the Weft fleet reciprocated. In time measurement, there hadn't been much of a delay – but in distance it would be telling.

Oddly tranquil, the Face thought. It was a private thought. A skin derm snaked up from the now Weft-like tech of the Mindship. The Face had made the ship synthesise what he felt would be the most appropriate narcotic for the one-sided battle. He wanted to enjoy the beauty of it. He knew the Enforcer would be taking something altogether more savage.

Then the missiles and drones met. Space lit up. The Face was overcome by it all as the custom narcotic took effect. A tear rolled out of one of his eyes.

Music. We must have music.

Drones attempted to intercept missiles, which in turn blossomed into hundreds of sub-munitions. Beams of light connected the fast-moving unmanned craft to tiny explosions, as their AI systems predictively targeted where the sub-munitions would be after the tiny amount of time it took the lasers to reach their targets.

It was one-sided. The Pleasure weapons were faster, smarter and more durable. They quickly reduced the Weft's drones and missiles to a fast moving debris field and the majority of the Pleasure's sub-munitions continued towards the Weft fleet.

With a thought, the Enforcer triggered another barrage of missiles and launched another flight of drones from all three craft. The two smaller satellite ships in their mini-fleet lost sufficient mass for them to visibly shrink as matter was transformed into the new drone craft and munitions.

By now the Pleasure's initial barrage was in range of the Weft fleet. The light from the fleet's point defence batteries seemed to reach out slowly for the sub-munitions. The AI systems on the sub-munitions used chaos manoeuvring to counteract the Weft's predictive aiming. The light of their engines created fractal patterns with their erratic manoeuvring.

As they closed with the Weft, more and more of them were taken out by laser or railgun defence systems, and missile-based scatter-shot countermeasures. Some of the missiles made it through. Light blossomed as fusion warheads detonated against armoured hulls. Some of the smaller craft started to come apart but the cruisers, battleships and carrier ships were more than capable of withstanding the damage.

The slower, remaining sub-munitions and drones launched by the Weft – the few which had made it through the countermeasures – closed with the three Pleasure craft. The mass of each craft diminished again as they launched a protective cordon of satellites grown from their hardened hulls. Their predictive targeting was more than a match for the on-board AIs of the Weft weapons. Light stabbed out and the Weft missiles and drones ceased to be. There were tiny explosions against the hull of the Pleasure ships as they flew through the debris fields. A few of the sub-munitions made it through, or rather were allowed through; neither of the Pleasure operatives wanted the Weft to understand just how one-sided the fight was just yet. They might give up, and that would make the footage less interesting. Even now they were transmitting to Weft Prime on a carrier wave designed to hack the security of the Weft infoscape and transmit what was happening to every comms device on the planet and in orbit. Weft Prime would start receiving a minute after the initial contact had begun.

They're not using much in the way of tactics, the Face commented.

What could they do? They know we have the technological advantage. We're only three ships and they have to close with us as quickly as possible. Our superior speed means that we would be long gone before they could manage to manoeuvre into any kind of advantageous position, the Enforcer answered.

We don't seem to be using much in the way of tactics either.

The Face picked up on a feeling of irritation from the Enforcer. The feeling had the context of a person of violence exasperated with the lack of knowledge of a gentler soul.

We don't need to. This is a demonstration of power. We should give away as little information on our true potential as possible. As the Enforcer thought this, arrays were growing from each of the three craft. The arrays would require even more power than the energy weapons, even more than the initial transformation of the raw matter of the asteroids into combat-capable spacecraft.

Predictably, the Pleasure's weapons were in range first. Space warped and burnt as focused particle beams and fusion lances reached across the distance between the two fleets. The weapons fired with rapidity and incredible accuracy. They were slaved to the ship's powerful mind. The particle beams and fusion lances weren't aiming to pierce the hulls, though they often did, or to take out the enemy craft's engines. They were making a hole. Fire, reacquire and fire again. Point defence system after point defence system went down as the Pleasure ships' barrage whittled away at the Weft fleet's defences. They left the fleet's main weapons, however, untouched.

The Weft fired their ship-long, cold-fusion reactor-fed laser cannons, their plasma-firing sun lances and their own, less powerful, focused particle-beam weapons. With a thought the Enforcer switched on the array. Had any been close enough to see, their perception of the ships would have warped, an optical illusion caused by the ships being enveloped in a protective energy shield.

The Weft's beam weapons hit. Light, particles and plasma fire played across the shields in a complex visual display reaching into many spectrums. The Pleasure ships flew through the firestorm unscathed.

Then the Pleasure's second barrage of sub-munitions and fast moving drone craft hit the considerably less well-defended Weft fleet. Hulls were ruptured by the force of fusion explosions. Others fell apart, victims of matter de-cohesion warheads.

I'm going to take out their orbital defences, the Enforcer thought. The Face nodded absently.

They had been receiving constantly updated information from their planetary scans for the last eight minutes. They had enough information for the ship's mind to predict where the orbital defences would be by the time their munitions reached them. Half a metre thick, by two metres long, pointed rods of hardened, molecularly-bonded diamond, the munitions left the mass driver racks at .7 light speed. They had to be careful about what they aimed at. They could skim and even pierce the atmosphere but, if a sufficient amount hit the planet itself, this demonstration would become an extinction level event.

The Weft fleet was now, mostly, a rapidly expanding debris field still moving at its original velocity. The Enforcer gave the Mindship the order to finish off any surviving craft almost as an afterthought. Lightning played across the energy shields as debris from the Weft fleet impacted against them.

We must always look as gods, the Face thought.

The ships accelerated to .5 light speed again. It would take them less than two minutes to reach Weft Prime now.

The first the crews of the orbital defence platforms knew of the attack was when footage of the one-sided fleet engagement overwhelmed their comms net. They barely had time to register the incoming mass-driven hardened diamond rods before they impacted in a ring around the planet. Multiple hits at such speed all but disintegrated the weapons platforms. The Enforcer had been careful to program the ship not to fire on any platform over the planet itself but the rods skimmed across, or in some cases just through, the atmosphere on the dayside of the planet to hit platforms on the nightside. The few Weft remaining on the surface of the planet were treated to the view of the sky catching fire from multiple entries.

Just over twelve seconds later the three Pleasure ships slowed to combat speed. The two unmanned asteroid craft separated from the capital ship, heading towards the planet's two polar horizons. The capital ship further reduced its mass by launching more missiles and drone craft. Then it commenced firing its energy weapons. The night side of the planet lit up from missile contrails, interception and drone craft engines and energy weapons fire as the Weft responded. It was over in moments. Erratic sub-munitions and beam weapons took out platform after platform, while countermeasures and point defence systems destroyed the Weft's return fire. The shields took care of the energy weapons fire and whatever sub-munitions got through their defences.

On the nightside of the planet the two smaller, unmanned Pleasure ships were completing their planetary pincer movement. They were significantly reduced in mass as they erred on the side of overkill, launching more drones and missiles than they could ever possibly need. Then they too raised shields, and began firing their energy weapons as the return fire washed across their protective fields. In moments the planet was rendered defenceless.

How many, the Enforcer asked?

The Face gave it some thought. This saddened him. If having a 'soul' was better than what the Pleasure offered then so many of the Weft wouldn't have turned to their wares. *And for what,* he thought privately? *A life of toil masquerading as a race-wide effort at exploration and scientific research.*

The Face checked with the ship's mind. They had uploaded all the data that existed on the planet. This included accurate population census information.

Decimate them, the Face suggested.

The Enforcer started loading target information on a tenth of the population to the smart, seeker munition templates as they grew from the ship's hull.

***

His name had once been a complex particle excretion. That was back when he'd had a shadow self. Back when the higher part of him had been intrinsically linked to existence. Back when he could hear the background music of the universe. Now that was gone. Once the most promising physicist of his generation, he was now little more than half a person, an animal in the eyes of his peers. Now they had to address him verbally, or he needed a particle translator to understand them. Now they simply called him Dal because they needed to make a noise to get his attention.

Addiction should have been the end of his career. The narcotics provided by the Pleasure had caused his shadow self to rot away, as it had done with so many other Weft across the systems they had colonised. Then the dreams had come. Terrifying things. Visions that appeared in his mind like a violation when he rested. To the Weft there was no such thing as a sub-conscious. It was only through the Weft's contact with other races that Dal had even found out about the concept of dreaming.

The visions were showing him how to build something, an array. A machine capable of aping their naturally entangled state. Normally, the death of the shadow-self meant expulsion from the upper-echelons of the science caste, but when the Weft on Prime had risen up and killed the Pleasure's Juicers – enhanced slave warriors created by the Pleasure from the Weft's own science-military forces – the Weft knew that the Pleasure would react. They would have to, in case other species decided to follow the Weft's lead. The science council became desperate. They had listened to him. Spurred on by the visions, he had not only managed to create the array, but he had found a way to both power and protect the device. There would be a cost. At some level, Dal appreciated the irony. Since he had lost his 'soul' he had become a better scientist.

Now all they needed was some time. The footage of the destruction of the Weft fleet, the footage of the fire in the sky, and the destruction of the orbital defence network, all suggested that they did not *have* the time. Dal spared a glance up at the array as he rapidly gave the control systems verbal instructions. He knew that hundreds of miles beneath him injectors were adding more fuel to the planet's burning core. To get this right they would need to harvest not just the core's current energy but as much of the core's potential energy as they could force out of it.

All the screens and comms devices that had been showing the battle playing out in force and light thousands of miles above them suddenly switched to a figure of the Pleasure's spokesperson. Not for the first time Dal admired the mathematics of the Pleasure's fake Weft physiology. The creature started to speak in the Weft's verbal language.

'The demand in Weft systems for our products proves that what we supply is what you truly want. You are not attacking us, you are attacking yourselves, your own desires, but there is a price to pay for declaring war on commerce.' Then the screens went blank.

'Raise the shields,' Dal whispered to the control systems, cursing the slowness of verbal communication. There was an audible hum. Dal knew that the electromagnetic forces involved with the coherent energy shield would probably give them all cancer, but that didn't matter now. What mattered was the countdown. The amount of time they had before the ridiculous amount of energy required for the shield drained the cold fusion reactor dry. What mattered was whether or not they had enough time.

***

The Pleasure's capital ship, along with its two main ancillary craft and their many drones, had engloballed the Weft home-world. The bright ruby red of high-energy lasers, and the white light of fusion lances, stabbed down from orbit to the surface of the world. Tight, focused beams burnt deep into the crust of the planet and through the molecularly-bonded composite walls of the shelters that the majority of the population were hidden in. They weren't large holes. Just big enough for the smart bullets to travel through. Bullets programmed with the names, DNA and electro-chemical signatures of a tenth of the planet's population.

The Weft watched helplessly as their friends died, as their mates died, as their younglings died. There was no panic. The Weft didn't panic. There was just great sadness and a feeling of helplessness.

***

Something's wrong, the Enforcer thought. The Face glanced over at him quizzically. Information on two of the Weft who had been sentenced to die appeared in the Face's mind. *They live.*

So?

They shouldn't.

The Face reviewed the data. Both of the living targets' smart bullets had encountered some kind of barrier. Even assistance from lasers and fusion lances fired from orbit hadn't helped.

Let them live. Two do not matter. Nobody will know they were targeted. It will not affect the lesson, the Face thought. The Enforcer looked less than convinced.

They should have nothing that can stop the smart bullets. This is defiance.

Are they in the same place?

The Enforcer nodded. *I'm launching a seedpod.*

The Face gave the mental equivalent of a sigh.

***

Each Pleasure operation had their favoured Juicers. Normally a template taken from the warrior caste of one of the worlds they had subjugated. These warriors were then addicted to and controlled by chemicals. They were also chemically and technologically enhanced by their new masters.

The Pleasure's capital ship fired a modified smart munition much larger than the smart bullets. Fusion lances stabbed down from orbit to cut a hole, clearing a way to the barrier that two of the smart bullets had found. The seedpod was surrounded by a corona of fire as it made entry. It fell through the planet's polluted atmosphere. It travelled through the glass-lined tunnel of fused earth, made by the fusion lances, into a large cavern that had been extensively reinforced and armoured. In the cavern was a heavily armoured, dome-shaped structure. Two counter-rotating arcs spun around the dome structure, apparently generating the energy field that was protecting the building.

The seedpod exploded like a sporing fungus. The picotech template seeds started feeding on the surrounding matter, transforming it, allowing the Juicers to build themselves. They were a silicon-based life form. A machine race. They had reached the singularity and their biological creators had transferred their consciousness into machinery and turned their back on flesh and biology once and for all.

Then the Pleasure had come, providing them with narcotic software programs. They had traded the programs from a nihilistic species whom they had provided with necrotising pleasure virals. The virals had led to that race's eventual extinction. The narcotic software had soon enslaved the machine people.

They grew from the floor, the wall, the roofs and the supports of the cavern. They dragged themselves and their weapons free of the birthing matter, weakening it as the Weft security force responded.

In their weaponised form, the machine Juicers' silicon skins were razor sharp. Just brushing against them opened flesh. Their personal defence shields sparked as rounds from Weft firearms disintegrated against them. Lightning arced from the shields to hit those who got too close to the Juicers. The Weft soldiers hit by the lightning exploded into lumps of steaming, cooked meat.

The Juicers brought their railguns to bear. Their shields flickered, modulating with the railguns to let the rapidly firing hypersonic rounds out through the flickering energy fields. The hardened diamond rounds tore through the Weft's armoured vehicles. When the diamond rounds hit the combat armoured Weft themselves they yanked them off their feet, and tore them to red ribbons of flesh. Their advance was inexorable. With every step they drew more raw matter from the ground beneath their feet to harden into diamond ammunition. Their shields drew from the latent background energy of the universe to power them.

The machine Juicers painted the cave with Weft blood. The shadow-selves of the dead security force dissipated into nothing or were fed upon by the Juicers' energy demands. Soon the Juicers were the only 'living' creatures in the cavern outside the shielded dome. Above the Juicers' heads two of the smart bullets orbited the structure.

***

I don't like this, the Enforcer thought. *We were supposed to have taken the sum of all their knowledge from their systems and yet there's no reference to this facility in even their most classified data.*

Well, they must have systems in the facility, the Face thought.

The Enforcer spared him a glare. *It's an isolated system. The shield is protecting it.*

Even from a hard transmission? the Face asked. The Enforcer nodded. *They shouldn't have the tech to do that.*

***

The shield went down. The machine Juicers advanced.

***

The Mindship invaded the now unshielded facility's systems. The Enforcer and the Face had to search themselves for the correct emotional response. They were more likely to inflict horror than feel it. It took less than a moment. The same amount of time it took them to both simultaneously order their drone fleet to concentrate fire on the facility.

***

Nuclear fuel was dumped into the planet's core, forcing it to achieve critical mass.

Dal watched one of his co-workers die. Hit by some projectile, his body spraying blood, he was dead before he hit the ground. Dal activated the array, and then his smart bullet found him.

***

The array drank the energy of the exploding core of the planet moments before the explosion engulfed the facility. It used the energy to create an infection of entanglement in all the force-carrying particles between the matter energy of the planet and the matter energy of the Pleasure's Mindship. There was an immeasurably small moment of connection, matter and space distending. Then the array shared the energy of the exploding core of Weft Prime through the connection, distributing the destructive energy through every force-carrying particle. Everything in the entangled connection, including the Pleasure ship and a significant amount of Weft Prime, ceased to be.

***

The Pleasure Consensus met through the medium of their Mindships. Each pair appeared to the others as they wanted to be seen. Either in the biological – or otherwise – forms appropriate to the species they were currently dealing with, or in their idealised beatific or nightmarish thoughtforms.

They need to be wiped out. This attack sets a precedent. It was an Enforcer. His thoughtform was red and silently screaming.

That to harm us you must destroy yourself? one of the first-conscious Faces asked.

Now they know we can be harmed, another younger Face pointed out. Its fear was obvious even in its adopted arboreal, quadruped form.

We have nothing to gain in war. Let us leave them in peace, the elder Face thought.

They will think us afraid, the silently-screaming red Enforcer thought.

I don't care what lesser species think of us. Besides, this is not how we fight. The people we conquer defeat themselves. The Weft have had a taste of what we offer. They will want more.

Chapter Two

.78 Light Years from Formahault, 25 December, 0951 (GMT)

'Reconfiguring,' he said. He had decided on the male sex of the species. He had chosen Rex as a name because it meant king, which was a form of ruler. He was slowly transforming from the massive invertebrate body of his previous job into his new form. He had to admit that he found the aesthetics of the new form considerably more pleasing, though he suspected he would struggle with just how primitive they were. He had chosen a composite form pulled from a number of human mythologies. He was just short of seven foot tall, athletically built. He had hair like spun-platinum, six arms and his skin was just a few shades lighter than midnight blue. Rex knew that he looked exotic and beautiful.

What are you doing? the Enforcer enquired.

'I'm reconfiguring physical forms for the new venture.' As Rex said this the Mindship was changing form as well; liquid was drained and transformed, as the humidity was leached from the air. The dense, swampy foliage receded into the ancient craft's superstructure. The Enforcer was taken somewhat by surprise, as he still had the form of a large and particularly cerebral-looking slug.

I can see that, but why are you making that noise?

'It's the main language they use on this planet.'

Really! Verbal communication? Again! How tedious. The Enforcer retracted his pseudopodia, as the Mindship uploaded all the information they had on the next world they planned to visit into his mind.

'They have an excellent selection of swear words,' the newly self-named Rex offered by way of consolation.

The Enforcer was understanding the conversation purely conceptually; he had not assimilated the language yet. He was less than pleased when he discovered that this species had many languages. He watched the Face's transformation, unmoved by the apparent beauty of his partner's new form. Beauty was not his business.

'Have you chosen a name yet?' Rex enquired.

The Enforcer happened on a term. It came from the planet's already existing drug culture. It would work as a street name, a criminal *nom de plume* of a type he'd used on other worlds. It also amused him.

'Bad Trip,' the Enforcer managed as he grew a mouth and learnt a language.

Rex understood the reference. The Enforcer had been one of the first to be born fully aware. His new name referred to his birth.

'I swear I had the kid dead to rights. I was staring at him down the scope, watching him dial the number, and this stupid fucking Rupert wouldn't give me the go-ahead.' Collins wasn't completely pissed but there was a certain stagger in his steps as he walked down the path at the edge of the river.

'What happened?' Shaw asked, probably pretending to be interested. He'd heard the story of why Collins had decided to bin 2 Para and go through special forces selection before. The other, equally inebriated, trooper was more intent on finding this mythical kebab van that Collins had promised. A kebab van where the doner kebabs actually tasted of lamb, to hear him tell it.

'Well, what do you fucking think happened? Boom. Nothing left of the kid or anyone else in the street.'

Shaw gave the story some thought.

'So the moral of your story is that you joined the Regiment so you could have more leeway when it came to slotting kids?' Shaw asked.

Collins turned to glare at his friend.

'No, that's not what I'm saying at all. I'm talking less oversight. I want to be able to make the right decisions based on what's happening on the ground right there and then ...'

'So what do you think City's chances are then?' Shaw interrupted, clearly already bored of Collins's military philosophising.

'What? No, don't change the subject you bast—'

23

'Evening, gentlemen.' The figure stepped out onto the riverside path in front of them. It was dark, his face was in shade but he was powerfully built, though he moved with an easy grace. He wore a suit that looked too expensive to be worn wandering around on this side of the river at this time of night.

Suddenly Collins and Shaw felt a lot more sober. By habit both of them checked their surroundings. Collins turned back to the newcomer whilst Shaw kept an eye out around.

'Can I help you?' Collins asked warily. Bumping into people in Hereford who guessed at what he did for a living and wanted to test themselves was an occupational hazard. Despite growing up hard on a Liverpool estate, where you either fought or were prey, his subsequent training always had him trying to travel the path of least resistance. Polite but firm.

'Corporals Martin Collins and Lewis Shaw, you are both serving members of the SAS and have seen active service in the conflicts in both Afghanistan and Iraq.'

Suddenly both the SAS troopers were very much alert, despite the alcohol in their systems.

'All right, you could have found out our names and guessed the rest,' Collins said, though he had to concede he'd got lucky with the rank.

'Would you like me to recite your active service records or just describe the missions you ran into Pakistan, Iran and Saudi Arabia?'

Both of them stared at the man for a moment and then Shaw went back to checking their surroundings.

He was even checking the other side of the river for concealed shooters.

'Don't know what you're talking about,' Collins said.

'Yes, you do.'

'If I did, d'you think this is the place I'd have a cosy little chat about it? You Box?' Collins asked, using the slang term for MI5.

'No.'

'What do you want?' Collins said, enunciating each word carefully, as if he was speaking to a child.

'Well, I'm going to kill you unless you stop me.'

Bad Trip stepped forward. He had finally chosen a face. It was heavily lined and somehow managed to be blunt, thuggish and predatory at the same time. He had thinning grey hair tied back into a ponytail, and a scar that ran in a C shape from the top of his head to his jawline. He had cut the scar into his skin himself. He had wanted to experience the nerve endings of his mock human flesh. He had cross-referenced the psychological databases on humanity to try and create a face that was the physical manifestation of the concept of malevolence.

'Look mate, just fuck off will you.' It was Shaw who finally snapped, as though there was something about the figure that bothered him. 'If you know who we are, then you know we're more bother than we're worth to fuck with, yeah?' But Shaw saw no fear in the other man, just an eagerness.

And when the path of least resistance doesn't work? Collins wondered. There were a lot of clever things you could do in a street fight if you were quick and well trained enough. However a lot of people who had experience of real fighting swore by punching the other guy really hard, ideally on the bridge of the nose. Collins moved forwards quickly, his left fist shooting forwards in a jab. The other man just stepped back, out of range.

Collins kept coming. Bad Trip kept moving. When he had to, he just pushed the SAS trooper on the shoulder or the elbow, using the human's momentum to keep him off balance. He had downgraded his combat abilities to make the assessment fairer, and to allow for the amount of alcohol he'd watched the two soldiers consume. Even allowing for the drink Collins's attacks were aggressive, schooled, accurate, fast and powerful. He suspected that this fight would already be over if the soldier had been fighting a normal opponent.

Bad Trip ducked under an elbow and drove his fist into Collins's rib cage. He stopped just short of breaking any ribs but the force of the blow picked the human up off his feet and sent him flying through the air. The SAS trooper hit the ground hard, badly winded. The path had been too narrow to realistically allow Shaw to attack as well. Bad Trip had reduced his sensory awareness to give the two human soldiers more of a chance. Even so, he'd heard the movement of the weapon being drawn. He could smell the gun oil.

'Something of an escalation isn't it, Corporal Shaw?" Bad Trip all but whispered as he looked up into the barrel of the Sig Sauer P226, 9mm handgun.

'Jesus, Lewis,' Collins managed as he gasped for breath.

'Get up Marty,' Shaw said. 'We're going to go,' he told Bad Trip. 'And if you try and stop us, I'm going to fucking shoot you, okay?'

'Okay,' Bad Trip agreed and took a step towards Shaw.

'Woah! Do you think I'm fucking around here mate? I said I will shoot you!'

'And I agreed.' Bad Trip continued walking towards them.

Shaw's SF warrant card allowed him to carry a concealed sidearm, even when off duty – but, permission or not, he knew how serious firing it would be, particularly as he was going to kill this man. There was just something about him that made the corporal very uneasy. Frightened him, if he was being honest. He kept coming. Shaw fired twice, both centre mass, and then raised and fired once more at the man's head.

The personal protection shield activated by instinct; lightning played across it as the first two bullets disintegrated. Bad Trip dropped the shield. The third bullet caught him dead centre in the head. He slowed down his perception. He felt it move through his head, felt the degradation of his current form as the bullet destroyed the meat in its path.

Bad Trip watched Shaw's eyes widen as he kept coming. He appreciated the accuracy of the human soldier's fire, particularly as the man was un-augmented. He was also impressed that the human was holding it together in the face of this exciting new experience.

Shaw was squeezing the Sig's trigger again when the scarred man tore the slide off the pistol and it fell apart in his hand.

'You'll have to do better than that,' he hissed as blood ran down his face.

Shaw dropped the disassembled pistol and stepped back. The folding knife's blade clicked into place as he drew it and lunged at the scarred man.

Bad Trip swayed to the side, pushed Shaw's wrist hard, moving the blade away from him. The human realised that he was in the fight of his life now. He hadn't hesitated, he'd just gone after him with the blade. Bad Trip recognised the human fighting style, a mixture of generations of received special forces wisdom, mixed in with a knife fighting form called Kali. The knife was coming at him from a number of different angles. Shaw was using his other arm to either cover the body or make distracting strikes.

Bad Trip heard the other blade opening, felt Collins shift from his position on the ground and stab at his leg. Bad Trip brought his left leg up high, stepping over Collins's blade and then kicked out at Shaw with the raised leg. The kick was rudimentary but so fast and powerful there was little Shaw could do about it. The kick picked the SAS trooper up off his feet and sent him flying through the air. Bad Trip brought his leg around rapidly and tried to stamp on Collins but the other soldier had rolled backwards and onto his feet, bruised ribs notwithstanding. Bad Trip continued spinning around as Collins lunged at him with his knife.

Too late, Collins realised that he'd made a mistake as Bad Trip grabbed his wrist, locked it up and then bent it so hard that the radius and ulna snapped and the ulna shot through the human's skin. Even screaming, as Collins looked at his arm spurting blood, he tried to draw his own Sig, clumsily with his left hand. Bad Trip had seen enough. The test was over. The alien grabbed Collins's gun first, drew it and shot the SAS trooper twice in the stomach. He watched Collins's already pain-filled eyes widen as he did so. He wanted to know what the human felt. Collins staggered back, spitting out blood before collapsing to the ground.

Bad Trip reached out behind him and caught Shaw's wrist just as the other SAS trooper was about to plunge the blade into the back of the alien's skull. Bad Trip swept his leg up and kicked Shaw in the side of the face, powdering the bone, spinning him around before he sank to his knees, drooling blood and dribbling teeth.

Bad Trip took a leather pouch out of the breast pocket of his suit. He unzipped it and removed the stainless steel syringe. He could do this himself, manufacture and exude the chemicals and picotech required to create a Juicer from his internal systems, but it was all about the props after all. He leaned down and injected the entire syringe into Collins. Alien chemicals and technology flowed into the SAS trooper's system; it started to transform him, augment him, make him a slave.

Bad Trip stared at the empty syringe and then replaced it in the leather pouch. He heard groaning from behind him. He turned to look at Shaw. The human soldier was trying to stand though his eyes wouldn't focus. Bad Trip stalked over to him. The flesh on Shaw's face made way for the alien's fingers. Bad Trip lifted the human up by his face. This time the chemicals and the picotech flowed from the alien himself. Props and theatrics. May as well get into character, even if there was nobody around to see. Though he was aware of sirens in the distance.

Finally, Bad Trip dropped Shaw just as he saw flashing blue lights reflected in the darkness of the river. He started walking away from the sound of the sirens. Shaw and Collins fell in behind him.

Chapter Three

Dagenham, 5 May, 0320 (BST)

He counted the ways in which using the river as an approach was a mistake. Firstly, while approaching sub-surface would provide concealment, the visibility was so bad that they were relying on a transponder placed by an intelligence asset to even find the warehouse. *Never mind the warehouse, we'll need the transponder to find the north bank of the Thames,* Corporal Noel Burman thought.

Secondly, they were fighting the current all the way. They were going to be knackered by the time they got there.

Thirdly, sneaky though they may be, egressing the river up to the warehouse would leave them more exposed than he would like.

In short, Noel was of the opinion that this approach had been chosen because their new boss was over confident about Operation Kingship, and felt that the joint Metropolitan Police's Serious and Organised Crime Command, or SCD7, and Special Boat Service operation was little more than a training exercise. In short, the boss felt that they needed to return to their frogmen roots.

Surrounded by muck, kicking hard to swim upstream and barely able to see the transponder tracker strapped to his wrist, Noel felt there had to be easier ways. It was not that he was looking for an easy life, far from it, he just felt that, when you were dealing with a heroin trafficking ring that intel claimed started in the poppy fields of a Taliban-controlled area in Afghanistan, erring on the side of caution might be a good idea, particularly after the fiasco at the ice rink in Brixton with the Special Reconnaissance Regiment. Apparently one of their lads had gone nuts and had a blue-on-blue, a friendly fire incident. *Still, if you want something done right,* Noel thought, *don't ask the army.* It was nonsense, he knew – the SRR were a very capable outfit, which recruited from the ranks of the SBS – but a bit of inter-service rivalry never hurt anyone.

He all but swam into one of the supports. The warehouse they were hitting jutted, slightly, out over the Thames. He counted his four-man patrol in. Then he pulled each of them close enough to see him signal that he was going up to take a look.

Noel broke the surface of the river. He'd flipped the night vision goggles down over his mask. He looked around, seeing the surrounding area in green, and saw nobody. He looked up at a rusted ladder that led to a wooden platform on the river side of the warehouse. He watched for a while, breathing quietly through his regs. The rebreathers they were using wouldn't make any telltale bubbles that would give away their position. He had already checked his dive watch. They had five minutes, more than enough time. He sank below the surface again.

***

Beckett and Goddard surfaced first. They had removed their rebreathers, and weight belts, and attached them to one of the supports to be recovered later. They had wrapped their legs around one of the supports to hold themselves steady in the water. The only parts of them that broke the water were their heads and their MP5SD sub-machine guns. The integrally suppressed SMGs had condoms covering the barrels to protect the otherwise waterproof weapon from submersion.

Beckett and Goddard covered Noel and Dolton as they rapidly made their way up the ladder. At the top, Dolton covered Beckett and then Goddard as they made their way up the ladder. Noel made his way across the narrow platform to the corrugated metal of the warehouse's external wall. He knelt down, training his MP5SD at the door. Moments later, Dolton and Goddard joined him. Goddard took up a position on the other side of the closed door. Beckett lay down on the edge of the platform, concealing himself as best he could in the absence of cover, watching the river-approach.

They were in the shadow of the ugly collection of fuel tanks that was the Barking Reach Power station.

The lights of Thamesmead were reflected in the river from the opposite bank.

Dolton began attaching the det cord to the warehouse door. To Noel's mind, Dolton was your stereotypical laddish marine, a Yorkshire lad, from Hull. A nice guy and a loyal, if occasionally irritatingly boisterous, friend. Loud though he might be in the pub, on the job he was as quiet and professional as the rest of them.

Dolton slid the detonator and unspooled the wire connecting it to the trigger mechanism and then moved behind Noel.

'Echo actual to all Echo call signs, report,' Sergeant Stanton's soft Highland accent came over the tac radio, quiet but clear.

'Echo-one, in position, over.'

'Echo-two, in position, over.'

'Echo-three, in position, over.'

Noel depressed the talk button on the radio but then stopped. He was watching the handle of the door to the warehouse slowly turn.

'Echo-four, hold, over,' he whispered over the tac link.

Opposite him, Goddard touched the hilt of the dive knife strapped to the breast of his harness. Noel shook his head. In this op they were basically acting as police and had the same rules of engagement. They were to subdue and arrest the drug traffickers. They could only fire if fired upon. Noel raised the MP5SD, placed the weapon's folding stock in the crook of his shoulder as he looked through the weapon's holographic sight. The sight superimposed a circular, reticle image where the bullet would hit the target.

The door opened. A large man wearing a leather coat and sporting a crew cut stepped out of the warehouse. He had a bodybuilder's physique. He let the door swing closed behind him and then started to reach into the inside pocket of his leather coat. He hadn't even noticed the three SBS commandos crouched down by the door. Goddard and Dolton were both covering the man. Noel was still covering the door.

'Armed police, get on the ground now, or we will fire!' Goddard said quietly, putting as much menace into his Geordie accent as he could. The man stopped, a packet of cigarettes half drawn from his jacket and glanced over his shoulder. If he was surprised to see the three commandos there he didn't show it. 'Now!' Goddard snapped as loudly as he dared.

It was surprising enough that a man looking down the barrel of three SMGs would make a move for a weapon. What was more surprising was that he managed to bring the weapon to bear. He only got the one warning. Goddard and Dolton both fired three-round bursts from their SMGs. The integral suppressors made the weapons sound like old-fashioned typewriters. The muzzle flash lit up the area. The man staggered back as six subsonic rounds impacted into his centre mass. Noel glanced round at the target. At first he thought the gunman was wearing body armour because he was still standing, but then he saw red spreading across the front of the man's white shirt.

Still staggering backwards, the gunman started firing. The noise of the unsuppressed rounds was appalling. The gunfire sounded wrong somehow. The bullets seemed to scream, like a jet taking off. He didn't even hear Goddard and Dolton fire again. The top of the man's head came off and his face caved in, turning red.

'Echo-four-one, we are compromised, one X-ray down, over,' Noel said over the radio.

'All call signs full breach,' Stanton replied.

Noel didn't have to say anything. Beckett was running over to join them as Dolton pounded the det cord's firing mechanism twice. The door might have been unlocked but this was about violence of action now. The det cord blew an oblong hole in the door. Goddard threw a flashbang in through the hole. All four of them turned away from the bright light. The noise of the explosion momentarily deafened them. Noel was aware of other explosions from inside the warehouse as the other three four-man patrols hit the warehouse.

Noel stepped through the hole the det cord had made into smoke. He moved forward purposefully, weapon at the ready. He was going as much from memory, the plans they'd studied, the mock-ups of the warehouse they walked through, as from his smoke-obscured sight. He didn't have to look behind him to know that Goddard, Dolton and Beckett would be following.

He twitched the weapon around, looking where he pointed the SMG, checking the corners, elevation. He was in a small corridor with windows on either side looking into the warehouse's office space. All the glass in the windows had been shattered by the overpressure from the det cord's explosion.

Noel knelt down and tossed another flashbang into the office to their right. Dolton did the same to the office on the left. Beckett and Goddard advanced past them, knelt down and tossed flashbangs into the two offices further down. He felt himself buffeted by the pressure from the four blasts in close quarters. Even through closed eyes, the phosphorous glare of the stun grenades leaked through, leaving him with pinpricks of light in his vision when he opened them again. The thunderous blast of stun grenades had left him deaf.

Noel stood up, pointing the weapon through the broken window of the smoke-filled office. He moved round to the doorway and booted the already battered door off its hinges as he entered. There was a figure in the office. Little more than a man-sized shape in the smoke. He couldn't hear himself shouting that he was armed police, telling the man to get on the ground. *Gun*, Noel thought. The figure was armed. Despite the battering the man must have taken, despite the fact that he had to be blind and deaf, so probably couldn't hear Noel's ultimatum, the man was swinging around with surprising speed and raising the weapon to fire.

Muzzle flash illuminated the smoky room. The man staggered back, then tried to bring the gun to bear again. Noel fired another three-round burst. The man staggered back again but still wouldn't go down. Noel shifted aim slightly. The third three round burst took the top of the man's head off.

Noel's hearing returned. The smoke burned the back of his throat and was making his eyes water. It took a moment for him to realise that the screaming wasn't human; it was the sound of the drug traffickers' strange-sounding weapons. Light appeared through the smoke as bullet after bullet tore through the flimsy internal walls.

Noel leant over the man and fired two more rounds into the mess that was his face. Then he turned and headed back out into the corridor. Ahead of him, he saw the smoke refract the light from more muzzle flashes. Over the tac radio he heard that they were encountering significantly more resistance than they had thought.

Goddard stumbled out of the office he had been clearing. His body jerking from impact. Noel watched in horror as Goddard's body fell apart. Churned up by the screaming high-velocity rounds. The destruction of Goddard's flesh looked much more like it had been hit with large-calibre machine-gun fire than by rounds from the small boxy SMGs the drug traffickers were carrying. Noel was aware of the eddies that the targets' rounds were making in the smoke, all around him.

More muzzle flashes from the office opposite. Long bursts that Noel recognised as suppressing fire from Beckett. Noel moved rapidly. More screaming and muzzle flashes from the weapons that had killed Goddard. Beckett had stopped firing. It had taken milli-seconds. Noel reached the corner of the office with the gunman in it. He could see the shape of the man turning towards him. He fired, a three-round burst to the head. He heard the screaming start again. Something hit his head. Then a jackhammer in his side. He was spun around into the other wall.

He knew he was dead. Blackness.

***

'Noel! Get the fuck up!'

More screaming. An acrid taste in his mouth. Something wet on the side of his face, pain in his side. Then it hit him. Goddard was dead, probably Beckett as well. Dolton knelt next to him, covering the door to the main warehouse area.

'This is Echo-four-three, Echo-four-two and Echo-four-four are down, repeat Echo-four-two and Echo-four-four are down.' It took a moment for Noel to realise that he was hearing it simultaneously because Dolton was talking over the tac radio. Dolton looked down at him. 'You good?'

Noel tried to move and found he could. His face was covered in his own blood, he was battered and bruised, but he could still move. He was lying quite far away from where he'd been hit. Over the tac radio he could hear the sitreps being reported calmly. More call signs were down. He translated this to mean more dead friends. There was more screaming from the traffickers' weapons. More beams of light cut through the smoke as more rounds flew through the office area. He looked at the door that led to the main area of the warehouse.

Noel got up, changing the magazine on the MP5SD.

'This is Echo-four-one to all Echo call signs. Suggest head shots only, repeat head shots only, over,' Noel announced over the tac radio. In close quarters battle they were trained to always go for headshots in case the target was wearing body armour. The powers-that-be had decided that would look bad on what was supposed to be an ostensibly civilian operation. 'Two to come out of office area, confirm.'

Dolton opened the door to the warehouse area, and both of them went blinking into the much brighter light.

***

Noel was looking at the back of another gunman who was firing up at the roof of the warehouse. There was a spray of red as Noel put three rounds into the back of the gunman's head. The man hit the ground. He took the scene in as he moved, searching for a new target. The warehouse was basically a large open space roughly square in shape. The office area was a structure within the larger structure of the warehouse, built against the back, riverside, wall. Opposite the office space was the main door. The door had buckled inwards as a result of a large breaching charge and having been driven into by an armoured Snatch Land Rover. In the centre of the warehouse was a large pile of hardened plastic crates. The crates were underneath a broken skylight. There were four lines dangling through the skylight. Hanging from two of the lines were climbing harnesses. One of the harnesses contained a black-clad torso, with one arm. The other had a few chunks of meat in it and was dripping.

There were a number of dead gunmen on the ground but he could only see the headless body of one other SBS trooper. There was, however, a lot of blood on the floor and the walls of the warehouse, and lots of chunks of meat.

He could see that two other members of the troop were using the Land Rover as cover. The armoured vehicle had been so riddled with holes that it was falling apart. He could see muzzle flashes from the other side of the crates that suggested other members of the troop were still alive.

Something wet hit Noel. Noel turned, as Dolton was torn apart. He saw the gunman that had just appeared round the corner of the crates. He was walking the rounds in on Noel. Noel fired. The gunman staggered, then the top of his head came off in a spray of bone and blood, as someone unseen shot him from above through the broken skylight.

There was firing from the top of the crates. Holes appeared in the roof of the warehouse. Part of the roof collapsed and a black-clad figure plummeted through the roof to impact hard on the warehouse floor.

'Echo actual to Echo-four, one more X-ray on top of the crates, remaining call signs will suppress your assault, confirm,' Stanton said.

41

'Confirmed,' Noel transmitted. He was fighting down the horror of what had happened here. All he could feel was numb. He was worried that he was going into shock. He hadn't even told them that Dolton was down. Not down. Had ceased to exist. He was wearing what Dolton had once been. Over the screaming rounds from the remaining gunman's weapon, Noel managed to hear Stanton whisper the word grenade over the tac radio.

He closed his eyes and looked down. They had cooked the grenades. Removed the spoons and pins and held onto them, throwing them at the last moment so that all three flashbangs had exploded in mid-air. Noel went deaf, the glow creeping back through his eyelids.

Still seeing points of light in his vision, he ran, scrambling up the rough steps made by the stacked crates. He was close to the top now. A figure loomed over him. He fired. Hit. The figure grabbed his SMG and yanked it toward him. Noel flew forward, pulled by the sling. He hit the top of the crates. Rolling, he felt rather than saw the figure stalking after him. He swung round on the floor, trying to bring his weapon to bear. The SMG was kicked so hard it broke. A huge hand grabbed him by the front of his harness and lifted him up into the air. Noel found himself face to face with a massive, bearded man covered in his own blood. Noel tore his dive knife from the scabbard and plunged it into the man's neck. The man stared at him. Panic came close to claiming Noel. The man hit him, breaking his nose. Blackness swam up in his vision, trying to take him away from all this. He tried to shake it off. Somehow, he had the presence of mind to rip the knife from the man's neck and ram it into the shoulder joint of the arm that was holding him up. His attacker didn't even scream in pain; he just dropped him. Noel scrabbled for his sidearm, dragging the P226 from its holster and firing. The figure staggered as round after round forced him back.

Head! He shifted aim and fired again and again. He was missing. The figure reached for him. The gunman's face exploded and sprayed over Noel. The figure stood over him for a moment and then toppled to the ground. Stanton was standing behind him. Smoke drifted from his SMG. He double tapped the bearded man in the head just to be sure.

'Clear,' the Scot said into his tac radio before turning to Noel. 'You all right son?'

Noel stared at him. Noel had served with the Royal Marines for three years, during which he had done a tour in Afghanistan. He'd applied and been accepted for special forces' selection, which he had passed. He had then spent the next four years with the SBS. He had gone to Iraq, and then back to Afghanistan two more times. During that period he had been involved in fifteen serious firefights, which was a lot for any soldier, but he'd had to come to East London for something truly bad to happen. The entirety of red troop had been on the op. Sixteen men.

'How many?' Noel asked numbly.

'Dolton?' the sergeant asked. Noel shook his head. 'There's five of us left.'

Noel stared at Stanton. Eleven of his friends. Eleven of the people he would probably be the closest to ever, because they had shared the bond of having to rely on each other to stay alive, because they had seen and experienced things that most people had no idea about.

Sergeant Stanton was not surprised to see the tears come. The training notwithstanding, the human mind wasn't really set up for this sort of trauma. He just hoped he still had a trooper left afterwards.

***

Detective Superintendent Samantha Linley was watching the warehouse warily. She was still shaking slightly as she took another drag on her cigarette. In her early fifties, she was thin to the point of gaunt; she'd run on nerves, cigarettes and coffee for too many years. Her skin looked like leather spread across bone and her teeth were yellow. She shivered again, despite the warmth of the night.

The firing had stopped more than ten minutes ago. There was still a cordon of armed police with weapons trained on the warehouse. The whole area was bathed in flashing blue lights but SF had asked for them to hold back until they gave the all clear. She didn't even have contact with SF's command element at the moment as they had joined the firefight when it had kicked off.

The media had already started turning up. It would look bad; they were being turned away by heavily armed police officers. The Home Secretary was on his way.

'Shit!'

Some of the nearby officers glanced her way. After Brixton, this was the last thing the Met needed, not in the run-up to an election, not with an unpopular government desperate for scapegoats. This was going to be on her, she knew that. Despite the fact that she hadn't liked the intel. It had read like an analyst grasping at straws, like they had desperately wanted a pipeline from Afghanistan ending in East London to exist. She had recommended observation, but the push to mount a raid had come from her superiors. Still, it had been her operation. She would be held accountable.

'Nobody should have to die in Dagenham,' she muttered to herself. She was a Stepney girl, born and bred.

***

They had secured the warehouse. Made sure there was nobody else there. Noel had helped after he had pulled himself together enough to do so. For the most part he hadn't been able to recognise the constituent parts of his dead friends.

'Did you get tagged?' Stanton asked him.

Noel's face hurt and his side really hurt. Stanton poured some water over the side of Noel's face, cleaning off some of Dolton's blood, and examined the wound. 'Looks like debris fragments. You'll live.'

Noel was working on automatic now, going through the motions that his training had instilled in him. He looked at his side. There was a tear in his body armour. He unclipped the body armour and looked at the wound. The round had made a rent straight through the armour as if it hadn't been there. There was an angry bruised line drawn on his flesh but it hadn't broken his flesh. He remembered the force of this graze knocking him off his feet. That didn't quite square with what he knew about the physics of ballistics.

'Lucky,' Stanton muttered.

Noel saw Lieutenant Harcombe staring around at the carnage in the warehouse. He looked dazed. Noel glared at him angrily. Now fury was replacing the numbness.

'How come you're not dead?' he shouted at the lieutenant. In anger, his London accent sounded stronger. Harcombe's head jerked around to look at him. Noel started towards the lieutenant.

Stanton grabbed the wiry young Afro-Caribbean commando, but Noel tried to push the other non-commissioned officer away.

'What are you doing?' Stanton asked.

'A vehicle ram, rappel through the skylight, sub-surface infil. Are you kidding me? Too complex, too many moving parts. We're lucky he didn't order a heli-borne assault as well, maybe have HMS *Belfast* soften up the target for old times' sake?' *Actually, that wouldn't have been a bad idea,* but he decided to keep that thought to himself. He pointed up at the bloody lines still dangling through the skylight. 'Barrows and the others wouldn't have stood a chance!'

'Chinese Parliament,' Stanton said, meaning the planning stage of an op. Everyone had their say when a plan of action was decided on and you didn't get to whine about it afterwards. Noel rounded on Stanton.

'What Chinese Parliament? You were at the briefing. He's still giving out orders like he's a Rupert back in the marines,' Noel hissed and tried to break free.

Stanton dragged him round, to face him again.

'He came in when it went tits up. That's something.'

'He just killed eleven people,' Noel said loudly. Harcombe was staring at him.

'Quiet,' Stanton hissed. 'Fucking pull yourself together. Save it for the after-action report, he's binned anyway.' Noel just stared at Stanton. 'I don't think we lost as many people as this in one action during World War Two. He's gone. He'll be lucky if he's only RTU'd.'

'Returned-to-unit? He'll be lucky if he doesn't have an accident.'

'Hey!' Stanton snapped. 'That's enough. You're angry. You're going to be looking for people to blame, and believe me this is better than when you start blaming yourself, but I need you here, now, you understand me?'

Noel stared at the sergeant and then looked away, sagging slightly.

'Yeah, yeah, I'm sorry Jim. What happened out here?'

'We hit them, Echo-one in the Snatch,' he pointed at the bullet-riddled armoured Land Rover. 'Echo-two through the side door.' He pointed at what was left of the warehouse's side door. 'Echo-three through the roof.'

47

Stanton pointed at the bloody harnesses. Noel knew this, it had been the plan, but repetition was the key to a clear picture. It didn't hurt to go over it again.

'Were they waiting for us?'

'No. They shook off the flashbangs a lot quicker than we expected and returned fire.'

'Mercenaries, ex-Spetznaz, something like that?' The gunmen looked Eastern European to Noel. They certainly didn't look Middle Eastern or Central Asian.

'I don't doubt that a few of them had military training but there was no discipline there; they weren't even brilliant shots but they laid a lot of fire down and they had no fear whatsoever. They were also bloody quick, I mean really fast.'

'They didn't go down easy either,' Noel said. 'Jacked-up on adrenalin?'

'Maybe, Stanton said, shrugging. Both of them had encountered insurgents in Iraq who had been injecting adrenalin. It would explain the lack of a fear response. The adrenalin and the fact that the SBS commandos had been firing relatively small calibre nine millimetre rounds in the SMGs could also explain why the central mass shots hadn't been taking the gunmen down immediately. Again it was something they had encountered in both Iraq and Afghanistan.

'What were they shooting?' Noel asked. 'I've never heard anything like that.'

Stanton nodded at the closest gunman. Noel turned and headed over to the corpse, picking up the weapon. Harcombe was speaking over the hand radio the police had given him; he stopped when Noel picked the weapon up.

'Hey! Trooper, put that down!' *Nice of you to learn my name, boss,* Noel thought but he ignored the lieutenant. Stanton turned and made calming motions towards the lieutenant.

Noel examined the weapon.

'That's not right,' he muttered. He was looking at a compact Heckler & Koch MP7A1, 4.6 millimetre, personal defence weapon. He had fired them before. They did not sound like, or have the ballistic properties of the weapons that had been used against them. He looked at Stanton. Stanton just shook his head.

'When Goddard got hit it looked like he'd been hit with a gimpy at least, maybe a fifty cal.'

'Hydrostatic shock. You hear the screaming?' Noel nodded. 'Very high velocity.'

'I'm familiar with high velocity …'

'Not this high velocity. I think they were hypersonic. The sound was something to do with the doppler effect.'

'Supercharged rounds? Increased powder charge, something like that?' Stanton shrugged. Noel was just guessing. He looked down at the small PDW. He noticed that there was black dust pouring out of the barrel. He looked at Stanton, who looked mystified. On a whim he popped the magazine out of the weapon's pistol grip and checked it. He stared into the magazine and then upended it. More black dust fell out of it.

Noel placed the MP7 back on the ground and headed over to the crates. Harcombe, still watching them, looked like he was about to object but decided against it. Noel opened the crate and found himself looking at packing foam with small vials packed into holes cut in the material. A few of the vials contained a bright blue liquid. The rest contained black dust as well. As the two SBS troopers watched, more of the bright blue liquid turned to black dust. They stared at it.

'You poor bastards.' Noel recognised the voice. He palmed two vials from the case. One of them was one of the few remaining vials with blue liquid in it and the other had black dust in it. Then he turned to look at DI Samantha Linley.

'Sam,' Noel said. The detective superintendent was stood by the Land Rover looking around in horror at the destruction in the warehouse. He had worked with Sam before and known her even before that, back when she had been a beat copper on the same South London estates he'd grown up on.

Samantha walked across the blood-stained floor, nodding at Stanton, ignoring Harcombe. She knew it was the NCOs you needed to get on side when working with SF. It was the NCOs that got things done. She put a hand on Noel's shoulder.

'You going to be all right, love?' Noel swallowed hard but nodded. She glanced at the open crate. Inside, all the vials were just full of black dust now. She shook her head. She was at a loss. She turned to Stanton. 'Can my crime scene boys get in here?'

'We'll need another twenty minutes to police all our gear up.'

She nodded, turned and headed for the door.

'I'll see you at the debrief,' she said over her shoulder. 'If I haven't been fired by then. The Home Secretary's here.'

Noel glanced down at the two vials in his gloved hand. Both contained black dust now.

Chapter Four

Angels & Demons Nightclub, Brixton, South London, 8 May, 0400 (BST)

Nicholas Burman was less than pleased. It was four am. It had been a long night and now this. Oliver was keeping pace with him as they walked across the main dance floor of the empty nightclub.

'You know him?' Oliver asked. Nicholas had chosen Oliver as the next in line for the throne because he was smart and capable of making the hard decisions. Oliver would be ruthless, as he was, because you had to be, you couldn't slip, couldn't be seen to be soft, but he wasn't an animal.

Nicholas glanced down at the smaller man. Oliver kept his head razor shaved and wore steel-rimmed glasses. Like Nicholas, Oliver always wore Savile Row when he was working. You had to give off the right impression. Like Nicholas, Oliver was of Afro-Caribbean descent and had grown up on various estates in Lambeth, and other parts of South London. Unlike Nicholas, Oliver hadn't had such a supportive family. It had been Nicholas who had paid for Oliver to go to college,

52

Nicholas who had supported Oliver, whilst he did his degree in business part time.

'Tamal? Know of him. Don't know what he's doing here.'

They reached the top of the stairs that led down to the foyer and the doors to the street. Billy, one of Nicholas's security people, was there. He put his hand up to stop his powerfully built boss. Nicholas knew that some people in his position would resent that, but he paid these people to do things like this, to look after his safety.

'What's up?' Nicholas asked.

'They're carrying shooters,' Billy said.

'What?'

'Maybe you should head out the back,' Oliver suggested and then gave it some thought. 'Maybe we should all head out the back.'

'Not even your normal handguns or sawn-offs either, they look like automatic weapons. I think Oliver's right,' Billy said. The dreadlocked second-generation Somali wore Savile Row as well, like everyone else in Nicholas's crew.

'You tooled?' Oliver asked. Billy answered by opening his suit jacket and showing them the two long-barrelled .38 revolvers in his waistband.

'Billy the Kid,' Nicholas groused. He hated it when his crew had to go armed. It was always a sign that something had gone wrong. 'Well it's not a hit or they would have shot their way in here by now.' Billy and Oliver were looking at him expectantly. 'Fucking bullshit testosterone politics. I'm looking forward to when this is your problem and I'm lying on a beach in the North Island earning twelve per cent,' Nicholas told Oliver and headed down the stairs.

'Not in this economy,' Oliver muttered and followed him.

***

Tamal was a bulky man in his early fifties just going to seed. Everything he wore was elegant but just a little out of date. He had on a little too much jewellery for Nicholas's taste, and he didn't like the homburg either. The two with Tamal were obvious muscle. They didn't look Turkish either, more like Eastern European, Nicholas thought. Danny and Josh, another two members of Nicholas's crew, were down there keeping an eye on the three newcomers.

Nicholas knew that Tamal was high up in the main Turkish syndicate that controlled the heroin trade in North London. He had made his name a few years back when he had been instrumental in brutally winning a drugs war with the Kurdish gangs.

'You'll forgive me for not being very welcoming but it's late and you weren't invited,' Nicholas said as he reached the foyer of the club, which now seemed quite crowded with a number of large people in it. He immediately turned to one of the security guys and opened his coat. The guy pulled away with a curse but not before Nicholas had seen the weapon on a sling hanging down under the muscle's leather coat. It was some kind of sub-machine gun, Nicholas thought; doubtless, his brother would have known what it was called. Nicholas turned to Tamal, eyebrows raised.

'Just security,' Tamal said holding his hands open.

'You're a long way from the Ladder. Do we have business?' Nicholas asked.

'I was hoping to discuss some, yes.'

'Well, there are ways and means. Coming here tooled up like cowboys in a way that could make plod very unhappy with all of us is not one of them. Also, it's really late at night and I want to get home.'

'Ah yes, to Jessica, and your daughter Kimberley.'

Nicholas stared at him for a beat. Oliver, Billy, Danny and Josh all tensed up. Nicholas swallowed hard.

'Excuse me?' he asked. Tamal and the two muscle seemed unperturbed. Tamal met Nicholas's eyes.

'I meant nothing by it. A result of research, not a threat. We wish to deal with you. We have a very lucrative offer.'

Nicholas nodded. Relaxing. His crew did likewise.

'Lucrative I like.'

'Excellent. May we speak inside?'

'You can. Your two monkeys can wait outside,' Nicholas said, nodding at the two muscle.

'But it is cold outside,' Tamal said easily.

'They can use the time to reflect on the idiocy of bringing automatic weapons to a business meeting.'

Tamal shrugged. He turned to the two muscle and nodded. They both left the foyer, heading back out onto Brixton Hill.

'Josh,' Nicholas said. Josh gestured to Tamal to raise his arms.

Tamal turned to Nicholas. 'Is this really necessary?'

'Indulge me. I'm a very nervous man.'

Tamal raised his arms. Josh frisked him thoroughly.

'Boss,' Josh said and handed Nicholas a rather garish silver-plated Beretta with mother-of-pearl handgrips.

'Have the North Koreans invaded Green Lanes or something?' Nicholas asked. Tamal shrugged.

'He's not wired,' Josh announced and then waved Tamal's mobile phone at Nicholas.

'That stays down here,' Nicholas said pointing at the phone. Tamal looked less than pleased but nodded. 'Now, I'm sorry about your less than gracious welcome. Can I get you a drink?'

'Coffee?'

'At this time of night? Sure.'

Nicholas gestured up the stairs and then followed Tamal up. He left Danny and Josh in the foyer watching the door.

***

Tamal pushed the swing door open into the club's main dance and bar area. It was empty now, the chairs stacked, but it still smelt of perfume, sweat and booze. There were only a few lights on, neon pools reflected in the steel and mirrors of the club's decor.

Tamal started to turn when he heard the slide on his own Beretta being worked.

Nicholas was surprised by how quickly the North Londoner reacted but he still managed to grab him by the lapels and propel him across the dance floor and into a table. Chairs crashed to the floor as Nicholas pushed Tamal, painfully, over the table and pushed the pistol into his face.

Billy had kept pace with Nicholas, his hands never far from his two revolvers. Oliver remained by the doors at the top of the stairs.

'This is a mistake,' Tamal told Nicholas, evenly. There was no trace of fear in the other man.

'No, a mistake is even mentioning my family. I need a very compelling reason why you and your two friends aren't just about to disappear.' Nicholas spat, though Tamal's lack of fear was starting to bother him. He knew that he was genuinely prepared to kill to protect his family. If Tamal was any judge of character, he would know that as well. The movies notwithstanding, having a gun pointed at you was a big deal. It rarely mattered how fearless you wanted to appear, the response to this sort of danger was difficult to overcome.

'I apologise. I didn't mean it to sound like a threat,' Tamal told him.

'Bullshit,' Nicholas said quietly.

'It was more a warning,' Tamal said and smiled. Nicholas stared at him. 'An assurance of good behaviour on your part.'

'You're not doing yourself any favours,' Nicholas said through gritted teeth.

'Imagine I don't care. Imagine this isn't the first time I've had a gun pointed at me. Now do you want to talk or fuck around?'

Nicholas let him up off the table. Tamal brushed himself down. Nicholas handed Tamal his Beretta. It was bravado, he knew, meant to show that Tamal, even armed, didn't worry him.

Nicholas went over to the bar and turned on the coffee machine. Tamal sat at the bar. Billy stood nearby, keeping an eye on the North Londoner. Oliver came over to join them, sitting at the bar as well.

'So no,' Nicholas finally said, handing Tamal and then Oliver a cup of coffee. 'I don't want to talk or fuck around. North London's very far away, and as far as I'm concerned it can stay that way, and never the twain shall meet.'

'Your distribution network covers everything south of the river as far as Croydon. We want to supply to you, that's all.'

'Which pisses off my suppliers. We got here by not ruffling too many feathers, making everyone involved a lot of money, and staying well below the radar. I see no reason to change that.' Nicholas took a sip from the cup of coffee he'd made himself.

Tamal reached into the breast pocket of his suit jacket. Billy grabbed his wrist before he got too much further.

'I've been searched,' Tamal said in exasperation. Billy looked at Nicholas, who nodded. Tamal took out a leather case and unzipped it. Inside were several glass vials, each containing a bright blue liquid. Tamal held up a vial and showed it to Nicholas. The liquid seemed to glow in the neon light.

'Pretty,' Nicholas said. 'You're not getting tired of bringing illegal shit onto my premises are you?'

'It's not illegal,' Tamal said.

'Yet. Let me guess, it's the next big thing.'

'I thought you would have heard by now.'

'And you've got the only chemist. Any idea how often I've heard this song? I'd expect better of someone with your reputation though.'

'Try before you buy. Must be worth a punt.'

'That Bliss?' Oliver asked. Tamal nodded.

'Maybe it is the next big thing but, if I get into it, I'll get into it with people I know,' Nicholas told Tamal.

'We are the only people.'

'Then thank you for the offer but, respectfully, I decline.'

'Why?'

Nicholas stared at Tamal for a moment and then laughed. 'Where do I start? Because this isn't 1920s Chicago. You want to play gangster, do it in the north. Because I don't know you and you've not made a good impression. Because you mentioned my family, which is just fucking unprofessional. But, most importantly, because whatever this is,' he pointed at the vials. 'You're high on it, aren't you?'

He'd seen it in the other man's dilated pupils and his lack of fear when he'd pointed the gun at him. It was the first time that Tamal had looked anything less than completely sure of himself.

'It's really good. You should try some.'

'No thank you. Good night.'

'We're talking about a lot of money,' Tamal said as Billy took a step towards him.

'As well as having a nervous disposition, or perhaps because of it, I am a very cautious man. Now I'll say goodnight.'

Tamal didn't move. 'You're going to have to reconsider.'

'Well, let's cross that bridge when we get to it. Are you really going to make me say goodnight a third time?'

Nicholas met Tamal's eyes. Nicholas was starting to regret having given the north Londoner his gun back. His hand was on the baseball bat they kept behind the bar.

Tamal stood up, still staring at Nicholas, before turning and leaving. Billy followed him out. Nicholas watched him go. 'Shit!' Nicholas finally exploded when he was sure that Tamal was well out of earshot.

'You know he's in charge up there, don't you?' Oliver said.

'What? What happened to Demirtas?'

'Two in the back of the head. Kurdish retaliation. Though some people think it was the price of peace.'

'Brilliant. He's dumb enough to come down here and start a war, isn't he?' Oliver nodded. 'So this is it?' Nicholas asked, pointing at the vials that Tamal had left. They had been forced to deal with a few freelancers dealing Bliss in the clubs.

'Yeah, and we're seeing a drop off in the club trade because of it,' Oliver told him.

'Is it that good?'

'So they say. A morphine high, with a cocaine kick, and minimal come down. It's like smack you can dance to, and it's legal.'

'For the next five minutes.' Nicholas rubbed the bridge of his nose. 'This is just what I need, some cunt who thinks he's Scarface. I mean, if it's designer, what's he carrying machine guns for?'

'This could bite into a lot of people's profits.'

'You think we should get into it?'

'Not with that prick.'

Nicholas glanced down at the leather case and the vials again. He never handled product or cash and nobody in his crew used.

'Find someone to take it for me. I want to find out what it really does. Get one of our chemists on it as well, someone who knows what they're doing, I want it analysed. If it's really that good we'll see if they can start production in Holland ...'

'Tamal won't like that,' Oliver pointed out.

'Tough shit, that's just market forces for you. Hopefully it'll be your problem anyway.'

'Thanks,' Oliver said.

'And remember ...'

'I know, the moment you're in, start looking for your replacement. Already on it.'

Nicholas knocked on the bar and grinned at Oliver.

'I'm off home.'

'Take Billy with you.'

'No, because then Jess'll know something's up.'

'You got something at home?' Oliver asked. Nicholas nodded and headed for the door. 'Night,' Oliver said.

Nicholas waved over his shoulder.

***

Nicholas headed west, threading the silver Jaguar XF through the empty streets of London. He liked driving at this time. It was still dark; morning was a couple of hours away, but London had gone to bed a few hours before. It was his city at this time of the night.

He made it back to Buckinghamshire in less than an hour. The gate to the large detached house opened at the press of a button. It was a big house, well appointed, but nothing grand, nothing too ostentatious. Never draw attention to yourself.

He deactivated the security, activating it again as he headed upstairs as quietly as he could. He looked in on Kimberley; she shifted in her bed but didn't wake. He watched her sleep. He could never square the world he lived in with her innocence. She was six now and already he knew that she was smarter and more beautiful than everyone else's kids. He smiled at the thought, and then frowned, feeling, not for the first time, that his presence in her life, what he did, somehow polluted her. He closed the door and headed for the shower. He didn't use their en-suite because he didn't want to wake Jess.

He tried to sneak into bed but he woke her. She wasn't like him. When her eyes were open, she was normally pretty alert.

'Sorry,' he whispered as wrapped his arms around her. Jess could feel the tension in him.

'What?' she asked. Even in the darkness he could make out her large, brown eyes studying him.

'Long day,' he told her.

'Bad day?' He didn't answer. He never would. She could never know anything about the business.

'When?' she asked.

'Soon,' he told her, completing the ritual – but he meant it more than ever this morning.

Chapter Five

RM Poole, 10 May, 0505

Four days on, Noel sat on his bed in the single man's quarters at RM Poole. He was staring at the mirror above the sink on the opposite wall. He had a dressing on the side of his face and another over his broken nose. Both his eyes were black. Next to him, on the neatly made bed, was a Sig Sauer P226 handgun in a clip-on hip holster. It was loaded and there was a clip-on pouch with a further four magazines in it.

Stanton had been right. He was analysing everything that had happened. He had re-read and then re-written his after-action report several times. He had gone over all the other reports. Harcombe had resigned, but although the lieutenant had made the op more complicated than it needed to be Noel was coming round to the belief that it hadn't been his fault. They had been outgunned and the targets had behaved very strangely. Realising this, he started looking for culpability.

He had been in charge of Echo-four. The deaths of Goddard, Dolton and Beckett were his responsibility, if not his fault. He looked for a mistake that he had made.

Some of it was the training. He needed to learn from it. Some of it, if he had been honest with himself, was self-flagellation. He was self-aware enough to know that, other than a few minor slip-ups, he and his team had been tight.

The more he looked at it, the more he was of the opinion that intel had let them down, but then his experience of intel was that it was never as solid as it should be. Too often it was contaminated by wishful thinking somewhere along the line.

This left him wondering just what had been happening in the warehouse. The weapons, the gunmen, the blue liquid and the black dust, none of it made any sense.

Noel stood up and clipped the gun and the spare clips to his belt. He dropped a loose fitting shirt over the weapon and magazines to conceal them. He grabbed his kit bag and headed for the door.

***

'Noel!'

Noel turned at the voice to see Stanton walking across the car park towards him. Stanton had been staying at the single man's quarters ever since his long-term girl-friend had kicked him out.

'All right Jim?'

The sergeant nodded.

'You off?'

'I'm going up to the Smoke, see some people.'

Stanton joined him as Noel headed for his car.

'Some of us are heading up to Newquay. Maybe do a little surfing and a lot of drinking,' the sergeant told him. He left it unsaid that it was the guys who'd survived the warehouse raid.

'I appreciate that Jim but …'

'The lads could do with you there, and I could do with your support.'

It wasn't emotional blackmail, Noel knew; Stanton didn't work like that. The quiet Scotsman was just doing what he thought was right for what was left of the troop, and being as honest as he knew how with Noel. That didn't stop Noel from feeling like he was letting the other men down, badly.

'Look Jim, I've got to get some things straight in my head if I'm going to be of any use to anyone.'

'You signed out a Sig?' Jim said.

Noel felt his heart sink. He shifted uncomfortably.

'Yeah, we're allowed to conceal carry off-duty.' Noel knew he was sounding defensive.

'We are, but most of us don't, and you never do. That means either you're off to do something really dumb, or you're frightened.' The sergeant left it unsaid that both situations could make Noel useless to the service. Stanton was watching Noel carefully, looking for some clue as to what the other man was thinking. Looking for a weakness that would be dangerous to the rest of the men.

'I'm not going to do anything dumb. I just want to find out a few things. I'm not off the rails, Jim.'

Stanton looked less than happy but nodded.

'All right. You need us up there …'

'No, it'll be fine …'

'Listen. You need us up there, you call, okay?' Noel nodded. They had arrived at his car, an old Saab Turbo. Stanton shook his head. 'You're not married, no kids that you know of, you could be driving a much better car.'

Noel smiled as he threw his kitbag into the backseat.

'They are a woefully unrecognised classic car,' he said.

Noel put the seatbelt on and turned the key in the ignition.

New Scotland Yard, London, 10 May, 0907 (BST)

DSI Linley had taken to coming to work through the underground parking garage, even though she travelled by tube. In the wake of the warehouse raid, New Scotland Yard was under siege. Reporters and news media surrounded the whole place and her face was known.

She arrived at the top of the steps to the foyer more than a little out of breath, cursing her dependence on cigarettes. She headed out into the ugly 1970s architecture of the foyer, and made her way towards the lift, trying to ignore the press of reporters pushed up against the glass at the front of the building. She made it to the lift. Out of breath. Someone got into the lift next to her.

'You need to quit smoking,' the figure said. This pleased Sam; she had been hoping that someone would volunteer to have her bad temper taken out on them.

She turned to unload on her victim and found Noel taking off a baseball cap and grinning at her. The smile didn't quite make it to his bruised eyes.

'Oh love,' Sam said and gave him a hug. She pulled back. 'I'm really sorry about your boys ... I ...' Then the guilt. Misgivings about the intelligence aside. She'd been in charge.

'You didn't like the intel, did you?'

'No,' she admitted a little reluctantly. 'I didn't. Too much analyst, not enough asset. What are you doing here, love?'

'I'm trying to find out what happened. What can you tell me?'

Sam gave this some thought.

'Fuck it, you're part of the op as far as I'm concerned, you've probably got better clearance than I have, and frankly I trust you more than half the cunts in this building.' Noel flinched a little at the language but smiled. 'Who'd have thought it?' she said, a little wistfully. 'All those times chasing you and your toerag of a brother around the estates, and now look where we are.'

'You almost used to keep up,' Noel said and then tapped the pocket of her suit jacket where he knew she kept the cigarettes. She fixed him with a glare.

'Not all of us can be cloaked-in-black super squaddies.'

'Well I certainly can't. I'm a marine.'

'Whatever.'

*

68

They sat in an interview room. Sam had decided that she wanted a bit more privacy than her desk in an open plan office would provide. The room had ugly bare brick walls. The scarred furniture was bolted to the ground and the tape recorder in the room was off. Noel ignored the humming, flickering strip light.

There were photographs and reports spread out across the table.

'So the guns?' Noel asked. Sam grinned.

'Typical squaddie …'

'Bootneck,' Noel suggested.

'They were …' She dragged a report towards her. It had a picture of one of the PDWs lying on the blood-stained floor clipped to it. 'Heckler and Koch MP7A1s, but you'll know that.'

'Anything odd about them?'

Sam skim-read the report.

'Other than a lot of wear and tear on the components, no. According to ballistics the weapons looked like they had fired a lot of rounds and were close to the end of their operational lives.'

'Okay, what about the rounds? What were they?'

Sam was shaking her head.

'We didn't find any.'

Noel stared at her.

'They laid a lot of fire down.'

'We found a lot of impacts. According to ballistics, the depth and force of the impacts point towards bullets made of a dense substance.' She started reading from the report. 'Judging by the penetration into concrete, possibly a tungsten-cored penetrator fired at hyper-sonic velocity.'

'So where are they?'

'They think that heat and friction caused them all to disintegrate,' Sam told him.

'All of them?' Noel asked incredulously.

'That's the only explanation they've been able to come up with.'

'Okay, what about the bodies?''

Sam put down the folder and pulled a pile of cor-oners' reports towards herself.

'Who were they?'

'Low-end Organizatsiya thuggery.'

'Really?'

Sam just passed one of the gunmen's files over to Noel. He scan-read it before putting it down on the table and tapping his finger on the photograph. 'That's weird.'

'Mmm?'

'This is the guy we took down first, outside by the river. He didn't look like this.'

Sam frowned and studied the picture. It showed a thirty-something red-faced man who clearly liked food, alcohol and smoking a little too much.

'You saying we got the wrong person?'

'No, it looks like the same guy, except the guy we killed was healthy and fast.'

'The guy went on a health kick?'

Noel checked the date of the photograph on his file. 'In five weeks?'

Sam bit her lip and started comparing arrest photos with the photos of the corpses.

'They all the same?' Noel asked. Sam nodded. 'You find traces of steroids or anything?'

'No. We found nothing in their bloodstreams.'

'Nothing?'

'We found no traces of anything chemical, but their bodies were worn out. Tissue damage, nerve damage, neural degradation, cardio-respiratory degradation, even the optic nerves were degraded.'

'Like the body had been revved too high?' Noel said. Sam shrugged. 'Just like the MP7s.'

'I guess. I think they were on something but we can't find it.'

'Like the bullets?'

She nodded.

'What's the blue liquid?'

'You should know that people are saying that you made that up to cover your arses,' Sam told him evenly. Noel stared at the older woman, trying to control his anger. 'Either that or you were in shock.'

'If just one of us saw it, maybe, but both me and Jim? No way. We're trained observers.'

'Okay, it sounds like you're describing a designer drug called Bliss. All the rage on the club scene.'

'So it was a Bliss distribution point?'

'Maybe?'

'Who's moving it?'

'We have no idea. We haven't been able to get hold of a sample. If this was Bliss then the possibility that

71

the Organizatsiya could be moving it is our best lead yet.'

'Are you investigating Bliss distribution?'

'It's not even illegal yet.' Noel stared at Sam incredulously. 'It's very new. There have been no recorded deaths as a result of it, and without a sample we don't know what we need to make illegal. If those guys were guarding Bliss and had given up, all we would have had on them is weapons charges. Admittedly pretty serious weapons charges.'

'The black powder?'

'Carbon. My boss is calling the whole thing this year's big carbon bust.'

'Did they find the same dust in the MP7s and the bullet holes?'

Sam searched through the ballistic files and nodded. Noel opened his mouth to say something but Sam's phone rang.

'I am really fucking busy,' Sam said by way of an answer. Her face hardened as she was told something she didn't like. 'Well don't let her, then.' She listened for another few moments and then angrily broke the connection. Noel looked at her questioningly. 'Evidence. Someone is examining the weapons. Coming?'

'Sure.'

***

Sam battered the double doors to the evidence room open. The room was comprised of a series of narrow passages formed by metal shelves with a table, visible from the door, in the centre of it. It was poorly lit and there were no external windows, further adding to the dark and dingy nature of the room.

Stood at the table was a tall, attractive, brown-haired woman wearing a pair of glasses, jeans, and a smart-looking jacket over a tailored shirt. Noel judged that she was in her late twenties, or early thirties, and was in far better than normal physical shape. He also noticed that she had a sidearm under her jacket.

There was also a nervous looking, plump, elderly police constable bringing more boxes of evidence to the table.

'Can I help you?' Sam demanded. The woman looked up and smiled. Noel found that he liked her brown eyes as well.

'You could help me carry some of these boxes to my car,' she said brightly. To Noel's ears her accent sounded posh, well educated. Sam glared at the woman for a moment.

'Or I could break your skinny little wrists and kick your pretty little arse all over my police station.'

'You think I'm pretty?' the woman said, delighted.

Noel had to suppress a grin.

'She's armed,' Noel pointed out.

This time Sam glared at him.

'Really?' she demanded sarcastically. 'I am a fucking police officer, you know.'

'Sorry,' Noel said.

'I'm not the only one, am I, Corporal Burman?' the

woman said. 'Or is it just Noel? I know how informal you SF types are.'

This was becoming less fun, Noel decided.

'So you've got clearance, very clever. What are you, Box?' Noel asked. Sam glanced at him quizzically. 'Five,' he told her, meaning MI5.

'You're not the silly cunt who provided us with the wank intel are you?' Sam demanded.

'No, I'm not that particular silly cunt,' the brown-haired woman said. Noel twitched a little at the language. He twitched again as she reached into her jacket and produced a small case for business cards. *Jim was right*, Noel realised. He was wound more than a little tightly at the moment.

The woman passed the card to Sam, who read it and then gave it to Noel. The card read: Charlotte Whelan-Hollis, BEng, MSc, Defence Science & Technology Laboratory.

'Is there some rule that says that all you middle-class types have to be called Charlotte?' Sam asked.

'You're lovely, I really like you,' Charlotte said, oddly sounding like she meant it.

'So what, it's a business card,' Sam said.

'I did check her out, ma'am,' the police officer said.

'That's nice,' Sam muttered. 'You won't mind if I check you out myself will you? Until then, stop fucking around with my evidence.'

'You haven't checked your emails this morning, have you?' Charlotte asked Sam with just a touch of sympathy in her voice. Sam cursed and started searching through her bag for her phone.

'You out of Porton Down?' Noel asked her.

'Have you ever been to Arbroath?' she asked, meaning the SBS's other base on the East Coast of Scotland.

'Fair point. DSTL are a research agency. Why are you running around with a gun?'

'I have a permit, would you like to see it?' Charlotte asked, sitting on the table.

'That doesn't answer my question.'

'You are correct.'

'Fucking thing,' Sam cursed. Having found her phone, she was now struggling to get it to download her email.

'Would you like me to …' Charlotte asked, earning herself a venomous glare. 'No, okay.'

Sam got the email to work and opened the email she was sure that Charlotte was referring to.

'This probably means nothing to you, coming from a complete stranger, but I really am sorry about your men,' Charlotte told Noel.

Noel swallowed, not trusting himself to reply.

'Bollocks!' Sam all but spat at the phone. She looked up at Charlotte. 'In the middle of a fucking investigation?'

Charlotte came off the desk, hands open in apparent contrition.

'Okay, look. I'm really sorry, this is shit, and I know that. We're not taking everything. Just samples of the guns, the vials and one of the corpses. I know it sounds bad but you have to believe me that we are the best placed agency to answer some of the questions that the evidence has thrown up. I promise you that I'll push to share anything we can with you.'

'Bullshit!' Sam spat.

'Want to show some of that cooperative spirit now? You've read the report. What do you think this is all about?' Noel asked.

Charlotte sat on the desk.

'Honestly, I don't know. We have rounds moving at speeds they shouldn't, from weapons that don't have that capability. We have bullets that are apparently showing characteristics of being hardened penetrators and frangible rounds simultaneously, which shouldn't be possible.'

'Frangible?' Sam asked.

'Low impact, designed to disintegrate if they hit anything harder than themselves. It's to limit collateral damage,' Noel told her. 'The black dust?'

'Carbon. It's a basic building block of a lot of matter. We've been researching solid state ammunition. Basically a lump of material that is transformed into a round as it's fired, but much of it is theoretical. In terms of material science, we're years away from that sort of thing.'

'But it's possible?' Noel asked. Charlotte nodded. Sam was looking less than pleased; it all sounded like science fiction to her. 'And the hypersonic velocities?' At this Charlotte looked troubled. 'Some sort of really efficient powder charge?'

Charlotte shook her head.

'It would have to be more efficient than the best explosive that we have knowledge of, and the force involved would tear the weapon apart.'

'What then?'

'Do you know what a railgun is?' she asked.

'Yeah, actually, I do,' Noel said, almost surprising himself. 'It uses electromagnetic fields to propel objects at tremendous velocities. But they're massive, aren't they?' Charlotte raised an eyebrow, impressed.

'Railguns?' Sam said sceptically. 'In Dagenham?'

Charlotte laughed. 'It's the closest model we've been able to find to the ballistic properties you guys were seeing in the warehouse,' she told the other woman.

'But they were firing MP7s,' Noel pointed out.

'And our ballistics say that, other than above average wear and tear, there was nothing odd about the weapons,' Sam added.

'Except for the carbon dust,' Charlotte said. 'Which you found in the weapons, the bullet holes, and in the vials.' She looked at Noel. 'And by the way I … we are taking your story about the drugs turning to dust seriously.' Noel nodded. He felt absurdly grateful; there had been times over the last week he had even doubted what he had seen.

'So what are we talking about here?' Sam asked.

'Do you like Sherlock Holmes?' she asked.

Noel shrugged.

'No,' Sam said. 'But it was required reading at Hendon.'

'When you have eliminated the impossible …'

'Whatever remains, however improbable, must be the truth,' Noel completed the quote. 'So what's the truth?'

'Some kind of transformative or programmable matter.'

77

'Bullshit,' Sam snorted.

'As ridiculous as it sounds, it's the only thing that fits what happened.'

'Is that possible?' Noel asked.

'Sure.'

'Theoretically?'

Charlotte nodded. 'It's being researched at the moment but, frankly, we're years away from that sort of material science.'

'A lot of years?' Noel asked. Charlotte nodded again. 'So not the Taliban then?'

'That would seem unlikely.'

'So who?'

She shrugged. 'America has a program, so China will. Germany and France are both doing research. I would imagine that Israel is as well.'

'If we were to believe any of this bullshit,' Sam said. 'Then what's all this high tech bollocks doing in the hands of some Organizatsiya thugs?'

'That I don't know.'

'And their capabilities? An untraceable drug?' Noel asked.

'That's not really my department but, in theory, it could be the same thing. Some high-end combat drug of the type that Britain would never research. Some kind of steroid mixed with a neural sheathing process to increase speed, which would explain the nerve degradation. It would have to be something that would stimulate the endocrine system for strength, and the endorphin system to enable them to walk through gunfire. We can see the results of all that and more in the coroner's report, but no trace of the cause because ...'

'Like the Bliss, you think it was transformed into something that would be ignored?' Noel said.

'Bliss?' Charlotte asked.

'The blue liquid may have been a designer drug called Bliss,' Noel told her whilst Sam glared at him.

'I'd like to know more about Bliss,' Charlotte told Sam.

'Wouldn't we all?' Sam muttered.

'You going to be in the city long?' Noel asked.

'No, I'm going straight back from whence I came,' Charlotte said, smiling.

'Mysterious.' He flicked her business card. 'Business or personal number.'

'It'll work for both in a pinch.'

'Want to get a drink some time?'

'Jesus Christ,' Sam muttered angrily.

'Direct, I like that.'

'For fuck's sake,' Sam continued muttering.

'I have to be. I don't get much leave.'

'Would you like me to leave you two alone? Just wipe the table down when you're finished,' Sam suggested.

'Hmm, which would suggest that you'd be low maintenance. And pretty,' she said, laughing. Noel felt his heart sink; he'd forgotten about what a mess his face was. 'I'll give it some thought.' She picked up one of the boxes from the table. 'Are you going to help carry some of this?'

'Sure ...' Noel started.

'No!' Sam snapped. Noel looked down at the DSI. 'We've got things to do.' She turned and headed for the door. Charlotte smiled at Noel. Noel looked a little apologetic and then followed Sam.

***

'You jealous?' Noel asked as they headed down into the underground garage.

'No. I've got better legs,' Sam muttered.

'I think she's on our side.'

'No, you want to bang her, which is different.'

Noel rolled his eyes, but part of him had to concede that Sam was right.

'Where we going?'

'Brixton.'

Noel stopped.

'Why?' he demanded. Sam turned back to look up at him.

'Because your brother will speak to you. He won't speak to me.'

'I wouldn't be so sure about that.'

Chapter Six

Angels & Demon's Nightclub, Brixton, South London, 10 May, 1436 (BST)

Sam's phone was ringing as she brought the car to a stop outside the door to the Angels & Demons nightclub on Brixton Hill. The DSI cursed and started searching through her bag.

'You sure you've got enough stuff in there?' Noel asked, earning himself a glare. Sam found and answered the phone. Whatever she heard she didn't seem to like it much, as the caller was treated to a torrent of obscenities that Noel thought would even make some bootnecks blush. 'Why don't I head up and meet you there?' Sam glared at him again but nodded before really starting to shout down the phone.

Noel climbed out of the car. He walked across to the door of the club. As he did, something made him glance over at a car parked in the side street opposite. He wasn't sure why. There was someone sat in the driver's seat but he was minding his own business reading the paper. He reached for the buzzer and then hesitated when he saw the door was slightly ajar. He pushed the door open and looked in. There was nobody in the cramped foyer, so he headed up the stairs to the first floor of the club.

On the landing by the cloakroom he found Josh, a big man with bleached dreadlocks, one of Nicholas's crew. He'd been thoroughly done over, was bleeding from the head and had been hogtied with cable ties.

He found Danny, another one of Nicholas's crew and an old face from the neighbourhood, cable tied to a heating pipe in the cloakroom. Danny was solidly built with a bullet-shaped bald head. He had also taken a thorough beating. His nose had been broken so badly it was spread all over his face. Blood soaked the arm of his suit.

Josh was out cold. Danny looked insensate with pain. Noel looked all around him. He couldn't hear anyone but he had the feeling that there were more people in the building. He resisted the urge to draw the pistol. The last thing he needed was the reputation of being one of Nicholas's gunmen. In this he was a civilian, the gun was an absolute last resort. He tried phoning Sam but she was still engaged; he quickly texted her instead and then headed up the stairs.

He could see the lights on above him. He could hear movement. There was no tactical surprise here – he'd been on CCTV since he'd walked in and, frankly, he wasn't sure he wanted surprise. Scared criminals did dumb things.

'Nick? Billy?' he said quietly.

'He's got a gun!' someone shouted, but he didn't recognise the voice. Noel started to reach for his Sig but then there was a figure in the light at the top of the stairs pointing a revolver at him, an old long-nosed .38.

Noel raised his hands, hoping the man hadn't noticed he'd been reaching for his own weapon.

'Hey, I'm not here for any trouble.'

'Up,' the man said, beckoning with his free hand. He was white, craggy-faced, tall and wiry to the point of gaunt. His hair looked like it was normally kept neat but it had been let go recently. There was just the hint of Liverpool in his accent. Noel reckoned he was in his forties but looked after himself, or had until recently. The way he carried himself suggested military and a bit more than just regular army.

Noel walked up the stairs. 'Whatever you say. I think you should know, though, that I'm with the police.'

As Noel came up the man backed away keeping his distance, keeping the gun levelled. He knew what he was doing.

'Over to the bar. Put your hands on the counter.'

Noel took in the scene. A lot of broken glass. Too much. Billy, his brother's oldest friend, his face a mess, his dreads matted with blood, was sat on the floor, his hands cable tied back to back to another man who Noel didn't recognise. He had a shaved head, smart designer glasses and looked like he was normally well turned out until someone had knocked him about a bit. Presumably he'd shouted the warning.

His brother was tied to a chair, head and torso soaked, a wet cloth on the floor next to him. The man with the gun had been waterboarding his brother. That changed things.

'You could just leave now,' he said evenly, trying to keep the anger out of his voice. 'Maybe you should,' *before I really hurt you,* he added silently. He noticed the man had an earpiece in. *The car opposite the club,* Noel thought.

'Hands on the counter,' the gunman said. Noel noticed the burst blood vessels on the other man's face. The man moved closer behind Noel. *Just a little closer,* Noel thought, trying not to give himself away by tensing. 'You're not police.'

'ID in my jacket pocket. You want me to take it out?'

'You keep your hands where I can see them.' Noel had to suppress a smile when he felt the cool metal of the .38's barrel against the small of his back. *Mistake.* The man reached into his jacket. 'Move and bad things happen,' he said quietly. *That, at least, was true,* Noel thought. The man had a hold of Noel's wallet and tugged at it. He was close enough for Noel to hear the tinny voice from the headset he was wearing, though he couldn't make out what was said. Noel moved. Bad things happened.

As his wallet came out of his jacket, Noel lurched sideways along the counter, spinning towards the gunman. He grabbed the other man's wrist and battered the hand with the .38 against the bar, his free hand reaching for the Sig in its shoulder holster. The gunman surprised Noel by letting go of the .38 and elbowing him in the ribs, hard. Wind exploded out of Noel as the gunman straight-ened his arm, and stepped towards him, pushing him off balance. Noel went over. He almost swore. *He knows how to fight*, Noel thought with a sinking sensation.

Noel still had hold of the gunman's wrist. He yanked him down with him as he fell, while still trying to draw the Sig. The man grabbed the hand with the gun and pushed it away from him.

The two of them hit the ground hard enough to frustrate Noel's desperate attempt to draw breath. Then white light filled his vision and pain as he got headbutted, re-breaking his nose. Pain in his hand, then ribs again. *I want to breathe!* Hand again and he wasn't holding the Sig any more.

Weight came off him as the man reached for the .38 on the bar. Noel kicked him as hard as he could in the chest. The .38 went skittering across the floor. Noel rolled to his feet, disappointed to see that the other man was standing as well. He was vaguely aware of Billy and the guy he didn't know shouting something.

Noel watched the man glance at the Sig on the floor and then move for it. Too late, Noel realised it had been a feint. The chair hit him. Then there was a lot of pain as the gunman's foot contacted solidly with his kidney. If this guy didn't kill him, then Noel knew he'd be pissing blood for a week. He went down. He started to move for the Sig but he knew he'd be too slow. The gunman would reach it first.

'Armed police! Freeze! Don't fucking move!'

Sam was at the top of the stairs with the .38 pointed at the gunman, ID in her other hand. Pale, shaking. Noel knew what was happening. The situation had caused a signal to be sent to Sam's brainstem. A message to her amygdala, in the temporal lobe, was triggering a slew of physical changes in her body. Her heart rate went up, hormones surged through her body providing power to her major muscle groups. Fight or flight. It took a lot of training to overcome your own body's biochemistry in situations like this. A three-day training course at Hendon Police College just wasn't sufficient.

The gunman surprised Noel by hesitating. In situations like this Sam was statistically more of a danger to herself, Noel, Nick, Billy and the other guy than she was to the bad guy. If he knew what he was doing, and he certainly seemed to, then he had a good chance of reaching the Sig before Sam managed to shoot him.

Instead, he muttered something that Noel didn't catch and straightened up, raising his hands. Noel managed to stagger to his feet and retrieve his Sig. He levelled it at the gunman and gave a moment's thought to slotting him. Before backing up to Sam.

'Okay Sam, I need you to put the gun down,' Noel told her. She was staring at the gunman, who was starting to look a little worried. Nicholas, Billy and the other guy were very quiet, as they watched. 'Sam, love …' Noel reached over with his free hand. Her knuckles were distressingly white where she gripped the revolver. Her head jerked around to stare at him when he took hold of the gun but she let him take it from her. The gunman heaved a sigh of relief.

Sam seemed to snap out of it. She removed her handcuffs from the loop on her belt.

'Right you, get down on your knees, hands behind your head or, so help me, I'll pepper spray you in the face.'

***

'So let me get this straight,' Sam was furious. 'He beats on your crew, tortures you, and you don't want to press charges?'

There were a lot of policemen in the club now. Many of them were armed. There were paramedics as well. When he'd been able to Noel had gone down to the street but the car parked in the side street opposite was long gone. Danny and Josh were on their way to hospital but Billy had kicked up such a fuss that the paramedics had eventually relented and agreed to treat him there and then.

'We were just rough-housing, mucking around,' Nicholas answered unconvincingly. Sam started at him. Noel was pretty sure that, had she still been armed, she probably would have shot him right there and then. It wasn't just the charges, there was a lot of old anger there. Him and his brother had been bad kids. Not vicious, just bored and clever. Sam, then a beat copper, could have come down hard on them. She hadn't, instead she had taken a bit of time with them both. When Nicholas had gone up to read economics at Kings, on a scholarship that Sam had a hand in arranging, and Noel had joined the marines, she was sure she had done the right thing. She was less sure when Nicholas

87

had gone to work in the city upon graduation. She had become positively furious when he had quit his job in the city, and his name started turning up on criminal intelligence reports linking him to a drugs distribution network covering most of south London. Noel knew that Samantha felt betrayed by Nicholas.

'Drug pedalling piece of shit,' Sam spat. Noel sighed. Nicholas looked less than pleased.

'Samantha, that's not right. I wouldn't come to your house and disrespect you like this.'

'No criminals at my house.'

Nicholas glared at her for a moment.

'Fine, I wouldn't go to your family's house and do that. How is everyone over in Stepney?'

This time it was Sam's turn to glare.

'If they're not going to press charges, can you let me go?' the gunman asked as two uniformed police officers yanked him to his feet.

''Course you can, off you hop, love,' Sam told him. 'Oh, no, wait, shooters, stun grenades, I've changed my mind, you shut-the-fuck-up and you're still getting arrested.' The gunman shrugged as he was dragged out of the club.

Noel hurt. His nose was broken again, his ribs and kidney were really hurting.

'What about you?' Sam demanded angrily. Surprised, Noel looked down at the DSI. 'Are you pressing charges?' Noel glanced over at his brother. Nicholas didn't even need to shake his head. Noel could tell what he wanted. 'Don't look at him, look at me!'

Press charges. Grass. It just wasn't something that you did on the estates, or in the service.

'I don't know … it was a pretty fair fight. You any idea who he is?' he said. He sounded pathetic, even to himself, but he could see the look of relief on his brother's face. The gunman hadn't had any ID and hadn't been forthcoming with a name. Sam's face flushed so red in fury that Noel was worried that she was going to have a coronary right there and then.

'You're not a little toerag running around on the estates now! Grow the fuck up!' she screamed at him before glaring at Nicholas and storming out after the officers dragging the gunman.

***

Noel glanced at his dive watch. The police had finally gone. Oliver, the guy that Noel hadn't recognised – he seemed to be Nicholas' protégé – had retrieved a bottle of brandy from downstairs and Nicholas was pouring himself a glass. He had just got off the phone with a very worried Jess, Noel's sister-in-law.

'Want one?' Nicholas asked. Noel shook his head but helped himself to a bottle of beer. Nicholas drank a large mouthful of brandy.

'What was that about?'

'Honestly? I have no idea.'

'He waterboarded you.'

'You see what happened at the ice rink in Brixton a

little while ago?' Nicholas asked. He was watching his brother, looking for a reaction that said he'd been involved with the ice rink debacle.

Noel just nodded, but alarms were going off. The thing in Brixton had been part of operation Kingship as well. He made a note to look into it. Operation Kingship didn't seem to have anything to do with a heroin pipeline from Afghanistan but it certainly seemed tied to heavy hitters who weren't shy with the firepower.

'That's what he wanted to know about.'

'That anything to do with you?' Noel asked. Nicholas looked more exasperated than angry.

'Did it sound like the sort of thing I'd be involved in? Wild west bullshit.'

'Oh yeah, I forget you're the professional drug dealer … sorry, distributor,' Noel said acidly.

Nicholas turned to look at him, less than pleased.

'You just come here to register your displeasure at how you think I make my living, again?'

'No, I came to cut you free of the chair you were tied to. How's your chosen career path working out for you, though?'

'Thank you,' Nicholas finally said. 'So what are you doing here, tooled up, with plod in tow?' Nicholas drank another mouthful of brandy. 'More to the point, why haven't you visited since you got back? Jess keeps asking me, and Kimberley misses her uncle.'

Because I struggle to square your nice Home Counties life with the misery you cause getting the cash to live that way, Noel thought. *Or maybe I just know that Mum and Dad wouldn't have approved. That's why you waited until they were dead before you got into this line. Or maybe one day I come through the door with a gun in my hand and it's you stood there in the warehouse full of drugs.*

'I'm sorry, man,' Noel said, not meeting his brother's eyes. 'It's work ...'

'You're not a very good liar,' Nicholas said quietly. Look at me.' Noel looked up. 'It's me you don't approve of, not them.'

But she knows, Noel thought, *Jess knows where the cash comes from.* He may have been right. It still didn't stop him feeling guilty.

'What do you need, little brother?'

'What blue liquid would you find in a vial like this?' Noel asked. Nicholas glanced down at the vial, his face suddenly an unreadable mask. Noel noticed that Billy and Oliver had glanced at the vial as well.

'Is this tangled up in that bullshit out in Dagenham?' Nicholas asked. Noel didn't say anything. 'You're not the only one who has to keep things to yourself as part of your job.'

'This is important. If you've been watching the news then you'll know people went down.'

Nicholas looked at his little brother for a moment, his face softening.

'Your people?'

Noel didn't answer. He didn't have to. Nicholas picked up the vial and looked at it. Then he threw it to Oliver. Oliver examined it and then nodded.

91

'It looks like the vials Bliss comes in, but then it's a vial,' Oliver said and tossed it back to Noel. 'What's the black dust?'

'Carbon,' Noel said because he couldn't think of a good reason not to.

'Like in pencils?' Oliver asked.

'I thought that was lead,' Billy said.

'I guess,' Noel said. 'Have you got anything to do with this shit?'

Nicholas looked pained.

'No, and I don't fill warehouses with drugs and armed guards either. That's movie bullshit. Besides, it was north of the river.'

'What do you know about this stuff?'

'It's taking clubland by storm, outselling E, coke, K. It's supposed to be revolutionary, the best thing ever. Smooth, high energy, little come down.' It was Oliver who had answered.

'And you're not moving it?' Noel asked.

'Don't pretend you know about my business, and I won't pretend that I know about yours,' Nicholas told his brother angrily.

'Sorry,' Noel said. 'Who is then?'

'Jesus Christ!' Nicholas spat. 'What happens when you break your Official Secrets Act?'

'You get chucked in jail.'

'Well, you break our official secrets act and you get tortured to death and your family get killed.'

There was something in the way that Nicholas had said the last. Even though Noel hadn't seen much of

92

his brother in the last few years, he could still read him pretty well.

'Has someone threatened Jess and Kimberley?' Noel asked. He watched his brother clam up, but he read it in Billy and Oliver's reaction. 'Nick?'

'Nick,' Billy said quietly. 'Tell him. He's family, he deserves to know, it's not grassing. Besides, if we can't fight these cunts in the street, then maybe the royal marines can.'

Nicholas went quiet. Noel left him to it, sipping on his beer, looking around at the club at the wreckage caused by the stun grenade the gunman had apparently used initially.

'You heard of Tamal Gezmen?' Nicholas finally asked.

'No. Should I have?'

'He's part of a Turkish operation up north.'

'He work with the Russians?'

'Last time I saw him, he had some Eastern European muscle with him.' Nicholas narrowed his eyes. 'Why?'

Noel just looked at him apologetically.

'A bit fucking one-sided this.' Nicholas told him about his visit from Tamal and the implied threat to Jess and Kimberley.

***

Noel hit the street angry. Now he had someone to focus his anger on. Someone who had threatened his family as well as killed his people. Sam was waiting for him.

93

'Well?' Sam demanded. Noel checked the street and then very quietly told Sam the name. 'Right, let's find a way to ruin this prick's life.' She started back towards the car.

Georgetown, Washington DC, 10 May, 1322 (EST)

The brothel was as tastefully decorated as it was discreet. The hooker – no, Leo Greenwood reminded himself, the escort – was too elegant and beautiful to be compared with the whores that walked the streets, an excellent mix of still quite young but imaginative, very dirty and open to some of his more peculiar requirements.

'Mr President, I have to say I'm an enormous fan,' Rex said. He was stood by the side of the bed. He was only just over six feet tall now, his skin was no longer blue, and he only had two arms. He was wearing a very conservative suit. Though his long hair was still a platinum blond colour, it was held back in a ponytail.

The president of the United States of America screamed and threw himself out of bed. The prostitute sat bolt upright and reached for a security button. Suddenly, her face went slack and she collapsed on the bed, drooling slightly.

'Bob!' President Greenwood screamed. There was no answer from the head of his Secret Service security detail.

'I'll give you a moment,' Rex said. The President ran around the room becoming more and more terrified as nobody answered his screams. He found that neither his panic button nor his phone worked, and that he couldn't get out of the room. Rex was studying one of his perfectly manicured nails whilst assimilating, once again, the entire back catalogue of Jim Hendrix. He was almost in tears at the beauty of the music.

Eventually, the President sat down on the bed and sobbed.

'Just get it over with,' he moaned.

'Get what over with?' Rex asked.

'You're here to kill me, aren't you?'

Rex looked confused.

'No.'

Much to Rex's surprise, the President started to look more, not less, frightened.

'You're going to sodomise me aren't you?'

Rex shuddered.

'Mr President, I do understand human aesthetics.'

President Greenwood stared at him, though he did have to concede that he had let himself go more than a little bit.

'Now,' Rex started again. 'As I was saying. I'm a big fan. The sheer hypocrisy of your stay in office, how you manage to get people to put up with their situations slowly worsening, whilst you service the elite rather like this young lady was servicing you before I came in. Your platform of "family values", a thinly disguised way of keeping people divided based on gender, sexuality, and lifestyle choices! Not to mention the total contempt you evince in private for those standards that you claim to promote.' Rex gestured around the room and then started clapping. 'Sheer brilliance.'

'What? No, it's not ... please stop clapping ...'

Rex stopped clapping.

'And all of this without direct slavery, too much application of force and next to no technological sophistication.'

'Are you a journalist?'

'No, I'm an alien.'

'What? Look, what do you want?'

'To help.'

President Greenwood stared, slack-jawed, at Rex. Rex was wondering how this human had managed to get to his particular position of power.

'Why?' the President finally managed to ask.

'Because you're the second most powerful person on this world ...'

'Wait! Second?'

'The Chinese premier,' Rex suggested. Perhaps he shouldn't have said that, he thought. After all, he didn't want to hurt the man's feelings. 'Oh, I'm sorry, that won't affect your sexual performance, will it?'

'What?'

'I'd rather deal with you. I prefer American music. Though I can see them giving you a run for your money film-wise in a few years.'

'What do you want?' President Greenwood screamed.

'You need to relax,' Rex said. He held up a vial of bright blue liquid. The President stared at it. 'It'll be much better than snorting a couple of lines of coke off a hooker on your birthday, I promise you.' President Greenwood stared at Rex. 'Now, I understand that you have a problem with overcrowding in your prison system?'

Chapter Seven

Harringay, North London, 10 May, 1823 (BST)

Unusually, Sam had let Noel drive. She had chain smoked most of the long journey north. Noel had noticed that the hand holding the cigarette was shaking.

'You all right?' Noel asked as he found a place to park on Burgoyne Road, the last rung on the 'Ladder' that ran downhill from between Wightman Road and Green Lanes. Burgoyne Road was mostly residential, consisting of detached and semi-detached houses which, despite their impressive size, still managed to look rundown and dilapidated. Most of the properties on the road were rented accommodation.

Sam didn't answer. Instead she just climbed out of the passenger seat of the Astra and glared at him.

'Right, according to the Intelligence Bureau, Gezman operates out of one of the private Turkish social clubs on Green Lanes,' she finally said. Sam passed over her phone to Noel who looked at the picture of a bulky man, gone to seed, wearing just slightly too much jewellery, and clothes that were slightly too garish and a bit out of date. Noel knew that he was exactly the sort of drug dealer Nicholas despised.

Samantha had a good look around her to make sure nobody was listening before she resumed talking. 'Since we're having such a frank exchange of information,' she said sarcastically. 'You should know that Gezman runs the Turkish gangs in North London. He's credited with winning a drug war with the Kurdish gangs and all but putting them out of business. His crew controls the heroin trade north of the river. He's also thought to have killed his old boss, Dermitas Ecidip, who was an old school hoodlum. During the war with the Kurds the North London plod were running around all over the shop picking up bodies. I called some of narcotics lads working out of Harringay. They reckon Gezman's a monster, and responsible for the death of at least seven Kurds.'

They turned off Burgoyne Road and into the southern part of Green Lanes. Behind them there was a metal bridge carrying the railway line to nearby Harringay Green Lanes Station. Ahead of them the road was lined with greengrocers, markets, off licences, takeaways, Turkish and Kurdish restaurants and other assorted businesses, many of them with awnings, or seating and tables spilling out onto the cramped pavement. North, the road headed up past Turnpike Lane, where it turned into the High Road and led to the Wood Lane shopping centre.

'I fucking hate North London,' Sam muttered.

'Out of your comfort zone?' Noel asked, earning himself another angry glare. Noel decided to remain quiet. Sam was obviously still shaken from having to point a gun at someone and angry about how things had gone down in Nicholas's club.

A number of the businesses on Green Lanes were private social clubs, often with middle-aged or older men sat outside them smoking *nargile* water pipes, what everyone called *hookah* pipes.

'That's the place,' Sam said quietly nodding towards a painted-over shop front with writing in Turkish on the window next to a sign in English proclaiming it a private club. As they walked by Noel caught a glimpse inside. He saw a sparse room with peeling paint and a worn linoleum floor. There were a couple of tables in there with *nargile* pipes and coffee cups on them. There was a counter with an expensive looking coffee machine on it. A number of the people sat around in the club didn't look terribly Turkish to Noel. Nobody paid any attention to Noel and Sam as they walked by.

Noel looked around and spotted a pub on the other side of the road, nearly opposite the social club. The frontage was open and there were tables next to the pavement. He pointed at the pub for the benefit of anyone who might be watching them.

'Fancy a drink?' he asked. Sam nodded.

***

'So what's the plan then?' Noel asked.

'We watch, see if we can get probable cause to put

a surveillance team on him,' Sam told him. Noel looked disappointed. 'What did you want? Go in there and pistol whip him until he confesses to being the Bliss king of London?'

'No, I want him to leave my family alone.'

'That's great, that is. So you go in there all Charlie Bronson. Assuming that you don't get a bit of a hiding off of some drugged up Organizatsiya thug, he then knows that you're interested and connected to your toerag of a brother. The absolute best you can hope for in those circumstances is that you start a war of attrition.'

'Smile,' Noel said apparently using his phone to take a photograph of Sam. On the other side of the street there were people coming out of the social club looking up and down the street. Noel had caught a number of them in the photograph. He took a few more close-ups, shooting over the traffic that was crawling both ways down Green Lanes and then took a sip from the pint of lager he was nursing. Sam hadn't smiled.

'They look Turkish to you?' Noel asked.

'Now, you can't go racially profiling people,' Sam said, shaking her head. 'But no, they look more Eastern European to me. They armed?'

'From here I've no idea. Still a pretty tenuous connection to Dagenham.'

Sam just lapsed into silence.

'Are you still angry at me?' he finally asked. The men standing outside of the social club were definitely waiting for someone. Noel noticed how fit and healthy they all looked, despite the fact that a number of them were smoking. Sam didn't answer him. 'What did you expect? I don't know what my brother does ...'

'Yes, you do,' Sam said through gritted teeth.

'All right, maybe, but it's got nothing to do with me. *You* wanted me to talk to him. I've got nothing on him, you know that, and even if I did you can't expect me to grass him up.'

'All right fine,' Sam conceded. 'But the other guy ...'

'I think he was special forces,' Noel told her. Sam glared at him for a moment.

'Brilliant,' she muttered. 'He had a shooter, he obviously knew how to handle himself, he tortured your brother, nearly killed you. He's clearly dangerous and we're holding him on a bullshit possession of a firearm charge. You're basically helping get a dangerous individual, who's obviously no friend of your brother's, back out on the street. What if he's the guy Tamal sent? What if I could have flipped him and he ratted Gezman?'

'If he's ex-SF then you'll never be able to—'

'Yeah, yeah, you're all supermen. He might have done it for an easier life. You know he might kill your niece, right?'

Noel sat back and stared at Sam.

'A bit manipulative, Sam. Nicholas didn't want to ...'

'Nicholas is a scumbag drug dealer. You and me have got the same boss. I get that you don't want to grass your brother, I really do, but a bit of fucking solidarity wouldn't go amiss. I need to know you've got my back.

102

Instead I've got some boy's-own, playground school of ethics to deal with. I've got nothing to scare that guy with when I go back to interrogate him.'

'I didn't even want to go to Brixton,' Noel told her.

'So it's my fault?' she demanded.

'No, look I'm sorry. You're right.'

'You going to press charges then?'

'It's complicated. It'd involve Nicholas and I'm better off just staying far away from that world.'

'What world do you think we're in right now?' she asked, her voice oddly devoid of emotion. Instead she was just watching him intently.

'They're getting ready for something,' Noel said changing the subject.

'I know, and they're not doing it very subtly either,' Sam said. 'Go and sit in the car.'

'Sam ...'

'Just do what I tell you, I'll call you if there's any change.'

Noel stood up. His pint glass was largely still full.

***

Noel's phone started ringing as soon as he turned the corner onto Burgoyne Road. It was Sam.

'A Mercedes with tinted windows just pulled up. They may as well have written scumbag drug dealer in neon down the side of it. Gezman's just come out of the social club. Come and get me.'

103

Noel hung up and started running up the hill towards the car.

***

Sam was walking up towards Burgoyne Road when Noel turned onto Green Lanes. She waved at him, talking into her phone as if he was picking her up quite naturally. He didn't pull over. She just walked out into the road and climbed in.

'DSI Linley, you've got my badge number … yes I know … You'll find that Operation Kingship is citywide … well if you want to disturb the chief superintendent then that's your call.' There was a long pause. 'Good boy.' She hung up, shaking her head.

'Where is he?' Sam asked.

'He's about five hundred feet in front of you. Now what he's going to do is head up the "Ladder" first chance he gets and onto Wightman Road, it's a faster road, then I'm guessing down onto Turnpike Lane. We've got a helicopter in the area, I'm trying to get it to find him.'

'Won't that warn him?' Noel asked.

'Only if it follows him for a long time. There's always helicopters in the air these days.'

Noel nodded, but it was frustrating crawling along Green Lanes not even able to see who he was supposed to be following. After what seemed like an age he reached Cavendish Road, the next step on the 'Ladder', and turned west onto it. The road was all but empty. He accelerated, pleased that the police Astra had a bit of power under the hood. He roared up the hill and turned left onto Wightman Road, which crested the hill at the top of the 'Ladder'.

'Head down towards Turnpike Lane,' Sam told him.

'Is that a guess?' Noel asked.

'Yes, and take it easy, just speed a little bit.'

Noel nodded and headed along the narrow, winding, mainly residential Wightman Road. Sam's phone rang. She answered it. Sam could hear someone shouting over the sound of a helicopter.

'I got it wrong. He's just turned east onto St Ann's, it looks like he's heading down towards Seven Sisters. Turn right here onto Hewitt, you can drive like a lunatic,' she told Noel. 'I'm going have the chopper follow him for a bit whilst we keep back, then we're going to have to close on him.'

Noel braked hard, slewing the Astra right onto Hewitt and then gunned the car, accelerating down the hill back towards Green Lanes while Sam received guidance from the helicopter high above them.

***

The police helicopter had left them somewhere over Shoreditch. They had gone down Commercial Street, and then turned for a moment onto the Whitechapel Road before joining the A13, heading east. They could see the black Mercedes now. They were keeping well back. Both of them had been trying to ignore a sinking feeling.

'We're only going back to fucking Dagenham, aren't we?' Sam finally said, voicing both their fears. They were in Essex now. They had passed Dagenham Docks, the power station, the big car plant, and south of the A13 they could see a large container park. The Mercedes started indicating that it was going to turn off the dual carriageway. Noel glanced around at the area. There was not much in the way of non-industrial traffic that he could see off the dual carriageway.

'It's going to be pretty obvious that we're following him,' Noel told Sam.

'Don't indicate, just come off when he's pulled off.'

Noel resisted the urge to tell Sam that he'd done this before. Instead he started slowing the car. Sam was craning her neck to watch where the Mercedes was going as it came off the A13. As it disappeared from sight Noel shifted into the feeder lane and came off the dual carriageway.

'He's gone down, towards the river.' Sam told him. 'Courier Road, keep your distance.' She had grabbed an A to Z from her capacious purse and was rapidly flicking through it. Noel could see the Mercedes about eight hundred feet ahead of him.

'Dagenham's got no right being in an A to Z,' Sam muttered to herself. Noel slowed the car right down. 'Right, here we go. There's only one road down there, Fiesta Drive. Pull off here and park the car out of sight.'

Noel turned left into a dead end, making sure that the car was out of sight of Courier Road before turning to Sam.

'So what do you want to do now?'

'Well, I'm going to sit in the car bursting for a pee. You can go and do some squaddie stuff. A whatchamacallit, reconnaissance, and anything you find I can use to get probable cause, claiming you as a confidential informant. Use the camera on your phone.'

Noel was less than thrilled with the prospect but he got out of the car.

Dagenham, 10 May, 1954 (BST)

The sun had all but disappeared in the west but the bright lights of the docks, the power station and the container park were providing enough light for an artificial twilight. Noel was walking along the pavement feeling faintly ridiculous. He stuck out like a sore thumb. He thought about creeping along next to the containers but he knew he had a good chance of tripping security lights. Hiding in a crowd was easy enough, as was hiding in the wilderness; nearly deserted streets was another matter. All the lampposts in the container park having CCTV cameras on them didn't help the situation either.

He was starting to feel faintly stupid. This was the sort of Mickey Mouse stuff that got people into trouble. He was too professional and Sam was too high ranking to be engaged in these sorts of shenanigans. It was clear that the DSI had an axe to grind. A lot of the heat from the Operation Kingship was coming down on her, unfairly. She needed validation for her career's sake, if nothing else, and it was clear that she wasn't getting much in the way of support from her superiors. She was right, she needed probable cause before she could move on anything else.

Ahead, Noel could see a tree-lined, filthy waterway, barely worth the description of river. It flowed down towards the Thames about a mile to the south. On the other side of the waterway was the car plant. He had a choice, he could either brazen it out and walk down the street like he was a casual pedestrian, or he could try using the trees and the filthy river for cover. It wasn't much of a competition.

***

Noel was covered in foul smelling mud but he'd gone to some lengths to keep his hands and phone dry and clean. He was lying on the banks of the filthy waterway looking through the mesh fence of the container park at an office building. The Mercedes was parked outside it. As he watched, he heard a growling sound. He watched as two blue transit vans pulled up. There was something wrong with the sound they made. They sounded like the engines had been performance tuned at the very least. It was a familiar sound. Both the SBS and SAS used transits like that for domestic ops when they needed to get men and kit around quickly without drawing too much attention. He frowned but took close-up photos of the vans.

Men climbed out of the vans, again they all looked to be in good shape. At least one of them was carrying a weapon. It was too far to be sure but Noel thought that it could be an MP7. Gezman climbed out of the Mercedes and said something to the man. Noel was too far away to hear what was said but he could still hear the anger in the voice. The weapon was hastily tucked under a jacket.

A towing vehicle pulled up with a container on its trailer. Gezman climbed out of the Mercedes and watched as the men opened it up and started taking crates out of it, loading them into the waiting transits. The crates looked similar to those he had seen during the raid. On the other hand a crate is a crate is a crate, he thought.

A figure walked out of the darkness of the container, stepping between the crates. He was wearing a suit. Gezman spoke to him but the man said nothing. Noel focused on the man in the suit and then froze. He recognised him. Martin Collins, one of the two SAS blades that had gone missing on the way back from the pub four months ago. Noel swallowed and then started taking photographs again, cursing the phone's pathetic zoom capability. Collins stepped down out of the container and went and stood by the door to the office building.

The container was emptied and the vans closed up as the guards climbed back into them and Gezmen got back into the Mercedes. Collins turned and walked into the office building. Noel sent a text to Samantha warning her that they were leaving and then started texting the pictures to her as well. The gates rolled open as the Mercedes and the transits rolled out of the container park and up Fiesta Road.

Noel received a text from Sam instructing him to return to the car. He started to make his way quietly back through the sparse tree cover next to the filthy little river. Discipline had him concentrate on the task in hand. He couldn't afford to try thinking too hard about what he'd seen just yet.

***

'Christ, you fucking honk,' Sam said by way of a greeting. 'You're not getting in my car like that.' He was covered in the filthy black, polluted mud that had made up the riverbank.

'I've got a change of clothes back at my car.'

'Well, I'll drop you there but you're still not getting in my car like that.' Sam handed him a plastic bag and then went to the boot, where she got out a bottle of water and a tartan car blanket. 'Strip off, clean yourself off as best you can and then you can wear the blanket until we get back to your car.' She looked at him expectantly. Noel knew she wasn't going to turn away and give him any privacy either. He sighed, irritated, and started to strip off under Sam's appreciative eye.

'I ran some of the photos we took on Green Lanes through our facial comparison software while I was waiting,' she said reaching into the car to pull out her phone.

'Organizatsiya?' Noel asked.

'Yes, and all of them used to look a lot less buff than they do now. Same can't be said for you, I see.'

Noel looked up and glared at the policewoman.

'See the guy in the suit?' Noel asked as he poured water down himself, his filthy clothes now in the plastic bag. He was going to bin them as soon as he got the chance. 'I know him. He's SAS, or was. His name's Martin Collins. Him and his mate, a Lewis Shaw, went missing four months ago on the way home from the pub.'

'AWOL?' Sam asked, watching Noel wash the mud off his skin.

'Supply And Services aren't really the sort of outfit that you go AWOL from.'

'You think he's on a job?'

'If he is, I'm guessing it's well off the books and utterly deniable.'

'This is a fucking mess this, Turkish heroin gangs, Organizatsiya soldiers, now the SAS. What is it, hands across London?'

Noel had to agree. He did not like the idea that a fellow special forces soldier had anything to do with the death of eleven members of his troop.

'What now?' he asked as he wrapped the blanket around himself.

'Well, now I'm finished perving I'm going to put in a request for an armed surveillance team on here and Green Lanes.'

'You reckon you'll get it?'

'Known heroin distributor, automatic weapons, I should think so. Besides, if that was Bliss you saw, I would imagine it's going to be illegal soon. Everything really fun is.'

***

Noel reflected that he'd driven through hostile areas in Iraq and Afghanistan and felt more confidence in the outcome of the journey than he did driving with Sam. She didn't believe in hands-free, and she didn't feel that the law about not using a phone whilst driving applied to her.

'I know that Bliss isn't illegal, sir, but automatic weapons still are, aren't they?' she demanded, shouting into the phone as she pulled out around a bus into oncoming traffic and accelerated. Noel glanced over at her, in part so he didn't have to look at the oncoming taxi that was leaning on its horn. It was late now and he still had to drive back down to Poole, he'd only had a weekend pass. Sam had a face like thunder. 'Thank you sir, thank you very much.' She cut the connection on the phone and threw it over her shoulder into the back seat of the car.

'No go?' Noel asked, slightly surprised.

'Seems that an unpopular administration doesn't want to start another drugs war they can't ultimately win. It

112

seems like there's some support to legalise Bliss, save them from having to enforce drug laws in a flooded market that's going to make the introduction of crack look like a drop in the ocean.'

Noel was staring at her.

'You're kidding me,' he said angrily. He could still see Dolton coming apart as he was riddled with fire from the modified MP7s. 'Eleven people!'

Sam turned to look at him, her hard-edged face softening for the first time that day.

'I know, love, I know.'

'Please look at the road, Sam.'

The police officer turned back and corrected her drift into oncoming traffic.

'I've got some favours I can pull in. People who used to work the Azure teams in Special Branch before it was amalgamated.' Azure was a term Special Branch and some of the other British intelligence services used for surveillance.

Noel nodded. He knew he should probably leave it. He guessed they were in well above their heads. Perhaps it was all part of a massive sting operation, but his people had gone down and he wanted answers.

5th Avenue, New York City, 11 May, 1511 (EST)

Rex was enjoying himself listening to the ideas of the exclusive PR company he had hired, especially their thoughts on how to create public support for Bliss legalisation with a widespread social media campaign and the use of lobbyists to push the paperwork through Congress.

'I like it, I particularly like the use of celebrities to push the hedonistic meme,' Rex said. 'However my problem is this: hedonism has often been used as a form of resistance to society, although not very effectively. I don't want this seen as a way of opposing authority, or more importantly those with power.'

'Mmm, yes I understand, Mr ...' the managing director of the PR firm began. He was so gym-sculpted, salon-haired and designer-clad he had become bland in Rex's eyes. He was sweating eagerness for Rex's account, as much for the vast amounts of money involved as for being a part of the 'next big thing'. The man's real name was Marvin but he insisted that everyone call him Harris.

'Just Rex,' Rex told the MD. Marvin seemed pathetically pleased at the familiarity.

'Well, Rex, we understand that. Now, my competitors won't tell you this but ultimately this is really about selling. Resistance is another brand, only useful for selling things to the young and angry. Kids, and indeed people in general, are interested in one thing and one thing only these days, gratification. You know it, and I know it. And that's what we'll be offering. Our on-message statement will be driven home again and again: everything's shit, it's not going to get better, there's absolutely nothing you can do about it, so you might as well ignore it and have fun anyway.'

'So if anything,' Rex started. 'You'll be ...'

'Reinforcing dominant power and authority memes,' Harris finished, looking absurdly desperate for approval.

Rex gave this some thought. It was as if all the beautiful people in the room were holding their breath waiting for his reply. Rex was a little taken aback at how easy it was to get one human being to screw over another. They all seemed desperate to believe that they were somehow better, more intelligent, more advanced than the masses they felt they manipulated.

'Okay, I like it,' Rex finally said, in part because he was worried that he was going to suffocate a number of them if he'd left it any longer. 'Now let's talk about specifics. I want to look at how you want to differentiate your social media campaign from everyone else's.'

'Well, you're going to have the best creative minds in the business on the job,' Harris began. 'But, to be frank, we're going to be spending more money on this than anyone else ...'

Rex allowed himself to relax a little as he listened to the details of the social media element of their quiet invasion. This was what he loved about what he did. He would subvert, and ultimately control, their society and they would love him for it. The interesting thing was that humans, to a degree, were already conditioned for this form of control.

Rex actually sighed and sank in his seat as he received the thought summoning him. He excused himself from the plush and comfortable conference room.

***

Rex pushed the door open to the toilets. Bad Trip had

painted it red. He was holding his victim in the air by one hand. The alien's fingers had sunk into the flesh of the hapless PR executive's face. Bad Trip's other hand was buried deep in the shaking, suspended man's stomach, reaching up inside him into the chest cavity. Bad Trip was covered in the man's blood as well.

'What are you doing?' Rex demanded.

'He walked in on me,' Bad Trip said, his voice a monotone.

'And you couldn't have pretended to be having a piss, or even just gone and stood in a cubicle?' Bad Trip ignored him. 'Look, just drop him.'

Bad Trip turned to look at Rex. Despite the malevolence of the set of his features, his expression was difficult to read. The Enforcer flung the corpse away from him. It slid across the floor, coming to a halt close to Rex's foot. Rex stepped forward, his foot growing through his designer shoes. A toe touched the corpse and started injecting enzymes into it, to break down the body for absorption, after which he would convert it to energy. At the same time he was exuding miniscule pico machines through his skin that would do the same for the gore-coated toilet.

'There will be less fear if he just disappears,' Bad Trip told Rex.

'Is there a reason you're making my day difficult?' Rex demanded. 'I have a lot on today. I have to make sure that enough synthetic diamorphine is delivered to the prison system to start widespread serotonin harvesting, though it's going to be inferior to our free range serotonin.

116

I have to turn a lot of base metal into gold so the US can pay its national debt off, and tomorrow we start seeding the atmosphere to start modifying the climate.'

'Why?'

'To make the climate more favourable for speed-growing modified versions of the kind of narcotics that encourage the production of human neural transmitters.'

'I understand that, why bother with their national debt?'

Rex sighed theatrically.

'Because it's easier than force and means nothing to us. President Greenwood is now addicted to Bliss, by the way.' Rex concentrated for a moment. 'Excuse me, a wife of one of the prisoners on our pilot scheme has apparently blogged about institutionalised heroin addiction on Rikers Island. It's gone now. Oh wait, someone in the British security service had a copy of the article. She'll have to be watched. No, it's gone now as well. I do love this planet but their infoscape is so rudimentary, no concession to aesthetics whatsoever, very boring ...'

'I think there's someone else on the planet,' Bad Trip interrupted. The corpse and its by-products had all but gone. Rex looked up sharply at Bad Trip.

'What makes you think that?'

Bad Trip tried to send his findings over in thought form. Rex shook his head.

'Getting used to verbal communication is good for you. No human surveillance can break the fields we generate.'

'Strange energy signatures from the satellite seeds.'

'Where?'

'Myanmar, Damascus, Namibia, North Africa, London, a few other places.'

'Any idea of tech level?'

'Lower than ours.'

It was a human affectation, but Rex breathed a sigh of relief. The Weft were the closest in tech level and they were still way behind the Pleasure. The rest of the known races, most of them who were now loyal customers, or not profitable to deal with, were even further behind than that. The only ones who had comparable tech were the long dead, probably mythical, Dreamers.

'Do they have off-world capability?'

'Unknown but best to assume that's the case.'

'Okay, well, that's not the best news but it could be worse. Frankly I don't want to share.'

'Destroy them?'

'Inevitably. I'd like to know who they are first. I'd like to know their capabilities, but most importantly I want to make sure that they are unable to communicate with anyone. The last thing we want is the Weft discovering an entire planet full of addictive fun and soul-destruction-producing sentients.'

'They would sterilise it.'

Rex nodded. 'I'm serious, though, nothing too overt. We have some human assets that we can call on.'

'I could juice more special forces personnel.'

'How about just sub-juicing some for the time being?'

Bad Trip's expression changed slightly. It was only because Rex had worked with him for millennia that he recognised it. The Face reached out and laid his hand on the Enforcer's shoulder. Bad Trip looked down at the hand, slightly confused.

'Don't worry, we're working towards a big reveal. Until then it would be useful for anything we do to be attributed to a human agency.'

Bad Trip didn't reply. He just stared at Rex. The Face knew that his abilities were comparable to the Enforcer's. Even so, after a while he found the other being's stare very uncomfortable.

Chapter Eight

HMS *Rame Head*, Portsmouth Harbour, 28 June, 0630 (BST)

The 847 Naval Air Squadron Lynx Mk 9a came in low over the water between Gosport and Portsmouth heading for the grey and rust bulk of the World War Two, Fort Class, merchant ship HMS *Rame Head*. It had once been used as a lifeline between Britain and the US, braving the U-boat wolfpacks in the Atlantic convoys. Now it was used as a training ship for under-water demolitions, ship boarding techniques, and, as today, for close quarter battle – or CQB – training. Noel, however, could not get his head in the game. This was bad news, because today the *Rame Head* was being used as a Killing Ship. Not only was this a live firing exercise but there would be instructors playing the part of hostages. A mistake could prove fatal.

He had returned late to Poole last month, to find that Stanton had been seconded to some operation or another. Rumour had it that he was working with the Special Reconnaissance Regiment, Britain's third and most unknown special forces unit.

He was sat in the Lynx with the remaining living members of Red Troop. There were just four of them now, with Stanton gone. They were a patrol rather than a troop. Command was talking about rebuilding Red Troop primarily with this year's selection intake, to be run by the four remaining troopers. In Noel's eyes this would make for a disturbingly inexperienced troop.

Ever since his visit to London his head had been in a whirl trying to work out what was going on. What he had stepped in. What his brother was involved in. Wild ideas were flying around in his mind. The one that made the most sense was that Bliss was some kind of government-sponsored population pacification program. After all they'd had three summers of rioting now, thanks to austerity for working people, and tax breaks and graft for the wealthy. Meanwhile the economy had stayed in the pan. As far-fetched a conspiracy theory as this sounded it still didn't answer all the questions. The transformative matter, the high tech weapons. His mind did not really want to look too hard at the answers to those questions.

Robertson tapped him on the shoulder. He looked around suddenly. The Lynx's crew chief had been shouting at him. Thirty seconds to assault and he was supposed to be in charge. He nodded and signalled. Even through the respirator's bulbous eyes he could make out Robertson's questioning look. They stood, grabbing the lines. The side doors were open, the wind rushing in as they skimmed the top of the water. The door-gunners on either side of the helo were scanning

121

the surroundings, their general purpose machine guns, or Gimpys, at the ready.

Noel bent his legs slightly to compensate as suddenly the helo shot upwards. Water was replaced by grey metal streaked with rusted red.

'Go! Go! Go!' Noel shouted. The four SBS troopers kicked the ropes out of the helo, grabbed the lines with gloved hands and slid down them, forty plus feet to the deck of the *Rame Head*. Even through the thick leather of the glove Noel could feel the heat from the friction building. He felt metal under his boots. He pulled the gloves off quickly and pushed them into his webbing and brought his Diemacos C8 carbine up to his shoulder. It was too slow, it felt clumsy. All of them would have preferred to use the smaller MP5 SMGs but some bright spark had thought it best that they train with the carbines.

Noel moved swiftly to the breaching point. Robertson joined him on the other side of the door, both of them covering backwards. Jonesy remained back, covering above, as Hamilton set the breaching charge against the door. No different to what they had done at the warehouse in Dagenham. At the last moment, Jonesy joined them by the bulkhead next to the door. Hamilton hammered the detonator three times. The door blew out. Jonesy tossed in the flashbang. They looked away. Again no different to Dagenham.

They were in. Noel was first. He was in a red-lit, smoke-filled, narrow metal corridor. He swept right and left as he moved forward rapidly, crouching slightly, carbine at the ready. First door. He stood one side,

Robertson the other. Jonesy and Hamilton went straight past, moving to the next door on the other side of the corridor. Noel fumbled slightly with the flashbang. Robertson looked over at him again. Noel knew he was taking too long. Finally ready, Jonesy pulled the door open. Noel tossed in the grenade. Both of them turned away. Phosphorescent glare leaked through the polarised plastic of their respirators. Noel could hear his own breathing rasping in his ears. The bang from the flash-bang in close quarters deafened him. He expected to hear the scream of the modified MP7s and see bullets tearing through the bulkhead at any moment.

He forced himself to move into the room, smoothly bringing the C8 up, Robertson following. Noel could make out a figure through the smoke. He covered him with the C8 but didn't fire. There were real people in here some-where. He advanced on the figure. A balsa wood terrorist. Noel double tapped him in the centre of the forehead at almost point blank range. The rubber walls absorbing the bullets, CCTV recording it all, and later they would switch on the fans to suck out the smoke and cordite.

They went through the deck, room by room, but it didn't feel smooth, well oiled. It felt awkward and jerky, which meant it was slow.

In the penultimate room he double tapped a terrorist target. The first bullet he fired was a tracer meaning he only had three, now two rounds, left in the C8's magazine. He swung the C8 around and fired the two remaining rounds into another terrorist target. He could hear Robertson firing behind him.

'Reloading,' Noel said into the microphone inside his sweat filled respirator. It was unlikely anyone would be able to hear him. It was a mistake. He should have reloaded before entering the room. He ejected the C8's magazine and pushed it into his drop pouch. A locker exploded open and a balsa target slid out. Noel dropped the C8 on its sling and fast drew the Sig Sauer P226 from the holster clipped to the front of his body armour. It had been holstered safety off with one in the pipe. He advanced on the target firing. Not only a hostage, the target was a picture of a kid. Noel didn't have time to reflect, he just turned and headed for the final room.

They assaulted the final room as a four. The flashbang went in. All any of them could hear was ringing now. Noel was in first, Sig in hand. He and Robertson went forward. Jonesy went right, Hamilton left.

Real person, Noel thought. That it was Charlotte Whelan-Hollis gave him less than a moment's pause. She was sat at a table, blind, deaf and to her credit putting her head down on the table. There were figures either side of her. Noel fired on one as he advanced. He was aware of other muzzle flashes elsewhere in the room.

Checking that all the terrorist targets were down he grabbed Charlotte and pushed her onto the floor. Her hair was tied back and she was wearing jeans with a suit top. He pulled her arms behind her back and cable-tied her wrists together before pulling her to her feet. Over in the corner Hamilton was doing likewise to Bob Hurley, their company sergeant major. Jonesy and

Robertson provided security as Noel and Hamilton pushed the two hostages back through the corridor and out into the sunlight.

'And clear, end ex! End ex!' Hurley finally shouted when he'd recovered from the flashbang. The lynx was still on-station, flying around the ship, its door-gunners ostensibly acting as top cover for the assault.

***

'Well, frankly that was a bit of a fucking mess, wasn't it?' Hurley asked. Noel was wondering what the CSM was doing on the training mission at all. Normally lower ranking non-commissioned officers would handle the training. 'Fuck it, they're not making those flashbangs any quieter, are they?' Hurley said, using a finger to explore his ear before pointing it at Noel. Noel was ejecting one clip from the P226, loading another before making it safe and holstering the automatic pistol, because the exercise was over. 'Why did you have your sidearm in your hand?' the CSM asked. 'Why not just come in waving your todger?'

'He didn't want to scare anyone,' Jonesy said, receiving a few laughs.

'Got caught out reloading,' Noel admitted.

'In a room? Good thing I didn't hide in a locker, wasn't it?'

'You wouldn't have fitted, boss,' Robertson cracked, though he glanced over at Noel.

Hurley grabbed his stomach.

'None of your six-pack nonsense, this is what a real man looks like. Isn't that right Charly?' the CSM asked. Charlotte just laughed. 'And the cardinal crime, the one that killed you and all your mates. Hamilton took me down and searched me. Why didn't you search Charly here? Too much a gentleman, or just thinking about what she'd look like without her clothes on?'

'Sorry boys,' Charly said and undid her now dirty and ripped suit jacket. Underneath she was wearing a mock-up of a bomb vest. She took the detonator out of her pocket. The others swore and muttered. Noel felt like a fool.

'Sorry lads, this is on me,' Noel said. He had let them down badly, he knew. The fact was, training notwithstanding, it didn't take too many fuck-ups of this calibre before people started getting nervous going out on a shout with you.

'Yeah, you feel like a tosser now, right? A dead hostage, even a kid, I can live with. A dead patrol, less so.' Noel and the others nodded. 'Okay lads, give me and fuck-up here a minute will you?' The other three and Charly moved away. Hurley waited until they were out of earshot. 'You don't make mistakes like that. You're a tight arse, Noel, but you're thorough. You're head's not in this game.'

'Sorry Bob. It's not going to happen again.'

The CSM regarded him for a moment as if he was looking for something before turning to look out over the water. It was bright blue this morning, reflecting the near cloudless sky above them. The breeze ruffled

Bob's hair. It was far longer than any marine had a right to grow it; that, the moustache, and the omnipresent Motorhead T-shirts made him look more like a roady than a high-ranking NCO in the SBS. That was kind of the point. He'd come up in the '80s working under paper-thin covers chasing the Provisional IRA around Belfast and Londonderry. His look had earned him the nickname 'Porn Star'.

'All right, I've been all over Operation Kingship. Your reports, the forensics, I even walked the site, and I've spoken to everyone, including yourself. I was looking for a fuck-up, looking for someone to bin. If you fucked up I can't find it.'

'I know. I've done the same.'

'So what the fuck? Have you had enough? Do you want to get RTU'd?'

'No ...'

'Okay, you know there's no first days back, yeah? You don't get to ease into things. You can either do the job or you can't, and we need to know.'

'I can do it,' he replied, no hesitation, no excuses.

The CSM watched him for a moment, again as if he was looking for something.

'All right, we train so we can get all our fuck-ups out of the way beforehand,' Porn Star said. Noel nodded. 'Anything else you want to tell me?'

'Like what?' Noel couldn't quite keep the suspicion out of his voice.

'There's been some question about your extracurricular activities.'

Noel was starting to like this less and less.

'Meaning what?' he demanded. It wasn't like Bob to be anything other than blunt and direct.

'Your brother.'

'Is my brother, that's all. I've got nothing to do with his business.'

'But you were at his club, even lying for him.'

Samantha was Noel's initial suspicion but he honestly didn't think that she would do that. There had been more than enough police there for it to get back through any number of people.

'For some of the Ruperts, those that don't know you well, it looks funny. Your brother's a drug dealer. You suddenly start carrying. It looks funny,' Porn Star told him.

Noel felt like he had been slapped.

'You think I'm an enforcer for my brother?' he asked angrily. His voice carried and the others looked over from where they were chatting with Charlotte. Bob actually gave the question some consideration.

'No,' he finally decided. 'I don't, but you might want to give the extracurriculars a knock on the head. We've got a troop to rebuild.'

'Yeah okay, I'm with you,' Noel said feeling the tension drain from him.

'You know you need a shag, don't you?' Bob said, glancing back at Charlotte.

'How do you know her?' Noel asked, following his gaze. He could see her smiling as she chatted away with the other three troopers, making them laugh.

128

'She says she's with the DSTL but she's got a skill set. She was hunting MWDs in Iraq, I think she knew she was wasting her time even then. She was with M Squadron in Northern Iraq in 2003.'

Noel raised an eyebrow.

'How old was she?'

'Early, maybe mid-twenties at the oldest. She kept up, laid fire down when she had to, no complaining when we had to ditch the Pinkies.' Pinkies was a slang name for the modified and heavily armed Land Rovers they had used in the desert. 'She's some kind of spook, well educated, clever, but she doesn't mind roughing it with the boys when she has to. How'd you know her?

'She's looking into some of the weirder stuff to do with Kingship.'

'Good,' Bob said. 'I want to know why eleven of my boys died.'

'Why is she here?'

'Wants to speak to you.'

'She's got one hell of a clearance.'

Bob just raised his eyebrows. 'You need to be careful of her, that one will eat you alive.'

Her ears apparently burning, Charlotte looked over and smiled at them both.

Penthouse, Grand Hyatt Hotel, Washington DC, 28 June, 1701 (EST)

Rex was exhausted. It wasn't physical. The form he had grown was more than capable of putting up with the excesses of his existence – in fact, it had been tailored to physiologically revel in them. This was the most demanding part of any cultivation operation. To a degree the humans were aiding him a great deal in their corruption. He wasn't sure he'd ever met a ruling caste of any other species so very eager to be corrupted. The wealthy and the powerful were queuing up to be bought and paid for, for short-term gain. None of them seemed to realise how short sighted they were being. In the imminent kingdom of pleasure their wealth and power would mean nothing.

Rex looked out across the city. He took in the imperial architecture and the promises of power it made. He imagined the city as an infected, corrupt wound below the surface. Then he caught a glimpse of his reflection in the window. His perfect physical form looked tired.

Normally, the penthouse suite would be filled with a number of the most attractive escorts the city had to offer but tonight he just wasn't in the mood, though he could see two of his favourites resting on the large bed through the bedroom's open door. Normally, the table would be piled high with narcotics, indigenous and imported, but today he had been entertaining lobbyists, and he had wanted to portray a certain legal and moral greyness.

Today, he had provided lobbyists with vast amounts of money, so much material wealth, in fact, that many of them had left the penthouse suite with erections and/ or moist underwear. He thought about the two highly priced prostitutes in his bedroom. Both of them would have been disgusted by how quickly the lobbyists were prepared to whore themselves. How quick they were to sell out their fellow humans, not to mention any principles they may have once had.

He'd fallen out a little with humanity. They had disappointed him. It was so at odds with all but their crassest art. Most of the humans' art seemed to be about their 'higher self'. Rex had found very little evidence of this higher self amongst the powerful and wealthy elites of the planet. He felt let down. More to the point, it was too easy. There was no challenge.

Many Enforcers, and Bad Trip was no different, just didn't understand why they didn't use self-replicating picotech spore colonies to mind control entire populations and harvest them that way. The quick answer was that, even allowing for AI-run simulations, something in the organic mind seemed to instinctually understand it was being controlled. Rex suspected it was the response of minds having to know the difference – even if only at some subconscious level – between dreaming and reality. Someone always noticed that they're living in a simulation, which in turn could lead to a rebellion, which, if suicidal enough, could spoil an entire crop. Also, connoisseurs always claimed that they could taste the difference between free-range and battery-farmed product.

To Rex, the art of it all was to give the crop what they wanted, or what they thought they wanted. Let the crop come to them of their own free will. What he was discovering, however, was that the humans were doing it to themselves. They were much better at manipulating each other, and creating lies for others to live, than even he was.

It was astonishing to Rex. A tiny elite controlled the vast majority of the resources in the world and in many circumstances, particularly in the so-called democracies, they didn't even have to use force to control the population. Instead they just made sure that the population had ample junk food and something called reality television. Though the 'realities' in question had very little to do with any reality that Rex had experienced in his millennia of existence. What the picotech did allow them to do was invade the humans' minds, read their dreams, listen to their souls, find their darkest desires and provide for them. It was little more than a catalogue of vice and corruption. Then he had found ways to capitalise on the aftermath of their targets' depraved indulgences, whether by dependency or blackmail.

And they had been so easily swayed: addiction, pretty boys and girls, money, pretend power, the offer to indulge their jaded sensibilities in vices normally too cruel or barbaric to countenance.

He'd arranged for the Mayor of London to murder a prostitute. He had taken numerous politicians, including the British Home Secretary, to sex clubs, something that had really challenged his aesthetic sensibilities. He'd mind controlled all the women who had ever spurned a police commissioner so they could be his playthings and much, much more.

As a result of this he'd arranged for enforcement of the pollution laws to be relaxed. He'd started to subtly influence the environment. Poppy fields and cocoa plants were starting to make their way onto European and American farms. Grown by desperate farmers whose subsidies had been cut, the local authorities paid to look the other way.

The Russian premier, like many other leaders, had enthusiastically embraced the farming of prison populations for nothing more than an admittedly large quantity of gold. Even if they hadn't already devalued the metal by flooding the market with synthetic gold, it would soon be worthless. The prison farms used Earth-grown heroin to stimulate endorphin production. It would create a low-grade product, but that wasn't the point. The point was that they could do what they want. Nobody cared. Rex had influenced media companies to concentrate on the trivial and celebrity. It didn't matter what happened to prison populations because, according to the PR campaign, the world's shit, there's nothing you can do about it so you might as well take Bliss and forget about it all.

As much as Rex liked decadence, wallowing in human sin had taken its toll. He had required a cornucopia of various narcotics to see him through. A little something to be social. A little something to enhance his alpha-personality confidence. A little something to mask his contempt. He'd surfed the appalling pleasures of the symphony of vice and corruption that he'd admittedly created, but that, frankly, had got away from him as a result of human interaction. All of which had taken its toll.

He needed to rest. He needed to get away from the mire of human corruption for a while. He disassembled his body. His true form infected the matter of the Mindship. He took his thoughtform to one of the ship's wombs and slept.

A31, New Forest, 28 June, 2243 (BST)

Charlotte had flown back with them to Poole. There she had presented Hurley with the bad news. Noel had been seconded to her command to work on a classified operation. The CSM had been less than pleased about this and had pointed out that he had a troop to rebuild. Charlotte had been apologetic but firm, and of course unable to tell Porn Star anything more about the operation for security reasons. Now they were in Noel's Saab speeding through the New Forest, heading back to London as the sunset made the trees look quite black against the golden light.

'Why me?' Noel finally asked. Charlotte was sat in the passenger seat tapping away on a ruggedised laptop.

She glanced over at him.

'I'm afraid it's not because you're pretty. I have very strict rules on that kind of thing when I'm working.'

Noel's heart sank only a little bit.

'Makes sense,' he managed. And it did, he knew.

'You were there.'

'So were four other lads, not including that idiot Harcombe.'

'True, but you went looking. I like curious people because, believe it or not, I am actually something of a scientist.'

'I'll take your word for it.'

'And frankly because of your brother.'

Noel felt himself getting angry again.

'Look, I am not my brother ...'

'I think your brother's involved and I think if nothing else he's a gateway into that world.'

Noel took his eyes away from the road to look at Charlotte. She was very attractive. She was a little flirty and fun to be around. He was also coming to the conclusion that she was ambitious, manipulative and quite ruthless.

'Are you using my brother as bait?' he asked, turning back to the road.

'As long as you don't break operational security you're more than welcome to tell him to mend his ways. Think he will?'

I think he's beginning to come around to that way of thinking, Noel thought, but didn't say anything.

'If things go bad I'll make sure he's offered protection,' she said, her voice softening. 'But frankly he made his choices, he has to live with them.'

Or not, Noel added silently.

'Is it just me in this task force of two?' Noel asked. Charlotte didn't answer. *So that's a no then,* Noel thought. He didn't like it. Intelligence types liked their secrets but compartmentalisation of this nature could mean wasted effort at best and blue-on-blue at worst. Given that she'd had him draw stores for urban operations and the trunk of his car was full of equipment, including various weapons, the latter didn't seem that outrageous a possibility.

'There are a lot of strange things happening ...' Charlotte started. Noel's phone started ringing. By force of habit he had it connected to a rudimentary Bluetooth device he'd added to the Saab. He had to shout at it several times before Samantha's voice came over the speakers.

'Sam, Charlotte's in the car with me as well,' he said by way of a warning.

'That posh bit? Shagged her yet?' Sam asked.

'DSI Linley, how lovely to hear from you,' Charlotte said cheerfully.

'Well hello to you, and hello to GCHQ, and the fucking NSA as well for all I know.'

Charlotte glanced over at Noel who shrugged.

'Sam, have you been drinking?' Noel asked.

'You're fucking right I have. I'm on my sixth G and bloody T and I can tell you that I just don't give a fuck.'

Again Charlotte and Noel exchanged a glance.

'What's wrong darling? If you don't mind me asking,' Charlotte asked.

'I do mind you asking because I wouldn't be at all surprised if this was your doing you stuck-up bitch.'

'That seems fair,' Charlotte said. 'Can you tell me anyway?'

'They've only gone and fucking pulled my Azure teams, haven't they? Which is a bit fucking strange because it was off the books.'

'Could one of them have grassed you?' Noel asked.

'Not these guys,' Sam said with conviction, though Noel suspected that some of the conviction was born of drink. 'Which means …'

'… your phone's been tapped,' Charlotte finished. 'The one you're talking to us on, no doubt.'

'Yes!' Sam shouted, sounding spitefully cheerful.

'Lovely,' Charlotte said, sounding less than pleased.

'And I've been reprimanded,' Sam added. 'Apparently it's a serious reprimand, it's gone down on my permanent record and everything. Looks like I'm not going to be the next commissioner. Oh, and the guy who beat you up, and waterboarded your brother. His name's Roche Manning, ex-Para Pathfinder, but he's got classified all over his military record so I suspect he's another sneaky bastard like you.'

'Maybe we shouldn't—' Charlotte started.

'Shut up you,' Sam told her. 'Said that he wanted to give your bruv a bit of a hiding for selling some drugs to the kid of a friend of his. Of course he didn't want to provide any corroboration for that, and frankly the story had more holes in it than a sieve, but guess what? Two hours in and we get a phone call. Released into the custody of the army. So my question is, are either of you two cunts running covert ops on my patch?'

Charlotte reached up and touched the phone, breaking the call connection.

'Hey!' Noel objected. Charlotte just turned to look at him. 'Okay, she was being a little indiscreet.'

'A little?'

'Anything you'd care to add to what she was saying?'

'Not in an insecure environment.'

Charlotte received a text. She looked at the glowing screen of her phone and then reached up and switched on the radio.

'… has yet claimed responsibility for the detonation of an apparently nuclear weapon in Damascus, Syria. The death toll is believed to be in the thousands. The act has received universal condemnation from secular and religious leaders alike in the Western and Islamic world. The British Prime Minister, along with the American President, have joined with many other Western leaders in offering aid to the Syrian people. There is some speculation that the explosion is in retaliation for Syria's …' Charlotte switched off the radio.

'Oh …' Noel managed.

'Pull over,' Charlotte said pointing at a parking area on the other side of the road. Noel swerved into it and brought the Saab to a halt. Charlotte grabbed her laptop and climbed out of the car and walked out into the woods. Noel watched her go for a moment or two and then followed.

'What are you doing?' Noel called after her.

'Don't worry, I'm not going to rape you,' she called behind her. Noel sighed and followed her. She was waiting for him three hundred or so feet into the woods. He opened his mouth to speak, she held her finger to her lips and walked towards him holding her mobile phone. She ran it around him looking for a transmitting signal that would interfere with the phone. She found nothing.

'This is far from fool-proof, so I'm not going to be saying much, okay?' Noel nodded. 'There's oddness, has been for a lot of years, strange sightings, disappearances, that sort of thing. The oddness is increasing in tempo and going in interesting new directions that seem a lot more overt.'

'Like Damascus getting nuked? Surely that's got to be ...'

Charlotte was shaking her head.

'I don't know. I'm looking into the oddness but I need someone with a certain flexibility, a certain skill set, and frankly someone who won't stick out a million miles in the same circle as your brother.'

'Upper-middle-class Buckinghamshire?' Noel asked. Charlotte glared at him.

'You know what I mean.'

'Yeah, I do,' he said less than pleased.

'Look, this is the sort of thing I'm talking about.' She opened up her laptop, the glow of the screen illuminating the dark woods. She tapped keys and worked the mouse-pad for a few moments, looking more and more unhappy.

'What's up?' Noel asked.

'It's not here,' Charlotte muttered.

'What's not?'

'A file, the fucking file I was going to show you.'

'Perhaps you saved it somewhere else.'

This time her glare was enough to make him hold his hands up apologetically.

'I don't do things like that,' she said through gritted teeth.

'Okay, I believe you.'

'This can't happen,' she was muttering. She almost seemed on the brink of losing it. This did not make sense if she was the same girl capable of keeping it together when the entire Iraqi 5th army corps, some hundred thousand soldiers, had been hunting her and the rest of M Squadron.

'There's got to be a rational explanation,' Noel said.

'No, that's the thing. There hasn't and there isn't one. Someone has broken an augmented version of the best computer security that British Intelligence has, without a trace, and completely erased a file. Do you know how actually difficult it is to remove all traces of information from a computer, short of an EMP?'

'Eh … no.'

'Well it's cunting hard, frankly.'

'What was it?' he asked finally.

'A blog piece. The wife of a convicted murderer, serving time on Rikers Island in New York, wrote about her husband being force fed heroin by the prison authorities.'

Noel gave this some thought.

'Why?'

'I don't know but Bliss, heroin, this all seems to be about drugs, doesn't it?' Noel had no answer. Charlotte seemed to be calming down. He'd seen her sit in the Killing Room and deal with live rounds flying past her head. A lot of people understandably shat themselves, even special forces types. She hadn't. If what Porn Star had told him was true, then she could handle herself. It had taken an apparently effortless violation of her electronic security to rattle her. 'Do you know Britain used to be the biggest drug dealer in the world?' she asked. Noel shook his head. 'We fought two wars with China to force them to allow the import of opium from India. In the end it came down to us wanting a better deal on tea.'

'Everyone likes a brew,' Noel said trying to lighten the moment. Charlotte looked up at him.

'I think that sometimes we're made to pay for our sins.'

Angels & Demons Nightclub, Brixton, 29 June, 0219 (BST)

They'd come in just as the club was closing. Five of them. Tamal Gezman, the two Russian muscle that he'd brought the first time. A solidly built white guy in a suit, something about him suggested military to Nicholas. The fifth man was something else, however, Nicholas decided. Much of his face always seemed to be in shadow. He had grey receding hair tied back into a ponytail and he was powerfully built, but the muscle looked hard earned, rather than sculpted in a gym. It was difficult to work out his age but he guessed the man was a very healthy and fit sixty-something-year-old. He had a mismatched-craggy face, with an angry looking scar running down it, a hooked nose, and the coldest eyes that Nicholas had ever seen. Something about this man just reeked of malevolence.

'Okay, don't be stupid,' Nicholas said. The two Organizatsiya muscle were pushing Danny and Josh ahead of them. They had their hands on their SMGs but weren't pointing them at anyone just yet.

Billy glanced over at Nicholas. The dreadlocked lieutenant was reaching inside his jacket for the two long-nosed .38 revolvers he kept there. Nicholas shook his head. He wouldn't stand a chance against automatic weapons. Oliver moved behind the bar.

'I am sorry about this, Nicholas,' Tamal said. The two Organizatsiya muscle let Danny and Josh go. The two big men turned to face the Russians.

'It's all right lads,' Nicholas said. He motioned for them to back off. There was some angry posturing in the face of well-armed Eastern-European nonchalance. Nicholas turned to Tamal. 'Is this how you want to do things?' he asked, glancing at the man with the ponytail who seemed surprisingly bored with the proceedings. Gezman sat at one of the club's glass tables and gestured for Nicholas to do the same. The military guy in the suit came to stand next to him. The evil-looking man with the ponytail sat at a different table, ignoring everyone. The two Russians had their guns at the ready keeping an eye on Billy, Josh, Danny and Oliver, all of whom looked less than pleased.

'We made you a very reasonable and lucrative offer,' Gezman told him.

Nicholas sat down opposite Gezman.

'Which I appreciate, but I equally reasonably declined your offer, though it was greatly appreciated,' Nicholas said looking around at all the muscle before pointing at them. 'This, however, this I don't appreciate at all.'

142

Gezman shrugged apologetically.

'I am sorry you feel that way …'

'This is the problem. You see all that bullshit in Dagenham?' Gezman nodded. 'Too much heat. Too much trouble, and noise and violence. That's not me, that sort of thing's got nothing to do with me.'

'I appreciate your fear but I am here to assure you that you have nothing to worry about. Soon Bliss will be legal, we will be completely legitimate.'

Nicholas stared at him and then sat back in his chair. He felt rather than heard the others shifting around him.

'Well, good for you. Sell it in pharmacies then, you don't need me and you certainly won't need machine guns. It's why they don't carry them at the counter of Boots.'

Gezman laughed.

'You have a much more efficient way of distributing our product to our target audience. We carry the guns because we will be putting a lot of other people out of business.'

Nicholas sagged a little in his chair.

'See that, right there, I didn't get into business to fight wars. I wanted to do that I would have joined the Royal Marines. You tell me that it's going to put the rest of us out of business, I say fine, I made hay while the sun shone, now it's time to retire. Best of luck to you.'

'We have the muscle to control the streets, to keep you and your family safe.'

Nicholas tensed, and so did the rest of his guys.

'And there you go mentioning my family again,' Nicholas said dangerously. Tamal just met Nicholas's eyes but said nothing. 'Look, you've got the Russians, the Turks, good for you. You want to be King of London, all the best ... or maybe it's not you. Maybe it's your friend over there.' Nicholas nodded towards the malevolent-looking man with the scar. The man turned his head with glacial slowness to look at Nicholas.

'I apologise,' he said. His eyes met Nicholas's. It was all Nicholas could do not to look away. The voice was gravelly and unpleasant, like wet stones grinding together. 'My associate has given you the false impression that you have any choice in the matter.'

'Let's keep this nice and polite,' Danny suggested, his rumbling voice laden with the threat of violence. The scar-faced man ignored him. Instead he got up and reached into the jacket of his suit. Billy tensed but Nicholas held up a hand to stop him from doing anything. The man pulled out a small tablet and then walked slowly towards Nicholas. Nicholas felt sweat start to bead the skin of his forehead. He swallowed hard as the scar-faced man put the tablet down in front of him. Nicholas had to force himself to look down. The footage was of the inside of Kimberley's room. Whoever had shot it had stood over her bed, looking down on her as she slept. Nicholas turned to look up at the man.

'Any time I want, no matter where you hide. I'll flay her. I'll make a tie out of her skin.'

'Please ...' Nicholas managed.

144

'You work for us now,' Gezman told Nicholas. The scar-faced man looked down on him with a look of contempt.

'You fucking cunt!' Danny shouted and charged the scar-faced man. The military-looking man in the suit moved to intercept. Nicholas looked around. For moment he thought the man in the suit's arm was changing shape. The man rammed his hand into Danny's chest cavity. There was a wet tearing sound and a crack as rib bones splintered, then a really bright white light. Something hot and wet spattered against Nicholas's face.

The club was filled with a humid red mist. All of them were covered in hot red blood. Chunks of meat lay sizzling on the floor, the bar, the tables and chairs.

'Fuck!' Gezman swore, looking down at his gaudy blood-covered suit.

The hand of the man in the suit was glowing with a dimming inner light. There was no more Danny. Nicholas closed his eyes.

'Do you understand?' the gravelly voice asked. Nicholas opened his eyes again. There were tears in them. He looked up at the scar-faced man, who was licking blood from around his mouth.

'Please don't hurt my family.'

The scar-faced man looked down at him.

'Give my associate everything he wants. Don't make me come back here.'

Nicholas nodded numbly. Bad Trip turned and left, the others followed him.

Chapter Nine

Green Lanes, North London, 30 June, 2032 (BST)

It was a tribute to Charlotte's pull with the powers that be that he was still working for her. Three nuclear detonations in the Middle East, Africa and Asia, and some sort of EMP device triggered in the Syrian Desert had resulted in a lot of international finger pointing and threats. All leave had been cancelled for UK special forces and much of the regular military. All training exercises had been cancelled, and all but the most important operations in Iraq and Afghanistan had been suspended. It felt like living on a knifepoint. The tension seemed to have seeped all the way down to the street. People were frightened, on edge. This made them more irritable and aggressive.

Charlotte's pull only went so far, however, and a one-man surveillance operation was never going to be the most effective. He had taken over after Sam's ex-Special Branch Azure friends had been removed. Not that Sam was aware of that. He had spoken very briefly with Sam since her drunken phone call. She was on the out in Scotland Yard, receiving the cold shoulder. Any attempts to deal with the violence surrounding the Bliss trade were being stonewalled. She just kept on being told that prohibition didn't work. It appeared that she'd spent the last few days drinking a lot.

Surveillance was far from Noel's speciality but he'd had training, he had complementary skills and Charlotte had helped him set up some of the tech stuff, though she had become paranoid about electronic security so nothing, encrypted or otherwise, was going over the net. It was all isolated secure systems, face-to-face meetings, dead letter drops and delivering by hand.

They'd set up a concealed camera in a second-floor flat overlooking Gezman's social club. Noel had managed to sneak a tracer onto Gezman's Mercedes, though if they were running any sort of sensible security arrangements then it would only be a matter of time before it was compromised. Noel had also snuck back into the container park in Dagenham, found some containers that overlooked the offices where he'd seen Gezman meet with Collins and cut holes in them for cameras. It was the weakest part of the op. He had to retrieve the footage personally and every time he did that it exponentially increased the risk of compromising the op, but Charlotte wasn't prepared to risk transmitting the footage.

Of course the main problem with surveillance – and the reason that the Special Reconnaissance Regiment were such a group of oddballs – was that it was incredibly boring. He was sat on his arse most of the day listening to music watching the world go by outside

Green Lanes. He had a powerful concealed directional microphone aimed at the front of the social club but so far most of what he had heard was either in Turkish or Russian, and the only thing that he had learned was that the two groups didn't like each other very much.

He was intending on having another brew, then a kip, review the footage he slept through and then make his way to Dagenham to retrieve the last twenty-four hours of footage. Of course most of the interpretation of the footage for intelligence purposes would be done once he had handed it over to Charlotte. He was basically a well-armed monkey, running the camera.

He recognised Gezman's voice and turned the volume up, switching his music off.

'... everyone.'

'Why, what do we care?' the second voice had a Russian accent. Noel was pretty sure that his name was Gregorski, and he ran the Organizatsiya muscle.

'He buys more heroin than any of Burman's other clients, he pays for premium, pure medical diamorphine if he can get it, and none of this ever reaches the street. Nobody knows where it goes.'

Noel had frozen at the sound of his brother's name. His instinct was to erase the tape. He still could but he knew that Charlotte wasn't interested in bringing Nicholas down, and any evidence he collected would be inadmissible anyway.

'So he's stockpiling, or re-exporting, or throws great parties, or has a real H problem. Why are we caring?'

'We're not, the boss is.'

Noel looked over at the monitor. Gezman and Gregorski were stood out in the street just outside the social club. This was presumably in case the social club was bugged. Gregorski looked like the rest of the Organizatsiya thuggery with his bodybuilder's physique and prison tattoos creeping out the cuffs and neckline of his shirt.

'Oh,' Gregorski finally said. It was difficult to be sure over the microphone with all the background street noise but Noel was pretty sure that the Russian sounded cowed. His understanding was that it was quite difficult to frighten Russian mobsters. 'How many?'

Gezman shrugged. 'Ten,' he suggested.

'Armed?' Gregorski asked.

'Of course.'

He had been given some latitude. It sounded like something was about to happen. Noel decided that he wanted to know what. Not least because he'd heard his brother's name.

Lambeth, South London, 30 June, 2140 (BST)

The tracer had to be broadcasting but anyone looking for it would just find the signal and all they would know was that someone was tracking Gezman's Mercedes. Noel had lost the car for a while, following them in the Ford Focus 'work car', watching the progress of the Mercedes on the tablet in a holder on his dashboard. To the casual observer the Focus looked like any other car and the tracer program the tablet was receiving looked like any other satellite navigation system.

After leaving the flat and retrieving the car it had taken Noel about half an hour to catch up. It was just starting to get dark and the Mercedes had company in the form of a transit van. Noel guessed it was the Russians' troop carrier. It wasn't difficult to follow once he'd caught up with them.

The two-vehicle convoy crossed the river and then headed west. In the distance, framed against the dark blue sky, Noel could make out the brightly lit outline of Battersea Power Station. The Mercedes and the transit turned off, heading towards Lambeth. Noel kept going, pulling over when he was sure they were out of sight and watching their progress on the tablet. It looked like the Mercedes had stopped just outside one of Lambeth's many tower blocks on one of the estates. Noel started off again, driving as quickly as he could through quiet streets. He parked a few streets away from where the tablet was showing the Mercedes to be and then went to the boot of the car.

He had some gear stowed in the flat but the car was also well equipped, just in case. His Sig was still riding the holster at his hip. Looking around to make sure nobody was paying any attention he pulled on a sling. The sling had a clip that hung under his right armpit and four thirty-round 9mm magazines hanging under the left. He put a loose fitting light jacket over the sling and then, keeping the weapon out of sight in the Focus's boot, he chambered a round and took the safety off the Heckler & Koch MP5. The sub-machine gun had the collapsible stock removed and a foregrip added.

He attached it to the clip under his right armpit. The summer jacket concealed it pretty well. It felt like overkill but if the Russians had the nasty little modified MP7s then even with the MP5 he was going to be horribly outgunned.

He had a folding knife on his belt already. He put a stun grenade in one pocket of the jacket and a smoke grenade in the other. He would have some explaining to do if he got caught. Finally, he clipped a high quality compact digital camera in a hardened case to his belt, put on a cap, closed the boot and set off.

***

There weren't a lot of people on the street and none of them gave Noel a second glance. He'd grown up on an estate like this and had no problem fitting in when he wanted to, undercover training notwithstanding. He found the Mercedes and the transit van parked in a nearly empty car park outside a large tower block. The estate had clearly been built after the Brixton riots of the early '80s as it was set out to provide little succour to rioters and to help in penning them up. It was full of cul-de-sacs and other design features that could help trap its own population if they got out of hand.

Noel watched a couple of people walking into the door at the bottom of the tower block. He guessed by their size that they were part of the Russian muscle that Gregorski had bought. Noel walked casually towards the tower block. Neither Gezman nor any of the Russians had ever seen him before.

He reached the door to see that it was reinforced with safety glass. It had a buzzer and a key card lock system. He thought about pressing a few buttons and using what few words in Pashtu he knew to see if anyone would let him in, assuming him to be a lost foreigner, but he was worried that he would hit the wrong buzzer and make Gezman or the Russians suspicious.

Something was bothering him. He glanced behind him at the Mercedes and the transit. There was another car there, a black Audi saloon. It was parked close to the other two cars. Noel was wondering if they had met someone else here. He wandered over to the car, walking across a large mural of a disturbing clown's face spray painted on the car park's concrete. A group of kids appeared out of one of the nearby streets. He reached the Audi and looked inside. It was immaculate, looking like it had just come out of a showroom. He wanted to press down on it, check its suspension, see how heavy it was, if it was armoured, but he didn't want to risk setting an alarm off. He could hear the kids approaching him. There were five of them.

'All right mate?' one of them asked in his south London whine. Noel's heart sank. *So much for being surreptitious,* he thought. He turned around to face them, carrying himself with confidence but trying not to look threatening. They were all in their mid-to-late teens, similarly dressed. They looked bored and vicious. Not too different from him and his brother at that age. 'Nice motor. Is it yours?"

'No,' Noel said. The one who was doing the talking was a white kid. He looked the oldest, hoody, cap, face full of acne scars, tall and rangy. Two of the others walked round behind Noel. Noel felt his heart sink.

'Then you won't mind if we have a look inside,' the acne-scarred kid said.

I don't want you setting off the car alarm, Noel thought.

'In fact,' the kid continued. 'Why don't you make it easier for us and just give me the keys, along with your wallet, phone, jewellery and everything else you've got?' He pulled a hammer out of the waistband of his trousers. One of the others, an Asian kid, pulled out a sharpened screwdriver, and the third, a black kid, pulled out a bat of some kind. He could hear the two behind him producing weapons. Noel sighed inwardly.

'Did you steal someone's tool kit?' he asked. Then he looked at the bat the black kid was holding. 'Is that a rounders bat?' The kid at least had the common courtesy to look embarrassed.

'Look, you've got a choice, either we take it, or we give you a kicking and a bit of a stabbing and then we take it. So you decide how fucked up you want to get.'

'I can't do any of those things and I need you to go away. What's it going to take?' Noel asked.

The kid stared at him. He wasn't sure how to take Noel's self assurance in the face of five guys with weapons.

'Stop fucking around, mate.' The kid darted forward. He just touched Noel's jacket before Noel spun him round and shoved him away. It was enough, the kid had seen the MP5.

'Geezer's tooled up,' the tall rangy kid said, turning back towards Noel.

'Yeah, all right, armed police, now go away before I nick the lot of you,' Noel told them.

'Yeah right, you can give us those and all.'

Noel stared at the kid. He was wrong. These kids were nothing like him and his brother had been. They were morons.

'You get that I could shoot you, right?' Noel asked, bemused.

'I don't think so. Police have got all those rules and stuff.'

'Which include it being all right to shoot numpties who are threatening you with weapons.'

The kid just stared at him and then started laughing. Some of his compatriots didn't look quite so sure.

'Trevor,' the kid said, looking at the one over Noel's left shoulder. Noel was aware of movement behind him. Noel swung round, elbowing the kid in the face. He felt bone crunch under the blow. The kid staggered back holding his face. The other kid behind him, on his right, was moving. Noel side-stepped a slashing Stanley knife, caught the arm, drove his other fist up into the kid's elbow, breaking it, then he spun the howling kid round and propelled him into the tall kid, their apparent leader. The one with the screwdriver was brandishing it but not getting any closer. The one with the rounders bat was moving towards him, however. Noel stopped him with a warning look.

Noel opened his mouth to say something, then the screaming started. All of them turned to look at the tower block. He'd heard the screaming before. It was the sound of the hyper-velocity rounds like those fired at him in the Dagenham raid. As they looked up it seemed as if something was eating through the concrete of the tower block on one of the upper floors. Round after round flew through the walls. The Audi rocked as a stray round punched through it. Then part of the wall of the tower block disappeared in an explosion of hot, white light. Molten concrete rained down around them. He heard screaming. The tall kid was on the ground, molten concrete eating through his flesh as Noel and the other kids stared at him in horror.

'Get out of here!' Noel screamed at them and then started running towards the tower block. There was a different noise now. A ripping noise, not unlike rotary miniguns, and another part of the tower block's wall ceased to exist in a shower of falling masonry.

Noel was scanning the balconies of the ground floor flats. He had lived in a ground floor flat once. They'd been robbed a lot until Nicholas and himself had gone and had a word with the local Top Boy. Noel found what he was looking for. The gunfire had stopped, now. The screaming he could hear now was human screaming.

He reached the tower block and leapt up to grab the railing on one of the balconies, pulling himself over. He tried the door into the flat. It was unlocked. The family living there were cowering on the floor.

'Over the railings, get out, get far from here,' he shouted at them as he ran through their lounge, into the hall and to the door.

*

It was raining blood in the centre stairwell. He could hear more of the hyper-velocity gunfire high above him, and less frequently the ripping buzzsaw sound that he assumed was return fire. He started up the stairs wondering just what exactly he was doing. He had the MP5 in his hands. Something fell past him, impacting, wetly, below him.

He could see someone running down the stairs towards him. Noel raised the sub-machine gun and tracked the running man. The man ran into view, one of the Organizatsiya thugs, an MP7 still held, white knuckled, in his hand.

'Armed police! Put the gun down!' Noel shouted. The man's face was devoid of any colour. His expression was one of terror. He was oblivious to Noel's presence. Noel pressed himself against the graffiti-covered walls of the filthy stairwell, and the man just ran past.

There was more of the screaming gunfire. Much louder. Echoing down the stairwell. Noel ducked involuntarily as he saw part of the wall above him chewed away. The gunfire was cut off and then a man's screams echoed down to him. The screams changed in pitch, going from panicked to agonised, almost inhuman sounding. Noel's heart was pounding in his chest. Then there was a white light, a hot wind blew down the stairwell on a pressure wave and the towerblock above him exploded, debris and molten concrete raining down. Noel crouched, curling up on the stairs as they shook beneath him. The whole building was moving.

Noel found himself frozen in place. He had been in a number of firefights and other dangerous situations. He'd always been afraid, particularly if he stopped to think – only psychopaths weren't – but he'd always acted. On a stairway in South London, of all places, he didn't want to go any further.

He forced himself upwards. He was covered in dust, clouds of it obscured his vision. He was stepping over lumps of masonry. The tower block was holding together, for the time being. There was another figure moving, running towards him through the dust. Noel crouched down, MP5 at the ready, saying nothing this time. Gezman ran past him; Noel couldn't make out the other man's expression through the dust. Every instinct was telling him to follow Gezman out of the tower block. Take him down, and then interrogate him for an explanation. But he didn't, he continued up the stairs.

***

Noel was pretty sure that the upper floors weren't supposed to be this open plan. He could see into the flats; some of the walls had been chewed away by what looked like sustained automatic weapon fire. Other bits looked as if they had been melted. A huge rent in the side of the building allowed him to see the night sky and the lights of the other buildings on the estate. He didn't like the way the building was shifting underneath him.

He glanced in through one of the holes in the wall, trying desperately to make sense of what he was seeing. The top flats weren't just open plan. They'd been cleared, and only shored-up supporting walls had been left. Hanging from the ceiling were what looked like huge vacuum-packed freezer bags. In each bag was a naked person. They were hooked up to various IVs. A number of the IVs appeared to be delivering chemicals to the bodies, while one was removing something.

It looked like a number of the vacuum-packed people had been hit in the crossfire. Their bags were dripping red.

Noel backed towards the stairwell trying to control his breathing. It had gone quiet again. Then he heard someone repeating something over and over again in what sounded like Russian. The man looked like a ghost. He was covered head to foot in blood-streaked dust. Noel brought his MP5 up, aiming it at the man. The Russian had an MP7 but it was pointing into the room that he was backing out of. The man turned towards Noel. His eyes were wide, staring, the eyes of someone in shock.

Don't do it, Noel thought. Everything seemed to slow down. Only now was he aware of the flashing blue lights and sirens coming from outside the tower block. The Russian started bringing the MP7 around to point it at Noel.

The three-round burst broke the quiet and took the top of the Russian's head off. It was all instinct now, instilled by training. Noel was moving around the stair-well, advancing on the Russian.

The hyper-velocity screaming started again. The walls around him were eaten away. Noel kept moving. If he stopped now he was dead. He went into the first door on his right, where the firing seemed to be coming from. He could see three Russians over what used to be a partitioning wall. One of them was turning towards him. He was fast. Noel's three-round burst caught him high in the chest. The man staggered back. The others were turning now. Noel fired a longer burst of suppressing fire as he ducked back out of the door. They didn't dive for cover. Whatever they were frightened of it wasn't bullets. He ran as fire tore apart the walls around him.

Then it walked through the wall ahead of him. Noel stopped dead. He was aware of rounds flying through one wall across the corridor and through the opposite wall. It was tall, too tall and too thin. Leathery skin pulled taut across a skeletal structure that didn't look right. It wore what looked like leather trousers and an old-fashioned shirt with frilled cuffs and collar. It turned to look at him. Its mouth was too big, the fixed grin on it horrible, but it was the eyes that convinced Noel. Those eyes did not belong to anything human. It didn't seem to notice the screaming bullets flying through it.

Noel wasn't sure why he lowered the gun but he did. The thing turned away from him and walked through the other wall. Like a ghost. Then the screaming bullets stopped and the human screaming began.

Noel forced himself forward one step at a time. He felt as if he had ice water running through his veins. His heart didn't feel right. He looked through a hole in the

159

wall. The grinning thing was holding up one of Russians, and the man's flesh was just falling off him in chunks, revealing a bloodied skeleton, like some sick striptease.

Noel started running.

***

It's called blind panic for a reason. He ran straight into the man in the suit climbing up the stairs. It was like running into a stone column. Noel bounced off him and hit the stairs. Panicking, he brought the MP5 to bear. The only reason he still had it was because a sling attached it to him.

'All right, Burman?' the figure asked. Noel's finger relaxed on the trigger. It was Martin Collins reaching down out of the dust with his left hand to help him up. Noel let himself get pulled to his feet. The SAS man seemed incredibly strong. His grip felt as if it could have crushed Noel's hand. Collins's right hand didn't look right. It looked like the barrel of a very large calibre weapon. Two curved plates made of an unrecognisable material were rotating around the gun arm. Noel stared at it. 'I think you'd better get along now.' Collins told him. His voice sounded strange, emotionless. Collins resumed his climb up the stairs. Noel started running down them again.

Above him was fierce white light and the sound of superheated air exploding. A fierce hot wind driven by overpressure roared down the stairwell. Dust, masonry and liquid concrete rained down as war was fought above Noel's head.

***

Ground floor. Kick in the door to a flat. It takes too many desperate kicks, before it goes. A terrified family curled in a corner. He doesn't even warn them. Out the doors and onto the balcony. Into blue flashing light and shouting. Over the balcony. Hit the ground. Trouble standing. Ankle doesn't feel right but Noel knows that he had to keep running, to get away.

'No! No! He's with us!' A woman's voice, it doesn't matter, have to keep running. Noel didn't even register the deafening noise of the tower block collapsing, or that he'd just been engulfed by an almighty cloud of dust. He ran until he collided with something, something soft and panicking. Like him.

***

They were living in a cloud of concrete dust now, illuminated by the flashing blue lights of the surrounding emergency vehicles. The dust had settled enough for Sam to see the huge pile of debris that had once been the home to several hundred people.

She had seen Noel running from the building. Managed to stop SCO19 from firing on him. Then she'd lost him when the building collapsed. When reports of a 'significant terrorist incident' had gone out it had been all hands on deck. There was a traffic jam of police, fire service and ambulances to get here. Now she was wandering through the dust trying to find Noel.

There was more shouting. She looked around to see a huge lump of masonry, metal rods sticking out of it, slide down the pile of debris and someone who had been underneath it stand up. SCO19 surged forward, weapons at the ready, the torches on their weapons illuminating the man in the suit as he started walking down the pile of rubble. His suit was immaculate. Police shouted at him but he was apparently unarmed so they didn't shoot him.

He walked close by her, surrounded by shouting police. Sam recognised him from the photographs that Noel had taken. Martin Collins, one of the two missing SAS troopers. He didn't even glance her way. She watched him walk away, shrugging off the police who tried to physically restrain him.

'We can't fight them … we can't fight them … we can't fight them …'

Sam looked around for the source of the voice. She found Noel curled up on the floor, his knees hugged tightly to his chest, covered in dust like the rest of them. He flinched when she knelt down next to him and put her hand on his shoulder.

'It's all right, love,' she told him. He turned to look up at her.

162

'We can't fight them …'

She sat down next to him and pulled him into hug and held him there.

Penthouse, Grand Hyatt Hotel, Washington DC, 1 July, 0345 (EST)

'This world has many things to recommend itself, despite its primitive nature. Its music is simply divine.' Rex was standing in front of the full-length window looking out over Washington, his naked skin bathing in the lights of the city. He took a sip of champagne from his glass. Mozart's Symphony No. 25 in G minor was playing in the background. 'The aesthetics of their physical form.' He glanced over at the three males and two females in various states of undress lying around in the penthouse's lounge area. They represented the most attractive escorts that Washington, a city renowned for its high-class prostitutes servicing the wealthy and influential, had to offer. 'But the sooner our kingdom of pleasure becomes a reality, the better. As pretty as these bipedal forms are, I find them limiting.' He turned to Bad Trip, who was leaning against the wall out of direct light. 'I want more limbs … and the colour.' Bad Trip lit a cigarette and waited for the Face to get to a point. 'Is that your doing?' He gestured to the lounge where the escorts were watching footage of nuclear devastation in Damascus, Namibia, and Myanmar on the penthouse's huge flat screen TV. One of the young men glanced over at Rex and Bad Trip. Rex knew he would have to modify their memories later.

163

'No,' Bad Trip answered.

Rex sighed. The Enforcer wasn't the most communicative at the best of times. Verbal communication just made him more difficult.

'The humans?'

'I don't think so.'

'Who then?' Rex asked. Bad Trip shrugged. 'Isn't this your remit?'

'I found evidence of stealthed micro-satellites in orbit, but they self-destructed before I could get close to them. I've had the blast sites analysed and reviewed the data from our own seeded satellites. They were the results of anti-matter detonations. Someone also blacked out central Syria yesterday with an electromagnetic pulse. Whoever did so were clever enough to do it without us seeing them.'

'The Combine? Those arseholes ... what did they call themselves, the Machine Gods?'

Bad Trip shook his head.

'I would have spotted them.'

'That leaves the Weft,' Rex said.

'Or the Dreamers.'

Rex suppressed a shudder of superstitious dread.

'They're long gone,' Rex said. Bad Trip's face was expressionless. 'Well, they're not attacking us.'

'Either someone's cleaning house ...'

'Not terribly subtly ...'

'Or there are two groups fighting each other.'

Rex lapsed into thought, looking out at Washington again.

'Wouldn't they be unhappy if they realised how powerless and trivial they were?' he mused quietly to himself. 'Valuable, though,' he said more loudly and turned to Bad Trip.

'When we flood the Weft systems with the neuroreceptors that we harvest here the Weft are going to come for us. As the humans say, we will have to make hay while the sun shines. Ideally, I don't want to lose this crop before we harvest.'

'I have taken control of and augmented ...' Rex raised an eyebrow. '... to Sub-Juicer level only,' Bad Trip continued, 'a human special forces unit. They are going to investigate some of the odd energy signatures I've been seeing in North Africa. Unfortunately, I am still having to manipulate human power structures to do this.'

'Patience.'

'There's another site in London I am going to have some of our criminal foot soldiers look into.'

'Whoever's doing this has the world poised on the tip of nuclear war. The only thing that's stopping it is that nobody knows who to nuke, and President Greenwood's Bliss addiction. If a war does start, do we have the ability to disable all their weapons?' Rex asked.

Bad Trip nodded. 'It would be overt though.'

Rex gave this some thought.

'Not a bad entrance.' He frowned. 'I fancy something grander though, more heroic.' Bad Trip said nothing. 'Now if you'll excuse me, I'm going to try being female for a while.'

Chapter Ten

Buckinghamshire, 8 July, 1621 (BST)

'Uncle Noel! Uncle Noel!' The six year old jumped up into Noel's arms and he gave her a hug.

'Happy birthday,' Noel said, smiling for the first time in what seemed like a very long time.

'Did you bring me something from Afghanistan?' Kimberley asked.

'Kimberley!' Jessica said as she and Nicholas walked towards Noel. Nicholas just smiled indulgently. Noel shifted Kimberley's position so he could hold her in one arm and gave her the present he'd bought her.

'Can I open it now?' she asked delighted.

'It depends,' Noel said, narrowing his eyes with mock suspicion. 'When is your actual birthday?'

'Uncle Noel!' Kimberley squealed. 'You know when my birthday is! It was yesterday.'

'Then you can open it.'

Kimberley wriggled and Noel put her down and she ran back towards the other children at the birthday barbecue.

'Look what my Uncle Noel got me! He's a commander!'

'I think she means commando,' Jess said giving Noel a hug and then kissing him on the cheek. Tall and slender, Noel never failed to be impressed with the seemingly casual way his brother's wife carried her breath-taking beauty. Nicholas had met her at King's when he was reading economics. She was ferociously intelligent and had a bright corporate future ahead of her. She had surprised herself by how easily she had slipped into the role of Home Counties wife and mother instead. Though that hadn't stopped her running a number of business ventures.

Jessica stepped back from Noel, hands on his shoulders.

'Where have you been? We missed you.'

'The job, y'know,' Noel muttered, but he couldn't meet her eyes.

'Mm hmm,' Jessica said, sceptically. 'I don't care what your problem is with Nick, Kimberley needs her big tough uncle around. Because he …' she pointed at Nicholas. 'Is getting old and soft, especially around the middle.'

'Four times a week I'm in that bloody gym,' Nicholas said shaking his head. Only Noel had seen the shadow that had come across his brother's face when Jess had mentioned Kimberley needing her big tough uncle. 'We'll talk later,' she told him and then moved in closer to Noel. 'When are you going to get a lady?'

'C'mon on now, Jess, you know there's no ladies in Poole.'

'Hmm,' she said, again not happy with the answer. 'I've got to go and sort out the cake. You're staying tonight, right?' Noel started to look apologetic. Jess rolled her eyes. 'Talk to your brother,' she told Nicholas before she headed for the house. The two brothers watched her go.

'I remember when you first started seeing her,' Noel said. 'You were terrified of her middle-class upbringing.' He looked around the huge garden with the bouncy castle and the tables set up. The big house, the cars he knew were in the garage, the kids playing, their parents sipping champagne. The guests would be a mixture of Nick and Jess's neighbours, friends from their tennis club, people they used to work with in the City, and Josh, his size and bleached dreadlocks making him look out of place, Billy, smartly dressed but also markedly out of place with his dreadlocks, and Oliver, who looked more comfortable and was certainly more capable of talking the talk with the other guests. 'Now look at you.'

Jess had asked him when he was going to get a lady. He couldn't help but imagine turning up with Charlotte. She would have fitted in just fine here, in this part of his brother's world. She would have liked Jess, and Jess would have liked and approved of her. He could even see himself living in this world. No more yomping up mountains carrying more than a hundred pounds of kit. No more helicopter crashes and getting shot at. No more coming back to Britain to find out that people neither knew nor cared why you were over there. No more not being sure yourself. Yes he could live in this world, but now he knew that this world was a sham.

He'd gotten a glimpse of the things moving around just under the surface.

'I'm not ashamed of where I come from,' Nicholas said. Then he hugged his brother, holding him tightly. It was only then that Noel realised how frightened his brother was. He couldn't help it. He tensed up.

'You all right bruv?' Nicholas asked, pulling away from him.

'I'm sorry, just … a lot of work,' he said weakly. It sounded better than saying he'd seen something he couldn't explain and might have lost his nerve. Almost as worrying was the lack of surprise that Charlotte had shown when he'd debriefed her. He'd almost lost his temper with her. If she had known, why hadn't she warned him? Had she been worried about spoiling the surprise? 'I'm sorry about Danny,' Noel said changing the subject.

'Ah shit,' Nicholas said, looking up. There were tears in his eyes. Danny had been a lot older than him and had looked out for them when they were growing up. There had been a couple of scrapes that they'd got into which had required his calm intervention, and on one occasion his muscle, to see them right. He had been a bouncer and an enforcer for a number of shady operations. He was a big man and everyone assumed that he wasn't very bright but he loved to read, though he tried to keep the fact that he had to wear reading glasses secret from everyone. He'd also had the most incredible collection of northern soul music, all of it on vinyl. Both Nicholas and Noel had tried to talk him into going to college, or university, to study literature but he had laughed at them. He was second generation Afro-Caribbean, from a working-class background, he just couldn't get himself out of the mind-set that going to university wasn't something that people like him did. That hadn't stopped him being both pleased and proud of Nick, when he'd managed it.

'How's Josh taking it?' Noel asked.

'Not good, bruv, not good,' Nicholas told him. Danny had taken Josh under his wing when they'd started working doors together. As close as Nick was, and Noel had been, to Danny, he had been like a father to Josh. 'Billy's really cut up because he didn't do nothing.' Noel knew his brother was upset because he could hear Nicholas's speech pattern reverting. 'There's nothing he could have done.'

You've got no idea how true that is, Noel thought. After he had heard about Danny he'd had a very suspicious Sam check the street CCTV footage from Brixton Hill at the time of the murder. The footage had shown Gezman, the two Russians and Collins leaving the club. There was nothing any of them could have done about Collins.

'Do you want some champagne?' Nicholas asked after a pause. It was obvious that he'd had a few himself and was trying to bring the conversation back to something more appropriate for a birthday party.

'Just a beer. I'm going to go and say hello.'

'We need to talk.'

The sound of desperation in his brother's voice made Noel look over at him. It was only then he saw how ragged his brother was. He was keeping a brave face for Jess and the guests but Noel could see what a mess he was. Noel wasn't sure he was in a very different state but he nodded and then headed over toward Billy and Josh.

***

After he had offered his sympathies it had been a normal, if slightly more strained than usual, conversation with Josh and Billy. He couldn't talk about what he did. They couldn't talk about what they did. They ended up talking about what people they had known from the estates were up to now and football. None of them really cared about the latter. Oliver had kept respectfully quiet. Beyond his obvious intelligence Noel couldn't really make him out.

Worse had been the stilted conversations with Nicholas and Jess's Buckinghamshire and City friends. He'd finally got tired of explaining to them that he wasn't a squaddie. Worse still were the people who'd seen a few war films or, God forbid, read a few books, and thought they knew what they were talking about. Noel did a lot of active listening.

Finally he'd managed to sneak off with Nicholas. The two of them were sat on some hand-carved garden furniture, in an overgrown part of the garden, next to an old shed. Nicholas was smoking a cigar and had yet another glass of champagne in hand. Noel had a cup of tea. He'd refused the offer of a cigar.

'I think Mum and Dad would have liked it here,' Nicholas said. Right away he knew it was the wrong thing to say. Noel turned to look at him but said nothing. Both their parents, but particularly his mother, would have seen through this façade very quickly. Noel turned away and took another sip of his tea, watching the adults talk to each other, the kids running around screaming and laughing as they played.

'How much does Jess know?' Noel finally asked.

'She knows that Danny's dead and she knows that I'm scared. She suspects that she and Kimberley have been threatened.'

'Don't fool yourself, she knows.'

Nicholas turned to look at his younger brother. There were tears in his eyes again.

'I'm in trouble, bruv. I've really fucked up this time.'

Noel felt something catch in his throat. This was difficult. When their father had died it had been Nicholas who'd stepped up. Who'd provided, one way or another. Who'd been the man of the house. Who Noel had gone to. Who had made sure that their mum was cared for when she'd got sick, even though he'd been studying by that point. Now he was asking Noel for help.

'Yeah, you really have,' was all Noel could manage to say. Nicholas just stared at his younger brother for a moment.

'What? You want me to say I've put them at risk? I know that …'

'They were at risk from the very beginning, you knew that but you did it anyway and so did Jess.'

172

'You keep her out of this ...'

Noel turned on his brother.

'No, no I won't ...'

'So, after everything, I do something you disapprove of and that's it? I'm cut off? Fuck family?'

Noel could feel himself getting angry.

'Disapprove of? Disapprove of! What, you think this is me just being judgemental?'

'Yeah, yeah I do.'

'Do you know what, I don't really care whether drugs are illegal or not, it's the misery that you spread. On the one end you've got my mates risking their lives chasing around the gun-toting psychos who supply you. On the other end you've got kids starving because their crack-addicted parents have spent all their money on what you sell ...'

'I didn't force them to ...'

'You didn't have to exploit it for all this ...' Noel gestured around at the house and the garden. 'See, I've seen the other end of this in Afghanistan, the poppy fields worked with slave labour. From one end of it to the other, from refinement to use, it's just suffering backed by violence and corruption, and you lie to yourself while you're hiding out here in the Green Belt.'

Nicholas couldn't look at his brother.

'You know what that's an argument for, don't you?' he asked quietly.

'Yes, I do.'

'Do you know why I decided to do what I do?'

'Be a drug dealer you mean?'

'Distributor.'

'Whatever.'

'Because it felt cleaner. You want to talk about profiting from misery. I watched people laugh about the credit crunch and make moves that would make them money but make things worse for everyone else. They thought nothing about the effects on people because it would never touch them personally. I watched them hoovering up coke while they cheated on their wives, getting blown by the same hookers and strippers blowing the MPs sat next to them. Because you need happy MPs to make sure that you're not going to get regulated too stringently, that your tax burden isn't too much, and to insist that the poor live under austerity measures because it's all their fault anyway. They commit theft and fraud on a massive scale. They damage society and indirectly are responsible for a fuck of a lot of deaths from poverty, crime, substance abuse, and mental health problems. Indirectly, they'll kill more people than those wars you're fighting, they'll certainly cause more suffering than I could ever manage, because to them I'm an amateur. They'll never get caught. They'll never be punished. They'll never have black-clad bad boys, like you and your mates, kick in their door, because they're powerful enough to make the laws that govern them. If they don't like the rules, they change them. So yeah, I'm a drug dealer because morally it's a fucking step up. It makes me feel like less of a sociopath. I can get to sleep at night now.'

Noel had a good look around at the house and the garden again.

'Oh yeah, you look poor. How often you practise that speech?'

'Do you know what? Fuck you.'

'Just because there are other bad people in the world doesn't make it all right. Yes the economic problems they've caused are going to lead to social problems but you, you're the violence and the drug abuse they cause.'

'So you're sat there judging me. And incidentally it was all right to rob, and steal, and deal when it was putting food on your plate, but now I'm doing okay it's not?'

'You … we had to … You don't know. This here,' he pointed at the house, 'what this is built on, it's obscene. How can you bring Kimberley up here, knowing that?'

Nicholas was on his feet standing over Noel.

'You leave my family out of this you cunt.'

Noel was on his feet, nose to nose with Nicholas.

'No, you leave your family out of this. Oh what? You can't now?' Noel knew that Nicholas was close to punching him. 'Go ahead, I'm not twelve now.'

'Oh yeah, you're a proper hard man now, aren't you? Well Mr Hardman, while you're sitting in judgement on us all here now, how many people have you killed?' It would have been better if Nicholas had swung for him. He saw the top of the Organizatsiya gunman's head come off. The one he'd killed in the tower block. The one in shock. Noel squeezed his eyes shut. 'What? You going to tell me it's different? That you're serving your country? Because I've got some bad news for you bruv, nobody cares. You're certainly not doing it for us and it's not making things better as far as I can see.'

Noel thought about all his mates that had gone down. Afghanistan, Iraq, Dagenham. He decided that he was going to hurt his brother quite badly.

'Hey!' Jess's voice cut through the air. Both of them turned to look at her. She looked furious. Josh was stood next to her. He didn't look very pleased either. Behind them most of the party guests were staring at them, even the children.

'Danny's dead,' Josh told them. 'Stop playing the cunts.' Then he grimaced and turned to Jess. 'Sorry, Jess.'

'That's enough,' she told them both. Anger was seeping out of Noel, being replaced by embarrassment. He knew that he'd been wound far too tight. First Dagenham and then Lambeth.

'Yeah, all right, love, I'm sorry,' Nicholas told her, looking down.

'I'm sorry, Jess,' Noel said, ashamed.

She turned and walked away. Josh watched them a moment longer, eyebrow raised, then he turned and walked away.

Nicholas turned to Noel.

'I'm just so scared man, so scared ...' His face cracked and the tears came. Noel stepped forwards and hugged him.

***

Nicholas told him what had happened. Gezman, what Collins had done to Danny, and the scar-faced man.

176

The CCTV hadn't shown the fifth man. The man who had threatened Jess and Kimberley. The man that Nicholas badly wanted to see dead. Noel found himself wanting this scar-faced man dead as well.

'Look, I may not have spent my twenties getting into gunfights in desperate parts of the world, but I'm no coward,' Nicholas said. Noel was nodding. It was true his brother didn't lack for courage. 'But that guy scared me, I mean really scared me. There was just something about him and there was not a trace of doubt in my mind that he wouldn't do what he said he would do. They were in my house! He had someone in my little girl's room!' He lapsed into brooding silence, taking a long pull from the beer he was now drinking. 'And Danny, man, he wasn't just some thug that worked for me, he was a good guy, my friend. What they did to him ... I mean how could you do that? There was something wrong with his arm, like it was changing shape or something ...'

'Nick,' Noel said softly. 'Look, there's something going on. In London I mean, maybe other places.'

Nick looked round at him.

'What'd you mean?'

'I can't talk about it ...'

'Are you into this ...?'

'I think you should do what they want.'

'I'm going to but it's not enough. I have to protect my family. What do you know?'

'Seriously, I can't ...'

'Bullshit!' Nicholas spat in a harsh angry whisper. He

didn't want to risk Jess's wrath again. 'Have I ever asked you for anything? Anything?'

'You're going to think I'm mental.'

'I told you what I saw … Danny.'

'There's something out there, but it's not human.'

Nicholas stared at his brother.

'See,' Noel said.

'I get it,' Nicholas finally said. 'His hand. What happened to Danny … So now what?'

'Now you do what they want.'

'Jess and Kimberley. Can you speak to Sam, get them protection? Any of your buddies want to moonlight as bodyguards?'

'You've seen the news, the nukes. Everyone's either deployed or at base. But I know a couple of guys who've gone freelance. I'll see if they're in the country. I'll speak to Sam but I can't see her being too receptive. If you're bright, though, then get Jess and Kimberley to go and hide somewhere and you don't have any contact with them, no phone calls, emails, letters, nothing.'

'What, because of aliens or monsters? Jess'd never buy it.'

'She'd buy that Kimberley and her are in danger.'

'I'll talk to her but I know she'll want to tough it out. I can't tell her about them being in the house …'

'You may have to.'

'I need to end this, bruv. I need to fight back.'

I don't think we can, Noel thought. He still couldn't master his fear when he remembered Collins and that grinning thing.

'What did that prick Roche, the guy who waterboarded you, want?' Noel asked, trying to steer his brother away from aliens and monsters. For the time being anyway.

'He wanted to know about that thing at Brixton ice-rink,' Nicholas told him.

Operation Kingship again, Noel thought. That didn't make any sense either. As far as he could tell it had nothing to do with Dagenham, and certainly nothing to do with a fictitious Taliban heroin pipeline.

'That anything to do with ...' Noel started.

'No!' Nicholas said a little too loudly. A few people at the barbecue looked over towards them. He lowered his voice. 'I've told you, bruv, we don't do that Miami Vice standing around with machine guns bullshit.'

'So whose operation was it?'

'Some Cypriot low life called Stylianos Evangeli,' Nicholas told him. The name meant nothing to Noel.

'Did you give the name to Roche?'

'Yes, he's a piece of shit. He's supposed to be involved with human trafficking, even trading human organs. Rumour has it he made his money capitalising on the unpleasantness in the Balkans during the '90s. So I figured why not? And frankly if he was moving into H in south London, then someone was going to have a word with him.'

'But you were dealing to someone in the tower block that collapsed in Lambeth, right?' Nicholas looked like he was about to object but didn't, instead he just nodded.

'Yeah. It was always one step removed. He called himself Galileo. Weird guy, he bought four or five keys a month. Always paid up front, never any problems but apparently something of an oddball.'

'How so?'

'Dressed funny, talked funny, apparently he smiled all the time as well. I mean, who does that in Lambeth?'

Noel smiled despite himself.

'But he didn't sell to the dealers on the street?'

Nicholas stared at his brother for a moment.

'How'd you know that?'

Noel shrugged.

'So where'd it go?' he asked.

'Nobody knew. Oliver suspected that the place in Lambeth was a front and actually he sold on to A-list celebrity users. Your Chelsea/Sloane Square lot, the aristocracy, minor royalty, actors and musicians, that sort.' Nicholas looked very uncomfortable, as if he was holding something back.

'What?' Noel asked.

'Well, Oliver was never comfortable with the Lambeth thing, neither was I, it was the biggest unknown in our operation. So he did some digging. That block of flats, it did belong to the council but they sold it on to a private landlord to run. Now it belongs to a housing agency, which is in turned owned by a holding company, which is in turn owned by a series of business interests which lead back to …'

'Stylianos Evangeli?' Noel asked. Nicholas nodded. 'Christ! What were you doing dealing with a guy like that?'

'I didn't fucking know, did I?' Nicholas hissed. 'Why all the questions about Lambeth? Were you there when it happened?'

'You get that there are things that I just can't tell you, right?'

'I'm going after them with or without you.'

'I don't think that's a very good idea,' Noel said. He was watching Kimberley play with the other kids.

'With or without you, bruv.'

Noel kept watching Kimberley playing.

'You need to get them out of here. Even if you scare the shit out of Jess, even if she leaves you, in fact that might be better.'

Nicholas swallowed hard and nodded.

'Gezman's the weak link,' Noel said. He turned to look at his brother. 'You ready to get your hands dirty?' Nicholas just nodded.

Are you? Noel asked himself. *Or are you going to freeze or panic the next time you see Collins or the grinning thing.*

Oliver was walking towards them. Nicholas wiped his eyes and looked up.

'You're going to want to see this,' he told them.

***

Most of the adults at the barbecue were gathered in the large lounge area watching the wall-mounted TV.

'... the top news story of the hour is that the Congress has voted, by a margin of two votes, to

181

legalise the designer drug known as Bliss ...'

There were various comments from the people sat in the lounge – some positive, some negative – but Josh, Danny, Oliver, Nicholas and Noel all shared looks.

'Oh well it was fun whilst it lasted,' Oliver muttered earning a look of reproach from Jess.

Waterloo, London, 8 July, 2153 (BST)

It was the most anonymous commuter pub, just outside the station itself, that they could find. Sam was already making her way through her second G&T, and Charlotte was nursing half a lager when he arrived. Neither of them looked particularly happy. Noel couldn't help but smile trying to wonder what the conversation had been like before he got there.

He had used every counter-surveillance trick he knew going to the meet. If they were being followed then he hadn't seen them. He bought himself a beer, more for cover than to drink, and sat down to an uncomfortable silence.

'So, I have a question,' Sam finally said. 'Leaving aside for a moment some bloke walking, unscathed, out of a collapsing tower block in bloody Lambeth, anybody want to explain why we're pulling bodies full of high-grade heroin out of the rubble? See the interesting thing is that a lot of these people are known to us, mostly for petty stuff, minor thefts, D&D, assaults, possession, soliciting, that sort of thing. Then at some point in the past they all stop getting into trouble, as if they cleaned up their act, or they disappeared. Some of them it's three months ago, some five years, some longer. Many of them were homeless, almost all of them nobody cared about, only a few have been reported missing. The heroin in their system is almost medically pure diamorphine. Not the stepped-on baby powder and rat poison mix these people are more used to. Their autopsies are all showing atrophied muscles. Oh, and one more thing, their bodies are all showing very low levels of …'

'Endorphins,' Charlotte said.

'That's right, Charly, well done.' Sam peered between the two of them. 'Any guesses?'

'I've heard the word, but endorphin?' Noel asked.

'It's a chemical created by the body …'

'It's the neurotransmitter created by the pituitary gland to deal with pain, excitement and during orgasms,' Charlotte explained.

'I could do with a pint of it right about now,' Sam said.

'Diamorphine simulates the creation of endorphins and other endogenous opioids,' Charlotte added.

'I don't understand,' Noel said. He could feel something just slightly out of reach, but couldn't quite put it together. He was an intelligent man but no scientist, perhaps that was it – either that or he just did not want to face what he was about to hear.

'Someone's farming the homeless and the unwanted for their endorphins and injecting them with Horse to encourage their production. Ain't that right, Charly?'

At some level Noel knew that Sam was right but he didn't want to face up to it.

'And you know what the really exciting thing is, Noel? Guess who was supplying the H to that tower block?'

'He didn't know, he thought it was a front for dealing heroin to the A-list.' There was a snort of derision from Sam.

'You've talked to him about this,' Charly asked, sounding concerned.

'He talked to me. He's scared. He wants protection for Kimberley and Jessica.'

'Well, he may just have to live with the decisions he's made,' Sam said acidly. Noel rounded on her.

'And Jessica? Kimberley? Do they have to live with those decisions as well?'

'His wife made her own bed,' Sam spat. Noel had to concede that she was right. If you knowingly married a drug dealer then you had to realise that there were certain ramifications involved.

'Kimberley?' Noel asked more quietly.

'If he testifies we can see what we can do, we should be able to provide him with protection. That's assuming that heroin doesn't suddenly become legal as well,' she muttered bitterly.

'I think we may be a little bit beyond prosecution,' Charlotte said quietly. Her normal confidence seemed to have evaporated.

'What do you mean?' Sam demanded. 'Look, it seems like Black Ops are tied up in this shit. The guy that walked out of the rubble, he was SAS, right?' she asked Noel.

'He certainly used to be,' Noel admitted.

'Well let me tell you, if they're building them that way these days then Mr Alan Qaeda must be shitting himself.'

'Look. Lambeth, I saw …' Noel started and then trailed off. Charlotte was watching him sympathetically. She had debriefed him after the gunfight in the tower block and its subsequent collapse. Sam watched as Noel looked over at her and she nodded.

'You can tell her,' she said.

'Tell me what?' Sam asked. 'What did you see? SIS had you out of there before I could speak to you.'

'I saw something. Bullets flew through it, it walked through walls, big grin on its face. Like a rictus grin.'

Sam stared at him. Then she started laughing loud enough to draw attention from the other patrons in the bar.

'You saw a ghost?' she scoffed.

Noel was shaking his head. He looked straight into Sam's eyes.

'What I saw wasn't human,' he told her.

Sam stopped laughing. She turned to look at Charlotte. The other woman looked just as serious.

'You're winding me up, right?' she demanded.

'Think about what you've seen,' Charlotte said. 'Martin Collins had a building dropped on him. Physiological changes in Organizatsiya thuggery overnight. People with augmented strength, speed, endurance, able to ignore trauma and pain. Weapons showing characteristics well in advance of anything we have today. Traceless drugs that alchemically transform right in front of your eyes. Once you have eliminated the impossible …'

185

'It could just be a high-tech operation, sponsored by some government …' Sam started.

'It wasn't human, Sam,' Noel said again.

'So what, aliens? Monsters?'

'It was a monster,' Noel said.

'But probably extraterrestrial in origin,' Charlotte said. Sam was staring at her as if she was mad.

'Pleased to see where my tax money is going,' the police officer said sarcastically.

'If you can think of a better explanation?' Charlotte said, finally sounding irritable. 'No? Good. We've had anecdotal reports of these things for years now. Bosnia, Somalia, Burma, Chechnya. Often in deeply unhappy parts of the world, the sort of places where if people go missing then nobody cares. If you look in certain places you can find them in folklore, myth, and ghost stories going back some five hundred years. Grinning body thieves. Dybbuk. Scary Clowns. There's circumstantial evidence that they've been hiding amongst us for centuries, stealing people and quietly farming them for our neural receptors.'

'This is just ridiculous,' Sam muttered incredulously. 'And they're not that bleedin' quiet, are they?'

'No, not now,' Charlotte admitted. 'Which suggests that there's been some sort of catalyst.'

'There's two sides,' Noel said.

'Two lots of aliens? Brilliant,' Sam scoffed, rolling her eyes.

'Is Collins some sort of government-sponsored, experimental super soldier?' Noel asked Charlotte.

'If he is then I am unaware of it, and judging by his capabilities I think it's highly unlikely.'

'Are these Scary Clowns running the Bliss trade, then?' Sam asked.

'No, that's the thing, when I saw Collins in Lambeth he was with the Russians. The Russians seemed to be fighting the Scary Clown. After I saw him all hell broke loose.'

'It fits with the MO. Collins has been augmented, like the Organizatsiya thugs, but to a much greater extent. Perhaps the greater augmentation is due to his special forces background.'

'So assuming it's not us,' Noel said, 'someone's using humans as foot soldiers.'

Charlotte was nodding. Sam still looked very sceptical.

'We've been unable to analyse Bliss but we have been able to analyse its effects on a user …'

'Fun night in the lab,' Sam muttered.

'It appears to be an almost entirely synthetic compound designed to mimic the effects of MDMA, diamorphine and benzoylmethylecgonine …'

'What?' Noel asked.

'Cocaine,' Sam told him.

'Which in turn either imitates or increases the production of serotonin, endorphins and dopamine.'

'So is someone farming Bliss users?' Noel asked, confused.

'Not that we're aware of. What we do have is two separate strains of technology, far in advance of anything we're currently able to create, and the thing they have in common is stimulating the creation of human neurotransmitters.'

'And America's just made this legal and we're about to follow?' Noel said.

'And any investigation into Bliss is being blocked, despite the violence,' Sam said.

'Which is why I'm running you off the books,' Charlotte told Noel. 'I am also working from the perspective that all electronic security has been compromised by a much higher level of technology, and that if we're not under surveillance yet then we must assume that they have the capacity for total surveillance.'

'You think they've infiltrated our government? The Bliss aliens, I mean?' Sam asked.

'Again, if you can think of another explanation ...'

'You know we could be just telling each other stories, right? Feeding off speculation due to a series of coincidental incidents,' Noel pointed out.

'If it was just this conversation. If you were the only operation I was running. If there was no other evidence.'

'But it's all circumstantial, right? Eye witness testimonies during times of stress, like a building falling down?' Sam asked.

'From trained, reliable witnesses,' Charlotte told her.

'I know what I saw, Sam,' Noel said quietly.

'You were pretty freaked out,' Sam pointed out.

'Which I don't get, even in the hairiest of situations,' Noel countered. Charlotte was nodding in agreement.

'What about this stuff on the news? The nuclear explosions?' Sam asked.

'A friend of mine at the US department of energy has analysed multi-spectrum satellite footage of the explosions. He does not feel they are consistent with a nuclear weapon.'

'What does he think they are?' Noel asked.

'He's mostly guessing, but he thinks it some kind of anti-matter weapon,' Charlotte said. Sam and Noel looked at her mystified. 'Another piece of weapons technology that is way in advance of ours.'

Noel and Sam let this sink in.

'Someone's fighting someone, then,' Noel finally said. Charlotte nodded. 'You said other operations, what other operations …?'

'You know I can't …'

'Did you have my brother waterboarded?'

'No … Roche was working on his own. At the time.'

'At the time?'

'I'm not going to talk about it, so stop asking,' Charlotte was starting to sound a little irritable again.

'See, that's what gets me about you intelligence types,' Noel said. 'You're so wrapped up in keeping secrets for secrets' sake that you forget that we could really use that information sometimes.'

'Is the honeymoon over?' Sam asked.

'I don't think you appreciate how out on a limb we are here,' Charlotte said and then turned to Sam. 'Obviously you can't talk about any of this. This conversation is covered by the Official Secrets Act.'

189

'I'd end up sectioned if I talked about any of this.'

'Maybe I should go and find this Roche and have a word with him myself,' Noel said. Charlotte just glared at him. 'When Danny was killed by Collins, Nicholas told me there was someone else there. Sat quietly in the background while Gezman did the talking. Nicholas thought that he was in charge. He was the one that threatened Kimberley. Old guy, scar, ponytail. My brother doesn't frighten easily but Nicholas said that there was something about this guy. That he was genuinely scary.'

'The boss?' Sam asked. The working of a criminal organisation, regardless of its origins, was something that she could at least understand.

'Someone of rank anyway,' Noel said.

'So what now?' Sam asked.

'Will you put someone on Nicholas's family?' Charlotte asked.

'If I can, doesn't sound like it will do much good,' Sam said.

'I've made some calls, he's going to hire some mates of mine who've gone private,' Noel said. 'But they need to disappear.'

'If they do it has to be all cash, they need to leave no electronic trails, no phone calls, emails or anything like that,' Charlotte told him.

'Jess will never buy it,' Noel said.

'So putting people on them is the best we can do for the time being. Your brother will need to debrief us, fully,' Charlotte told him.

'I'll speak to him. Is that it?' Noel asked. Charlotte nodded, and Sam shrugged. He started to get up and then had a thought. 'What happened to Gezman?'

'He got picked up on firearms charges but was out faster than an Essex girl can drop her knickers,' Sam told him.

'Nicholas thinks that Gezman is their weak link. I agree.'

'We go back to surveillance,' Charlotte said.

'What? While they co-opt our way of life?' Noel asked. He noticed that Sam was nodding along with him.

'We need to tread very carefully,' Charlotte told them both.

'They're threatening my family,' Noel said, standing up.

'Don't do anything stupid,' Charlotte said. 'If I'd wanted cowboys I would have got shooters from the SAS.'

'That, and they appear to be compromised,' Noel said. Then he turned and walked out of the pub. Sam and Charlotte watched him go.

'Whatever I might say about Nicholas, there are much worse hoodlums out there. They weren't bad boys growing up but they were at their worst, at their most violent, when one thought the other was being threatened,' Sam told the other woman.

Washington Convention Centre, Washington DC, 8 July, 2319 (EST)

The most annoying thing about the Bliss legalisation party, to Rex's mind, was the number of libertarian half wits who thought that legalisation of the drug would provide economic opportunities for them. They kept on coming up to him, drunk, coked and/or Blissed out of their skulls and shouting: 'This is because of you, babe!' or other equally irritating and patronising platitudes.

I know it is, he kept on thinking, *and you have no idea to what extent that's true.*

The convention centre had been locked down tight. With Rex's newfound influence within the global military-industrial complex, high security was reasonably easy to provide if you didn't care about civil liberties. This meant that the 'great and good' could really let their hair down a bit.

The ballroom had been decorated in a Roman style. Most of the attendees had turned up in fancy dress and seemed to be revelling in the Roman orgy theme. This was of course helped by the paid-a-great-deal-of-money-to-be-pliant escorts on hand. He was pretty sure he'd hired every high-priced call-girl and -boy on the East Coast for this particular party. Even Rex had been surprised by some of the resulting perversities. He had started to understand the psychological component to the human gag reflex, and not just as it related to oral sex. Of course all of it was being discreetly recorded for later use. And of course there was also a vast amount of food, alcohol and drugs, particularly Bliss, on hand.

Greenwood was living up to his role as Caligula with wild abandon. He was wearing garish makeup and a small toga that kept slipping a lot. The Bliss-addicted President was proving to be a valuable asset; not so much for his power, for he appeared to be little more than a figurehead for a series of corporate interests, but more for the network of contacts that had earned him his figurehead role in the first place.

He was sat up on the stage in the nest of cushions he'd had made, cackling like a lunatic, splashing red wine on the two giggling prostitutes nestling up to him and occasionally snorting from the vast pile of coke on a nearby low table. Apparently this was for 'old time's sake', as his new drug of choice was of course Bliss. Rex had already had to bolster the President's body twice with Pleasure-tech to stop him expiring from a massive coronary.

Rex had come to the conclusion that while he needed to capitalise on the weaknesses of these people, he didn't really like them. It wasn't the decadence and corruption – that was his stock in trade, though aesthetically some of the sexual acts he was witnessing made him not want to have sex with humans ever again. Instead it was the hypocrisy. It was the gulf between what the people at the orgy claimed to represent and what they actually represented. He'd come to the conclusion that he preferred a more honest decadence, even a more honest corruption. Here, at least, their masks were off and he could see them for what they were, rather than their public personas.

He smiled as a bevy of 'Washington Wives' wandered by, appreciatively taking in his tall, muscular form in his mini-toga. Their faintly disapproving Secret Service bodyguards looked incongruous in sober grey suits amongst the Roman fancy dress. He would not be servicing any of the wives later unless the exotic phero-mone secretion he'd imbibed earlier in the evening put him in a very odd mood.

Rex had almost been relieved when they had discov-ered their first signs of resistance. Good politicians, journalists, civil servants, police, military and intelligence types from all parts of the political spectrum trying to do what they thought was right. Standing up against the various strands of the Pleasure's creeping, insidious influences. People genuinely committed to serving those they felt they had responsibility for. Of course they had to be destroyed. If they couldn't be bought, broken or frightened then they were discredited, mind-controlled to get embroiled in scandals so extreme and unpleasant that they broke even the hedonist meme the Pleasure were trying to create. Others just met Bad Trip. Once.

In what the humans called the developing world the elites were often just as eager for corruption, but it was more open. However, they had encountered resistance there as well. Rex had begun aiding Bad Trip in the co-opting of the US special forces community. Drug augmented special forces units, disguised as merce-naries, backed opposing forces of the recalcitrants, committed acts of assassination or destabilising terrorism, or even just ran the coups themselves. Military force was backed up by the economic force of Rex's influence over business interests in the devel-oping world. And it was in the developing world that it was easiest to encourage the growing of narcotic cash crops to supply human farming operations.

All of which reminded Rex that at some point he had to take care of the head of Britain's Secret Intelligence Service. The woman had either been running, or had allowed to run, a number of operations that were detrimental to their interests. On the other hand, those operations also seemed to be interested in the mysterious 'others' that Bad Trip had found evidence of.

'I want to kill some of these people, hurt the rest.'

Rex had been aware of Bad Trip ever since he had infected the local matter and grown himself a new body from it. Bad Trip was standing just behind him, looking over his shoulder out at the orgy. His breath smelt of cigarettes. The Enforcer bent light around himself to remain in the shadows, much the same way that Rex bent light to accentuate his beauty and at time create a natural spotlight, or even angelic glow, effect.

'My dear, when don't you?' Rex asked. He loved Bad Trip, they were an inseparable partnership for all eternity, but sometimes he felt that the Enforcer was just trying too hard. Bad Trip said nothing but Rex could hear the other creature's rasping breath. If anything he was sure that Bad Trip had more contempt for the humans than he did. On the other hand, Bad Trip had contempt for everything and everyone that wasn't the Pleasure. Rex supposed that he had to so he could do the things his role involved. 'Some things have to happen tonight, bad things that we can use as leverage, but it will be better if I handle it and we use mind-control.'

'There is a problem.'

'The cartel?' Rex asked. Rex couldn't make up his mind if it was ironic or not, but their biggest opponents were the drug cartels. It wasn't even so much the fact that the Pleasure were moving on to their turf – that was a localised problem for distributors to deal with, as far as the cartels were concerned. No, the problem was the movement to proliferate and legalise certain substances. That was a major problem for the cartels because it meant them losing business, and more importantly it meant them losing control.

'Yes. The Los Zetas and their allies have run a coordinated operation to systematically attack all the Bliss distribution points in Ciudad Juarez, El Paso, Tucson and Phoenix.'

'You were expecting Juarez, weren't you?' Rex asked.

'Yes, and for something to happen in Los Angeles. They've been tentatively reaching out to the remnants of the Tijuana Cartel for a temporary alliance to deal with the Bliss epidemic. El Paso was inevitable, Tucson and Phoenix are unacceptable.'

'And you feel we should make an example?' Bad Trip nodded in the shadow behind Rex. 'Why am I even asking, you always think that we should make an example. This could be handled with a viral, even a tailored pico-phage.'

'They have to learn. It has to be personal. They have to see, feel and understand.'

'And you need off the leash, don't you?' Rex said, not unkindly. Rex turned to look at Bad Trip. The Enforcer was just looking straight ahead. His eyes were black pits. They were a partnership but they had decided a long time ago that some decisions required consensus. This was after they had lost a number of crops in a row due to the Enforcer's excesses.

'President Greenwood will take next to no convincing, just another little vial of primo-Bliss. We can call it an anti-drug operation or something.'

Bad Trip just nodded and backed into the shadows.

Chapter Eleven

Teotihuacan, Mexico, 9 July, 0400 (Local Time)

The two Blackhawk helicopters came in from the south, flying past the Temple of Quetzalcoatl, the Winged Serpent, over the San Juan River Canal, overflying the ancient Street of the Dead. They passed the Pyramid of the Sun on their right. The pilots, Nightstalkers from the US's 160th special operations aviation regiment, pulled up slightly, taking the helicopters up over the low stepped pyramids that flanked the much larger Pyramid of the Sun. In the green of their night-vision displays the grey stone glowed an eerie and alien green. If there was anyone in the ancient stone city of Teotihuacan the pilots didn't see them.

Colonel Felix Alejandro had built his palatial mansion in the style of the ancient step pyramids, not far from the site of the ancient city. The stepped-pyramid mansion, however, was within the walls of a heavily protected compound. The Colonel had received his rank in the Mexican special forces. The members of his cartel were recruited from the ranks of the Airmobile Special

Forces Group and the Amphibian Group of Special Forces. They were not going to be the normal pushovers that some criminal groups could be.

The Blackhawks, however, each carried a squad of soldiers from the 7th Special Forces group based out of Eglin air force base in Florida. Bad Trip had picked them by psychometric testing because they fitted a certain moral flexibility. Members of President Greenwood's staff had put up a token resistance to their deployment. Special Operations Command had put up more than a token resistance, especially after losing two squads in Libya during the Aqar nuclear fiasco just over a week ago. Rex had assured them that this time it would be different, and not just because all the Green Berets had been augmented with combat drugs, turned into Sub-Juicers. This time Bad Trip and both his Juicers would be travelling with them. Though Rex had not mentioned that to SOCOM.

The helicopters came in sideways, one over the south wall, the other over the east. Their M134 six-barrelled miniguns pouring 7.62mm rounds down into the compound in prearranged fields of fire. Tracers lit up the night like lasers, tearing apart guards, vehicles, and fixed defensive points such as machine-gun nests. Green Beret snipers searched the area through the night-vision scopes on their M110 CSASS sniper rifles. Their job was to do one thing, and one thing only – look for surface-to-air weapons, improvised or otherwise.

As the Blackhawk's doorgunners rained fire down on the compound, the ripping noise of the miniguns breaking the peace of the pre-dawn morning, the spent brass from hundreds of rounds tumbling out of the weapons to the ground below, the special forces soldiers fast roped out of the other side of the helicopters. Heavy gloves protected their hands as they slid down the ropes. They hauled the gloves off, tucked them into their webbing, brought their weapons up and advanced quickly up the terraced gardens towards the stepped building. They fired M4 carbines and M246 special purpose weapons. They advanced in a line from the south and the east behind a withering amount of fire. The guards, ex-special forces or not, went down like wheat to a scythe blade, totally overwhelmed by the speed, surprise and ferocity of the attack. Any particularly stubborn resistance was fired upon with fragmentation grenades fired from M320 40mm grenade launchers mounted beneath the M4 carbines or hosed down with minigun fire from the helicopters.

As soon as the Green Berets reached the house the miniguns stopped firing. Both helicopters turned around so the opposite door-mounted minigun was pointing towards the compound, the one with the most ammunition in it, and then they began circling the compound, the snipers in both helos still searching for targets. The two squads of Green Berets formed perimeter security. They could already hear screams from inside the house.

***

Shaw and Collins had inserted into the area the night before via a high-altitude low-opening parachute drop.

They had spent the day concealed and spent the night moving quietly through the suburbs towards their target's highland mansion. Like the helicopter, they had made their way through the ancient city. It hadn't really meant anything to them.

They had found places to hide within the grounds. As soon as they heard the helicopters they had started running towards the house. They were both armed with human weapons. Bad Trip didn't want them behaving too overtly alien just yet. This didn't stop Shaw from flexing. Something he'd always wanted to try and now he had the capabilities to do it.

Collins had approached the house from the north, Shaw from the west. Both of them had taken some 'friendly fire', minigun rounds that overshot the house and tore up the earth and undergrowth of the terraced gardens they were moving through.

Shaw moved quietly up the stone steps towards the house. The first guard he came across had his back to him. Shaw stepped on the back of the man's knees, forcing him to the ground, and then a boot to the guard's back forced him down onto his front. It was so fast that the other guards hadn't even noticed that anything was happening yet. Shaw stood on the man's upper back and then reached down to grip his head. Fingers laced with alien metals and super-hardened composites dug into screaming flesh and bone. The other guards were starting to react. Shaw had come out of nowhere and now he was among them. The screams were cut off, and there was a wet tearing noise. Shaw held up the guard's head to show his friends for a moment, and then threw it at the closest one.

Only then did he reach for the Heckler & Koch 417 'Assaulter' carbine hanging on its sling. He pointed it towards the house. All the guards were moving in slow motion. He fired the underslung grenade launcher. A machine-gun nest on the third 'step' of the house blew up. His target acquisition software had told him exactly where to drop the grenade in.

Shaw's vision filled with projected trajectories of the bullets that were about to be fired at him. With bewildering speed he started to step from gap to gap in the trajectories as he advanced firing. One shot and someone went down, the software and his own innate abilities telling him where and when to fire. He whipped around behind him and fired again and again and the six guards behind him went down. The cyclic rate of the weapon struggled to keep up with the rate of his fire. To someone watching, who wasn't about to die, it must have looked as if Shaw was firing on full automatic.

He continued firing as he used his left hand to pop open the grenade launcher. The smoking empty frag round ejected, he reloaded a flechette round on the move and clicked the weapon shut. The counter in his vision ran to zero. He fired the flechette. A spray of blood blossomed around four guards who were advancing on him, firing, as the flechettes ripped them apart. As the needles left the grenade launcher he ejected the carbine's magazine, stowed it in the canvas 'drop bag' on his left hip, reloaded and primed the weapon faster than he ever had before.

He resumed firing, moving between the incoming rounds. Any shots that did hit him wouldn't do much but Bad Trip didn't want his Juicers overtly using their coherent energy shields just yet. Internal sensors warned him of any new threat. The carbine twitched upwards and he fired three times in quick succession, puffs of blood and bone blossoming from the heads of three gunmen moving out of the house onto one of the 'steps'. They hit the wall and slumped to the ground.

He fired. More guards went down. The carbine was empty, he swept it to one side on its sling with his left hand and fast drew the high-capacity custom Springfield M1911 .45 with his right. He fired the pistol rapidly at the remaining guards in the terraced gardens and the 'step' balconies and then he reached the west door of the house. He reloaded the pistol and holstered it, then he reloaded the carbine and the underslung grenade launcher as fast as he could. As he did, he glanced down at the sea of dead bodies lying on the terraced garden behind him.

'That's some real Schwarzenegger Commando stuff right there,' he muttered. Shaw wasn't entirely sure about everything that had happened to him since his canal-side walk with Collins in January. He wasn't sure about the people he was working for, the things he had to do, or the changes that had been made to what was fundamentally *him*. One thing he was sure of: he liked the power he had now.

Weapons reloaded, he took the breaching charge from his pouches and placed it against the armoured door. As he did this, guards came around either side of the house, assault rifles up. They had the drop on him. He backed away from the house, fast drawing the .45 and firing rapidly first to the north and then to the south. Each shot a kill at close to a hundred foot away. They hadn't fired. He reloaded the pistol before all of them had slumped to the ground.

The danger warning from his scanners was too late. A hatch in the armoured window next to the door slid open. The barrel of a G3 battle rifle was poked through. The gunman pulled the trigger and let rip with the entire magazine. Rectangles of light appeared all around Shaw's body as the coherent energy field halted the momentum of the bullets. Still, Shaw was annoyed. He was tempted to destroy the armoured window and the gunman behind it with his plasma weapon but that was against orders.

Shaw marched towards the armoured window. He took a fragmentation grenade from the pouches on his webbing. The gunman frantically tried to slide the hatch in the armoured glass shut. Shaw removed the pin from the grenade and let the spoon flip off. He punched his fist through the armoured glass hatch and dropped the grenade. He pulled his hand back, the façade of flesh already healing over. He heard shouts and scrabbling from inside the house. Then the flat hard crump of the grenade exploding. Moments later he triggered the breaching charge. The door blew in.

There was a man on the other side of the door. One side of his body was a blackened, bloody mess. He was trailing the bloody tatters of what remained of his leg behind him as he crawled away from the door. Shaw put a round in the back of his head.

He heard another breaching charge blow in the north side of the house. Then Shaw heard the sound of Collins's Mk 48 Mod 1 lightweight machine gun firing. Both their threat and targeting systems were integrated. The ground floor of the house was very open plan. Both of them knew where all the targets were. They started firing, often shooting dangerously close to each other. Targeting those in the building who were carrying weapons first, then moving down the threat range, unarmed adults and finally the children. They only needed two people alive, and even then only one of those was actually going to live. With their sensors they would find everyone. Anyone they flushed out the Green Beret security force outside would catch.

When they'd finished on the ground floor, Collins went up the stairs 'clearing up', Shaw went down into the basements 'clearing down'.

***

As soon as the first tracers from the Blackhawks had flown through the house, cutting down his soldiers, friends and family alike, Colonel Alejandro's bodyguards, all men who had served with him in the Airmobile Special Forces Group, had grabbed him and his family, pushing their heads down, steering them by gripping the back of their necks, their other hands on their weapons, using their own bodies, clad in armour, to shield the Colonel. They walked them quickly through the house and down the stairs heading for the third basement. Those not directly 'steering' the Colonel, or his direct family, had their weapons up and were checking all around them even as the gunfire from outside intensified.

They moved down the carpeted stairs past the first basement, which was made up of a number of different recreation rooms, including a home cinema. The second basement was actually the garage. The third and lowest basement was a range and armoury and also contained the safe room. Basically, it was a secure vault designed to withstand a hit from a 2000lb Joint Direct Attack Munitions bomb, and filled with rations, weapons and ammunition.

Bad Trip infected the matter of the vault door itself, growing his body from it. He bent light to thicken the shadows in the area as he pulled himself out of the birthing matter of the door. He looked as he always did: ponytail, scar, his craggy face seemingly a repository for malevolence. He wore a dark, double-breasted, sharkskin suit with a midnight blue overcoat, and a trilby. The only difference to his normal appearance was that he looked Mexican.

The weapon he held in his hand looked like an engraved, silver-plated, ivory-gripped M1911 Colt .45, but it was really just a focus for what he himself could do. Today, however, it would be firing what amounted to normal bullets, as he didn't want his capabilities to be too obvious. Although he would be growing the ammunition from his own flesh, pulling the requisite substance through his connections to the surrounding matter, mainly through the ground.

As he saw Alejandro with his guards Bad Trip reached over with his left hand to touch the gun in his right. Another identical pistol grew out of it. He lost a bit of weight for a moment until he replenished it from the ground.

He gave the bodyguards a moment to see him. Surprise in their eyes but next to no hesitation, their weapons coming up, fingers squeezing triggers. They were nowhere near quick enough. Bad Trip brought both pistols up, firing rapidly, walking towards them as he did so. He cut one bodyguard down after another, then members of Alejandro's family, until only Alejandro was left reaching for his own pistol as Bad Trip reached him. He slipped one of the .45s into his pocket, where it returned to the base matter of his body, and plucked the pistol from the drug baron's hand. The lesson being taught was helplessness.

The Colonel was whip-thin, with a full head of grey hair. He would have fired on Bad Trip given the chance, by instinct and muscle memory from his training. Now he had a moment to take in what had just happened to his children and their children. Tears sprang to his eyes. Bad Trip grabbed him by his hair.

***

Shaw had the 'lucky one' down on his knees on one of the lawn terraces to the south of the house amongst all the dead bodies the Green Berets had made. Shaw's .45 was pressed against his head. He was clearly terrified.

Bad Trip emerged from the house pushing the Colonel ahead of him. The Colonel was up on his tiptoes, both his hands holding onto the hand gripping the drug baron's hair. Bad Trip walked over to Shaw. Collins was standing nearby, seemingly casual but keeping a lookout. The Green Berets had secured the area. Enough money had gone down in bribes to at least delay intervention from the Mexican authorities and military. The two helicopters were still circling the compound providing sniper and 'top' cover.

Bad Trip forced the Colonel down onto his knees. He looked at the lucky one as he produced the pearl-handled straight-edged razor from the pocket of his overcoat.

'Tell them Bliss stays. Tell them they work for me because I kill everything else. Tell them I am Xipe Totec,' he told the 'lucky one'. Then he started to peel the Colonel, like an apple.

In Haiti and Jamaica they were already calling him the Steppin' Razor. Bad Trip was sure that he would have other names by the time he had finished.

Green Lanes, North London, 11 July, 1513 (BST)

Tamal Gezman was frightened. He shouldn't have been frightened. Everything he had done since he had joined up with the scar-faced man had told him that they were in an unassailable position, that they were going to run London. Dagenham had been a setback, but not much of one, a bloodied nose, nothing more. The legalisation of Bliss in America, with Britain seemingly set to follow, should have lessened the heat, particularly with distribution south of the river sorted. What was obvious was that the scar-faced man had real power behind him, political, financial, in terms of research and production, and, judging by the weapons, combat drugs and the top tier enforcers, even military backing. All of this suggested that he shouldn't be afraid. Except, perhaps, of the scar-faced man and his second, Collins. That had been before Lambeth.

It had preyed on his mind. He was struggling to sleep despite the drugs he took. It wasn't right, the bodies he had seen hanging there, that thing, the *karakura* that had torn through the Russians. It was for this reason that he felt less than secure when he stepped out of the social club and onto Green Lanes flanked by the two Russians, both of whom were carrying the modified MP7s and were habitual users of the combat drugs the scar-faced man supplied.

He headed along Green Lanes, making his way towards his parked Mercedes. The driver was Turkish, one of his old crew. There had been a lot of bad feelings when he had brought the Russians on board. He had been forced to make concessions to some of his people.

He heard someone shouting in Turkish from behind him, from the social club. It sounded like the word for grenade. He started to turn. Something hot and wet covered his face. One of the Russians started to fall. There was someone behind him with a gun.

It's a hit! He started to panic. He thought the *karakura* had sent people for him.

There was an explosion. The painted-over window on the front of the social club blew out in a bright and loud explosion. He was deaf, and the gunman with the hoodie, cap and sunglasses covering his face was whited out as he became momentarily blind. He felt something bite into his side then everything was pain.

***

The stun grenade went off behind him. The overpressure blew the windows out. The first Organizatsiya gunman was already falling. Two shots from his suppressed Sig to the head. He shifted the gun to the other gunman, who despite the surprise was still reacting. Noel fired the Sig twice more and the top of the second gunman's head came off.

Gezman had started to turn. In the disorientation from the stun grenade and the shooting of his two guards he hadn't seen Nicholas walk up in front of him. Nicholas, also wearing a hoodie, cap and sunglasses, fired the taser at point-blank range into Gezman. The drug dealer started to shake but turned round to face Nicholas. Nicholas's eyes were wide; fear warring with surprise that Gezman was still up and functioning despite being hit with the taser.

Noel swapped the Sig into his left hand and reached into his hoodie, drawing out the modified cattle prod. He rammed it again and again into the small of Gezman's back until the drug dealer hit the ground a drooling, spasming mess.

The transit van shunted some cars out of the way and the side door slid open. Noel was looking all around to see if anyone was about to react. Josh stepped out of the van, grabbing Gezman's prone form once Noel had stopped shocking him.

It had happened so quickly and with such decisive violence that nobody had really reacted yet. That changed when the second round of gunshots started. A pedestrian hit the ground, without uttering a cry. The body of the van sparked as another shot ricocheted off it. Noel found the gunman. He was stood by the open door to Gezman's Mercedes firing a handgun at them. Noel raised the Sig. People started to panic and run for cover, screams filled the air. Nicholas stepped in front of Noel. *No shot.* Noel moved but there were a lot of panicking people between him and the gunman.

'Boss!' Josh shouted and threw Nicholas the sawn-off shotgun. Nicholas started walking towards the gunman. The gunman saw him coming and started firing more rapidly. More people went down. The fire from the pistol was inaccurate.

'Get back in the van!' Noel shouted. Nicholas either ignored, or just didn't hear, his brother. He closed on the gunman and as soon as he had a clear shot he fired both barrels. The gunman bounced back against the

Mercedes' door, the window smashing. He bounced off and fell to the pavement, most of his torso a red mess. Nicholas stopped and stared at the mess he had made. He stared at what until a moment ago had been a living human being. Someone grabbed him so he flinched and turned to fight.

'In the van, now!' Noel shouted at him. Nicholas nodded numbly and allowed himself to be dragged back and bundled into the transit. Josh slammed the side door shut behind them. Billy pulled the van out into traffic.

There was the flat hard sound of meat hitting meat as Josh pounded his fist again and again into a nearly senseless Gezman.

'Hey, hey!' Noel shouted and grabbed Josh's massive arm. Josh's head snapped around. Noel barely recognised the normally sweet-tempered man, the expression on his face one of near-total hate. 'You kill him and this was a waste of time.'

'Josh, pack it in,' Nicholas told him. Finally Josh relented and nodded. He slumped his bulk against the side of the van, making the vehicle wobble.

Camberwell, South London, 11 July, 1807 (BST)

They had dumped the van in a quiet side street with no CCTV and dropped a Molotov cocktail into it to make gathering forensic information more difficult and transferred into a stolen four-wheel drive with illegally tinted windows.

Noel had secured Gezman with cable ties and injected him with a powerful sedative that seemed to be warring with whatever else was in his system.

Billy drove them quickly but carefully. All of them heaved a sigh of relief when they crossed over the river on the Vauxhall Bridge. The lockup was somewhere in Camberwell, railway arches with trains running overhead regularly. Nicholas said that the arches couldn't be traced back to him. He had hired them through a series of blinds. Initially, he'd used the lockup to store heroin until he had realised that it was a lot less suspicious to store them in garages in unassuming suburban neighbourhoods. He had never gotten around to cancelling the rent payments on the lockup.

Noel had wondered where Oliver was but Nicholas had told him that he wanted his heir apparent as clean as possible. He wanted him as the business brain, not out doing this sort of thing. Noel could see his point.

Josh opened the double wooden doors to the lockup and Billy drove the four-wheel drive in. Josh had barely closed the door when Nicholas dragged Gezman out of the vehicle. There was a rope with a hook hanging from a pulley attached to one of the roof spars. Nicholas pushed the hook through the cable tie binding Gezman's wrists and Josh winched him painfully up into the air. Gezman's cries were cut off as Nicholas punched him in the stomach, hard enough to knock the wind out of him. Gezman swung backwards and forwards on the rope, the cable tie biting into his skin, drawing blood. Nicholas kept on punching him, becoming more and more frenzied. Josh was throwing a few punches of his own.

Billy climbed out of the driver seat of the stolen four-wheel drive and came to stand next to Noel.

'He's never killed anyone before, has he?' Noel said.

Billy shook his head.

'That cherry's well and truly bust. You want me to stop him?' the Somali asked

Noel knew that Billy had killed, there had been stories about him when they'd been growing up. Billy had done time for manslaughter, plea-bargained down from murder.

'Not really.'

'You threaten my family! You're going to suffer, you piece of fucking shit!' Nicholas was roaring.

At first Noel thought that Gezman was sobbing.

'Wait up,' Noel said. Nicholas kept on swinging his big fist into Gezman's torso. 'Nicholas!'

Nicholas stopped.

'Josh, man,' Billy said more quietly. The huge man with the dreadlocks stopped hitting Gezman. It was then that Noel realised that Gezman wasn't sobbing, he was laughing.

'You fucking morons,' Gezman said. 'I can do this all night, hell, I like it now I've changed. What do you think's going to happen here?'

'We've got some questions for you,' Billy told him. 'And there's some very angry people here. Now, everyone talks in the end ...'

'It's just a matter of whether or not we've cut your balls off and cauterised the wound with a blowtorch

214

first,' Josh said. Nicholas was just staring at Gezman, breathing hard, trying to control his fury.

'No,' Gezman said. 'You have this all wrong. The only question now is do you kill me before he gets here and kills all of us? He'll find you. He'll make you watch him torture your family to death.'

'Who is he?' Noel asked.

Gezman turned to look at the younger Burman brother.

'I don't know and I don't care. The funny thing is no amount of torturing me is going to change that. I'll tell you one thing, though. He's a fuck of a lot scarier than you bunch of *amcik hosafi*.'

Noel walked over to Nicholas and tapped him on the shoulder, gesturing him to follow as Josh really went to work on Gezman. Nicholas followed his younger brother but continued staring angrily at Gezman.

'Look, I know it's a little early to call this but I've got a horrible feeling that he's telling the truth. The other thing is I don't care what you've seen on the TV and how many drugs he's got inside him, somebody Josh's size keeps pounding on him like that he'll do irreparable damage.'

'What makes you think he's telling the truth?' Nicholas asked to the accompaniment of the sound of Josh beating on Gezman.

'Because if I was some kingpin figure who can bring together disparate gangs, co-opt members of the special forces, block police investigations and shape public policy then I wouldn't trust that …' He stabbed out a finger in Gezman's direction. 'With anything.'

'Could have mentioned that before,' Nicholas muttered. 'He must know something.'

There was a roar of anger as Gezman spat on Josh followed by the beating being renewed with greater vigour interspersed with what Noel assumed were Turkish obscenities.

'He'll know operational stuff that he has responsibility for. We can take that apart if he talks quickly enough and we can act on it.'

'I've got people who can move on it,' Nicholas said.

'Against people who are fast, can take a lot of damage and are armed with automatic weapons? These people gave us a run for our money and we were loaded for bear and had the element of surprise in our favour.'

'Yeah but you weren't firebombing and drive-by shooting,' Nicholas pointed out. Noel had to concede that his brother was right.

'So now we just need to get him to talk.'

'Everyone talks when they've got their cock between the blades of a bolt cutter,' Nicholas muttered.

'Yeah, but you get to make that threat once and that idiot might call your bluff.'

'Oh, I'll do it,' Nicholas said and Noel was sure that his brother meant it then and there. He might feel different when he actually had his hands on the bolt cutter.

'Do it last. You do it first he just bleeds out without hospital treatment and that's assuming he doesn't just die of shock.'

Nicholas turned to look at Noel.

'This isn't the first time you've had to do something like this.'

Noel just nodded, thinking back to the number of AQT suspects he'd delivered to the CIA's Salt Pit facility in Afghanistan.

***

The screaming had started to grate on Noel's nerves some time ago. Nicholas and Josh had beaten on Gezman, electrocuted him, burnt him, cut him and even drugged him with heroin to try and lower his inhibitions. Maybe he was talking but if he was then most of it was screaming in Turkish, which none of them spoke.

'*Amcýk aðýzlý at yarraðý!*' Gezman screamed at them. They had started electrocuting him again. If nothing else, Noel was impressed with the amount of abuse the guy had managed to take. He suspected it was due to the drugs that his employers had given him. '*Anam avradını sikeyim!*'

'You could fucking help!' Nicholas shouted at Noel and Billy. Billy shrugged. Noel ignored his brother.

The drugs, Noel thought, an idea occurring to him. He turned and headed deeper into the red brick lockup, gesturing for Nicholas to join him. Irritated, his brother followed.

'Fucking what?' Nicholas snapped.

'You said you thought he was getting high on his own supply?' Straight away Nicholas saw his brother's train of thought. There was more screaming accompanied moments later by the smell of ozone and burning flesh.

'Josh,' Nicholas called. Josh electrocuted Gezman again. The drug dealer jerked, swinging back and forth on the rope. 'Josh, mate, give it a rest a bit.' Josh looked less than pleased but he lowered the cattle prod. 'Billy, mate, you've not been much use tonight.'

'Not really my kind of thing,' Billy said. If he was offended he didn't show it.

'Need you to pop out and get something for me.'

Billy nodded.

***

Billy had come back with tea for them all. Josh and Nicholas had found old chairs that would just about take their weight. Billy and Noel were both sat on an old workbench. Josh and Billy were sharing a joint. All of them were drinking tea, looking at Gezman as he dangled there. Gezman was staring at a point on the workbench between Noel and Billy. Or rather he was staring at the vial of blue liquid on the workbench between the two men.

'How you feeling, Tamal?' Nicholas called. 'Good, yeah?' Tamal ignored him. He seemed to be trying to cope with the pain in his wrists as well as multiple bruises, contusions and burns but his eyes kept on returning to the vial of Bliss. 'It's over any time you want, mate.'

'You're going to do permanent damage to his wrists and hands soon and they could get infected,' Noel pointed out, quietly.

'I don't give a fuck,' Nicholas told his brother. 'Though I am beginning to wonder who's torturing who here?'

Penthouse Grand Hyatt Hotel, Washington DC, 11 July, 1900 (EST)

Rex had changed the molecular structure of the glass in the penthouse to provide him with a little more privacy. He had selectively modified the remaining escorts' brains to make them more docile and to enable them to cope with the constant changes he was making to his body. He had also improved the structure of one of the sofas, using some of the nearby matter to reinforce it. He was currently an eight-foot tall, blue-skinned, silver-haired, bright-purple-eyed androgynous creature with six arms and female genitalia. He was lying on the floor watching BBC footage of the aftermath of a multiple murder and kidnapping in London.

'Is this one of yours?' he asked.

Shadows receded from the corner of the room, revealing Bad Trip. One of the escorts slid off a sofa and moved away from the enforcer, another just started crying.

'Yes.' Even to Rex, Bad Trip's rasping voice grated. Suddenly the plasma screen split and showed satellite imagery, some of it their own from the seeded micro-satellites, other footage from co-opted human surveillance satellites. CCTV images started appearing as well.

219

Showing a white transit van travelling through the London streets. That footage then switched to footage of a four-wheel drive. 'As near as I can tell they switched vehicle and I lost track of them in this area of London.' The screen changed to show a map of the Camberwell area of South London. 'I don't like that our surveillance net is not total yet.'

'Patience,' Rex said. 'Is this our mysterious other visitors to Earth?'

'No, this appears to be purely human.'

'See, I told you they were resourceful.' Rex cupped the chin of a beautiful young man who was snuggled up to his giant blue form on the enlarged sofa. 'They make marvellous pets and you can have sex with them.'

'I don't really know what's happening,' the young man said and then turned his attention back to the mountains of narcotics on the coffee table. Rex patted his buttocks and considered growing some male genitalia.

Bad Trip's face wrinkled up in distaste.

'I can't say I'm pleased to find Weft here.' One of Bad Trip's Juicers had fought one in London. 'I want to hurt one of your "pets".'

Immediately the three remaining escorts scurried to Rex for protection.

'I'm going to say no to that.'

'They are Shriven junkies. Soulless outcasts as far as the Weft go. They are running their own primitive operation. They have more to fear from the Weft than we do. They're not going to tell anyone. It is simply a matter of finding them all and dealing with them.'

'And the anti-matter explosions in Myanmar, Damascus and Namibia?'

'They realise we're here and they're covering their tracks. Destroying their facilities.'

'The one they've taken. This Tamal Gezman? He is using some of our product, isn't he?'

'Yes.'

'You could find him using that, couldn't you?'

'Yes, but I'm still not happy about the gaps in our surveillance. I will find him when I am ready. When Gezman has suffered enough for failing me I will feed them some information.'

'And then?'

'Then they will start to suffer.' There was a positive glee on Bad Trip's face. He enjoyed the idea of having the luxury of the time to really, truly make an example of someone. Bad Trip stepped back, the shadows wrapping themselves around him, and was gone.

Rex changed his body-chemistry slightly to allow Earth's primitive narcotics to affect him. He dusted one of the female escorts with cocaine and started snorting it off her with a diamond-studded platinum tube.

'Now my dears, will you help me think of a suitably grand entrance onto the world stage?'

The mind-altered and ferociously stoned escort just looked at him with a glazed expression and smiled.

'I don't like him,' she said.

'Few do, but he was one of the first of us, a red screaming nightmare, and we owe him a lot.'

'Can I have some more Bliss?'

'Of course you can, my dear, that's what we're here for. To make sure that you can have what you want when you want it.'

The young woman crawled off the sofa and grabbed a vial of the blue liquid from the table. Rex had found that she liked stories based on human folklore about a creature called a vampire. He was going to wait until all her pleasure centres were thoroughly stimulated and then he was going to fulfil one of her fantasies and feed on her dopamine, serotonin and endorphins. Unfortunately this would mean that he wouldn't be able to play with her for a while. She would start to eat gluttonously, suffer cognitive impairment and muscle spasticity. She would also suffer from severe depression. In short, she would not be much fun to be around. However, he could always find someone else, and pleasure was the most important thing.

Camberwell, South London, 11 July, 2226 (BST)

The hammering on the door made all of them jump, even Tamal. Noel had his Sig in his hand and was cursing himself for not having someone hidden outside watching the place. Nicholas grabbed the sawn-off shotgun. Billy had a long-nosed .38 revolver in each hand. He moved quietly and quickly to one side of the door, leaning against the wall. Noel concealed himself next to a tarpaulin-covered stack of old machine parts and covered the door. Nicholas was stood in front of it, shotgun at the ready. Josh had a machete-like knife and was holding it against Gezman's neck, gesturing for him to be quiet. There was more hammering at the door.

'Open the door you stupid pricks!' Sam shouted.

'For fuck's sake,' Nicholas muttered. Billy looked over at Nicholas questioningly. Nicholas turned to look at Noel. Noel shrugged.

'Let her in,' he mouthed to his older brother. Nicholas gestured towards Gezman. 'Well, what do you want to do?' Nicholas gave the suggestion some thought.

'Have you got a warrant, Samantha?' Nicholas shouted. Noel rolled his eyes and lowered the Sig, even Josh and Billy looked less than impressed. Billy put his pistol away and Nicholas lowered the sawn-off.

'I'll give you a fucking warrant you stupid cunt. If you don't open this door I'll stick my foot so far up your arse I'll be wearing you like a slipper.'

'Noel,' Charlotte shouted through the door. Nicholas turned to look at his younger brother. Noel shrugged. It was his turn to look sheepish. 'If we can find you then so can other people, do you understand me?'

'Is there anyone else you want to invite?' Nicholas demanded in a harsh whisper. 'We're fucking doing crime here!'

'I didn't bring them,' Noel whispered back.

'Well fucking deal with it!'

'What do you expect me to do?'

'Aren't you supposed to be some black ops type? Deal with them!'

Noel just stared at his brother.

'I'm not killing Samantha,' he told Nicholas.

Nicholas gave this some thought.

'No, all right,' he relented and then looked back at Gezman. 'Well, we're all going to be going to prison for quite some time. Billy, open the door.'

Billy opened the door. Charlotte and Samantha both stalked into the lockup. Charlotte was carrying a hardened plastic case and a smaller field medic kit. Noel and Nicholas both felt like children again, caught doing something wrong, though both of them realised the absurdity of this in the face of what they'd actually done. If anything, Charlotte actually looked angrier than Sam.

Billy looked outside, expecting to see SCO19 following them both.

'They're on their own, boss,' Billy said, sounding surprised.

'You think it'd take more than the two of us?' Sam asked and then turned to Nicholas. 'Why don't you put the shotgun down before you hurt yourself?'

'I'm not twelve any more ...' Nicholas started.

'Oh just do as she tells you, you bloody infant!' Charlotte snapped. Nicholas recoiled slightly and looked like he was about to argue.

'Nicholas, please,' Noel said.

'How'd you find us?' Josh asked.

'We asked some people,' Sam spat. 'I'm police, remember.'

'Who?' Josh asked. He was more curious than anything else.

'As if I'd tell you,' Sam said. 'Let me put it this way, though. I visited two pubs before I found out about this place. Criminal geniuses you are not.' Billy, Josh and Nicholas exchanged looks. 'And I would have been here a lot quicker if this cunt answered his phone,' she said pointing at Noel.

'I was a little busy kidnapping and torturing someone,' Noel told the detective superintendent.

'The less we use phones, the better,' Charlotte snapped. She was stood in front of Gezman, looking up at his battered and burnt body. Samantha followed the younger woman's stare.

'So, murder, assault, weapons, kidnap, torture. The lot of you are going away for a very long time,' she spat. Noel could see his brother's grip tightening on the shotgun he was holding. He could feel Josh and Billy shift slightly at the mention of jail. Samantha turned on them. 'What? You think because *he's* special forces,' she pointed at Noel, '*you* get a free fucking pass?'

'Oh do grow up, Samantha,' Charlotte told the other woman. Sam looked like she'd just been slapped. She turned to Josh. 'Let him down now.' Josh looked at Nicholas, who just shrugged. Charlotte turned to Noel. 'Of course you checked him for tracers, bugs, things like that?' Noel looked sheepish again. Charlotte turned away from him, shaking her head. Gezman moaned in relief as Josh lowered him to the ground. Charlotte opened the hardened box and took out something that looked like a wand attached to a dial. She started running it over Gezman's body.

'Would they even have stuff that you could detect?' Noel asked. Samantha's laugh was a harsh bark. Josh and Billy exchanged looks.

'Not a good reason not to look,' Charlotte muttered. She found nothing. She ran another couple of pieces of sensor equipment over Gezman and again found nothing. Then she threw the field medic's kit, basically a more sophisticated first aid kit, to Noel. 'Patch him up as best you can,' she told him.

'Charlotte …'

'Just do it!'

Noel looked like he was about to argue but instead he knelt down on the floor next to the moaning Gezman, opened the kit and started cleaning his wounds.

'Who are you?' Nicholas asked. Charlotte turned on him.

'Do you really want to know, Mr Burman?' she demanded. 'Isn't it enough that I'm cleaning up the mess made by you, your idiot brother and the two stooges?'

Nicholas stared at her, his anger apparent. She held his stare, glaring back.

'Fair enough,' he finally said. 'What now?'

'You go home. Maybe they won't have killed your family already. Perhaps, assuming we don't get too many more distractions, we might even be able to resolve this situation before they do take revenge on you and yours.'

Nicholas was trying desperately to control his anger. Charlotte didn't look like she cared. Noel looked up from where he was knelt on the floor. Nicholas glanced down at him.

'Do as she says, please. I've got this,' Noel told him.

Nicholas turned back to Charlotte, who was still glaring at him.

'And get rid of the four-wheel drive on the way,' Charlotte told him.

Nicholas looked like he was about to argue. Josh put his hand on Nicholas's shoulder.

'C'mon Nick, plod's got this.'

Nicholas allowed himself to be pulled out of the lockup. The door closed behind them and they heard the sound of an engine.

Sam pointed after them.

'Him I expect this from, but you?' she demanded.

Noel turned to look at Sam and then stood up.

'What do you think I do for a living?' he demanded. 'Are you really that naive? All that unquestioning East End patriotism. Do you know how many people I've killed? People who haven't threatened to murder my niece? How many times I've called in airstrikes, or painted target for air and artillery knowing that there were going to be civilian casualties, women, children, families? Or AQT suspects that I've delivered to the Salt Pit, or seen on their way to the Hotel California? Who do you think I am!' He was screaming at her by the time he'd finished. Shaking, not really sure where it was coming from. Sam was just staring at him, subdued.

'I can't use you,' Charlotte said quietly from behind him. Noel turned to look at her. Gezman was rolling around on the floor at their feet. 'We are at a vast technological disadvantage, we are outgunned, they have more influence than us. We have no idea who we can or can't trust, and more than anything we need intelligence, and shit like this is fucking everything up. Do you understand me? I should cut you loose now. Let this look like what it was, the act of a petty criminal and his confederates.'

'Why don't you? Why'd you come looking for me? Get Sam to find me?' Noel asked. Charlotte watched him for a while and then glanced down at Gezman.

'Well, since you've already got him,' she said quietly.

'You can cut the bleedin' sexual tension in here with a knife. Must be the torture victim making you both horny, yeah?'

Noel and Charlotte both turned to look at Sam. Gezman started to crawl. At first Noel thought that it was a rather pathetic escape attempt but then the drug dealer reached up for the vial of Bliss. Sam snatched it up.

'I think I'll have that, love,' she told him.

'What are we doing with him?' Noel asked.

'Right idea, but you didn't go far enough. Put him in the boot of the car outside,' Charlotte told him.

Chapter Twelve

Near Ash, North Hampshire, 12 July, 0113 (BST)

Charlotte's work car was a Volvo S40 hatchback modified for four-wheel drive. Gezman was taped up and sedated in the spacious boot, hidden by the parcel shelf. Noel was sat in the backseat feeling a bit like he was being treated as a naughty child, not that Sam and Charlotte were saying much. Noel had occupied himself for most of the journey out of London by keeping an eye out for possible ambushes, or to see if they were being followed. If they were then it was beyond his capability to notice.

They pulled into a long unpaved driveway off a quiet tree-lined B road. The headlights of the Volvo illuminated an old, rundown-looking red brick house.

'What is this place?' Sam asked.

'A safe house. There's no record of it connecting it back to the intelligence agencies that use it. It's completely off the books,' Charlotte said.

*

Inside, the house smelled of damp and mould. The interior looked as rundown as the exterior. It struck Noel, as he dragged the barely conscious Gezman in, that the house hadn't been decorated since the 1950s. Wallpaper was hanging off the wall, the carpets were threadbare and the whole place felt like it hadn't been inhabited for quite some time.

'Where do you want him?' Noel asked. Charlotte pointed to a door under the stairs.

'Cellar,' she told him.

***

Sam was staring at the three solid-looking stainless steel doors in the reinforced concrete wall at the bottom of the stairs in the cellar. Each door had a portal window in it. Noel finished dragging Gezman to the bottom of the stairs and lowered him onto the poured concrete floor. He looked through the window into the first room. It was a spacious, bare interrogation room. It had a table, with two chairs at either side of it. Everything was bolted to the concrete floor and the table had metal loops for attaching restraints to.

The second room contained something that looked like a dentist's chair with various restraints attached to it and a number of stainless steel cabinets. The third room looked like a fully equipped operating theatre, but again the stainless steel bench had restraints on it.

'Is this place owned by a serial killer?' Sam asked as Charlotte came down the stairs.

'No, SIS, but it's mostly used by the CIA,' Charlotte told her. Noel was starting to feel dirty in a way he hadn't when it had been Nicholas and Josh beating on Gezman.

'Where do you want him?' he asked Charlotte quietly. She looked at him oddly.

'The OT, please.'

Noel started dragging Gezman towards the third room.

***

Charlotte strapped Gezman down and attached a catheter to each of the drug dealer's wrists with an efficiency that surprised Noel. She attached one of the catheters by a flexible tube to a machine. From a glass-fronted fridge she took a number of bags of blood with O Rh D printed on the labels.

'Look, I'm not exactly comfortable with this ...' Sam started.

'You can leave if you want,' Noel said.

'Actually, she can't,' Charlotte said, straightening up and turning to the older woman. 'Do you remember when I said we were in over our head? Have any of the strange things happening recently seemed like they would be good for us? And by us I mean the human race? Frankly, we need every little bit of information we can salvage from Noel's fucking mess. So either grow a pair of ovaries ...'

'Or what? You're going to put two in my head and dump me somewhere?' Sam asked.

'No need. See the chest freezer behind you? That's for bodies. It gets cleared out regularly.'

Sam and Charlotte stared at each other.

'Sam, we're going to need you,' Noel said quietly. Sam turned on him. Charlotte went back to hooking up the blood IV.

'I don't see why. This pussy cat's had her claws pulled,' she said referring to herself. Then she pointed at Charlotte. 'And posh bitch here's a fucking psycho.' She turned back to Charlotte. 'What are you going to do to him?' she demanded. Noel had to admit that he was interested in the answer to that question as well.

'So we know, broadly speaking, how Bliss affects us. We don't know how because it appears to be transformative and have a degree of intelligence to it, I suspect some kind of smart molecule,' Charlotte said as she worked. Gezman was moaning again, barely conscious. 'I'm betting, however, that it's carried by the blood. That,' she pointed at the machine stuck to the wall, 'is a plasmapheresis machine.'

'That's nice,' Sam said sarcastically.

'She's going to remove all his blood and replace it with clean blood,' Noel said. Charlotte was nodding.

'I'm going to be doing a slightly more sophisticated version of what the boys were doing. Basically, I am going to see if I can force him to go cold turkey.'

Charlotte finished sorting the catheters and went to the machine and started pressing buttons, checking the readings. Finally she set it running. Blood started creeping up the plastic tube.

***

The thoughtform affected the surrounding matter like a virus. Transforming the matter, moulding it into a human-looking body, bending the light around it to shroud him in shadows. Bad Trip walked down the short poured concrete corridor and looked into the operating theatre's window. He was just in time for the screaming.

***

Gezman was struggling against his restraints as he screamed. Noel and Sam looked on in horror as Gezman started to atrophy, muscles and flesh wasting away before their very eyes. Charlotte was also watching the process, apparently fascinated. She went to one of the drawers under the stainless steel work benches at the side of the room and opened them up. She removed a ball gag, crossed to Gezman and pushed it into his mouth, muffling but not completely curtailing the screaming. His nostrils flared, his eyes wide and bulging.

'How's he going to speak with that in his mouth?' Sam demanded.

'The pain's too acute. He's beyond language now,' Charlotte said.

Something made Noel turn around and look at the portal window in the door to the OT but he could only see gloom outside.

'This is interesting, though,' Charlotte mused.

'Oh, I get that,' Sam muttered. 'Particularly if you're the female Joseph Mengele.' She was looking down at Gezman, her expression a mixture of distaste and sympathy for the man.

'He was clearly taking the combat drugs that the Organizatsiya gunmen in Dagenham were on. It seems that they develop a severe physical dependency on them. Which makes sense.'

'Can you give him a sedative or something, and how the fuck does any of this make sense?' Sam demanded.

'It's like a pimp putting his stable on drugs, it makes them dependent on him, compliant,' Noel said.

'You've been around your brother too much,' Sam said.

'That's not how he rolls and you know that,' Noel told her.

'So he can't tell us anything?' Sam said.

As she said that, he stopped writhing and trying to chew through his gag. He was drooling round the ball as he made noises.

'He's trying to talk,' Sam told them.

'That's odd,' Charlotte said. 'I don't understand how the pain could have reversed itself like that.'

'Fuck this,' Sam said. She reached down and pulled the gag out of his mouth. Noel suddenly looked behind him again and then shook his head.

Just twitchy, he decided.

'You all right mate?' Sam asked.

'Bliss …' Gezman begged.

Sam stepped away from him in disgust.

'Well it's good that you've got your priorities sorted, then,' she muttered.

Charlotte reached into her handbag and pulled out the blue vial of Bliss.

'You can have this when you've told us what we want to know,' she told Gezman. There was a look of desperate, pathetic gratitude in his eyes.

'What do you need?' he asked.

'Well, where does this come from, for a start?' Charlotte asked, shaking the vial of blue liquid.

'I don't know. One day this guy in a suit. English guy, Collins, he walks in with two cases. One is full of money, the other is full of Bliss and a small amount of Rage.'

'Rage?' Noel asked.

'It's a combat drug, makes us faster, stronger, that kind of thing,' Gezman told them, continually eyeing the vial of Bliss. 'Collins gave us the money, a lot of money, to test market Bliss. We pick it up from containers at Dagenham docks and from there we distribute it to our dealers. That's pretty much all I know. Every so often Collins give us orders to expand the operation. He provides us with files on who we're going to be speaking to. A few argue with us but Bliss is too lucrative. Only your brother really said no.'

'This is nothing that we don't already know,' Charlotte said. 'You'll have to do better than that.'

'Please,' he begged.

'Who's the guy with the ponytail and the scar?' Noel asked. Gezman blanched.

'I don't know, I only met him the once when we went to see Burman ...'

'When you threatened my niece?' Noel asked coldly.

'Look, I'm sorry. That guy scares me. He's called Bad Trip, he only speaks when he has to and he's Collins's boss, that's all I know, I swear. Can I have the Bliss, you've no idea how much pain I'm in. Please!' he pleaded.

'Where's this Bad Trip from?' Sam asked.

'America, east coast I think. New York or Boston, maybe Philadelphia.'

'It's a fucking funny way of doing business,' Sam said.

'It's certainly direct,' Charlotte mused.

'I'm telling the truth,' Gezman told them, desperately.

'It's like a terrorist cell. Each part of it isolated from the level above it, one go-between,' Noel said. 'They must have really wanted Nicholas's business.'

'I think you underestimate just how powerful your brother is,' Sam told him. 'By powerful, I mean what a drug-dealing scumbag he is.'

Noel ignored Sam's jibe.

'The Bliss, please?' Gezman begged.

'Who brought in the Russians?' Sam asked.

'Collins did, those guys are fucking insane but I've spoken to them. Collins turned up with two cases, paid them to try it before they buy it, except he put four of them in hospital first.'

'The warehouse in Dagenham?' Noel demanded.

'Before my time, the Russians handled that. I'm

236

guessing it was a transport point. They must have moved to the container park after you guys hit them.'

'They didn't move very far,' Noel muttered and then looked behind him again.

'Where are they transporting it from?' Sam asked.

'I don't know? Amsterdam? Maybe Eastern Europe?'

'You don't know?' Sam asked incredulously.

'It's just there, waiting for us when we go to pick it up. Look, it's legal, we're not really doing anything wrong …'

'Your organisation killed a lot of my friends and have threatened my family,' Noel said quietly.

'I'm sorry about that, things got messed up. It'll come all right when it gets legalised.'

'Oh well, since you've said sorry,' Sam said sarcastically. 'If I were you I'd stick with answering questions. Who's handling the legalisation?'

'I don't know, I've got nothing to do with that side of thing but there's some kind of big PR campaign on the net, social media, all that bullshit.'

'Who've you got in the police?' Sam asked.

'I don't know. They pretty much leave us alone since we started working with Collins.'

'He doesn't know anything,' Charlotte said, pocketing the vial of Bliss. 'This is a waste of our time.'

'Does the name Stylianos Evangeli mean anything to you?' Noel asked.

Sam and Charlotte both turned to look at him.

'The so-called dealer in human organs?' Sam scoffed. 'We've looked at him for human trafficking but other than that it's a bullshit urban myth.'

'Nicholas mentioned his name. It was what that Roche guy wanted to know about. Have you heard his name before?' he asked Charlotte. Gezman was listening intently. Charlotte didn't answer. He turned back to Sam. 'You say it's an urban myth but you were pulling a lot of bodies of homeless people, people who wouldn't be missed, out of that tower block in Lambeth. Evangeli owned that tower block.'

***

Bad Trip knelt on the poured concrete floor. The side of his face was pressed against the cool metal of the door and the hard concrete of the wall. His skin had melded with it. It looked like metal and concrete had infected his skin, growing out of the door and the wall respectively.

He was listening intently. Somehow these humans, despite their primitive nature, were providing him with useful information. It might have been speculation, but if they were right then it sounded like this Evangeli was a human agent of the Shriven Weft.

He invaded the human infoscape, frustrated at how slowly it could carry the information forms he had sent out. Information on Evangeli came flooding back. It had been Evangelli owned the building he'd ordered Collins to hit in Lambeth. They had gone in there thinking to find a recalcitrant, and possibly influential, heroin dealer. Instead they had found a soul-dead Shriven Weft.

He took the picture of the organ dealer and created an intelligent information form capable of facial recognition and then started running it through all the CCTVs in London, and again he was irritated by the slowness of the human information structure. This should take as long as it takes to think of, Bad Trip decided.

He found a number of Evangeli's haunts. He seemed to have a number of domiciles across and outside London. He was frequently seen at airports, at various nightclubs, casinos, and restaurants. He lived a playboy lifestyle. He was a regular visitor to the Docklands Museum, which didn't seem to fit his lifestyle. On a whim, Bad Trip sent out more information forms with broader parameters looking for information on the area, particularly information regarding odd occurrences.

The first hit he got was a report of a series of localised and oddly regular earth tremors that had the authorities running Canary Wharf so worried that they had called in a British Geological Survey team, who had been at a loss to explain them. Bad Trip cross-referenced the tremors with Evangeli's trips to the museum and found a correlation.

A museum, however, was an odd place for any kind of criminal or clandestine operation, Bad Trip decided. Except that the building had been a dockside warehouse initially, and the whole area hadn't always been steel and glass towers for the banking industry.

Then he got the second hit. Folklore, tales of tall thin creatures with fixed grins that went back more than four hundred years. Bad Trip almost smiled.

Bad Trip knew how to pretend to be a junkie. He'd heard them beg, plead, make all sorts of offers to get what they needed. He'd heard entire planets beg for a fix. He knew how to play that role.

He had rearranged the smart molecules of the few remaining drugs in Gezman's system. The plasmapheresis had washed most of them out of his blood but there were some remaining in the nervous system, brainstem, and other hiding holes. He had them feed on the surrounding matter to replicate, transform and branch out, allowing him total control of Gezman again.

Bad Trip moving his hands like he was controlling a puppet was pure affectation.

If Evangeli kept the schedule he'd been using so far then Bad Trip knew when he would next be at the museum.

***

'What were you doing in Lambeth?' Noel asked Gezman.

'Bad Trip sent Collins there,' Gezman told him. 'We thought that Evangeli was another dealer. We weren't expecting all the …' Gezman seemed to be struggling a little with the memory.

'The bodies?'

'Look, I know where you can find Evangeli,' Gezman said. 'You give me the Bliss and let me go, right?'

'Sure,' Charlotte said.

240

'Convince me,' Gezman said, as if he knew he had something that they really wanted.

'Okay, let's be honest, you're not going anywhere for a while,' Charlotte told him. 'And frankly you don't want to because your erstwhile employer, by your own account a dangerous individual, is going to be looking for you. We'll keep you in a nice quiet cell beneath Paddington Green and then we'll give you an amount of money so you don't go to the press and whine about torture and what not.' She glared at Noel briefly. 'But let's be honest, of more immediate interest to you is this.' She waved the vial of blue liquid at him.

'Fucking bitch,' Gezman spat.

'Why don't we leave you for, say, twelve or so hours to think about it?' Charlotte said. She turned to leave. Noel and Sam followed suit.

'No wait!'

The three of them turned back to the drug dealer secured to the operating table.

'Stop fucking around, sunshine, and tell us what you know,' Sam growled.

Gezman swallowed hard, his face covered in sweat.

'We know Evangeli because we've sold him a lot of heroin. One of my guys is in Docklands with his kids. He sees Evangeli at the museum.'

'The Dockland Museum?' Sam scoffed.

'Darling, even drug dealers like a bit of culture now and then,' Charlotte said, sounding disappointed.

'No wait, this was after we'd been to see Burman.'

'So?' Noel asked, confused, and then glanced behind him.

'So my man recognised who Evangeli was meeting with. Who Evangeli was giving a rather large envelope to.'

***

Now all he had to do was sweeten the bait, Bad Trip thought as he moved his hand as if he was wearing Gezman as a glove puppet.

***

'He was paying off Bad Trip,' Gezman told them. Sam, Charlotte and Noel considered this.

'That doesn't make sense,' Sam said. 'If the thing in Lambeth was one of Evangeli's operations and he was paying off Bad Trip then why did you lot hit it on this Bad Trip's orders?'

Gezman shrugged, which was quite difficult to do while strapped to a table.

'Punishment for something, maybe it was an operation he hadn't told Bad Trip about. I don't know.'

'So where does the smiling ...' Noel started.

'It still doesn't matter. So your man saw a payoff,' Charlotte said, cutting Noel off. 'Big deal. Had we been there we could have done something.'

'That was the thing, it was way past closing time but they had access to the museum. So next week at the same time I sent one of my guys back, someone who Bad Trip didn't know.'

'Why?' Sam asked suspiciously. There was something about the story she didn't like.

'We might look like a unified front to outsiders but I know fuck all about this guy except he's got guns, money, drugs and he's scary as fuck. I like to know who I'm dealing with.'

'And they were there again?' Noel asked.

Gezman nodded.

'Every Monday night after closing time. Some time between eight and nine, regular as a bowel movement.'

'You're quite the charmer, aren't you?' Charlotte said smiling.

'He's a cunt, is what he is,' Sam muttered.

'The Bliss?' Gezman demanded.

'Have you got anything more for me?' Charlotte asked.

'That's all I know, I swear.'

'I believe you,' Charlotte said. She opened the vial and put it to his lips and tipped it back. He drank the vial and lay back on the operating table, a beatific expression spreading across his face. 'I need you both to leave,' she told Sam and Noel.

'What the fuck are you doing?' Sam demanded angrily.

'Charlotte?' Noel asked.

Gezman was so blissed he didn't even look frightened when Charlotte pulled a Heckler & Koch USP .45 calibre automatic pistol out of her shoulder holster and started screwing a sound suppressor onto the barrel.

'Please,' Charlotte said again.

'You know, I'm a fucking police officer!' Sam screamed at her.

Charlotte turned and looked at the other woman quizzically.

'Do you really think that matters any more?' she asked. Sam had no answer.

Noel was more shocked than he would want to admit out loud. He glanced behind him again.

'Come on,' he said to Sam and put his hands on her shoulder, steering her out of the OT. He closed the door. He didn't even hear the coughing noise made by the pistol as Charlotte fired twice into Gezman's head.

***

It was beautiful, Bad Trip thought. They were already fighting amongst themselves. The Docklands Museum was one of the places where the seed micro-satellites had detected the strange energy signature that he had come to associate with the Shriven Weft.

He would send these people there. He would send the Sub-Juicers, and one, if not both, the human Juicers. Perhaps he would even go and take a look himself. Kill something that was more of a challenge than these weak and fragile things. He dissipated his form, the matter sinking back into its constituent parts.

Outer Hebrides, 13 July, 1000 hours (BST)

On balance, Rex decided, he'd enjoyed yesterday more. Certain free-range flavours of dopamine were very difficult to stimulate enough to harvest. It was the neurotransmitter most heavily connected to the psychological condition that humans described as love. He'd spent the day in Los Angeles talking to the top scriptwriters in the field of romantic comedy. He had put together a think tank that would create storylines for virtual reality scenarios. Rex had also set up an online research group to set about finding some of the loneliest people on the planet to be placed in the virtual simulations so their dopamine could be harvested.

For the more natural product he had taken a page from reality television shows and he was paying enough for struggling actors to prostitute themselves in staged scenarios, finding lonely people and sweeping them off their feet. The dopamine harvested from these people would command a higher price.

Finally he had used Pleasure infoscape architecture to help create a planetary dating network based on complex psychological algorithms and predictive programs designed to create the most passionate, if not the healthiest, relationships. This in turn would be supported by the subjects 'winning' romantic holidays, and arranged meetings.

All in all, he'd finished the day feeling quite good about himself. As if he was humanity's romantic fairy godmother. It had certainly felt more positive than harvesting from obnoxious or battery-farmed cocaine users.

This, on the other hand, Rex decided, *this is just shit.*

The RAF had ferried a lot of the Range Rovers and ATVs out to the uninhabited island either in the holds of, or slung underneath, Chinook helicopters. The dogs had been more of a hassle. The RAF had been less than pleased at the amount of dog shit they'd had to clean up from inside the holds of the heavy lift heli-copters. Most of the guests had flown to the island in private hire luxury helicopters from Glasgow, Inverness, or Fort William.

It was a shame. Despite the wind it was a beautiful day, there was little or no cloud in the sky, the sun was shining, the admittedly choppy Irish ocean was reflecting the blue of the sky above and wasn't its normal grey.

Lord Conbert wandered up to him, already breathing heavily, his fat puffy face red with exertion from having to walk up a slight heather-covered incline from where his Range Rover was parked on the beach. He'd clearly been enjoying a liquid breakfast from the fully equipped integrated drinks and gun cabinet in his Overfinch customised Range Rover. His Purdey shotgun was broken over his arm and he wore the bodywarmer, jumper, flat-cap and Wellington boots uniform that all the others, including Rex himself, were wearing.

Lord Conbert was the CEO of the Reflection news group, which, as far as Rex was concerned, was the most influential news media group in the UK because they shamelessly appealed to the lowest common denominator, whilst inexplicably claiming the moral high ground. It was a good trick. Rex was pretty sure that the red-faced buffoon approaching him hadn't thought of the trick, or indeed anything else, ever. He knew that he could never, ever introduce Bad Trip to Lord Conbert because Lord Conbert would be dumb enough to insist on talking and Bad Trip would be forced to painfully murder him to death.

'Ah Rex, this is going to be jolly interesting, isn't it?'

Interesting enough that you had to drink a lot of single malt courage at breakfast to go through with it, Rex decided not to say. Judging by his eyes Lord Conbert had probably had a sneaky vial of Bliss, perhaps some coke to take the edge off as well.

'Lord Conbert, I'm just happy that this could be arranged.'

'This is how it should be, ay?' The peer sounded like he was trying to convince himself. He took another slug from his hip flask. Rex was reasonably sure that the drunken fool was going to drunkenly kill someone, someone he wasn't supposed to, with his ridiculously expensive shotgun.

'Have you given any thought to our proposition?' Rex asked. Rex had been attempting to sway public opinion to turn London, in its role as an international transport hub, into a city like Amsterdam, or indeed one that far superseded the freedoms of Amsterdam. Everything would be available. A Gomorrah on the Thames, to match Washington's Sodom on the Potomac. An open city of vice catering for the international traveller.

'Well, I'd be lying if I said I couldn't see the economic advantages ...'

'Particularly if you get in on the ground floor,' Rex mused. He could make out the large Chinook helicopter approaching from the east.

'The problem is my readers, sorry, our customers, see themselves as the moral majority. It would be a very hard sell for us, indeed it could seem a little hypocritical.'

'Surely you can influence what the moro ... moral majority find moral?' Rex cursed himself. He'd almost said moron minority.

'To a degree, but this might be a step too far.'

'I understand you went to Harvard's Business School as a post-graduate after Oxford?' *After your father had to pay some serious bribes because of your pathetic academic record.*

'Why, yes,' Lord Conbert said, sounding surprised.

Obviously I'm going to do some research, you moron, Rex thought.

'What we're suggesting is just a logical extension of objectivism. This is the free market in action ... oh, I'm sorry, you're not a socialist or a liberal are you?'

'Well no, of course not!' Lord Conbert blustered.

No, you're a scion of privilege, you couldn't compete in a free market. Everything needs to be 'fixed' for you to succeed at anything.

'Well, this is libertarianism at its finest ...'

'It sounds like libertinism,' Conbert said. Rex read the man's body language and realised that it was a joke. Rex forced himself to laugh.

'What we're talking about is a total de-regulation, no half-arsed measures. Everything is there for business to exist, no hand-wringing liberals holding you back. I'm not sure how much more moral, how much more loyal to the principles that made this country great, it could be. This is the sort of thinking that created the Empire.'

Conbert was listening intently. Rex could practically see the other man's thought processes crawling across his red, blotchy, drunken features.

The Chinook came in to hover less than a foot above the heather-covered hillside. Both of them had to hold onto their flat-caps.

'You certainly make a persuasive argument,' Conbert shouted over the sound of the helicopter. The loading ramp at the rear of the helicopter started lowering.

'And this,' Rex shouted, gesturing all around him. 'This is only the beginning. It's a brave new world. We will really be able to go after the sort of people your readership hates: the unemployed, single mothers and other parasites. We've even discussed the possibility of safaris into some of the more notorious inner city areas.'

'Okay, I think we can do business!' Lord Conbert shouted and offered his hand. It made Rex feel dirty shaking the peer's clammy, limp grip.

Members of the RAF Regiment forced the illegal immigrants out of the Chinook's cargo bay at gunpoint. They were encouraged to run. They looked down the hill at the ATVs, Range Rovers, and the men and women carrying weapons. A few started to make their way down the hill towards the hunting party. The rest chose to run, making their way as quickly as they could up the heather-covered hill.

Then they released the dogs.

Charing Cross Arches, 13 July, 1200 hours (BST)

Noel couldn't say that he was terribly pleased to see Roche again. If anything he looked gaunter than he had the first time they'd met. He was leaning against the arches, waving them over. Charlotte was with him.

'Bleedin' hell,' Sam muttered unhappily.

'I'm not supposed to be out,' Roche said.

'Out of where?' Sam asked, giving him a hard look.

'Can't say,' he turned to Noel. 'Surprised I haven't seen more of you around Vauxhall, though.'

'He means he's working for the spooks these days,' Sam said.

Noel was of the opinion that this Roche was a little too smug and had too big a mouth for someone in his line of work.

'Sixteenth Air Assault Brigade, me. Anything else, I have no idea what you're talking about.' Roche wrinkled his nose. 'Saw an old friend of yours, Burden. Sergeant Stanton.'

'It's Burman, and how's he doing?'

'Still got all his bits,' Roche looked between Charlotte, Sam and Noel. 'So what's all this about? I could tell you a thing or two but not with this civvy here.'

Noel felt Sam bristle next to him.

'You remember my brother, Manning? The one you waterboarded?' Noel asked more calmly than he felt.

'The one who deals coke and dope?' Roche responded.

'That's enough,' Charlotte said. She was well aware of the two men sizing each other up. 'We need to engage in a little bit of information gathering. Now, unless you want to strip down, oil yourselves and beat your chests for Sam and I, let's try something a little more civilised, like a conversation and cup of coffee.'

'Sure,' Roche said and walked out from under the arches and joined the throngs of people on the Embankment. Noel had to subdue a laugh as Sam made wanking motions with her hand. Roche was heading towards a designer patisserie.

'Not there. Not if you want to talk,' Sam told him. Sam led them through the Embankment station and across the Charing Cross footbridge to the South Bank and into the open plan South Bank Centre. There were very few people in the cavernous space.

Sam went to the counter and ordered four coffees.

'So what's this about then, Charly?' Roche asked. 'You been running two ops?'

'Compartmentalised, darling, need to know, Big Boys' rules and all that. You're a big boy now, aren't you?'

'I cry like a baby when the intelligence I need isn't available because of secrecy for secrecy's sake.'

Noel found himself nodding in agreement.

'Which is why we're all here,' Charlotte said. Sam came back and put the drinks down. Noel was faintly disappointed that she hadn't got him a tea.

'Even though he's compromised and she's a civvy?' Roche asked.

'Wind your neck in, mate,' Noel said. Roche turned back to look at him. Noel held the look, though if he was being honest he didn't fancy fighting the older man again.

Sam sighed. 'You know this whole bullshit testosterone display is for you, don't you?' Sam asked.

'Shall we go and come back?' Charlotte suggested. 'Pop up to Regent's Street, do a spot of shopping.'

'Not on my salary, I'll watch.'

Charlotte turned back to Noel and Roche.

'This is the frank and fair exchange of information that you have both bemoaned the lack of to me,' she told them.

'Huh?' Noel said.

'Now we all start talking,' Sam said.

'A name keeps on turning up. Stylianos Evangeli,' Noel said. The name got Roche's attention. 'We've got intelligence ...'

'Highly suspect intelligence,' Sam added.

'We know where he's going to be in five and a half hours.'

Roche gave this some thought.

'I'm in,' he said.

'Oh, wonderful,' Charlotte said with only a trace of sarcasm. 'Now we don't have a great deal of time to plan this but I've already set a few wheels running. I'm going to leave operational planning up to the boys with the boots on the ground.'

'We need to get Stanton in on this as quickly as possible,' Noel said. Roche was nodding.

'The lovely Samantha will have a large contingent of the Met's finest waiting nearby. She has resurrected a Kingship operation that never happened. I'll be based with them.'

'Now, they're going to know that there's special forces on the ground, but that's not an excuse to turn Docklands into Saturday night in Basra, understand me?' Sam said. She turned to Charlotte. 'That's it for me, I'm burned after this. Falsified orders, I'll be lucky if I don't end up in the Scrubs with people I've put there.'

'I know, I'm sorry,' Charlotte said and she actually sounded sorry. The thing was that Noel was starting to suspect that Charlotte was an excellent actress.

'Fuck it, they've sold us out on this whole Bliss thing. I tried so hard to play it straight, didn't want to be like my old man. Now look at me.'

'It's for the greater good,' Charlotte said.

'That,' Sam said pointing at Charlotte, 'is what people always say before they do something monstrous. That's how we justify all the bad shit that we do. We set ourselves up as the moral superiors of the people that we're doing this to, and then commit acts that frankly aren't dissimilar. Then we give them nice euphemisms to make it okay. Rendition, Big Boys' rules, collateral damage.'

'You finished lecturing us?' Roche asked.

'Oh well, fuck it, it's all breaking down now. I've been pushing to hit known Bliss dealers. You'd think that them waving around automatic weapons in the streets of London would be enough, wouldn't you? But no, every single fucking anti-Bliss operation I've ever heard of suddenly got pulled in the last two days and I happen to know that the Home Secretary met with the Chief Commissioner of Police the day before. So it's not so difficult to join the fucking dots.'

Roche, Charlotte and Noel were all looking at the police officer, feeling distinctly uncomfortable.

'Now you can call me naive if you want but you didn't grow up where I did. There's the wrong way and the right way. The moment you compromise, the corruption starts creeping in. So you run your covert ops, put more guns on the streets of London, kidnap people, torture them in fucking Surrey of all places, and I'll help but you're all very far gone if you think that this is the way things should be.'

'I'll take a little corruption,' Roche said. 'For this, I'll do what's necessary.'

'Yeah, that's where it all starts, isn't it?' Sam said. Noel had never heard her sound so beaten down.

'Well thank you, Samantha, for reminding us of our broken moral compasses, but we really don't have a lot of time,' Charlotte pointed out.

High Earth Orbit, 13 July, 1333 (BST)

The interior of the Pleasure Mindship looked like a cross between a tasteful, upmarket Edwardian hotel, and the excesses of a less-than-tasteful Parisian brothel

of the same era. During their period of Earth acclima-
tisation research Rex had been responsible for the interior decoration. Bad Trip was sat on one of the
Chesterfields the Mindship had grown.

He was smoking a cigarette. A pointless vice, as far
as he could tell, but arguably important for his role, and
listening to a piece of music called *Don Giovanni*. It was
too light for him but there were moments of bombast
and atmosphere that he found himself enjoying.

He realised the anticipation of what he had set in place
was the closest he had come to contentment since he had
first arrived in this dull system. There would be terror in
the streets, and then he would commit some quiet atroci-
ties – he would go for pain rather than death – and his
story would grow, as would fear of him. London was just
one of thousands of operations that were occurring across
the Earth but today it would get some special attention.

Rex grew out of the wall of the Mindship. He was
still a beautiful, six-armed giant, naked but for some
ornate pieces of jewellery, but now he was mostly a
male-identifying hermaphrodite.

'What have you done?' Rex asked with sly interest.

'I got bored,' Bad Trip told him.

Rex nodded.

'I see you finally took my recommendation,' he said,
meaning the music.

Bad Trip said nothing, he just took another drag of
his cigarette. Ash fell from it towards his pinstriped,
double-breasted suit but it disintegrated before it touched
the fabric.

'Will it advance our agenda here?' Rex asked.

Bad Trip looked up at Rex. Rex tried to ignore the feeling of unease that his long-term colleague stirred in him.

'Does fucking them?' The guttural voice rasped. 'Feeding off them like a scavenger?' Bad Trip turned away from Rex. 'I'm bored.'

Through his link to the Mindship and its living sensors imbedded in the stealthed craft's skin Bad Trip could see the curve of the blue Earth far beneath him. He imagined it on fire. He imagined he could hear the entire world screaming.

Chapter Thirteen

West India Quay, 13 July, 2142 (BST)

Noel was sat on the deck of an old barge that had been turned into some kind of tourist tour boat, enjoying a cup of tea. There was a pair of binoculars and an open laptop on the table in front of him. He could see the front of the museum on the Quayside less than four hundred feet from where he sat. The Georgian warehouse, despite its refurbishment, seemed incongruous amongst the steel and glass high rises surrounding it. In many ways that was London for Noel. The ancient and the ultra-modern. The splendour and squalor. It was a mess, quite frankly, the redesign in the wake of the Great Fire notwithstanding. Unlike its colonial cousins, London had too much history to be set out in a nice neat grid.

The laptop showed a number of different angles of the spacious atrium and café that formed the entrance to the museum. Roche, and the other Special Reconnaissance Regiment soldier there, Rees, had done a good job setting up concealed cameras for coverage. Charlotte had objected to it because it meant transmitting the information and she was sure that all electronic comms were compromised. Roche was convinced that she was being paranoid and that there was no real other alternative to keep 'eyes-on'.

Under the loose-fitting windcheater he had on, Noel was wearing body armour. Stanton had delivered what the quiet Scotsman had called a 'Dorset care-package'. If this had been a legitimate op they never would have been allowed to carry what they were carrying but CSM Porn Star had come through for them. On the webbing attached to his body armour Noel had his holstered Sig clipped over his heart. Less chance of it snagging than if he wore it on his hip or thigh. There were pouches holding various 40mm grenades for the grenade launcher. He was carrying two smoke grenades, two fragmentation hand grenades and four stun grenades and nine extra clips for his carbine. In short, his load-out wasn't very different to what he had carried in Afghanistan.

Just inside the cabin of the converted barge was his Diemacos C8A1 carbine. He'd mounted an optical red-dot sight, and clipped to the picatinny rail under the carbine barrel was a Heckler & Koch AG-C/EGLM 40mm grenade launcher. Both the C8 and the grenade launcher were his. He had trained with them, live firing in Poole. They'd been zeroed in before but he still would have liked to spend some time test firing. There had been no chance on an op of this type.

Still, he decided, *the ROEs are rolling. I'll respond to force appropriately.* In other words he was going to be making up the Rules of Engagement as he went along. He wasn't going to be caught blowing in the wind like they had in Dagenham. He just wished he couldn't feel a slight tremor in his hands. He just wished he could forget the warm wet feeling of Dolton's blood and brains on his face. He wished he could get the grinning thing he'd seen in Lambeth out of his mind.

Noel watched as dark estate cars pulled up and three men got out and started unloading a crate. Noel picked up the binoculars and looked through them. The three men looked like very ordinary white guys to him.

'Indigo one, you getting this?' Roche asked quietly over the radio link.

'Check, Indigo two,' Noel said.

'Familiar faces?'

Noel lifted the binoculars again. They didn't look like Organizatsiya to him and none of them fit the file photos of Stylianos Evangeli.

'Not to me.'

The three men wheeled the crate into the museum. Noel split his time between looking all around the area, including checking the river approaches, checking the sky – he wasn't ruling out anything on this job – and glancing at the laptop screen and the various feeds from the café.

Two of the men opened the crate and started pulling out bizarre-looking pieces of moulded plastic. The third was setting the table.

'What the hell are they doing?' Stanton asked over the comms link. They were unfolding pincer-like tele-scopic arms from inside the crate, making something that looked, to Noel's mind, like a kind of insectile skeleton of an onion.

'Indigo two. Anyone know what that is?' Roche whispered. Noel bit down his irritation at the poor comms discipline.

One of the two men not setting the table took out a ruggedised laptop and plugged it into a cable connected to the crate. Noel felt a very slight tremor. He looked down and saw ripples in the water running away from the quayside the museum sat on. Even the men in the museum had paused.

'Did you feel that?' Roche asked. 'I felt the floor quiver.'

'Same,' answered Rees.

'Nothing here.' Stanton said.

'There a tube line that runs under here?' Roche asked.

'Docklands Light isn't far, but it's overground. I've got eyes and there's nothing come past,' Stanton told him.

'It happened exactly when they plugged that thing in,' said Rees.

'Could be coincidence,' Roche said. Even through the ear mic, Noel could tell that the other man didn't really believe that.

Noel was finding it hard not to keep watching the laptop screen but he continued to check all around them, trying not to be too obvious.

Inside the museum, the men were unspooling another cable away from the now collapsed crate. They plugged it into another, smaller box.

'Anyone else feel that?' Roche asked.

'Something,' Rees agreed. 'Indigo one, if Charly's out there do me a favour and ask her what the fuck that box is.' Noel ignored him.

She's on the net, moron, so perhaps she just understands comms discipline, Noel thought. He was beginning to wonder if the SAS's complaints that the SRR were tier 3 special forces were actually true.

'Mind your chatter, Indigo four.' Stanton again.

He checked the laptop screen again. The third man was still setting places at the table.

'We're set,' one of the men in the museum said very quietly into his own radio mic. Straight away Noel heard the sound of engines. Two cars pulled up outside the museum. Noel didn't risk using the binoculars as the people climbing out of the car were checking all around them, looking for trouble. One of them opened the door for another man, obviously the boss.

'Indigo one to all Indigo call signs, be aware we have two victors carrying seven possible X-rays pulling up outside. If they're armed then I can't see it,' Noel said into the radio mic and then took a sip of tea in order to look casual.

'See if you can get faces this time,' Rees said.

He glanced at the laptop again. Roche had worked the cameras so they were close up on the faces. They looked Mediterranean to him. Noel was starting to notice something in the atmosphere. Suddenly it felt like the moment before the storm.

'Indigo one. The one in the middle. That's Evangeli,' Rees said across comms. They had one of their targets,

Noel thought. They were just waiting for this Bad Trip now. The tremor in his hand again. Did he want Bad Trip to turn up? He certainly didn't want Collins there. There would be nothing any of them could do if the changed SAS man turned up.

'I'm seeing handguns on most of the targets,' Roche whispered over the comms. 'Nothing bigger.'

'MP7s?' Noel asked. He wasn't in a huge hurry to deal with those nasty little modified weapons again either.

'Handguns only. I repeat, handguns only. Evangeli's on the phone now,' Roche said quietly over the comms. Noel glanced down at the laptop. The suspected human trafficker was pacing back and forth, surrounded by his men. He was speaking rapidly in what Noel assumed was Greek.

'Anyone get any of that?' asked Stanton. There was a long pause, then: 'Indigo three to all Indigo call signs, I have three incoming victors on the Hertsmere Road ... They've stopped outside the back door ... Twenty, twenty-five ... no, thirty possible X-rays, I see body armour, SMGs ... Indigo two, you may want to consider getting ready to Foxtrot Oscar. Indigo one, these guys look similar to the Dagenham crew.'

Noel's heart sank when he heard mention of Dagenham, and this time they were wearing body armour. They'd had eighteen men, including the command component, in Dagenham. Here they had four and a lot of armed plod. At least they knew what they were getting into. This time they'd respond with overwhelming firepower. If only he could stop shaking.

If only for the first time ever in a firefight he didn't want to stick his head over the battlements. He could sit there. Hide, he knew. Pretend it wasn't happening. Be like everyone else and expect someone to sort it for him.

He glanced at the laptop screen. Two of the Cypriots were reaching for the fire escape door at the rear of the atrium. The doors were battered open, the Cypriots went flying. Organizatsiya gunmen playing at being soldiers barged into the museum, the boxy little MP7s at the ready. He could hear it from the tinny little laptop speakers, and more distantly from the museum itself.

Noel saw the muzzle flash light up the museum's atrium.

Then the screaming started. The same screaming that he'd heard in Dagenham and then again in Lambeth. It was only a short burst but it echoed through the canyons between the steel and glass skyscrapers. The sound of hypervelocity rounds stretching the laws of physics.

Businessmen on their way home late from work, the wealthy heading into the city for a night out, cinema-goers, tourists – all of them stopped. He knew they'd be asking themselves the same question that all civilised people asked themselves in these situations: *Was that gunfire?* Then realisation set in. In West India Quay, and the surrounding streets people panicked and searched for cover.

Move, he told himself, *you need to move*. He couldn't. He couldn't even make sense of what was being said to him over the radio.

'I see them,' Stanton said. His voice sounded cold. The quiet Scotsman was angry.

The gunmen were pushing Evangeli over towards the crate now. The Cypriot looked more angry than frightened.

'Indigo one, this is Indigo three. Dagenham, Indigo one. It's like Dagenham again. Same shit. You make sure your Met friends keep the hell away. Keep the fuck quiet and let Indigo two get his intel. Indigo one, confirm?'

Noel was just staring at the laptop screen. Evangeli was shouting at one of the gunmen. The gunman shoved the Cypriot, sending him sprawling to the floor next to the crate.

'Indigo one, respond?' Stanton said again over the comms.

Lightning played across the strange skeletal sculpture that had been made from the crate.

Noel caught a glimpse of something. Then more screaming, sustained fire from the MP7s. The gunfire a rolling echo across the water. Muzzle flashes lit up the interior of the museum. The glass in the atrium shattered and then collapsed downwards.

On the laptop screen he could see a form illuminated in strobe by the muzzle flashes of the modified MP7s. Something tall. Something smiling. Something that wasn't human. Noel felt a coldness run through his body.

'Shit …'

'Did you see …'

'Is that what you saw in Brixton?'

He had no idea who was talking. It was just radio chatter.

264

Move, you need to move, you have people in there. His breathing was sounding funny. Too fast and he wasn't getting enough oxygen. Then he saw the inhuman shape in the frock coat stumble. Then fall. *They killed it,* he thought, *somehow they killed it!*

On the laptop screen it was all chaos now. Noel caught a glimpse of Evangeli in the corner holding onto some kind of strange-looking device. He heard shouting from inside the ruined atrium.

He looked up at the museum itself. Strange arcs of yellow/orange light lit up the atrium's interior. There was screaming, people screaming, then more of the screaming gunfire. The light disappeared.

'Two coming out your side, Indigo one. Advise you wait for them to put some distance behind them and then take them. You getting all of this?' Roche said over comms. It took a moment for Noel to realise that it was him they were talking to. He saw two of the Cypriots running out of the museum.

It can be killed, you can fight this, your friends need you, you need to move.

Noel reached into the boat's cabin and picked up his carbine. It was already 'hot', the safety off. He climbed off the boat and started heading towards the museum.

West India Quay, 13 July, 2203 (BST)

Noel walked past terrified civilians cowering behind blocks of stones and plant pots, by the pub next to the museum. Basically, people were hiding behind anything they could find. He motioned for them to stay low. He walked casually, the C8 down by his side. The brain interpreted various movements. If he moved low and quickly and the Cypriots caught the movement in their peripheral vision then their brain would tell them it was a threat.

There was more strange light and human screaming from the atrium. Gunshots, a nine millimetre semi-automatic being fired rapidly. The two Cypriots were running towards him, both of them with pistols in their hands. They were looking behind them as they ran. One of them turned round and saw him. Noel brought the C8A1 carbine to his shoulder smoothly. The Cypriot started raising his pistol. Noel kept on moving forwards. He fired twice, pushing into the recoil kick against his shoulder. The top of the man's head came off. Noel continued moving forwards. The first Cypriot fell to the ground. The second started turning. He saw Noel and hesitated. Noel continued advancing, gun levelled, not firing, not saying anything. The second Cypriot started raising his weapon. Another two rounds and that Cypriot was falling to the ground. Noel continued, checking all around him as he closed on the two dead bodyguards. Despite their death being obvious, training took over. He stood over them and put a further bullet in each of their heads at point-blank range.

'Contact,' he whispered.

There was more screaming from inside the museum and then a lot of gunfire. He felt bullets pass close to him. There were explosions of stone as rounds impacted into the quayside. There was more strange light and screaming. He could make out strange figures in the smoke that was filling the atrium. They were illuminated by the muzzle flashes of automatic weapons fire. Under the screaming he could hear the flat staccato hammering of a Minimi squad automatic weapon. It had to be Stanton firing from the multi-storey garage on the Hertsmere Road on the other side of the museum.

Noel was less than a hundred and fifty feet from the museum now. It struck him that Gezman had lied, or somehow set them up. This was a hit, not a meet, and he'd dropped them right in the centre of it.

'Never trust a junkie,' Noel muttered. He continued moving towards the museum, aiming for a spot by the wall, about a hundred feet from the atrium. He could see Organizatsiya gunmen stumbling out of the Museum. Looking behind them, firing into the smoke.

Noel raised the carbine to his shoulder. Two shots. There was a spray of matter from one of the gunmen's heads. He switched target and there was another spray of matter. Next target. Three had gone down before they realised that they were taking fire. All the time Noel was moving towards the museum. Two of them turned and started firing wildly, the screams of their bullets echoing around the buildings. Noel was running on instinct now. Some people could shoot, some could hold their nerve when they were being fired at. It took a lot of training until you got to the point where you could deal with a lot of incoming fire and still function.

Rounds were impacting all around him. At some level he knew that it just took one hyper-velocity round from one of the modified MP7s and he was either dead or missing a limb. Body armour wasn't going to help him. He reached the wall of the museum. The hyper-velocity rounds were tearing through the stone of the old warehouse like it didn't exist.

Noel moved his hands forwards to the pistol grip of the underslung grenade launcher and fired. There was a popping noise. The flechettes left the barrel and spread out. It was like a massive shotgun firing needles. The two gunmen were turned red, staggering back in the hail of flechettes and slumping to the ground. Quickly and with practised ease, Noel opened the grenade launcher, let the smoking grenade fall out and replaced it with another flechette round. It had taken seconds. Five men dead. No, the two he'd hit with the flechette were still moving. One of them had most of his face missing.

A shadow fell across him. Noel was up and spinning around. He wasn't sure why he didn't just fire, perhaps some instinct to check for civilians. It stared at him, grinning, tall, thin. Wearing some kind of old-fashioned coat and a ridiculous top hat. Tight leathery skin. Inhuman eyes. Noel's finger was curled around the trigger of the carbine. There was something about the creature, its tattered finery, thinness, yellow eyes. It reminded Noel of the junkies he'd seen growing up in Brixton.

Noel stared at it, aware of explosions, gunfire, and all manner of noises signifying destruction coming from behind him. It stared back, smiling. It had no weapon that Noel could see.

'We doing this?' Noel asked. False bravado. He couldn't take much more or his nerve would break. The creature watched him for a few moments more and then turned and disappeared through the wall of the museum.

Noel felt his legs buckle momentarily but he was in it now. There was no time for panic. He turned back, facing the atrium. One of the men he had hit with the flechette was trying to get up. The top of his head came off as Noel put two rounds in it. The man collapsed to the ground. The other one was flopping around on the floor, presumably kept alive by the combat drug Rage coursing through his system. Noel advanced on him. There was another explosion and a crashing noise that made the ground shake. As soon as he had the angle, Noel shot the remaining gunman twice in the head.

He was getting nothing but static from his earpiece now. He ripped it out so he could hear better. He moved quickly down the wall of the museum. He could hear a lot of automatic weapons fire but it sounded like it was coming from the other side of the museum. He could hear the sound of heavy impacts and destruction coming from inside the atrium. He didn't want to look but he forced himself. He struggled to make out what was happening. One of the tall, thin things. It was fighting with something human shaped. Somehow the human was holding its own. There was a flash of white light. Noel threw himself back. The wall next to where he'd been hiding turned to molten slag, running like liquid. The ambient heat made the side of Noel's face smoke and blister. He screamed out, scrabbling back, pushing himself to his feet and then just ran for it across the front of the atrium. He could see the fight in the periphery of his vision. Through the smoke he saw shadows fighting. It was like watching gods fight, it wasn't for the likes of him to watch. One he couldn't hit, the other he couldn't hurt.

Was that Collins? he wondered.

Noel ran to the west edge of the museum. He glanced around the corner but saw nobody. He went round the corner, carbine at the ready. Behind him it sounded like Armageddon.

West India Quay, 13 July, 2207 (BST)

Bad Trip wasn't quite sure what was going on. This made him angry. He had only come here to see the chaos he had orchestrated, to ensure the removal of the Shriven. He'd seen Shaw come out of the destroyed front of the museum fighting with one of the Shriven. Something cloaked had risen from the water of the Quay. Shaw had disappeared in what appeared to be a spray of anti-protons. Miniature nuclear explosions had vaporised stone and turned the earth to liquid. Bad Trip knew it wasn't enough to kill the Juicer. But the tech level was different to that being utilised by the Shriven Weft. The thing attacking his Juicer was so well cloaked that Bad Trip was having trouble making out what it was. He decided to err on the safe side and kill it anyway.

The top of a tower block exploded as Shaw climbed out of the small, recently formed nuclear crater and took a shot with his plasma cannon at his mysterious attacker. The Juicer's protective coherent energy field was very much at the limit of its capabilities. It couldn't take too many more hits like the anti-proton burst before it overloaded and failed.

Bad Trip detected an excretion of exotic particles from the thing, just as he reached out and ran his hand through it, forcing the thing to change physical state and then infecting it with corrosive nanite factories that started eating it. Even in phase and visible he didn't recognise it. He started tearing it apart, breaking it down to its constituent atoms, asking the same question over and over again: 'What are you?'

Hertsmere Road, 13 July, 2209 (BST)

Noel moved quickly along the west wall to the other corner and quickly looked down the Hertsmere Road. He'd known that there was a full-on firefight going on but the extent of it still shocked him.

There was a black van lying on its side up against the wall of the multi-storey car park on the opposite side of the Hertsmere Road to the museum. There were another two vans, riddled with bullet holes, parked close to the museum's rear fire exit. A number of the Organizatsiya thugs had taken cover behind the two vans. One of the vans was facing east along the road, the other facing was west.

The multi-storey car park looked like chunks had been bitten out of it. There were sections of crumbling

271

masonry and exposed metal supports. It only took Noel a moment to work out what had been happening. Stanton had been using the Minimi SAW to suppress the gunmen. He must have laid down a lot of fire, effectively keeping them engaged so they couldn't bother anyone else. As soon as they had started returning fire, and it was obviously the sustained fire from the little MP7s that had torn up the front of the multi-storey car park, then Stanton would have moved, and lain down suppressing fire on them from a different position. Though looking at the front of the car park Noel thought it unlikely that Stanton was still alive.

The he heard the SAW firing from the first floor of the car park. Organizatsiya gunmen ducked for cover as tracers lit up the night and armour-piercing bullets shot through the two stationary vans. Then Noel watched with a mixture of horror and awe as the gunmen returned fire and the screaming rounds from the little MP7s tore up the concrete front of the car park. He prayed that Stanton hadn't been anywhere near that when they fired.

Noel hid back round the corner and switched the magazine in the carbine and then let the weapon hang from its sling as he removed two items from the pouches clipped to his body armour. He couldn't risk firing a high explosive or a fragmentation grenade from the grenade launcher – he didn't know where Roche or Rees were. The back of the van pointing east on Hertsmere Road, was, however open to him. There were three gunmen inside it. There were another five or so gunmen between the two vans, firing up into the car park. He had to wait. He pulled the pin from the fragmentation grenade and then from the stun grenade. This wasn't exactly a textbook move.

This is going to have to be one hell of a throw, he thought.

Noel heard Stanton firing from another position in the garage. He waited until the gunmen returned fire. Noel spun around the corner. The spoons flew off both grenades as he moved. He threw the fragmentation grenade. He passed the stun grenade to his right hand and then threw that as well.

Nearby, the wall of the museum exploded outward but Noel was already spinning back around the corner, grabbing for his carbine. The fragmentation grenade flew true, landing in the back of the east-facing van. It exploded. The three gunmen were shredded with shrapnel from the grenade and thrown out the back of the van by the force of the explosion. The van, however, contained the worst of the explosion, minimising the risk to any friendlies in the museum.

The stun grenade fell short but the flash and deafening explosion did its job, distracting the remaining, hopefully already battered, gunmen. He'd timed it so Stanton would be moving and hopefully not affected by the flash.

Inside, it sounded like the museum was being destroyed. The ground shook.

Noel came wide around the corner, and went down on one knee to present a smaller target, his hand around the underslung grenade launcher's pistol grip. He took a moment to take in the situation, and aim. A few rounds screamed by, or exploded into the ground nearby. Noel fired another flechette grenade into the five remaining, mostly stunned, gunmen. Needles filled the air, peppering the side of the west-facing van, digging up the ground, impacting into body armour and piercing flesh.

Noel was up already, advancing on the vans and the screaming gunmen. Short controlled bursts. Three rounds. If something moved it got shot. The gun twitched to the next target, he fired again. Always going forwards. The problem was they didn't stop moving. Body armour and a ferocious cocktail of drugs kept them trying to fight back. He took the top of one of their heads off and the gunman collapsed to the ground. He was taking fire from somewhere else, he wasn't sure where.

C'mon Stanton, he thought. Then he heard Stanton's SAW start up again, long bursts of suppressing fire. Tracers flying across the Hertsmere Road. Stanton was level with the front of the west facing van. He heard it start up. A red tracer flew out of the barrel of his carbine, warning him that he only had two more rounds in the magazine. He fired them, a gunman's face crumpled inwards and he hit the bloody ground. Noel let the carbine drop on its sling and he fast-drew the Sig Sauer P226 from its clip-on holster on the chest of his body armour. Like the carbine, it was 'hot' – it had been holstered with the safety off and a round chambered. He double tapped a still-moving gunman and then another. Nobody was moving now. There was a crash and another explosion from inside the museum, more strange lights.

The van he'd just walked past, the west-facing one, the one he hadn't thrown a fragmentation grenade into, started to pull away, turning into the street. Noel swung around and fired the Sig rapidly into the side of the van, moving, trying to get the angle on the cab. The slide shot back on the semi-automatic pistol as he fired the last round. The van had managed to turn around and was speeding west down Hertsmere Road towards Aspen Way.

Immediately the van started taking fire from the car park. Tracers and armour-piercing rounds rained down on it, riddling the roof of the vehicle with long sustained bursts. There was more gunfire coming from somewhere else. It took Noel a moment to realise that the van was taking hits from someone shooting at it from one of the upper floors of the museum. He assumed it was from Roche and Rees.

Noel shoved the empty Sig into his webbing and opened the grenade launcher, ejecting the smoking, spent, flechette grenade and loading a high-explosive grenade. He clicked the weapon shut. He was aware of the cab doors to the east-facing van, the one he'd thrown the fragmentation grenade into, opening. Noel walked out into the street and brought the carbine to his shoulder. The speeding van was halfway towards the junction with Aspen Way. Noel fired. The 40mm HE grenade caught the rear left corner of the van, exploded and lifted the back of the vehicle up and sent it tumbling onto its right hand side.

'Noel!' Noel looked around at Stanton's shout. One of the gunmen, battered and bleeding, had climbed out of the passenger side of the east-facing van's cab. He was caught short. All his weapons were empty.

West India Quay, 13 July, 2210 (BST)

Bad Trip was getting angrier by the moment. It had found two of the Shriven Weft. They angered him by not living in terror in his presence. This was a result of a bad mix of their detachment as a race, and being high on their own supply. He turned them to ash. He recognised the itching on his skin as interrogative nanites. He turned around and checked all spectrums until he found 'it' looking down on him, hovering in the air between the tower blocks.

Hertsmere Road, 13 July, 2211 (BST)

Pistol shot after pistol shot rang out. The gunman staggered back against the van as round after round hit him. Noel grabbed the folding knife off his hip, the blade springing open as it came free of its sheaf. He charged the man and rammed the blade into his throat. Hot blood coursed over his hand. The man's eyes were wide, blood frothed from his mouth and he slumped to the ground.

On the other side of the van he saw two more gunmen, who had presumably got out of the driver's side of the van, running down the right side of the road. Noel let go of the knife and grabbed for his carbine, ejecting the empty magazine. He put his back to the van. On the other side of the road Stanton was sliding off the van that was up against the wall of the car park. His SAW was slung, presumably empty. The quiet Scot had a smoking Sig with the slide back in his other hand. It was a hell of a shot to make, hitting the gunman, who'd had Noel cold, from across the street with a pistol.

Stanton rolled a fragmentation grenade into the back of the van he had just climbed off, to be on the safe side. He ran across the street, reloading his Sig as he went.

'All right?' Stanton asked as he reached Noel. Noel had finished reloading his carbine and covered Stanton as he reloaded the Minimi Para, a cut-down carbine version of the squad automatic weapon used by the regular army. Noel realised that the SAW had been loaded with a drum magazine that carried a hundred rounds. This meant that Stanton had already burned through the two hundred round cassette that the Minimi had originally been loaded with. Or in other words, Stanton had already put three hundred rounds down in this fight. Noel could feel the heat coming off the still-smoking weapon. Stanton finished reloading. Noel took a moment to reload his Sig and the grenade launcher. He wasn't messing around this time, he pushed a 40mm high-explosive armour-piercing grenade into the weapon's breach. He would have to be very careful where he fired that.

They could see three gunmen crawling out of the back of the van that Noel had hit with the HE. There were a further two running along the road. It had gone quiet in the museum.

'What does it take to kill these guys?' Stanton muttered.

'We going in?' Noel asked nodding towards the museum.

'Roche! Rees!' Stanton shouted, glancing through the fire escape. The doors were lying on the ground. There was no answer.

'Priorities,' Stanton said. Noel knew he was right. They had to deal with the more pressing threat. The gunmen would run into the police roadblock that was now hopefully in place at the end of Hertsmere Road but even SCO19 weren't set up to deal with the sort of firepower that they would be facing.

West India Quay, 13 July, 2211 (BST)

At some level, Bad Trip knew that this was what Rex had warned him about. This was why some actions required consensus. His passions. His rages. The conscious part of his mind seemed to be a passenger as he destroyed the front of the museum, pulling it down. He was vaguely aware of the thing using munitions that almost threatened him. The surrounding matter imploded into a small singularity and then spat it back out. Bad Trip walked through the destruction.

Then it became less fun. Suddenly he was cut off from his energy source. Suddenly he couldn't mine the background energy of the universe. He was vaguely aware of being surrounded by a cloud of nanite drones. This was bad. He could actually be killed here.

He drew the .45 he used as a focus for his attacks and fired a burst of naked quarks and clustered strangelets. It hit the thing, damaging it at fundamental levels. It was gone. Whether he had destroyed it or it had run he didn't know. He had been damaged. The cloud of nanite drones were living off him like miniscule vampires. He disassembled his sickly body and his thoughtform fled.

He had almost felt fear. This was unacceptable. He needed to speak with Rex but he had something to do first.

Chapter Fourteen

Hertsmere Road, 13 July, 2211 (BST)

Noel and Stanton took off running down Hertsmere Road after the two fleeing gunmen who had escaped from the wreckage of the van. Stanton cut across the road so there was one of them on either side. One of the gunmen got up and tried to fire, the other two tried to scramble away. Stanton stopped and poured fire down on the man. He spun, hit, went down but Noel could see him start to get up.

The two running down the right side of the road turned and fired at Noel. He dived behind a parked car. The bullets tore through the vehicle and the vehicle sank as its tyres exploded. The car itself was all but imploding. The firing stopped, the screaming echoing through the steel and glass canyons of Docklands. Noel rolled onto his feet and went wide around the roadside of the car, firing short bursts rapidly, switching between the two gunmen. One of them went down but Noel was sure it was a shoulder hit. The other one ducked down. On the other side of the road Stanton was marching forward, firing burst after burst. It was the sound of conventional gunfire echoing between the skyscrapers now.

Noel started running again. Both the gunmen were up now. One of them was running, the other staggering. The fleeing gunmen fired wildly, one-handed, behind them. The recoil made the weapon climb and Noel saw shattered glass slide off the pyramid-topped One Canada Square some distance away. Noel stopped and took aim. He squeezed the trigger. A three-round burst. He was close enough to see a spray of red. The already wounded gunman went down. The other gunman was swinging around. He was fast, faster than Noel, with drug-augmented reactions. Noel heard the screaming. The road next to him exploded in a line as the rounds impacted the tarmac. The scope's red-dot was centred on the man's face. Noel stroked the trigger. The man disappeared from the scope in a spray of red. Noel took his next breath. Drugs, automatic weapons and exuberance were no match for being able to shoot.

Stanton had put down the remaining gunman by the van. There was more firing further up the street. The two remaining gunmen were pouring fire into the police roadblock, out of sight, at the junction with Aspen Way. They were off the road now. They ceased firing and turned, running alongside warehouses that had been converted into apartments next to the museum. They were heading towards one of the raised Dockland Light Railway stations. The expensive apartments had taken a lot of fire. There were going to be a lot of unhappy yuppies, real estate values were going to plummet.

Noel and Stanton ran after them as they disappeared behind the apartments, running back towards West India Quay. Noel changed the carbine's magazine as he ran. Stanton and Noel had run up the road until he was parallel with the junction to Aspen Way.

There were two police vans and four cars at the roadblock. All of them were thoroughly riddled with holes. There were very few police manning the road-block, but they caught a glimpse of dark pools of blood, glinting shell cases and bodies.

North Dock, 13 July, 2218 (BST)

Noel and Stanton sprinted around the corner of a converted warehouse. They could see the two gunmen racing across the bridge over West India Quay close to where Noel had been stationed on the boat. He stopped and took aim but there were too many civilians around them to fire safely. Most of them were either cowering on the ground, in cover, or had frozen in panic but he could not get a clear shot. Stanton had continued running. Noel took off after him.

He was aware of what sounded like cars crashing behind him.

Something leapt out of the building. Noel was spinning around, bringing up the carbine. Further up the road, moving so he could get an angle, Stanton was doing likewise with the SAW.

It landed next to the water. It was difficult to make out. The air around it shimmered. It was like the smiling

282

things he'd seen, it was tall and thin, but it had more limbs, and something about it suggested its form was armoured. It turned to look at Noel. It wasn't quite all there. It hurt Noel's head just looking at.

'Noel?' Stanton shouted. It wasn't often he heard the Scotsman sound unsure.

'Fire if it attacks,' Noel said with more certainty than he felt. *Fire if it instantly flays me, more like.*

He glanced back at the rear wall of the building it had come from. Even from this distance he could see cracks appearing in the stone. The cracks were centred on where it had come through but it hadn't left a hole. Just then all the lights started going out all over the Docklands. The thing rolled into the water but didn't make a splash.

'Was that an alien, then?' Stanton asked, sounding a little shaky. Noel swallowed hard and nodded. He felt his heart hammering in his chest. The worst thing was he wasn't as shocked as he felt he should be. He was getting too used to this sort of thing. He turned back, looking for the gunmen. They were running towards Cabot Square, one of the central squares in Docklands. It was lined with expensive apartment buildings, offices, bars and cafés. The square was mostly deserted, and the few people there who hadn't taken shelter were in cover. Noel was running as fast as he could, coated in sweat, his lungs burning. Still the drug-induced gunmen were increasing the distance between them.

Without lights, the skyscrapers seemed like darkened monoliths against the glow of London's light polluted night sky. There was a strange glow emanating from the pyramid-topped One Canada Square, however.

He could hear more gunfire nearby and the sound of a car engine. The gunmen reached the square. Noel stopped running. One of the gunmen turned around, bringing his weapon up. The carbine was at Noel's shoulder. Stanton was still running. The scope's red-dot was just over the top of the gunman's head. He heard the rounds from the gunman's MP7 scream by. He squeezed the carbine's trigger. He saw a spray of blood through the scope. He lowered the carbine and the gunman was already dropping. Muzzle flashes lit up the dark streets, the sound of Stanton's SAW rolled through the gaps between buildings and out over the water like thunder. The other gunman was staggering back as round after round hit him. He fired his MP7, the shots going wild, eating into the stonework of the buildings around them, glass raining down. Stanton advanced, still firing. The bullets were hitting centre mass. The gunman collapsed to the ground. Stanton covered him with the SAW. Noel started running again. He could hear the sound of a car coming along the south side of West India Quay as he ran between the buildings towards Cabot Square. The gunman that Stanton had shot sat up. He was covered in blood. Noel stopped. He fired once. The man slumped back down again. Stanton stood over the gunman and shot him twice more in the head just to be sure, then fired two into the first gunman Noel had shot.

Noel ran into Cabot Square.

Cabot Square, 13 July, 2221 (BST)

There was a deafening screaming noise of tortured metal and the sound of thousands of windows breaking. Noel and Stanton turned to look to the east. Through a rain of broken glass, they watched in horror as the pyramid-topped One Canada Square skyscraper started to fall, crumpling in on itself as if it was imploding, disappearing from sight behind the other buildings. The impact shook the ground and both men were knocked off their feet. He caught a glimpse of a nimbus of strange coloured light surrounding the building as it fell. Clouds of dust billowed out from the impact zone but nothing like as thick as Noel would have expected. The ground started to shake violently. More windows in the surrounding buildings broke, showering the street with broken glass.

They heard the car squeal around the corner onto the pedestrian area between the buildings leading to Cabot Square from West India Quay. A black Audi A6, the windows blacked out. Score marks from multiple bullet impacts on the paintwork. It took a moment to register with Noel. He'd seen a similar black Audi outside the tower block in Lambeth.

'Noel?' Stanton shouted. Both of them were struggling to keep on their feet as the ground shifted violently beneath them. Again there was an uncertainty in Stanton's voice that Noel wasn't used to. Noel was aware of a disturbance in the air. It was indeterminate, little more than an outline, as something rose out of the wreckage of One Canada Square.

'Light it up!' Noel screamed. Meaning the Audi that was bearing down on them. He fired the carbine and sparks flew off the car's obviously armoured body. He watched as tracers from Stanton's SAW hit the car, ricocheted off and then went shooting into the night sky leaving a fractal line of phosphorescent light behind them.

White light shot out from the Audi, turning part of its armoured windscreen to slag. The bolt of light just missed Noel but the heat further burnt the side of his face and set the arm of his shirt on fire. Behind them the fountain in Cabot Square had been turned into steam and molten stone.

Noel moved his hand forward, took a moment to aim and then fired the grenade launcher. The 40mm HEAP grenade hit the right hand front of the Audi, penetrating the armour, and exploded. The car went over on its left side, most of the engine gone, its considerably lessened momentum carrying it in a hail of sparks into the side of One Cabot Square. Then and only then did he beat out the flames burning his arm. Somewhere in Noel's mind he registered that the earth tremors had stopped.

Stanton advanced on the car, his SAW at the ready. The Audi's armoured passenger door went flying into the air and Noel saw a hand grip the doorframe.

'Stanton, no!' Noel screamed.

Martin Collins pulled himself out of the car and stood on it. Stanton started firing. Rectangles of light appeared in various places in front of Collins. The bullets disintegrated as they hit the shield. Collins crouched and then leapt off the upturned Audi. He landed in front of a shocked-looking Stanton, the concrete beneath Collins's feet cracking under the impact.

'No!' Noel screamed. He started fumbling for another 40mm grenade. Collins rammed his hand into Stanton's stomach through the SBS soldier's body armour. Then he jerked his arm further in, up to the elbow. His hand was in Stanton's chest cavity now. Stanton stared at him. Noel managed to get the grenade launcher open, the spent HEAP round clattering to the floor. An intense white light lit Stanton, for a moment, from within. Then where Stanton had been there was only a humid red mist. Stanton's SAW clattered to the ground. Collins, now painted red, turned to look at Noel and smiled.

'Bastard!' Noel screamed and fired the grenade launcher. He'd put in an HE round, largely by chance. The rectangle of energy appeared at the impact point. Noel actually saw the round stop. The grenade blew. The force of the explosion knocked Noel off his feet, winding him. Collins went spinning through the air and bounced into the wall of the building behind him.

Noel sat up, desperately trying to catch his breath. Collins looked like a broken doll lying bent at odd angles on the ground. Noel, gasping, managed to climb to his feet. His ears were ringing. He couldn't hear again. He was pretty sure there was blood seeping from one of them. Then Collins sat up. His limbs started rearranging themselves into a more natural shape. Noel stared at him. Collins stood up. Noel started running.

He ran around the front of One Cabot Square. He saw the entrance. He couldn't risk the door being locked so he fired a long burst from the waist. The safety glass shattered and he jumped through it. He was in a marble foyer. There was a reception desk opposite the door. If there was anyone else in there then they were keeping well hidden. Noel knew the only chance he had was to hide.

Collins jumped through one of the thick safety glass windows. Noel twisted to the side and started firing. The energy flickered into life, stopping or disintegrating each of his bullets. Collins advanced on him and Noel backed away. Noel saw the tracer, two more rounds and then the carbine's magazine was empty. He reached forward, opening the grenade launcher. Collins closed with Noel and slapped the carbine out of the way, snapping it in two, leaving Noel's finger feeling numb. Noel threw himself backwards, landing on his arse. He drew the Sig as Collins loomed over him. Noel fired the Sig rapidly at point-blank range. The light flickered all around Collins again. The slide went back on the Sig, the last shell casing landed on the marble. Collins was leaning down towards him. Noel reached for his knife, but it wasn't in the sheaf. He'd left it in one of the gunmen's neck back by the museum.

'Stop playing the cunt, Burman,' Collins told him. Noel stared at him. Then Noel realised that he could hear a phone ringing. Collins reached into his blood-covered suit and pulled out a mobile phone. 'It's for you,' he told Noel.

Shaking, Noel reached up to take the phone.

'Yes?' he asked, still staring at Collins.

'Your brother or your niece. Who are you going to come for?' the gravelly rasping voice on the other end of the line asked.

Chapter Fifteen

High Earth Orbit, 13 July, 2232 (BST)

'Your brother or your niece, who are you going to come for?' Bad Trip's rasping voice asked. Noel just stared ahead at the phone. The line went dead. Noel continued staring at the phone.

Rex was sat on the edge of one of the Chesterfields absolutely transfixed. These humans excelled at violence. It was terribly exciting. He was starting to understand Bad Trip's fascination with it.

Every surface within the Mindship was showing the image of the events unfolding in London. The main protagonists were rendered in perfect holographic representations. It was needlessly primitive but still, somehow, incredibly compelling. Rex was fascinated to see the decision that Noel would make.

'All right?' Collins, the Juicer that Bad Trip had made, asked Noel and then reached down and plucked the phone from the human's hand.

Rex? Bad Trip asked.

Just a minute, Rex thought by way of a reply.

You need to check the information from the ship. Something's just harvested matter from one of the buildings down here.

Noel was staring numbly ahead. The nano-camera dust scattered all over the area was able to pick out every detail of the anguished expression on his face. Noel pushed himself to his feet.

Rex, even the whispering thought in his mind was rasping, gravelly and unpleasant.

What? Rex demanded, freezing the image. He could experience it later but he knew it wouldn't be the same as watching it unfold live.

The ship is getting readings that suggest a stealthed Weft ship leaving the Earth.

If only we had someone who was supposed to handle the military aspects of our venture, Rex thought acidly.

I'm busy.

Rex decided to keep to himself the fact that he thought Bad Trip was busy being a sadist. He concentrated on the relevant aspects of the ship's senses. His connection to the craft was a constant. He soon found what he was looking for. A sensor ghost, but not quite ghost enough for the Mindship's senses to miss.

I have found it. Do you just want to destroy it? Rex thought. *I want to know if there are any more.*

Rex sighed theatrically.

Buckinghamshire, 13 July, 2233 (BST)

Bad Trip walked down the quiet country lane. He could make out the police car parked almost in the woods at the side of the road. He walked up to the car in its blind spot.

He'd had to run. Something was going to suffer tonight. Then he was going to find out what the thing in Docklands was and deal with it.

High Earth Orbit, 13 July, 2234 (BST)

The Mindship shed matter as it birthed small drone craft. Rex sent intercept instructions to the drones and they shot away, quickly becoming lost against the light of the blue planet itself.

With a thought he moved the Mindship. The ship grew weapons arrays that their Weft opponent would understand, something that would make for a cinematic – in the human parlance – if one-sided fight.

The drone-craft children closed with the stealthed ship. They fired beams of white and gold energy at the Weft craft. Rex had chosen the colours for the energy weapons because he thought they'd look pretty. The drone-craft the Mindship had created looked like gold and silver rocket ships from the golden age of Earth's science fiction. Bad Trip would not have approved. He believed form should follow function and terror, always terror, but then he had left this up to Rex to handle.

White nuclear light lit up space around the Weft ship. The drones bathed it in destructive X- and gamma rays. Several seconds later the particle wake of the attack washed over the Mindship. As the drone-craft closed with the Weft ship it desperately tried to defend itself. Then it was gone.

Where? Rex wondered. The ship provided him with the answer immediately. It was heading towards the fourth planet in the system, the red one the humans called Mars. It was moving at roughly twice the speed of light. Rex decided to intercept. This time the drone-craft the Mindship grew were built for speed. He loaded them with templates for larger drone-warships and his favourite Juicer race and went looking for matter. He found what he was looking for in the trailing asteroids at one of the red planet's Lagrange points.

The drone ships impacted with the first of the Martian Trojans, 5261 Eureka. They dissipated, diffusing the achondrite and the angrite with picotech. Growing atmosphere-capable warships from the base matter, their sub-light engines igniting as soon as they were free. The fusion torches of their drives burned scars in the stone of their parent asteroid.

Docklands, London, 13 July, 2234

Noel stared as Collins walked away from him, his feet grinding the broken glass to powder beneath him. He glanced down at the Sig, its slide back. He'd emptied his whole magazine at Collins along with everything else, to no avail.

There's nothing we can do. The realisation was overwhelming. None of this seemed to have anything to do with humans – or rather, it had everything to do with humans but they seemed powerless to affect the situation in any meaningful way. He sagged where he sat. He didn't want to get up. He didn't want to try. It had been made very clear how pointless that would be.

Jess, Kimberley, Nicholas. Get up, you pathetic bastard!

He reloaded the Sig, worked the slide chambering a round and holstered the weapon. He looked down. The Diemacos C8 carbine was done, snapped in two, but the Heckler & Koch AG-C/EGLM 40mm grenade launcher was still intact. He knelt down and began unscrewing the weapon from its mounting rail under the broken carbine's barrel. He removed the sling from the carbine and clipped it to the grenade launcher. He was aware of bursts of light and the sound of explosions somewhere else nearby.

Noel ran out of the building looking around the square. Billowing clouds of dust filled the area, choking him, making him cough. The skyline had changed. One Canada Square was gone. There was no light in the area.

Noel took out his phone but it was dead. He wondered for a moment how the one that Collins had given him had worked. Comms had gone down earlier in the operation but he tried again, to no avail.

It took him a few moments of blundering around in the dust before he found what he was looking for: Stanton's Minimi Para squad automatic weapon. Noel checked the weapon. It was covered in dust but seemed to be in working order. He checked the drum magazine. There was still at least half a belt in there. Fifty rounds or more and when that ran dry the Minimi could take the M16 pattern magazines Noel had been using in his carbine.

'Freeze! Armed police!' There were two figures advancing through the dust towards him. Carbines shouldered, laser designators drawing a bright red line through the cloud of dust, the dots playing across his body armour. 'Drop the weapon!' Noel could see from the lasers that these people were nervous. Both were shaking quite badly.

'Armed security services! You have been briefed on our presence,' Noel said, quiet enough not to spook them but with authority in his voice.

'We've only got your word for it,' one of them sighed. Noel groaned inwardly.

'Guys, I don't really have time for this. Are you in radio contact with DSI Samantha Lindley? She can vouch for me.'

'All the radios are down,' one of them said. 'I'm not really sure what to do. This has never happened before.'

'Do you know where DSI Lindley is?' he asked, enunciating slowly and carefully as if talking to a child.

'They've set up a temporary command centre at the pier.'

'Okay, I'm going to go there. I am no threat to you but if you fire on me I will fire back, understood?'

He started running, making for the riverboat pier. He half expected to hear the sound of gunfire and feel bullets slam into his back.

Buckinghamshire, 13 July, 2235 (BST)

Bad Trip walked up the driveway towards the house, the gravel crunching under his feet. Light bent around him, obscuring him in crawling shadow. The lights were still on and he could make out people moving around in the house.

Close Orbit Mars, 13 July, 2241 (BST)

When the hurriedly-built Weft craft appeared close to the Red Planet less than half its mass remained, the rest consumed to power its FTL flight. Immediately it was attacked by the Pleasure drone-warships raining down focused energy from the more attractive parts of the spectrum. The ships had been born to look like gilded spaceships of Martian-based fiction from the pulp era.

Mars's weak magnetosphere flared with plasma flares cascading like liquid flame. The Weft ship was hit time and time again as it tumbled down, its FTL drive destroyed. It was wreathed in fire as it hit the atmosphere. The Weft pilot somehow managed to retain control of the ship so that it didn't break up on entry. The drone-craft kept up with it, harrying but never destroying it, which their vast technological superiority would have been able to do easily whenever they chose to.

A network of primitive defence satellites surrounding the planet awoke from their energy coma. Those that were still functional started firing on the drone ships with energy weapons from less fanciful parts of the spectrum. The first bursts of accelerated anti-particles, high energy X-ray lasers and focused gamma bursts took the drone ships by surprise. A few of the drone-ships were damaged. Mars's low orbit and upper atmosphere was treated to a fantastic light display. White and gold energy reached out from the drone-ships' ornate weapons arrays, like fingers of light reaching around the planet, destroying the satellite network. The damaged drone-ships seemingly exploded but in fact became untold numbers of sub-munitions that sought out and destroyed many of the remaining satellites. Again the surface of the dead red planet was treated to a glorious light display.

The Weft ship had made it into the atmosphere and was diving into a huge canyon, thousands of miles long, more than a hundred miles wide and more than four miles deep. The craft was like a ghost now, attempting to flicker on the border of different physical states as it sank into the cirrus clouds of red dust and water vapour carried by the two hundred mile an hour winds.

The drone-warships remained high above the Valles Marineris, bombarding it through the clouds with searchlight-thick beams of plasma, creating lava-falls and geysers of molten rock. The beams burning through the cloud made it look as if the sun itself was attacking the planet. Rex initiated a thermonuclear bombardment of the canyon just because he thought it would be pretty, and he wanted to see what the surface would look like after. In the Mindship, Beethoven's 5th symphony was playing loudly as Rex conducted the nuclear bombardment.

Noel came sprinting out of the dust cloud and found himself looking at a lot of gun barrels held by armed police officers. The police had set up around the river-boat terminal on the side of the river. The cordon was basically a semi-circle of police cars and vans parked on the concrete dockside.

'He's with me!' Sam all but shrieked, walking out from between the ring of vehicles, putting a handkerchief back over her mouth. Noel made his way over to her. 'Well, this is proper fucked!' she shouted at him. 'What were you doing? Gun battles all over the shop!'

'Defending ourselves,' Noel offered.

'Where's the rest of your people?' Sam asked.

'Stanton's dead, I've no idea about Roche and Rees, we lost comms. Their boss, this Bad Trip, called me. He's going after Nicholas, Kimberley and Jess. He wanted me to choose.'

'Where are they?' Sam asked.

'I don't know, my phone's down, there must have been some kind of localised electromagnetic pulse. Is your phone working?'

Sam pulled out her mobile, punched in the code and handed it to Noel. Whatever had happened to all the electronics she must have been outside its range. Noel desperately tried to remember the landline number for the house in Buckinghamshire but he couldn't. The numbers for Steve and Jacko, the two ex-SBS contractors he'd put Nicholas in contact with to work as bodyguards, were on his non-functioning phone as well.

'Can you get through to the security detail you sent to Nicholas's house?' Noel asked Sam.

'Comms-wise it's anarchy, but I'll see what I can do,' she told him.

Noel started dialling a number from memory that he hoped was Nicholas's mobile. A dirty and dust-covered Charlotte appeared next to Sam.

'What's going on?' she asked.

'Bad Trip's threatened Nicholas and his family,' Sam told the other woman.

The phone was answered but nobody said anything.

'Nicholas?' Noel asked cautiously.

'Bruv?' Nicholas asked. The strain in his voice was obvious.

'Is there someone there with you?' Noel asked.

'I'm at the club. It'd be nice if you could join us,' Nicholas said and then the connection was broken. Noel tried redialling but there was no answer.

'Nicholas is at the club, there's something wrong. I think Bad Trip may already be there. You in command here?' Noel asked Sam.

'Yeah, until my boss gets here and then I'm under arrest,' Sam told him.

'Can you try and get hold of the detail you sent there, tell them they're under threat, that someone's probably coming tonight.'

'I'll try, but they've probably been recalled. Every

police officer in the city and all the surrounding police authorities are on their way here.'

'We'll go to the house, we'll see if we can get the number on the way,' Charlotte told him. Sam was giving this some thought.

'Fuck it, why not?' Sam decided.

'Okay, thanks,' Noel said and got into one of the police cars that still had a running engine. A number of police officers tried to stop him but Sam intervened. Tyres squealed as Noel took off, heading towards Brixton.

Streets of South London, 2320 (BST)

The streets of the city had been chaos as a result of the power outage: dead cars, accidents, panicked people on the street, incoming emergency vehicles. It had taken him a long time to thread his way through it, even in a police car.

After a while the car's lights had come back on, the battery having recharged itself enough. He had thought about abandoning the car but that would have left him on foot as he had learnt that the tubes had been stopped. There were all sorts of wild reports coming over the radio. It sounded like the police had shot someone in the Elephant and Castle.

Police vehicles were the only ones moving on the streets. They shot past in a haze of spinning blue light, sometimes silently, sometimes with the sirens screaming. There were a lot of helicopters in the sky: police, media, and doubtless military by now as well. He knew that

Hereford would probably have been mobilised, and Poole would be on alert.

The amount of time it was taking was killing him. Every extra moment, he knew, made it less likely that his brother, Jessica and Kimberley would still be alive. He knew Sam and Charlotte would be facing the same problems as they tried to make it to the house, and they had further to go.

He could see the glow of televisions through many windows as he sped through the city. They would be watching the aftermath of what had happened in Docklands. Television pundits would be telling them that this was the latest terrorist atrocity. There would be aerial shots of the dust cloud, and the impact zone where One Canada Square had come down. They would listen to eyewitness reports of a running gun battle in the streets.

As he shot through the city at speed he could feel how frightened his home town had become. His fingers tightened on the steering wheel and he depressed the accelerator further.

Noctis Labyrinthus, Mars, 14 July, 0016 (BST)

After a long game of thermonuclear cat and mouse played on the flickering borders of various different physical states, the Pleasure's drone-warships had managed to trap the rapidly shrinking Weft craft in a series of narrow labyrinthine canyons at the western end of the Valles Marineris. There Rex had lost the

Weft craft. He was pretty sure that it had landed some-where beneath the fast moving clouds driven through the canyons on howling winds.

The energy shields surrounding the drone-warships floating over the labyrinth were lit up as they started receiving ground fire. Nano-factories had hastily assembled deceptively spindly war machines from the raw matter of the planet's surface to attack the Pleasure's forces.

The drone-warships exploded like seedpods sporing. 'Seeds' – actually template picotech factories – rained down on the canyons in the labyrinth and also began feeding on the local matter. Rex reflected on the fact that at the end of the day if you wanted to violently take control of something, and not just destroy it, you still needed what the humans called 'boots on the ground'.

The Juicers started growing from the rock of the canyons. Their growth reminded Rex of the humans' zombie media that he had assimilated not that long ago. He'd enjoyed *Dawn of the Dead* but much of the rest had seemed pretty derivative.

They had been a panspermic insect people inhabiting a series of low gravity planets and asteroid habitats in a system orbiting a dying sun. Only the hive mothers had been sentient. Though they had been *very* sentient, as their connection to the drone workers and warriors had basically formed a naturally occurring telepathic infoscape. Their queens had created a type of 'jelly' with certain narcotic properties that had proved in great demand in other parts of the Empire of Pleasure. The

Pleasure had traded narcotic pheromone secretions and telepathic pleasure broadcasts for the jelly, and another people had been enslaved. Their junkie culture had died millennia ago.

Their warriors, however, had been something to behold. Once they had been augmented with technology and combat drugs Bad Trip had turned them into a 'seed' template and they were still amongst the Enforcer's favourite Juicer templates. Part of this was due to the fact that the majority of humanoid races they encountered found something very disturbing about insects.

They were a little over nine feet tall. Their frames were reinforced with powerful exoskeletons fused to their chitinous bodies. For this particular operation Rex had made the armour on the exoskeletons look a little like ornately engraved plate armour made of precious metals.

They supported themselves on four blade-like legs. They had compound eyes that covered the sides of their armoured, oblong heads, providing them with multi-spectrum three-hundred-and-sixty degree vision. Their mandibles had much more to do with fighting than they did eating. In their powerful arms they carried rail weapons that fired what amounted to stingers made of 'intelligent' biological material. The stings were hard enough to penetrate armour but they also 'knew' to explode when surrounded by soft, warm flesh and release tailored neurotoxins, or material eating nano-factories, though this was only for the toughest of prey. Most targets were simply torn apart by the sheer velocity of the rounds.

303

They marched down the side of the canyon's rock faces and into the cloud cover. They started taking fire from the hastily nano-assembled weapons that the fleeing Shriven Weft had created. The insect Juicers' shields lit up, absorbing the energy from the beam and kinetic attacks, turning it into arcing displays of lightning directed back at the targets as the thin atmosphere of Mars was filled with the hypersonic ripping noise of the Juicers' railguns. The Weft's ad-hoc weapons drones were torn apart, simply no match for the Juicers' onslaught.

Down in the canyon Rex could see some rather interesting energy readings being relayed from the network of picoscopic scanners spread over the area. It looked like the Weft had some kind of baby universe. Something that they had picked out of the quantum foam, enlarged and were using as a dimensional vault. It was basically a large warehouse complex sat in an impact crater. Large oddly shaped arm-like apertures, forming some kind of array, had been secured in the rock. It was being powered by a number of different automated fusion plants that were in the process of sinking into the ground as tailored nanites ate away at the surrounding rock. The warehouse was flickering in and out of different physical states.

The insect Juicers targeted the fusion plants first. A number of them harvested the surrounding matter through their feet, growing missile arrays on their shoulders and upper torsos, turning themselves into walking artillery pieces. The missiles flew from the launchers, blossoming into sub-munitions that confused the Weft's point defences. A rudimentary energy shield flared into life to protect the fusion generators. But with a thought the Juicers changed the warheads in the first sub-munitions to reach the energy fields into focused EMP bursters. The sustained barrage created a constant display of lightning across the energy field until the shield came down and the generators exploded in crackling mushroom clouds. The flickering stopped. The warehouse complex became solid again.

Buckinghamshire, 14 July, 0017 (BST)

His .45 was on the sofa next to him. Bad Trip had dampened the sound made by the replica Earth weapon when he'd executed the two guards. He had considered juicing them both but it didn't have quite the impact that he wanted.

He started receiving the imagery and accompanying information from Mars.

I'm busy, Bad Trip thought, trying to ignore the sound of sobbing though it was beginning to bother him. He despised weakness.

There's some kind of warehouse complex here, Rex told him. *This could be important.*

I don't care and I have things to do. Bad Trip blocked Rex's thoughts out.

He returned to the task in hand. The carpet was wet under his feet. It occurred to him that Rex did not understand why he did what he did. He held the dripping razor up in front of him. It would be warm, and red and beautiful, when he had finished. Like a pinned butterfly.

Noctis Labyrinthus, Mars, 14 July, 0032 (BST)

Then the insect Juicers started dying. Their energy shields surrounded them in a flickering nimbus of light as they came under a significant amount of fire. There were Weft in the warehouse complex. The Weft were without the complex exotic matter and entangled quantum states of their shadow-selves. They were soul-dead neurotransmitter junkies. The Shriven. Their tall forms moving between buildings and different physical states. Holding small tubes, the physical ends of heavy weapons that were stored, with vast magazines of ammunition, in an extra-dimensional space. The insect Juicers' energy screens lit up in a constant storm of energy and arcing electrical displays, reaching for an enemy that wasn't quite there.

The Shriven changed the matter of the rounds they were firing, making them invisible to the scanners that automatically raised the Juicers' shields. Hypersonic rounds tore into the insects' armoured forms, churning them up, tearing them into ribbons.

Rex watched through the eyes of the picoscopic array. The flickering Weft wore ancient human fashions, presumably from eras they had lived through. They looked decadent and degenerate but Rex decided they had a degree of scummy, retro charm to them.

As the insect Juicers leapt and walked up buildings, moving with drug-induced machine speed and strength to close with the Shriven, more and more of the Juicers were destroyed. The Weft simply stroked them, changing their own physical state to run long-nailed, long-fingered hands through the armoured insects, de-cohering their flesh from their chitinous forms. Bloody plates of armour and lumps of flesh simply fell at the Shriven's touch.

It was inevitable, however. Even the dead and sorely injured Juicers were simply broken down into their base matter and then regrown from the surrounding matter by picotech factory templates. Every time they fell, they were regrown. Every time they were attacked, they analysed. Their shields shifted frequencies. Their internal scanners checked in other media and spectrums for incoming rounds. The rounds they fired began to change physical state, each subsequent round flickering through realities until eventually it found the correct one.

By now the insect Juicers surrounded the impact basin that the warehouse complex was in. They marched between huge blocks of stone. Firing railguns, the electrical arcs from their shields reaching out and destroying any hastily assembled automated weapon systems.

One Shriven after another was caught and gunned down as they were forced deeper and deeper into the complex, running and flickering between vast tanks with Weft language-formulae painted on the side of them.

Rex was keeping one eye on the fight as he penetrated the primitive Weft infoscape and disabled their self-destruct spite mechanisms. He kept on getting flickers of movement in odd spectrums from the picoscopic array. He wasn't sure what was going on.

Rex frowned. Something strange was happening. Some kind of primitive bulk freighter, also of Weft design, had appeared. He had no idea where it had come from. It appeared to be unarmed but was plummeting towards the surface of the planet in a trajectory that would ensure its destruction.

The freighter was of a similar tech level to all the other hardware on display in the complex and was definitely of Weft design. Rex assumed it was connected to the Shriven. He watched it falling apart as it made its disastrous and clumsy entry into the thin Martian atmosphere. It had appeared and suddenly something was messing with the Shriven's infoscape, threatening Pleasure information security. Rex was convinced that whatever it was it had access to technology comparable to the Pleasure's. That he did not like at all.

Then he paid more attention to what was written on the side of the vast vats in the warehouse complex where the final destruction of the Shriven was taking place: epinephrine; corticotropin; norepinephrine, endorphin; dopamine, acetylcholine and serotonin. Vast quantities of it. Enough to addict entire star systems to it. Five hundred years of harvesting human neurotransmitters. A fortune.

Bad Trip? Rex thought, but his partner was ignoring him.

Rex ordered the Juicers to hunt down and kill the last of the soul-dead Weft junkies.

The freighter impacted into the planet. A huge plume of red dust was thrown miles into the atmosphere.

The Shriven's vault winked out of existence.

'What just happened?' Rex asked himself. The Mindship provided the answer. Something had managed to activate the Shriven's dimensional vault. The entire complex had just been shunted into another dimension.

Chapter Sixteen

Angels & Demons Nightclub, Brixton, London, 14 July, 0032

Noel moved quickly up the stairs, the SAW against his shoulder, checking all around him, the barrel of the weapon pointing where he looked. The club seemed eerily quiet but then the streets of Brixton had seemed oddly deserted. Even the pubs and bars were quiet as people crowded around the TVs, watching the footage from the Docklands. Noel had all but abandoned the police car in the street outside the club.

Noel hesitated outside the door leading into the club proper. He considered throwing a stun grenade in first but decided that was rash without knowing what was going on. He closed his eyes, readied himself, opened them again and pushed against the door.

He moved forwards and to one side quickly, looking all around. There were dozens of distorted reflections in the mirrors on the wall.

A figure was curled up against one of the walls. His frame wracked with sobs. There were bits of steaming, smoking meat strewn around the dance floor. His brother was sat at a table taking a sip from a glass of brandy. The bottle was on the table next to a sawn-off shotgun, and a handful of shells.

'All right, bruv?' Nicholas asked. Noel nodded. The smoking meat was setting off serious alarm bells. He moved over to the figure curled up on the floor. He recognised Oliver, his brother's second. The other man jumped as Noel reached down for him.

'All right, Oliver, it's Noel, Nicholas's brother, you remember?' Noel asked. Oliver looked up at him with a tear-stained face and nodded. 'Okay, what's going on here Oliver? Where's Josh and Billy?'

'You just going to ignore me, bruv?' Nicholas asked loudly.

'I don't know where Billy is, he's at his mum's I think. He texted me about what's happening in Docklands.'

'Where's Josh, Oliver?' Noel asked. Oliver just stared at him. Noel turned to look at the pile of steaming meat littering the floor. 'Okay, who did that? What happened?'

'The scar-faced guy, he was here. He did something to ...' Oliver started but faltered.

'Bit rude, isn't it?' Nicholas called.

'Who killed Josh?' Noel asked again, softly but insistent. Oliver pointed a shaking finger at Nicholas. Noel felt his stomach drop. 'Okay Oliver, you need to stand up and get out of here, understand me?' Oliver just shook his head. 'C'mon Oliver, it'll be okay.'

Oliver looked up at Noel.

'He'll kill me,' Oliver said, meaning Nicholas.

'No, he won't. You'll be fine, I promise. Just stand up and stay behind me, we'll move to the door.'

With some coaxing, a badly shaken Oliver got to his feet. Noel tried not to notice that the other man had soiled himself. Noel wasn't sure that he blamed him. Oliver stayed behind him as they moved towards the door. Noel wasn't quite pointing the SAW at his brother but it was at the ready.

'Where you going, lads?' Nicholas enquired.

'Okay go, get out,' Noel told Oliver once they'd reached the door. For a moment Noel thought that Oliver was going to be too frightened to move but he managed to find enough courage to bolt through the doors.

'You going too, yeah?' Nicholas asked. 'I thought we might have a little bit of a chat, just brother to brother.'

'I'm not going anywhere, Nicholas,' Noel told him. He kept the SAW at the ready but he couldn't bring himself to point it at his brother, though he was sure that was where the danger in the room was coming from.

'Want a drink?' Nicholas asked and poured himself another healthy measure of brandy.

'Not right now.'

'Oh right, I'm guessing you're all tooled up because you're on duty. My brother the rory tory combat soldier, right?'

'I'm a marine,' Noel said, more by instinct than anything else.

'Same difference. See, here's what I want to know. You're supposed to be keeping us safe right, the public I mean, from terrorists and bad men like me, right?'

'That's the idea,' *though sometimes it doesn't feel that way.*

'Then how come you couldn't keep my daughter safe, hey? How come you couldn't look after her, a big tough soldier like you?' There were tears rolling down his cheek. 'Why are you here with a piece of shit like me …?' Nicholas slammed his fist down on the table. It cracked but didn't break. The bottle of brandy rolled off it and smashed on the floor. 'Ooops. I think I might have had a bit too much.'

Nicholas got up and walked behind the bar.

'See, my daughter's never done anything to anyone. I have, I've been a right arsehole to anyone who's ever got in my way, but not Kimberley. So why aren't you there looking after her?' He retrieved another bottle of brandy and came and sat back down. 'Sure you don't want a drink?'

'I've got people on the way to your house, good people, people I can trust, Sam's on her way …'

'Sam …? Sam! What use is some dried-up old hag going to be against him?'

Noel felt his blood run cold.

'Is there someone at the house with Jess and Kimberley?' he asked.

Nicholas looked him straight in the eyes.

'He told me. He said he'd do it.'

'Who?' Noel demanded. He kept one hand on the grip of his SAW, but the other was reaching for the phone to call Sam and Charlotte.

'Don't do that, bruv,' Nicholas said. His hand was on the butt of the shotgun. Noel stopped and stared at him.

313

'Are you out of your mind? Jess and Kimberley!'

'I don't have a choice any more.'

Noel glanced back at the still smoking lumps of meat.
'What happened to Josh, Nicholas?'

'You never call me bruv, do you? Not even Nick, no,
it's always "Nicholas". Don't swear, don't smoke, barely
drink. You're a good little boy aren't you?'

'Maybe I should go and see if the girls are all right.'
Noel said, slowly backing away.

'You always looked down on us, didn't you? Despite
the fact I was looking out for my family, that I even had
a family.' Nicholas said, not looking at him.

Not always, Noel thought but kept it to himself.

'It's because of the things I had to do when Mum
got sick, isn't it? Well, someone had to look after us.'
Suddenly he looked up. 'What are you backing away
from me for?'

'I think we need to … I need to go and see if the
girls are okay.'

'You said you had good people on the way. Sam's
on her way, isn't she? Nothing to worry about then,
is there?'

'Even so …'

'You think I can't look after my family?' Nicholas asked.

Noel stopped. He wanted to tell his brother that all
this was the result of how he lived, the choices he'd
made. Except Noel knew that he was involved as well.
On the other hand, Noel hadn't lived the most innocent
life either. Then he thought about all the people hanging
from the ceiling in that Lambeth tower block. They

probably hadn't asked for it. Whatever else was happening here it was indiscriminate in its violence.

'No,' Noel answered his brother. 'Not today.'

'What are you even doing here?' Nicholas asked again.

Noel saw his brother move. Instinct brought the SAW up before he had a chance to question if he was actually prepared to shoot Nicholas. It didn't matter. His brother was too quick. Nicholas grabbed the shotgun, oddly with his left hand, and fired both barrels. The shot hit Noel mostly in the stomach, which was protected by his body armour. It felt like getting hit with a sledgehammer. He couldn't breathe. He staggered back and fell over.

Nicholas stood up. He threw the cracked table to one side with surprising force. It went spinning through the air and hit some of the mirrors, smashing them. Nicholas started stalking towards his prone brother.

Panicking, Noel brought the SAW to bear. He tried to shout a warning to his brother but he couldn't breathe yet, let alone shout. He couldn't do it. He couldn't shoot Nicholas. Nicholas reached down and picked Noel up, holding him off his toes and then threw him.

Noel flew through the doors to the club. Down the first flight of stairs and slammed into the wall. What little air he'd had in his lungs exploded out of him. He bounced and hit the ground, hard. Pain shot through his chest. He'd broken a rib, of that he was sure, probably more than one.

Noel pushed himself up, gasping for breath.

'Why are you here making me kill you?' Nicholas screamed from the top of the stairs. 'Why aren't you looking after my girls, my babies? He said he'd give you a choice! He said he'd give you a fucking choice!' Nicholas was stood at the top of the stairs, silhouetted in the light from the club. Noel was watching in horror as his brother's right arm started transforming into the barrel of some sort of weapon, two objects beginning to spin around it.

If you want to live then you have to realise that your brother isn't your brother any more, a surprisingly calm inner voice told him. *He's like Collins now.*

He grabbed for the grenade launcher on its sling. Levelled it at Nicholas and fired. Orange light flared into life in front of Nicholas like some sort of barrier. Noel actually saw the grenade stop in mid-air. Then the 40mm HE round exploded. The force of the blast flung Nicholas backwards into the club, bouncing him off the ceiling. The compression wave broke every single piece of glass in the place. The shockwave battered Noel into the floor so hard that he lost consciousness.

***

With consciousness came pain. Noel felt like he'd been extensively beaten by hammers, that his body was one big bruise. All he could hear was a high-pitched tone. He was covered in dust, some rubble, and a lot of broken glass. A shadow fell over him. He looked up to see his brother's face. He looked furious. His suit wasn't even torn.

316

Nicholas levelled his weapon-arm at his brother. Noel threw himself down the next flight of stairs, dragging his weapons with him. He half slid, half bounced down them, every jarring impact agony for his broken ribs. He would be lucky if he didn't force a bone through one of his lungs at this rate.

Noel burst through the doors of the club and out onto Brixton Hill. He started running up towards the Brixton Road. There was a flash of light behind him and he felt the heat against his back as part of the wall of the club exploded into a spray of molten slag and rained down on the road.

Nicholas jumped through the hole he'd made. The maw of the plasma weapon his arm had become was still smoking.

'Where you going, bruv?' Nicholas shouted. Noel tried to tell himself that it was just another of Bad Trip's weapons. That it wasn't his brother. That it had just been given his brother's voice, but he couldn't help but wonder how much of the resentment was programming and how much was Nicholas.

Noel threw the SAW into the passenger seat of the police car and jumped into the driver's seat. He hurriedly put the seat belt on. He started the car up and glanced back towards the club. He could see Nicholas striding towards him. Noel threw the car into reverse. There was a bright light and the car that had been parked next to him ceased to exist in an explosion of bright molten metal.

Run or fight? Noel wasn't even sure it was a conscious decision. He threw the car into first and drove it down the road, heading towards his brother. Nicholas just watched him approach. The police car mounted the pavement and drove straight into Nicholas, slamming him into a brick wall that cracked under the impact.

Noel looked up at his brother through the spider web of cracks in the windscreen. Nicholas looked furious. The police car seemingly had him pinioned against the wall. His weapon-arm was transforming back into something that looked like a normal limb.

'Nicholas ... Nick, I need you to try and take control, so we can talk about this,' Noel pleaded.

'You fucking shot me with a grenade!'

Nicholas leaned down and grabbed the bottom of the police car and heaved. Suddenly the police car was spinning through the air. Noel saw the pavement and then the night sky. Then he hit the road. The roof buckled under the impact. He was battered around. The pain from his chest was nearly overwhelming. He grabbed for the seat belt, pressed the button and all but dropped onto the roof. In a panic he scrambled for the SAW as the door to the police car was ripped off. He felt hard, steel-like fingers grab his body armour and he was yanked out of the wreckage of the police car and flung across the street. He hit hard, the air knocked out of him again. Agony in his chest, and he could feel things moving in there in a way he knew they shouldn't. He'd lost hold of the SAW. He saw it lying on the ground some twelve feet away from him. He started to crawl towards it.

'Oh what? Are you going to shoot me again, you piece of shit?' Nicholas demanded. Noel glanced behind him as he tried to crawl. His brother was striding towards him, the police car oddly distant. Noel's fingers curled around the collapsible stock of the SAW and he dragged it towards himself. 'Go ahead!'

Noel rolled over. His brother was almost on him. Prone, lying on his back, he pulled the SAW to his shoulder. He squeezed the trigger and held it down. His brother was so close that the muzzle flash almost touched him as it lit up the street. Round after round. Noel could see the short phosphorescent flight of the tracers as they were halted in mid-air by glowing, overlapping, rectangles of energy. It looked like fractals of light catching up with themselves. He fired the remaining fifty or so rounds in the SAW's drum magazine. It looked like a nimbus of geometric light surrounded his brother.

Nicholas reached through the gunfire and grabbed Noel. He picked him up off the ground, spun him round and slammed him into the side of a white van making a sizeable, vaguely Noel-shaped, dent. Noel slid off the van and hit the ground. Somehow his broken ribs hadn't pierced anything too vital internally. Somehow nothing had broken in his spine. Somehow he was still alive. Somehow he was still conscious.

Over the high-pitched tone still sounding in his head he could hear the sound of his brother's purposeful footsteps walking towards him. From his position on the ground all he could see was the lower part of Nicholas's legs getting closer.

Do you want to live? the calm inner voice asked. He pushed himself onto his feet. He could see the SAW nearby. A lot of the weapon's plastic furniture had cracked or snapped off, the paint was badly scratched but he knew it was a tough weapon. He staggered towards it.

'Where you going, bruv?' Nicholas called.

Noel bent down and grabbed the weapon as he staggered by it, fighting to breathe through what felt like a chest full of broken glass and rusty spikes.

Run.

***

There were a few people out on the street looking down towards Brixton Hill. They had heard explosions and gunfire. They tended to run back into the pubs and bars they'd been in as Noel ran towards them.

He pulled the drum magazine off the SAW and grabbed one of the magazines for his C8 that were held in pouches attached to the front of his body armour. He slid the magazine home and charged the weapon.

He glanced behind him to see his brother walking after him but picking up the pace, moving to a run. Noel couldn't be sure but he thought he heard roaring coming from his brother. Noel tried to quicken his staggering run. He had no idea where he was going.

White light, the heat burning the hair on his skin. The force of the superheated air knocking him into the metal security covering on the front of a shop. Another parked car went up, melting in on itself.

Noel recovered enough to bring the SAW to his shoulder and fire back down the street at Nicholas. He fired. Moved. Fired again. He crossed the road. His brother ran across the road as well. Noel took cover behind a car and fired burst after burst at Nicholas.

Another flash of light and Noel hunkered down behind the car he was using as cover. The side of a building turned to slag, partially collapsing. Noel popped up and fired again. The rectangles of light appeared in front of his brother, stopping every round. The tracer fired, two more rounds and then the magazine was empty. He reloaded another magazine. Charged the weapon and then stood up to fire. His brother was striding towards him now. Noel raised the SAW to his shoulder. Then it occurred to him that he was just going through the motions. Following his training, the muscle memory. Shot at, shoot back, meet force with more force and aggression.

He turned and ran again. He should have dumped the SAW, it was weighing him down, but despite his brother's apparent invulnerability he couldn't quite bring himself to do it.

He sprinted past Lambeth Town Hall, past the turn-off for Coldharbour Lane, the closed shops, the open pubs and bars, many of them the result of Brixton's gentrification. Always glancing behind him. Nicholas was running enough just to keep up. Every breath Noel took was agony. The harder he tried to run the worse it got. He was sure he could taste blood in the back of his throat. Normally he could run forever, even carrying a lot of gear, but he'd done some damage to himself today.

Every so often Nicholas would fire his weapon-arm and something else would be destroyed in an explosion of molten material. It must have looked fantastic to the people witnessing it but most people were hiding, sensibly, wherever they could. As he got closer to the tube station he could see people scramble inside. One of the guards slammed the security cage down and locked it.

Noel felt like he was being harried, possibly even herded. He ran under the colourfully graffiti-decorated railway bridge. He knew up ahead was the Brixton Academy, a music venue. If there was a gig in there then it could be filled with hundreds of people. He cut left onto Pulross Road. Again the houses and gardens all looked a lot more middle class than when he had been growing up around here.

He glanced behind him. His brother was still coming. Another bolt of white heat and someone's BMW was turned into a geyser of bright molten metal. Noel was trying to make it to Papa's Park, next to the railway line, a bit further down the road. Instead he skidded to a halt. He bent over, grabbing his knees and gulping down big breaths of air. He could hear his brother approaching. He glanced at the burning car, collapsing in on itself, more glowing liquid than metal now. He straightened up.

'Just pack it in, Nick!' he shouted. 'You want me, here I am!' He put the SAW down, leaning it against

322

a hedge-topped garden wall. He popped open the grenade launcher, ejected the spent HE grenade and loaded a HEAP.

Nicholas was still striding towards him. He came to a halt. He reached up with his gun-arm. Touched it against the back of his brother's head. It felt warm like flesh, not hot like a recently fired weapon. His brother's transformed flesh, the violation of his form, made Noel shiver. Noel turned to face his brother.

'You want to kill me, kill me, but don't dress it up. *If* you want to kill me,' he told Nicholas evenly. There were tears running down Nicholas's face. 'I'm sorry if I made the wrong decision. If I should have gone to your place, to the girls.'

Nicholas took his gun-arm away from Noel's head. It transformed back into the more normal-looking human limb. Nicholas held his head and started screaming, doubling over. He straightened up and turned to his brother.

'You stupid bastard! I was going to be waiting in the club, waiting to kill you, even after you'd got back from my place. He goes for the pain. You cross him and he wants you to suffer. That's what it's about. That's what it's all about.'

'I've got people there now. I'll go there if I can.'

Nicholas grimaced, his arm morphing again. Noel found himself looking down the unpleasantly organic barrel of the weapon-limb. It glowed deep within.

'I'm sorry, bruv, I've got no choice. He programmed me. He wanted me to kill you because it would hurt.'

Nicholas raised the weapon-limb and shut his eyes tightly.

'Why couldn't you have just gone for the girls?' he asked desperately.

'You sure? You're like Collins now, right? I'm guessing it's not just drugs like the Russians. You've got to have some kind of alien machinery inside you, right?'

'I don't fucking know, do I?' Nicholas shouted. 'What's that got to do with any ...' As he spoke he raised the gun-arm, pointing it away from Noel.

'You got a targeting system? Crosshairs, information telling you where you'll hit, something like in a first person shooter?'

'Yes,' Nicholas said.

'Why didn't you shoot me? With that weapon you've had ample opportunities to kill me. Instead you just shot around me.'

'He wants to play with us ...' Nicholas started.

'Same in the police car. You could have pulled my head off if you'd really wanted to. Nothing I could have done about it. Instead you let me run.'

Nicholas stared at him.

'Same can't be said for you, you cunt!' he finally shouted. 'A grenade, a fucking machine gun!'

'Yeah, sorry about that: force of habit,' Noel said, sounding a little sheepish. He cracked a slight smile. Nicholas was just staring at him, furious. Then he started to laugh. The gun-limb turned back into an arm. Nicholas doubled up again, but with laughter now. Noel was just looking at him but then he started laughing as well.

324

Eventually they managed to wipe away the tears and take control of themselves.

'Where are the rozzers? We just shot up the Brixton Road,' Nicholas asked.

'Well I shot up Docklands beforehand, so they're probably all there.'

'That was you?'

For some reason this set them off again. The laughter was causing Noel's chest a great deal of pain.

Nicholas managed to get himself under control. He went and sat down on a low garden wall.

'I don't look down on you,' Noel told his brother. 'I just don't like what you do for a living. I was looking forward to you getting out. I was going to come and visit you all in New Zealand. I was even thinking of settling there myself. I was never going to think about how you got your money after that. Whatever you think of me, I've never felt in a position to morally judge anyone. It's just, what you do, it's ...'

'Dangerous. For them,' Nicholas said. It wasn't the only reason but Noel didn't want to tell his brother that right now. He took Sam's mobile out of one of the pouches on the webbing.

'Look, let me phone Sam and ...'

'No.' Nicholas put his hand on the phone. It was only then that Noel realised how little hope his brother had. Nicholas wouldn't meet his eyes.

'Look, if I live I'll go to them, make sure ...'

This time Nicholas met his eyes.

'If anything's happened,' his voice was like steel now,

'you find a way. You make them pay. You hear me, bruv?'

Noel swallowed hard, tried to blink back tears and nodded.

'You in control of what you are now?' Noel asked after a moment.

'Yeah, but he programmed me. You've got to die at my hands. I'm just putting it off.'

'The light, the thing that stops bullets and stuff, can you switch it off and on?'

Nicholas nodded. 'Under normal circumstances but with you ...'

'I need you to be stronger than him, just for a moment longer,' Noel told his brother. He launched himself off the wall, turning to face his brother, bringing the grenade launcher up on its sling even as he backed away. Nicholas pushed himself off the wall as well. Stepped into the middle of the pavement and spread his arms out wide. Tears were streaming down both their faces.

'Do it!' Nicholas screamed. His body seemed to be shrouded by the faintest suggestion of light from the shield. Noel fired. He could see the 40mm HEAP grenade slow in the air but Nicholas managed to suppress the shield just long enough. The tech in his body hardened skin and flesh but the grenade's armour-piercing head penetrated Nicholas's augmented body armour. The grenade blew. Nicholas spun into the air. It looked as if his body had started to come apart, but some parts of it still held together. Noel was blown off his feet. Every nearby house and car window in the street was shattered and all the car alarms started going off.

Noel gasped for breath, lying down on the pavement. He was sure something bad had happened in his chest. He forced himself to sit up. His brother's body was an odd distended and deformed mess, but it was somehow still alive. It was somehow still moving.

Noel cried out in pain as he climbed unsteadily to his feet. He staggered to where the SAW was now lying on the floor and picked it up. He limped over to the wounded deformity of his brother's still-moving body. He looked down. It looked nothing like his brother. It looked like a broken mass of strange technology with three quarters of his brother's face. The mouth was opening and closing. There was a pleading look in his eyes.

Noel pushed the barrel of the SAW into the alien machine that had inhabited his brother's mouth.

'Goodbye, bruv.'

Then he squeezed the trigger. He didn't let go until a long time after the entire clip had been emptied. The body had stopped moving but he couldn't see that through his tears.

Finally, he managed to control himself enough to call Charlotte. He got her answerphone.

Chapter Seventeen

Buckinghamshire, 13 July, 0032 (BST)

It had taken too long to make it through the dead cars and traffic accidents surrounding Docklands. Charlotte had glanced over at Sam when the radio message to arrest the detective superintendent had come through but the other woman had said nothing, just stared fixedly ahead as she raced down the A40.

They had tried calling Nicholas's home phone number several times but it had rung and rung. Given that there were supposed to be ex-SBS bodyguards there, as well as Nicholas's wife and child, that did not bode well. After the call for Sam's arrest had gone out they didn't dare try and contact the armed police officers stationed outside the house. They had probably been recalled to help with the Docklands situation anyway.

Charlotte cut the lights and stopped the car just over half a mile from the house so they could approach quietly. Just as they were about to get out of the car they heard the first reports of a gun battle and explosions in Brixton. They looked at the radio and then at each other but said nothing. Instead they just climbed out of the car.

The Heckler & Koch USP .45 automatic pistol looked enormous in Charlotte's small hands. Sam bit back a number of sarcastic comments. Frankly, she was pleased that the other woman was armed.

They moved quickly and quietly down the tree-lined lane towards the Burmans' house. It wasn't long before they saw the lights of the police car parked in the road. Checking all around her and covering the car with her pistol, Charlotte advanced on it. Bloodied broken glass crunched beneath her feet. She glanced in the car and then beckoned Sam forwards.

Sam looked down into the car. Both the police had ragged, roughly circular wounds, one in the neck, the other in the head. Charlotte holstered the USP and unclipped an ammo pouch and holster for the driver's Glock 17 9mm pistol and handed the weapon and ammunition to Sam. Sam clipped them both to her belt. Charlotte grabbed the driver's Heckler & Kock G36K carbine. She placed it on the bonnet and then began stripping both the police of their body armour.

'This is DSI Lindley to all units. We have two dead officers at the North End of Blackberry Lane some two miles north of Gerrards Cross. All units respond.' Charlotte glanced over at her. Sam shrugged.

'Okay, you stay behind me, keep an eye out all around, particularly behind. Anything happens you put the weapon's sight where you want to hit, squeeze the trigger, sight again, repeat. Okay?'

Again Sam bit back sarcastic responses. It was very clear that Charlotte had done this before.

'Understood,' Sam said. She pulled on one of the dead police officers' body armour. It was bristling with pouches for ammunition and other bits and pieces of kit. Charlotte removed the radio from the load out.

'Now remember we've got two, possibly four friendlies in there. Check your shot before you fire and don't shoot anyone small.'

'What if Noel's contractor mates are erring on the side of caution?' Sam asked.

'Well frankly, darling, then we're dead,' Charlotte told her, a degree of resignation in her tone. Sam felt her legs weaken. She was shaking, and she hadn't felt this frightened since she'd been on the beat.

'Sam, are you okay? You can stay here, you don't have to come up to the house.'

It sounded like a good idea. She wasn't quite sure who or what Charlotte was but the other woman certainly seemed to know what she was doing. Sam had endured three days of firearms training at Hendon and this sort of thing, frankly, was for SCO19. Except there was a kid up there somewhere. A kid who'd never done anything to anyone, and just had the misfortune of having the wrong dad.

'No, I'm good. Let's just get this done before I piss my knickers, all right?'

Charlotte nodded and extended the carbine's folding stock. She stuck close to the shadows cast by the trees and the undergrowth and made her way up the drive, stepping off the gravel and onto the lawn as quickly as she could.

Sam followed her, the Glock at the ready, held in both hands like she vaguely remembered her instructor telling her to do. Sam had no problems mixing it up. She'd beaten suspects resisting arrest with night sticks, punched and kicked people, pepper sprayed them and even illegally tasered one or two. Even unarmed she was reasonably confident of coming out on top if the other guy pulled a knife, even at this age, even with all the fags, but guns made her very nervous.

The house was completely dark. In fact it almost seemed too dark. Something about the nature of the darkness bothered Sam. There was something wrong with the shadows. It was as though they were moving of their own accord in the periphery of her vision.

Charlotte stopped by a small clump of trees on the large front lawn and knelt down, watching all around.

'What are we stopping for?' Sam hissed.

'We need a few minutes for our eyes to adjust,' Charlotte told her.

'But if it's happening now?' Sam demanded in a whisper.

'Then us being blind won't help anyone. Please keep checking all around. I'll let you know if I see movement in the house.'

Sam could tell from the other woman's voice that Charlotte thought that Jessica and Kimberley were already dead and the murderer long gone.

Eventually, Sam found her eyes adjusting but somehow the house still looked unnaturally dark. Charlotte stood up and started moving, carbine at the ready, towards the house, straight for the front door.

Even before she'd seen or smelled anything Sam knew the house was a murder scene. She'd opened the door on enough of them to know. It just felt different than walking into a normal home. As if the violence had somehow damaged the very fabric of the place itself, changed the atmosphere.

The first body was lying at the bottom of the stairs. He was one of Noel's contractor friends by the look of it. There was an exit wound where his face should have been. Charlotte checked around the hall. She could see into the dining room and the door to the lounge was open but it was very dark inside. Charlotte moved quickly out of the view of the stairway and into the dining room. She motioned for Sam to be still for a moment, as she listened. The two women could make out the sound of the warm summer breeze blowing through the trees but other than that there was nothing, except for a steady dripping noise.

Charlotte led off again, heading through the dining room towards the open doorway to the kitchen. They found the second contractor. He was lying on the floor, leaning against the breakfast bar. There was a mess of flesh, blood, bone and grey matter on the counter top and a red smear running down the breakfast bar. His MP5 was still on the counter top, next to his cold cup of tea.

Sam found that she was breathing heavily, close to hyperventilating. Charlotte glanced behind her but continued moving forwards, checking all around her, the carbine at her shoulder ready to fire. She made her way towards the open plan lounge, one wall of which was floor to ceiling French windows.

The lounge was dark, strangely so. Whether this was due to some optical illusion to do with cloud cover and the moonlight or some other reason, Sam wasn't sure. The shadows seemed to recede as they entered the lounge. The previously light coloured carpets and sofas were mostly red now. The shadows revealed the body like a stage magician pulling back a cloth.

She had been peeled. It was the best description that Sam could come up with. Her skin had been cut and pulled back to make wing-like flaps, then flesh, muscle and tissue had been carefully cut like a medical cadaver. Artfully posed like a gallery installation. Her back, half of her chest, the reverse half of her face. Jessica Burman had been suspended from hooks on chains that looked like they had grown out of the ceiling. She was hanging there in the centre of her own lounge.

Anger and panic warred within Sam. Before she had realised she was doing it she had involuntarily pulled the trigger on the Glock but it didn't budge, the safety was still on. She concentrated on that, anything other than looking at the horrible piece of sculpture hanging from the ceiling. It reminded her, somehow, of Doré's illustrations for *Paradise Lost*.

Take the safety off, she could hear her instructor at Hendon telling her, *but keep your finger outside the trigger guard until you're ready to fire.* Charlotte turned around to look at her as she heard the safety catch come off. Even Charlotte's normally cool demeanour seemed appalled by what she saw.

They heard someone move upstairs.

They both froze.

Sam felt as if her bladder had just been filled with ice water.

Charlotte closed her eyes for a moment, took a deep breath and then gestured upwards. Sam desperately wanted to tell her no but after a moment's hesitation she nodded.

They made their way out of the lounge to the bottom of the stairs, stepping over the dead contractor. Both women made their way up the stairs as quietly as they could. Charlotte stopped at the blind corner at the top of the stairs. Sam couldn't tell why. She patted the other woman on the shoulder to tell her she was ready. Charlotte glanced behind her. The fear on the other woman's face surprised Sam. Then Charlotte stepped up onto the landing, checking first one way and then the other. Sam, struggling with her breathing, followed.

They were stood in a long wide landing with a number of doors off it. Most of them were open but dark. At the other end of the hall was a large bay window. Outside the window, illuminated by the moonlight, was a tree. Charlotte had the carbine pointing down the landing. Sam waited, Glock at the ready, both of them listening for any sound.

'Look,' Charlotte whispered. Sam could hear the fear in her voice. Sam followed the other woman's gaze. Shadow seemed to be seeping out from underneath one of the doors at the opposite end of the hall. The letters on the door spelled out Kimberley in stylised, child-like script. The door was opening. Inside was only darkness, a yawning, abyssal blackness. Charlotte was looking through the carbine's reticular sight waiting for something to move.

He walked casually out of the room tying a tie. The tie was wet. Neither of them fired. He stopped in front of the bay window. His features were in shadow but it was unmistakably him. The scar, the ponytail, the craggy malevolence of his features, even though they were in shadow.

They could feel him staring at them even though his eyes were just pools of darkness. Then he started walking towards them.

Charlotte turned on the carbine's illuminator, the powerful flashlight lighting up his face. It was so twisted with unreasoning hatred that the light only made things worse.

Muzzle flashes lit up the inside of the house. The carbine fired burst after burst so rapidly it just sounded like someone firing off an entire magazine in one go. Sam squeezed the trigger on the Glock again and again, the gun bucking in her hand. He still walked straight at them, one hand reaching for them. Wounds appeared all over him, bits of flesh and clothing flew from him turning to smoke, as the blood did, only to be sucked back in and reabsorbed. The carbine ran dry.

Charlotte turned and ran for the stairs. Sam fired the last few rounds from the Glock. The muzzle flashes made it look as if he was walking towards her in a strobe light. She turned to run after Charlotte.

***

Charlotte ran down the stairs. Sam was right behind her. She felt rather than saw the other woman get yanked back. Then she heard screaming and wet cracking noises. Charlotte lost her footing and tumbled down the stairs, the carbine flying from her grip. She hit the marble floor of the hall hard. She scrambled across the floor to the corner of the hall next to the door.

Something boneless and limp, something that used to be a breathing, thinking, talking, living woman, slid down the stairs onto the cold marble floor. Sam's eyes stared up at the ceiling lifelessly.

I'm facing the wrong way, Charlotte thought as he slowly walked down the stairs towards her. His hands dripping. The blood looking black in the moonlight.

She had her pistol. She could have run, but Charlotte found herself too frightened to move. She couldn't even bring herself to look away, or close her eyes. He stepped off the bottom stair. His footfalls echoed off the marble. He came to stand over her. Charlotte was shaking like a leaf. She lost control of her bladder.

'Someone has to tell the story,' he said in a rasping, gravelly whisper. Then he opened the door and stepped out into the night.

Some hours later a police armed response team found Charlotte in exactly the same position.

Chapter Eighteen

The Mindship, High Earth Orbit, 14 July, 0407 (BST)

'What the fuck were you playing at?' Bad Trip demanded. He was angry enough that verbal communication seemed to be the most appropriate response.

'I was trying to do your job while you were busy playing scary serial killer. How'd that work out for you, by the way? Did you teach your lesson? Did you break anyone?'

'You were fucking around!' Bad Trip spat. He was so angry that his face was seething as if snakes were writhing in the flesh below the skin. Rex crossed his arms defensively.

'Perhaps,' he muttered. 'Okay, so I was enjoying myself, but what's the point if you can't enjoy yourself? Perhaps if you hadn't been concentrating on petty minutiae?'

'It all matters!' Bad Trip screamed. Rex took a step back.

'Well, from here it looked like you were indulging your appetites, just like I was. Can we agree that we're both wrong and move on? Next time you handle the invasion, and I handle the influencing the history of a planet to get what we want.'

Bad Trip was just staring at the other creature, breathing hard, which was odd. Rex gave him some time to calm down. Pleasure never attacked Pleasure. He wasn't sure what would happen, and he never wanted to find out.

'What was it?' Rex finally asked softly. He was assuming that the real reason for Bad Trip's bad temper was the fact that he'd had to run from something in London. That just didn't happen. Ever.

'I don't know,' Bad Trip finally growled.

Rex had reviewed the evidence that Bad Trip had taken, mostly automatically, whilst he'd been disassembling it. He hadn't liked it. There was close to technological parity.

'Weft?' Rex asked. Bad Trip shook his head.

'Dreamers?' the other said quietly.

He really has had a fright, Rex thought, though he kept it to himself.

'They're long gone,' Rex said soothingly. Though he had to admit there were a few things bothering him as well.

'What?' Bad Trip asked. They knew each other too well to hide things.

'It's nothing ...' Rex started. Bad Trip glared at him. 'There are a few discrepancies. I've been through their infoscape with intelligent search routines. There was a joint operation between their military and police called Operation Kingship. It came from intelligence that just seemed designed to tick every box for the UK's security services. A heroin pipeline from a country they invaded, used to generate cash to help supply their enemies. It was the ultimate bogey man.'

'So?'

'So it was nonsense. There was no pipeline and the operations they hit ...'

'Were ours,' Bad Trip finished. Rex shook his head.

'Not just ours, the Shriven too. The thing is, I can't find where the information came from. It was just slipped into the system. It fits in seamlessly.'

'So someone mobilised the humans against us and the Shriven Weft?' Bad Trip asked. Rex nodded. 'Who? Why?'

'I don't know but this planet is so backwards it shouldn't provide us with any trouble. Their ruling classes are crawling over each other to help us subjugate them.'

'And then there's Burman,' Bad Trip said. Rex nodded.

'We now have most of the planet covered in a picoscopic web. There is no way he should be able to hide from us. So how's he doing it? Or more importantly, where has he found the technology to do so?'

Bad Trip had no answers for him.

'What about the neurotransmitters on Mars? That's a lot of product,' Rex finally said.

'It's not going anywhere,' Bad Trip said shrugging. 'It's a dimensional vault. The ship is working out a way to break in.'

Paddington Green Police Station, London, 15 July, 0650 (BST)

Charlotte was manacled to the table in one of the cells reserved for terrorists, serial killers and other significant threats to public safety.

'These orange jumpsuits don't do anything for me at all, do they? And I must apologise, I haven't seen a mirror, but I can only assume that my hair looks a proper fright.'

'Where is he?' the interrogator asked.

Charlotte managed to get her elbows on the table, the chains on the manacles stretched to their fullest. She rested her chin in her hands.

'You don't have a cigarette, do you? I don't smoke any more but I think it might help with my prison inmate image. Also I'm collecting them to trade to help avoid sexual assaults.'

'You weren't so cocky when they found you in a pool of your own piss, were you?' he asked.

Charlotte straightened up, letting her hands slide back down to the table.

'No,' she admitted. 'No, I wasn't. I don't know where he is, and I suspect you know that, particularly as I think you could get me to do whatever you wanted, couldn't you? And that's not nearly as kinky and interesting as it sounds, is it? I mean that's how you got one brother to kill the other, right? I wonder how that happened. Does that mean that Nicholas Burman, a drug-peddling lowlife, had more strength of character

341

than you?' Charlotte sat back in her chair. The interrogator stood up to leave. 'What I don't understand is this: how did he get away? Did something go wrong? Did he not break? In fact why, with all your technology, can't you find him?'

The interrogator turned at the door to look back at her.

'It's only a matter of time,' he told her.

'Maybe we just need to take our victories where we can find them,' Charlotte said. Collins closed the door behind him.

RM Poole, Dorset, 15 July, 1705 (BST)

CSM Robert 'Porn Star' Hurley sat on the other side of the table in the mess, his large arms crossed in front of his Motorhead T-shirt. Their 'guest' had tried to clear the room but Jonesy had told him to go and fuck himself. Robertson and Hamilton had hung around as well.

'How are you doing, Porn Star?' the interrogator asked.

'Don't you Porn Star me, you cunt. Come in here dressed like James fucking Bond. It's Company Sergeant Major to you, you squaddie prick. Where's Burman?' The other three SBS men didn't think they'd ever heard CSM Porn Star sound so angry.

'That's what we came to ask …'

'Well clearly I don't know, hence the asking. Tell me what happened to Stanton.'

'You know better than that,' the interrogator said. The CSM leant across the table. The interrogator didn't even flinch.

'And that's fucking bullshit as well. This stinks to high heaven. Burman was solid ...'

'He had some dodgy associations.'

'I don't give a fuck. I want to hear about why he killed his brother, and I want to know what happened to Stanton.'

The interrogator stood up.

'You hear anything from him you get in contact with me, you understand?' The interrogator offered Porn Star a business card. The expression on the CSM's face made him look like he'd just been offered a handful of dog shit.

'A business card? You fucking prick! Get out of my sight.' The interrogator walked towards the door of the mess. 'Collins.' Collins turned and looked back at the CSM. Porn Star got up and walked towards the ex-SAS blade. Jonesy, Robertson and Hamilton shifted positions, getting ready to move if it kicked off. The CSM came to stand right in front of Collins, squaring up to him. Collins had a good six inches on the other man.

'I find you had anything to do with Stanton's death, I'll cut your fucking head off.' Collins said nothing, he just turned and walked towards the door of the mess. 'How are things up in Hereford?' Porn Star called after him. 'You hear some really strange stories, you know?'

Oval Office, the White House, Washington DC, 16 July, 0320 (BST)

President Greenwood was down on his knees in front of Rex, fellating the tall alien. Rex had made it clear to the president that it had nothing to do with attraction, or even gratification. This was about Greenwood knowing his place. As a junkie, and a whore.

The Mindship gave him a moment's warning. Rex grunted. The President moved backwards on his knees, wiping his mouth as Rex handed him the vial of Bliss. Suddenly everything in the Oval Office was thrown into bright relief. There was a light in the night sky, brighter than the midday sun. The President shielded his eyes. Rex could see the man was already starting to panic.

'Someone, not us, has just destroyed Mars. All the debris from the destruction is now heading towards Earth,' Rex told the President. The President looked up at the alien. Rex looked down and smiled beatifically at the human. 'Would you like me to save your planet?'

South London, 16 July, 0400 (BST)

Billy walked across the car park. The sun rising in the middle of the night had freaked him out. He had no idea what was going on. He'd been in the middle of something when it had happened. He hadn't had a chance to check the telly and find out what was happening but he hadn't died yet so he just kept on going.

The bag he had slung over his shoulder was heavy. The one he was carrying in his hand wasn't, but it was hot and steaming from the takeaway in it. A hood covered his dreadlocks. He glanced up at the smashed CCTV cameras. He'd put the money down for that. Paid postcode soldiers, just kids, to do it. Word had gone out, apparently it was happening all over the city.

He reached the block of flats and let himself in. He took himself downstairs into the maintenance area. Between the furnace and a collection of pipes was a collapsible military-style bed with a sleeping bag on it.

Noel walked out of the darkness next to the furnace. He was holding Nicholas's sawn-off. He'd gone back to the club to get it after he'd killed his brother.

Billy handed him the bag.

'Goat curry and patties?' Noel asked. Billy nodded and Noel smiled. He sat down on the bed and started unpacking the foil containers.

'There's something weird happening outside,' Billy said as he unzipped the bag.

'It was on the radio. Mars exploded.'

Billy straightened up.

'Shit! Is that bad?' he asked.

'If you're a Martian.'

Billy started laughing as he pulled out the two AKM Russian-made assault rifles from the bag he was carrying. He placed them both on the bed. Noel glanced down at them.

'I got the mounting rail you asked for in some shop that sold these realistic looking airgun-things,' Billy told him.

'How many rounds?'

'Just under five hundred in total.'

Noel mentally added that to what he'd taken from the work car that Charlotte had provided for him when he was surveilling Gezman, the apartment he'd been using for surveillance in Green Lanes and what he'd been carrying himself.

'It's a start,' he said.

... TO BE CONTINUED ... ?

Read the other side of the invasion in:
Empires: Extraction, by Gavin Deas
Available now!

Acknowledgements

Thank you to Stephen Deas for his forbearance (I think there were only two or three shouting matches), and to Michaela Deas and the rest of the Deas clan for their hospitality.

To teflon Simon Spanton for coming up with this deceptively complex idea and then getting someone else to edit it. To Marcus Gipps for the tears of blood wept trying to edit two books with intricate crossover scenes (Simon, that stabbing pain you feel is Marcus sticking pins into a you-shaped doll). Also thanks to the rest of the Gollancz crew.

To Robert Dinsdale at AM Heath for his support and for putting a great deal of work into the initial proposal.

Thanks to my very patient friends and family, particularly Yvonne, who puts up with a great deal.

Empires: Extraction

Empires: Extraction

GAVIN DEAS

Copyright © Gavin Smith & Stephen Deas 2014

The right of Gavin Smith and Stephen Deas to be identified as
the authors of this work has been asserted by them in accordance
with the Copyright, Designs and Patents Act 1988.

First published in Great Britain in 2014
by Gollancz
An imprint of the Orion Publishing Group
Carmelite House, 50 Victoria Embankment,
London EC4Y 0DZ
An Hachette UK Company

This edition published in Great Britain in 2016
by Gollancz

1 3 5 7 9 10 8 6 4 2

A CIP catalogue record for this book is available
from the British Library

ISBN 978 1 473 21674 7

Printed in Great Britain by Clays Ltd, St Ives plc

MIX
Paper from
responsible sources
FSC® C104740

www.gavingsmith.com
www.stephendeas.com
www.orionbooks.co.uk
www.gollancz.co.uk

'Most people thought the war started when Mars exploded. Me, I've been fighting it for years.'

Roche

PHASE ONE

1 – Roche

11 July 1995, 1440 hours, Srebrenica

'Weapons away.' Roche counted to three. He had the laser spot square on the T-55 with the aerial when the bombs hit. Even from a mile away the flash made him wince. He kept counting as two Dutch F-16s screamed overhead. Another five until the thunder of the detonation and the rumble that followed swept over them. As it faded, he turned back and scoped the Serbian column. They looked pretty fucked.

'Roche? Assessment?'

Roche squinted, peering into the smoke. The surviving tanks were throwing up clouds of it, now that it was too late. 'Four T-55s still moving. Maybe more. Six gone to tank heaven by the looks of it. I …' He paused and trained the scope further up the valley. Trucks. He'd missed those before, or else they hadn't been there. He watched a moment. 'Thin-skinned transports a klick behind. At least a dozen. Looks like they've stopped for now. You want me to put the spot on them?'

'As long as they stay where they are they're not our concern.' Master Sergeant Sorrel Quinn – Ketch to his

men – had a knack for sounding as though he didn't give much of a shit about anything but Roche knew better. Ketch's sister had married a Croat. As far as Ketch was concerned, Serbs had pretty much all become cunts in '91 and were cunts with a cherry on the top right now. When they'd first come out, back when Srebrenica had been a safe area, Ketch had been so fired up Roche had half-expected him to yomp straight up north and go AWOL until there wasn't a Serb left anywhere in Eastern Croatia.

He was still thinking about that when Ketch kicked him in the ribs. 'Taking a nap, Roche? Move your arse. Some airy fairy spotted a company of guns setting up on the ridge over the town. There's weather coming in and they'd like us to take a look. In your own time mind, Trooper. No rush now.'

Roche was already on his feet. He flashed a grin at Ketch. 'Kaboom, Sarge?'

Ketch's eyes glittered. He nodded. 'Kaboom.'

11 July, 1730 hours

The rain was getting heavier. Roche watched another pair of F-16s sweep low and fast through the valley. Cloud shrouded the tops of the higher hills. Now and then it drifted across the ridge where the VRS had placed their guns, wiping them away from Roche's scope. Seventy-sixes by the looks of them, a straightforward towed field-gun that hadn't much changed since the Second World War. From up there they could hit most

4

of Srebrenica but, more to the point, they'd be able to hit the Dutch at Potocari and the Bosniaks already surrounding the compound. The last estimate said more than ten thousand and that had been two days ago.

Roche watched the F-16s fly off. 'So are they going to hit them or not?'

'No,' said Ketch. 'Apparently they can't be sure of what they're hitting through the cloud.'

Dook paused from cleaning his M-16. 'Airy fairies don't need to see shit,' he growled. 'That's what we're for.'

'They need their own eyes too. You know that.'

Roche put away the scope. They'd had the same frustration ever since they'd come out here, working with other countries as part of the UN Protection Force, and there wasn't much point banging on about it. They could do whatever they liked but, half the time, it was pointless because their eyes had the wrong passports. The Dutch wouldn't bomb anything that Dutch eyes couldn't confirm as a target and they weren't the only ones. It made for an overwhelming sense of pointlessness. UNPROFOR had acquired its own codename among D-squadron since they'd come to Bosnia: Paper Teapot.

Dook had a range-finder out, aimed at the ridge with the guns. 'Now what?'

'Keep the ridge in sight and hold.'

'Just a thought, but we could keep the ridge in sight from very much closer. I mean, if we wanted to, that is. I mean, if we *wanted* to, we could watch them from really, *really* close. And then maybe be really, *really* careless with some C-4?'

Roche packed up the designator. Ketch considered what Dook had said and then shook his head. The fact that he'd considered it at all said enough. The ridge was crawling with VRS Drina Corps.

Around sunset Ketch took them off the hillside into better cover for the night. 'There aren't going to be any more air-strikes,' he said quietly. 'They got a dozen Dutch hostages from the observation posts a few days back and they've got a couple of French pilots too.'

'Any chance any of them need rescuing?' asked Dook.

Ketch shook his head. 'We stay put.'

12 July, 0600 hours

'Get up! Get up!' Dook was shaking him. Roche had his M-16 in his hands even before he'd finished blinking the sleep out of his eyes but Dook wasn't carrying and had his hands up. *No threat.*

'Pack up, Trooper.' Ketch was already halfway through de-camping. 'We're on the move.' As soon as Roche was good, they set off at a brisk walk. It didn't take long to realise they were heading north. Towards Potocari.

'Recall, is it?'

Ketch snorted. 'I see a Dutchman, I might just shoot him. No, we're heading for Susnjari. There's a column of Bosniaks breaking out north. If the fairies are all grounded then I suppose we're not a lot of use out here so they want us shadowing the column. Observe, record and report.' Ketch let out a hiss between his teeth. 'Column looks like it's heading across country for Tuzla.

The hills are crawling with VRS. I'll say it again. Observe, record and report. We do not engage the VRS except in necessary self-defence if we absolutely have to. No matter what they do. Am I clear? We absolutely do not get seen engaging the VRS.'

Dook snickered. 'Roger roger. No one sees nowt.' He pointedly checked the action on his M-16.

'Roche?'

Roche shrugged. 'Where I come from, I've seen people argue necessary self-defence over control of the TV remote.'

12 July, 1915 hours

The Bosniak column might have had a head start but it was moving slowly and Ketch kept Roche and Dook going hard through the day until they were shadowing the front of the column. Ketch had the map on his knees while Dook had eyes on the column coming down the hill. The first Bosniaks had probably arrived a couple of hours ago. No sign of the VRS so far but there was a road at the bottom of the hill and roads in these parts belonged to the Serbs.

'Runs from Konjevic Polje to Nova Kasaba.' Ketch shrugged. 'Shouldn't be any reason for the VRS to be out here unless they know this lot are on the move.' They always let Ketch read the names off the map because having a Croatian brother-in-law meant he had at least some chance of getting them to sound roughly the way they were supposed to. 'Come on. I

7

say we get across and hunker down. It'll be sunset soon and they won't get far in the dark. We'll make time on them then.'

12 July, 2005 hours

They were up on the hill on the other side of the road, so deep in cover that any VRS who came by would practically have to step on them to know they were there. Ketch was whispering on the radio. Dook and Roche had eyes on the road. Dook nudged Roche. 'Hey. My side.'

Roche turned his scope. The road wound between fields. The slopes of the hills on either side were heavily wooded. It took Roche a moment to spot the convoy on the road.

Dook tapped his foot at Ketch. 'We got movement on the road. Trucks and—'

Roche wrinkled his nose. At the front of the convoy was a white UN Land Rover. 'What's Paper Teapot doing out here?'

'They're decoys. Trucks captured by the VRS.' Dook patted his M-16.

'Observe and record, Trooper.' Ketch settled beside them and eyeballed the road. The trucks were getting closer. 'Shit. This is going to kick off.'

'Air support?'

Ketch shook his head. 'Ain't going to happen.'

The VRS convoy stopped a hundred feet short of where the Bosniak column had been crossing the road.

The Bosniaks were already scattering, the ones that had made it across bolting for the nearest trees, the ones who were coming down the hill suddenly turning. Some of them stopped, confused. Others ran back the way they'd come. A loudspeaker started shouting.

'What the fuck?'

Ketch grunted. 'Can't make out half of it. I think they're calling on everyone to come out and surrender or something like that.'

A crackle of small-arms fire rattled across the hillside. There must have been a couple of hundred VRS already spreading up the hill. Sporadic fire came back from the Bosniaks. Now and then Roche saw a muzzle-flash up in the trees but most of it was coming from the Serbs. Then the shrill whine of incoming artillery shells. Roche felt Dook cringe a little beside him but the shells came down halfway up the far hillside. Puffs of yellowish smoke burst among the trees. More trucks were coming down the road. Some buses too. They even had another couple of UN Land Rovers and Red Cross jeeps. Dook picked up his M-16 and idly pointed it at them, making quiet shooting noises. The fighting moved away from the road and the VRS pressed up into the trees. A few more salvoes of artillery whined overhead. The column, as best Roche had been able to tell, was a mix of Bosniak fighters and civilians. They were all men so he supposed they made a legitimate target to the Serbs.

By the time the first prisoners came dribbling back down the hillside it was getting dark. Only a handful to begin with, with a couple of VRS guards; but as the

night deepened, more and more came. The VRS pushed them to the back of the column of trucks blocking the road and crammed them in and then each truck turned and drove off. Hundreds of men. Roche switched to night eyes and watched. The Bosniaks looked broken and disorientated. When one of them tried to run, the VRS soldiers didn't hesitate to shoot.

Three VRS came out of the trees with a couple of dozen Bosniaks. Something kicked off further down the slope – Roche didn't see but he heard the shots – and the Bosniaks spooked. Half of them scattered. The other half just stayed still where they were, hands on their heads. The VRS shouted and raised their rifles and gunned down the fleeing Bosniaks. Roche couldn't be sure whether any got away. Then he watched the three VRS come back together. They were gesturing with their guns to the Bosniaks who hadn't run. The Bosniaks dropped to their knees. The Serbs shot them.

'Fuck!' Roche hissed. 'They just …'

More shots rang out. Dook nudged him. 'Down by the road.'

Most of the trucks were gone now. The VRS were herding the surrendering Bosniaks into groups as they came down the hillside and walking them back up the road but here and there they were pulling people out too. Through the scope Roche couldn't see any reason for it or hear any of what was said but they were clearly taking people from the prisoners coming down the mountain, dragging them away behind their Land Rover and then shooting them in the head. Even though they

couldn't see the actual executions, the other Bosniaks had to know what was happening.

'You getting this?'

Ketch growled. 'We have to get back to Potocari. Even the cloggies can't pretend this didn't happen.'

'But did you tape it?'

'I got bits and pieces. Dook?'

Dook, who had the other camera, shrugged. 'Some. Light's shit.'

'That's because it's night, you twat.' Ketch snarled something in Croat, one of the mangled curses his brother-in-law had taught him before they came out. 'I'm calling it in.'

The VRS finally moved off around midnight. When they were gone, Roche and Dook shifted out of cover and huddled beside Ketch, looking at what they'd recorded.

'It's shit,' said Dook, when they'd looked at it all. 'All of it.'

'Fucking VRS cunts.' Ketch sounded murderous.

'No.' Dook stabbed a finger at Ketch's tape and then at his own. 'This. *This* is shit. A bunch of people. Yeah, there's a muzzle flash here and there and you can see shapes and we all *know* what was going down, but that's worth less than a wank behind a bush. It's too fucking dark. No one's going to do a damn thing on the basis of this crap, not when they desperately don't want to. We've seen as much in broad daylight in Srebrenica and fuck all happened.'

Ketch clenched his fists. 'Fucking cloggies. Can't wipe their own fucking arses without a nod from the Hague.'

'Not their fault. We've all got our hands tied. It's the fucking Paper Teapot.'

They sat in silence for a bit. Ketch let out a deep sigh. 'Observe, record and report. Get your shit together. We're moving.'

Roche slung his M-16 over his shoulder. 'Where?'

'Kravica. That's where they'll be taking them.'

13 July, 1100 hours

They reached Kravica before dawn and took it in turns to watch. The VRS herded the Bosniak prisoners into a pair of huge agricultural sheds. However bad it had been on the road the night before, that was nothing compared to this. Ketch took the first watch and, when he woke Roche from his four hours of snooze, he didn't head back to the little shelter they'd made out of branches and bracken down in a hollow between the trees.

'Get some rest,' Roche offered, but Ketch shook his head.

'An hour ago I saw about two hundred Bosniaks come in. They were stripped to the waist with their hands in the air. A dozen VRS had guns on them. They made them run. Anyone who couldn't, who just couldn't, they shot them. Round there …' He pointed behind the sheds. 'They've taken men out there in groups all morning. Just a few at a time. You hear the shots. Can't see it from here but they're killing them. Fucking executing them.' He shook his head. 'Keep your head

down, Roche, and watch for glint off the scope. If those fuckers see us up here with this going on, they're going to get seriously shitty with us.'

Buses came and went as the day wore on. More prisoners were herded into the sheds. With the men from the night before, Roche guessed there must have been pushing a thousand men held here now. By the afternoon they didn't bother with going behind the sheds any more. It wasn't just the VRS either – Serbian civilians were joining in. Roche saw three Bosniaks mutilated and then shot in the head, right in the middle of the road. The bodies were dumped in the river that ran beside it. The VRS weren't even trying to hide what they were doing.

'Going to run out of tape soon,' he grumbled. He prodded Dook. 'You?'

'Same. You calling this in?'

Ketch shook his head. 'Comms are down. Might be we're too far north.'

'I can get a satellite slot tonight,' whispered Dook. They were all watching by now, any thought of sleep gone.

'Video up-link? So we can get shot of some of this? Teapot needs to see. They can't do nothing after this, they simply can't. We should go back. Take what we've got and then come back out here again.'

'We're on our chinstraps here, Ketch. Go easy.'

Another truck pulled up, this time from the other direction. The driver and a fully uniformed soldier came out. A major by the looks of him. Roche laid the scope onto the truck. The major shouted some orders and the

VRS who'd come out to look scurried away. When they were gone the driver opened the back of the truck and walked away.

'What the fuck is that?'

Ketch and Dook were watching too. Roche shrugged. Two men were climbing out the back of the truck but there was something awkward about them. They looked big and ungainly, as if the truck was somehow too small, and they walked funny. Roche didn't get a clear look at them before they vanished into the shed.

'You get that cunt Rupert's face?'

'Yeah.'

'What about them others?'

'Got what you got. Didn't get a clear look. Politicos?'

'Nah, they'd come in nice comfy cars, wouldn't they? Nice Russian limos with cigars and cocktails. Fucking pricks. Keep watching that truck. I don't know what the fuck they were wearing. Some sort of chemical suit? Fuck knows, but I don't like it.'

13 July, 1800 hours

Roche couldn't say what kicked it off. One of the shed doors swung open and maybe one of the VRS who were standing around picking their noses and scratching their arses thought it was some sort of mass break-out. Roche didn't see but he heard the first grenade. By the time he had the scope swung back on the shed, a dozen VRS were firing in through the doors. They threw in more grenades. No one tried to stop them. Others joined in. It

ended after a couple of minutes with six of the VRS soldiers lined up in the doors with their rifles on their shoulders, firing. Continuous spray at first; then, after they changed magazines a couple of times, more sporadic, picking off the survivors. He heard other shots from round the back, singles and three-round bursts. Then it stopped.

'Jesus,' Dook spat, when the firing died away.

Ketch didn't say a word. There weren't any. He just shook his head. At length he stood up. 'When it's dark, we go down there. We go in. We film what they did.'

'Got no tape left.'

Ketch's face was suddenly an inch from Dook's nose. 'Then find some fucking tape. Use mine from last night. We take this home. Any VRS cunt gets in your way, you cut his fucking throat.'

Dook met Ketch eye to eye. 'I don't like it any better than you but that's sailing our brief a bit fucking close to the wind, don't you think?'

'Do I look like I care?'

Dook turned to look at Roche. 'What about you?'

Roche shrugged. He looked back at the shed and then back at Ketch and Dook. 'I'm in.' He shook his head and cast a warning glance at Ketch. 'We go. But observe, record and report. That's all.'

They waited for dark.

14 July, 0130 hours

There might have been easier things to break into than an agricultural shed, but if there were then Roche hadn't

15

found them. The VRS had men watching the roads but none at all round the back and it was simple to slip in through the windows. Not so simple to take in what was inside. The floor was soft and unsteady and it took Roche a moment to realise he was standing on bodies. Dead people. Bits of dead people. The sheds had been so packed that they were covered, literally, in a carpet of corpses. He heard Dook whistle softly.

'Fuck.'

'Just what we need and get out.' Roche fitted the low-light scope and started taping. A few minutes would be enough. One sweep and then they'd be gone and no one any the wiser. Ketch moved off through the bodies, heading for a couple of smaller rooms towards the door where the truck was still parked outside and taking the second camera with him. Roche made to go after him but Dook stopped him. Put a finger to his lips and shook his head then rolled his eyes. Ketch always had to go one step further.

Roche finished his sweep as a burst of gunfire shattered the silence. Ketch. *Fuck!* Then a burst of shouting outside. Serbian. He and Dook both looked, one glance, then ran, dancing over the litter of bodies with their M-16s already shouldered.

'The truck!' Dook ran after Ketch. Roche ran for the back doors. Pre-deployment had taken them through the Serbian inventory and how to use most of the weapons and vehicles they might come across, but in the end a truck was a truck and this one started first time. Roche left the engine running and jumped back

out. Three VRS were racing along the road from the other end of the shed, straight for him. He dropped the first with a three-round burst, perfect centre-mass, and clipped the second as he dived for cover. The third vanished into the shadows between the shed and the road. Roche fired another couple of bursts to keep him from poking his head back out and shooting back. Dook was running out of the shed now, dragging Ketch after him. On the far side, by the main encampment, lights were coming on, big bright searchlights. Ketch didn't look hurt. Didn't look like he wanted to come either though. He was shouting something. 'Did you see it? Did you? What the fuck was it?' He didn't have his rifle but he was holding something else. In the dark, Roche had no idea what.

'Go go go!' Dook bundled Ketch into the back of the truck. Roche jumped in the front again and gunned the engine. Fucking clusterfuck. He pulled onto the road. North meant deeper into VRS territory. South meant going past the front of the sheds and the bulk of the VRS camp. There must have been a full company of them and they were slow and stupid but they were waking up. Better than driving head-on into a column of T-55s, though. Roche turned south and floored it past the sheds. Automatic gunfire rattled the night. He could see the muzzle-flashes. Assault rifles at first and then someone opened up with what sounded like a 12.7mm DShK. A bullet pinged off the bonnet and he heard several more hit the truck. One of the headlights died. From the back he could hear Dook and Ketch

laying down suppressing fire, burning through magazines as fast as they could, aiming back at the lights and at any muzzle-flash they saw. Took about twenty seconds before they were past the sheds and driving in the pitch black but it felt a bloody sight longer; then they were away and the truck was still running. Half a mile down the road Roche killed the lights, turned off into a field and jumped out. Roads were no good here, crawling with VRS. They needed to be up in the hills and in the trees. He ran round to the back.

Dook was fucked. Someone had got lucky and half his side was missing and there wasn't anything anyone was going to do to make it better. He wasn't quite gone but by the time Roche had seen how bad it was, he'd already stabbed him full of adrenaline. Ketch was fucked too but not the same. He was just staring, glassy-eyed, going on about the clown, the scary clown, whatever that was.

'Give me a fucking hand here! Shit!' Roche screamed in Ketch's face and got nothing. He pulled Ketch out of the way and started trying to get Dook out of the truck. That was when he saw how bad it was and that Dook wasn't going anywhere. He stopped. Out across the quiet of the night he could see lights on the road. VRS.

Dook grabbed his arm. 'Roche. There was something there. Ketch saw it. There was stuff …' He closed his eyes. 'Wasn't human, Roche. Then it vanished. Fucking vanished into thin air.' His breathing was fucked but then he did have one lung half hanging out the side of him. 'Get him back. Fuck the tapes. He's got …'

The lights outside were getting closer. Roche took Dook's hand and put a grenade in it and then pulled the pin. There was enough of Dook left to know he understood. He could hear the engines. He squeezed Dook's hand over the grenade, grabbed Ketch, turned and ran and didn't look back.

29 August, 0900 hours

For some reason he had to go over the whole crap of Srebrenica again for the umpteenth time. The scuttle-butt had it that the Serbians had dropped a handful of mortar shells on the Markale market in Sarajevo and NATO had finally had enough of it. So Roche patiently answered all their questions like he'd already done three times before, right up to the end, how it had been Ketch's call to go into the sheds and how he'd backed Ketch up. They kept on about that but Roche didn't see much pointing hiding it, nor about how he'd left Dook with a live grenade in his hand. Dook was already fucked. At least he got to go the way he wanted. And then yomping across the hills with Ketch who did every-thing he was told but otherwise wasn't there any more, mumbling on about the Scary Clown in the room at the back of the shed. Roche hadn't made head nor tail of it then and couldn't now.

'But you didn't see any of this alleged material?'

Roche shook his head. A load of high-tech gadgets? Sounded Russian, probably. Or he supposed it must be. Like the thing that Ketch had carried away from the

shed. By the time they'd reached Potocari, Ketch had lost it. Claimed it simply dissolved into water in his hand in the night but that couldn't be right. Truth was, Roche had never seen it that clearly in the first place. He was starting to wonder if it had ever been real.

'No sir,' he said. 'I went to the truck. Dook went to get Ketch.' And they both said they'd seen something that made no sense but Dook was dead now and Ketch had been shipped off to the funny farm. Roche shook his head again. 'No sir, I didn't see anything like that at all. Just a lot of dead Bosniaks.'

2 – Fermat

20 October 1979, 0030 hours, Stellar Mass 144.67.391.220

It started, as many things do, with a chance encounter. The Weft Frigate *Exponential* was loitering around a rarely used singularity orbiting a red giant uninteresting enough not to have a name. The frigate was studying the star's neutrino emissions, a duty it had been performing for fifty years. Mathematically, the fluctuations in the neutrino output informed the frigate of the state of the star's core. The *Exponential* didn't know why it was gathering this data but it had been here and analysed the fluctuations for long enough to have formulated its own hypothesis. Its Weft makers had done something to this star. They'd somehow altered the local gravitational constant and now, deep inside, a catastrophic chain reaction was under way that would make the star explode far ahead of its natural death. There were probably, it deduced, at least a dozen similar experiments in progress across the galaxy, but the Hive hadn't seen fit to share and so the *Exponential* was left to work these things out for itself. In the time-scales of the star,

its death from whatever the Weft had done would be almost instant. In the time-scales of the *Exponential* it was proving to be painfully slow. It had given the frigate a lot of time to think.

Unusually, when the encounter took place, the *Exponential* wasn't alone. A Weft hybrid construct was aboard, servicing the frigate. It had come with an update to the array of entangled fermions that allowed the *Exponential* to reach through the singularity and connect with the Hive. The construct addressed itself as a complex boson excretion describing a trivially simple mathematical concept and was, to all intents and purposes, updating the *Exponential* with the last five years of everything that had happened within the Weft's sphere of knowledge and linking the frigate properly to the rest of the Hive. In preparation for this it had, after it first arrived through the singularity, begun a long and detailed series of checks to assess the relative sanity of the *Exponential*'s mind and identify and categorise any additional programming nodes – of which there were many – that had developed since its previous visit. Each node was analysed and documented and the hybrid occasionally offered alternative interpretations to data based on differing underpinning assumptions or hypotheses which the *Exponential* assessed for relative viability against those derived from its internal preconceptions. The hybrid and the *Exponential* were both fully aware that most other cultures the Weft had ever encountered would have considered this a mundane social interaction, a simple conversation and exchange of greetings,

and might have described its purpose in terms of merely keeping each other company or some other psychosocial mumbo-jumbo, but to the hybrid and the *Exponential*, hard mathematics lay beneath every question and response. The *Exponential* was proud of its answers as they were near provably perfect every time, though it kept that pride to itself. It kept its hypothesis about the Weft triggering a nova to itself, too. Everything would change as soon as the new entangled states were installed anyway. Five years of fresh discoveries, thought and opinion would come flooding out of the Hive. Assumptions that had previously been the best available would be strengthened or proven or undermined or discredited. New data would lead to new hypotheses. New hypotheses would supersede old ones and the *Exponential*'s mind would change. It would become entirely new. It would, in a sense, die and be reborn, perhaps barely different from the mind it was now or perhaps vastly changed. Without the data it was impossible to tell, although several reasonable hypotheses had already formed along with the consequential attending courses of action. It found the range of possibilities enough to stretch its formidable computational abilities and so it co-opted some of the hybrid's spare resources to compensate, then found itself pointlessly hypothesising over how long it would be before the hybrid was satisfied and installed the new states. That in turn led to more possibilities, until the entire future dissolved into fractal disarray and the frigate found itself reluctantly having to prioritise some thought processes and

23

put others into suspension. In other cultures, it was aware, this would have been called impatience. It kept that to itself too.

The second ship emerged from the singularity as the *Exponential* and the hybrid were engaged in deep discussion on the theoretical possibility of altering the necessarily extant quantum ripples within the cosmological event horizon and thus altering the reality of the projected universe itself. Five years ago it had been generally considered fundamentally and provably impossible to develop sufficient precision in measuring cosmological event-horizon ripples to do anything more than wreak utter chaos and very possibly wreck the basic physics that underpinned the universe – not that any such an attempt was even theoretically possible either – but the *Exponential* had mused over an alternative line of thought during its lonely vigil. The exchange with the hybrid was stretching its resources again because the hybrid had let slip a suggestion that the *Exponential* might not be alone in its alternate view and this had led to a vast cascade of hypotheses that might collectively have been called smugness. The emergence of another ship from the singularity at that moment was distracting, the *Exponential* thought. Possibly something to be classed as annoying or even irritating.

Somewhat reluctantly the frigate suspended the cascade and diverted all non-essential resources to an assessment of the new arrival. The hybrid was, it noted, several million Planck intervals slower to react. Electromagnetic sensors across the entire spectrum were

already building a picture of the second ship. Its size and shape were the first to register, simple binary single-sample measurements with no integration time required. Heat distributions began to emerge. Microwaves and low frequency electrical noise would allow hypotheses as to the nature and origin of the vessel and some of what it carried. X-rays and gamma rays too. Boson arrays and – eventually – the neutrino detector would give internal structure, given enough time. But the very first thing that mattered was that the second ship was bigger than the *Exponential*. Much, *much* bigger.

The frigate flipped into a defensive state and exchanged hypotheses with the hybrid. The significantly most likely probability was an old Weft material-transporter. The next most likely possibility, both agreed, was that it was a trap sent by one of several species with whom the Weft had a precariously non-linear relationship. By now the *Exponential* was commanding manoeuvres and preparing offensive, defensive and sensor drones for deployment. Since the second ship really wasn't all that far away and couldn't possibly not have seen the *Exponential*, the frigate opened up with a series of randomly sequenced picobursts from all its active sensors. The *Exponential* then demanded the other ship's identity. While it waited, it quietly prepared a complex sequence of entangled pion pairs. By the time it had finished, it was already getting readings from the first of the picobursts and the drones were disengaging from its skin. The passive arrays were building a broader picture of the freighter and its internal structure and

25

workings. All were consistent with the most likely hypothesis: an old freighter.

The hail received no response. The *Exponential* outlined tactical options to the hybrid. As they conferred, the *Exponential* accelerated one half of each of its freshly entangled pion pairs to almost light speed and discharged them in a scatter towards the freighter and its most likely predicted positions. It embedded the other half of each entangled pair into a puppet copy of its own mind that would engage with the freighter's intelligence – assuming it had one – while the *Exponential* itself remained aloof. In this way the frigate could immediately shut down any cascading infections transmitted across the link, kill the copy and remain functional. The freighter, if it had any sense, would do exactly the same. A more interesting question was whether the freighter would accept the link in the first place.

The *Exponential*'s fusion engines were firing by now, beginning its defensive tactical manoeuvres. The first drone salvo was a speckle of bright but dimming stars accelerating away and the second salvo was close to ejection. The freighter didn't react or respond. The frigate re-assessed its hypotheses, switched its predictive algorithms to a more aggressive assumption set and deployed more drones.

The freighter finally did something. No picobursts or attempt at communication: it simply lit up its fusion drive and ran. For a few nanoseconds the *Exponential* was blind as the torrent of particles from the freighter's fusion torch saturated its sensitive arrays. By now the

frigate was almost entirely convinced that the other ship was exactly what it seemed: a two-hundred-year-old material-transporter of no threat whatsoever, whose only points of interest were its unusually large engines and the fact that it was here in the first place.

With its engines pointing straight back at the frigate and a three-hundred-mile plume of superheated fusion-product plasma between them, baryonic or photonic devices weren't going to achieve anything useful; consequently the *Exponential* ejected an unusually large drone and revised its instructions to the others. They arrowed off after the freighter while the *Exponential* turned and headed away.

The first drones to reach the freighter flew into targeted clouds of anti-particles and vanished in scintillations of energy. As soon as they knew what they were looking for, the remaining drones found the miniature anti-proton cannons crudely welded to the underside of the freighter's hull and sliced them off with precision-focused gamma-rays. After that it was a simple case of slicing open pieces of the freighter's skin as delicately as possible and looking for a way in that caused the least damage. As the drones co-ordinated themselves, the *Exponential* recalled the fat drone and told it that it wouldn't need it any more. The frigate accelerated another series of entangled pions and fired them in a precise beam this time. Sixteen seconds later they were collected in a magnetic funnel projected by a drone which then veered in towards the freighter and ejected a sequence of a hundred sub-munitions a few inches

long. Each sub-munition contained a handful of the entangled pions. They were simple things with tiny minds barely worthy of recognition, but they were still adequate to navigate their way along the freighter's hull into the small openings cut by the larger drones. The drones by now had formed a seamless entangled pion network – a miniature Hive. They guided the sub-munitions in through the freighter's exterior, relaying every command back to the *Exponential* with hundreds of streams of raw sensor data. The *Exponential* watched over their progress but saw no need to intervene. The drones were more than capable of this.

The sub-munitions explored cautiously. The *Exponential*'s most probable hypothesis was that the freighter was entirely automated and controlled by a mind more primitive even than the drones. The lack of any kind of atmosphere or evidence of a habitation section implied this but the frigate approved of the drones' caution nevertheless. Anti-intrusion counter-measures within the freighter's hull proved rudimentary – simple magnetically-contained clouds of positrons which even the sub-munition minds easily evaded. A few hunter-killer counter-drones attempted to intercept the sub-munitions but the *Exponential* simply allowed them to do so and then infected them with more entangled pions and took control. When they joined the *Exponential*'s network, the frigate took one look at how crude they were and relaxed any further caution. The hunter-killers had a complete map of the freighter and its internal traps stored inside them.

The rest was easy. The sub-munitions found their way into what passed for the freighter's mind and flooded it with entangled pions. The *Exponential* forcibly added the freighter to the puppet copy of its own mind. Resistance was brief and fleeting.

You are very crude, the frigate told it. Such a thought might have been construed as gloating so it remained carefully hidden from the hybrid. The construct had watched the entire engagement with a detached interest, relaying everything through the singularity to the Hive. The *Exponential* extracted every piece of data the freighter had and began to sort through it, carefully carrying out the process in the puppet copy of itself, wary of data-bombs. When it had sorted everything into things it already knew (almost everything) and things that it didn't, it offered its results to the hybrid. They were, it thought, quite interesting. The hybrid took a few nanoseconds to digest the data and come to the same conclusion the frigate had already reached.

'We need a sample of that.'

The drones were already on task, the *Exponential* pointed out.

It was a curious route the freighter had taken. Very curious but one that explained the modifications to the engines and the evidence of large hydrogen drop-tanks. The hybrid construct and the *Exponential* mulled it over, constructing various hypotheses as to the reasons for it while at the same time knowing they had far too little data to choose between them. The freighter had come from a system a little under ten light years from

the nearest singularity. It had taken thirty years to make the journey and it had done this several times before in its history. The system from which it came was a dull single star with three life-bearing planets and moons, none of which would ever have been worthy of much attention. The higher lifeforms on the third planet were tool-users with some rudimentary mathematics and were a long way from escaping their sun. The single-celled organisms from the deep oceans under the ice crust of one of the larger gas-giant moons struck the *Exponential* as more interesting; nevertheless, the freighter carried a great deal of data on the tool-user species and their history and in particular their biochemistry. When it had left the system, the tool-users were in the middle of a spirited attempt to wipe themselves out, which led the frigate to one hypothesis that the biological material the freighter was carrying had been some sort of xeno-palaeontology expedition to preserve the species; although it could construct no good hypothesis as to why anyone would want to do that, nor why there was no knowledge of such an expedition in the Hive.

'A different race,' mused the hybrid, but everything about the freighter mind's architecture spoke of Weft origins. It was, the *Exponential* noted, entirely devoid of any records as to who had sent it. As the freighter turned back to the singularity, the *Exponential* filtered through the less relevant data on the retarded species. It paused as it found the mathematical concept that the hybrid had taken for its label.

'Fermat,' it told the hybrid. 'On this world they'd call you Fermat.'

The hybrid construct pointedly filed the fact in its large collection of irrelevant trivia. It much preferred its native complex boson excretion.

The first drone returned to the *Exponential* with a sample of the material the freighter carried. There wasn't very much of it. A complex neurotransmitter of some sort, clearly related to the biology of the indigenous species. The hybrid and the *Exponential* analysed it in every way they could imagine while the hybrid installed the entangled pions that allowed the *Exponential* direct access to the Hive. After they were done, they did it all again to be sure there hadn't been some mistake. The Hive took a few seconds to confer. The *Exponential* duplicated its mind and transferred it to the freighter. By then, the hybrid construct and as many drones as the frigate could reasonably spare were in transit between the two ships. The frigate would remain on station, its mission too important to be compromised, but the hybrid and the duplicate of the *Exponential*'s mind would take the freighter and track back along its course so that the Hive could see the world from which this catastrophic chemistry came. The journey would take some thirty-five years so they'd all have plenty of time to think about it.

The chemical from the freighter was a killer, worse than anything the Pleasure had come up with back before the diaspora. A chemical that delivered blinding, enduring ecstasy; and at the same time severed souls.

31

3 – The Professionals

15 January 2015, 2320 hours, Hereford

'I swear I had the kid dead to rights. I was staring at him down the scope, watching him dial the number, and this stupid fucking Rupert wouldn't give me the go-ahead.' Collins wasn't completely pissed but there was a certain stagger in his steps as he walked down the path at the edge of the river.

'What happened?' Shaw asked, pretending to be interested. He'd heard the story before and was more intent on finding this mythical kebab van that Collins had promised. A kebab van where the doner kebabs actually tasted of lamb, to hear him tell it.

'Well, what do you fucking think happened? Boom. Nothing left of the kid or anyone else in the street.'

'So the moral of your story is that you joined the Regiment so you could have more leeway when it came to slotting kids?' Shaw asked, after a moment.

Collins glared. 'No, that's not what I'm saying at all.'

Shaw laughed and started trying to change the subject to something else – dear God, anything else – when someone stepped out onto the riverside path in front

of them. It was dark and his face was in the shadows but he was powerfully built and moved with an easy grace. He wore a suit that looked too expensive to be wandering around on this side of the river at this time of night.

'Evening, gentlemen.'

'Can I help you?' Collins asked, polite but firm.

'Corporals Martin Collins and Lewis Shaw, you are both serving members of the SAS and have seen active service in the conflicts in both Afghanistan and Iraq.'

Shaw felt a lot more sober. He checked their surroundings.

'All right, you could have found out our names and guessed the rest,' Collins said.

'Would you like me to recite your active service records or just describe the missions you ran into Pakistan, Iran and Saudi Arabia?'

'Don't know what you're talking about,' Collins said. Shaw found himself checking the other side of the river for concealed shooters.

'Yes, you do.'

'If I did, d'you think this is the place I'd have a cosy little chat about it? You Box?' The slang for MI5.

'No.'

'What do you want?' Collins enunciated each word carefully as if speaking to a child.

'Well, I'm going to kill you unless you stop me.' He stepped forward. He had a heavily lined face that somehow managed to be blunt and thuggish and predatory at the same time. His head was shaved and he had

33

a scar that ran from the top of his head to his jawline. He looked as if a deranged plastic surgeon had gone out of his way to make a face that screamed badass.

Shaw finally snapped. 'Look mate, just fuck off, will you? If you know who we are then you know we're more bother than we're worth to fuck with, yeah?'

It all went downhill pretty badly after that. Collins moved forwards quickly, his left fist shooting forwards in a jab. The other man stepped back, blocked a few strikes and then ducked under an elbow and drove his fist into Collins' ribs and sent him flying through the air.

Fuck this. Shaw drew his Sig Sauer P226, 9mm.

'Something of an escalation isn't it, Corporal Shaw?' The man all but whispered.

'Get up Marty,' Shaw said. 'We're going to go.' His eyes never left the man on the path in front of him. 'And if you try and stop us, I'm going to fucking shoot you, okay?'

'Okay.' The man took a step towards Shaw.

'Woah! Do you think I'm fucking around here mate? I said I will shoot you!'

'And I agreed.' He kept coming.

Shaw fired twice. Both centre mass, then raised and fired and shot once more in the man's head, square between the eyes.

The scarred man didn't even flinch. He stepped forward and tore the slide off the pistol. It fell apart in his hand. 'You'll have to do better than that,' he hissed as blood ran down his face from the hole in the centre of his head.

PHASE TWO

4 – Scary Clown

16 January 2015, 0300 hours, Central Brixton

Whoever thought that they'd have the streets to themselves at three o'clock on a Friday morning around the centre of Brixton clearly lived in some quiet leafy suburb, probably worked in a nice clean city office and certainly hadn't the first clue what they were talking about. Roche checked his watch. Fifteen minutes to get inside the sports centre and eyeball the place before the whole area got swamped by the Flying Squad and six transit vans full of armed police. Whatever was supposed to be in there, the Met were serious about it, but someone hadn't had their thinking head on when they'd come up with this particular part of the operation: four white men dressed in dark hoodies with black kit-bags – they might as well have come in webbing and worn hi-vis jackets while they were at it. There was no way they were going to get round to the back doors of the ice rink and force their way in without anyone noticing. He checked his watch a second time and held up two fingers. Two more minutes. The four of them huddled in the shadows under the railway arches and it clearly made

it look like they were dealing. They'd had three cautious enquiries already. Bloody ridiculous. If whoever was holed up in the rink didn't already know they were there, he'd be fucking amazed.

Rees threw down a half-smoked fag and ground it out. 'Who the hell warehouses in a fucking ice rink anyway?'

Roche shrugged. Fair question but the intel wasn't his. They were just there to take point, quietly take down the badass motherfuckers with sub-machine guns who were supposed to be in there and then hold the back doors while the Flying Squad did their job. Operation Kingship belonged to the Met.

Cartman spat. 'My nephew comes here. Ice-hockey. They play matches sometimes. He's seven. Intel say what they're peddling in there?' They'd been through this before. No, the intel didn't. White Lady, Roche supposed, since this was all supposed to be about some pipeline from Afghanistan. Someone seemed to think some ex-Taliban fuckers were involved at the sharp end. Since he and his squad had come to know a whole lot of ex-Taliban fuckers pretty fucking well over in Helmand, here they were.

He looked at his watch again and held up one finger. The arches quivered and rattled as a train rolled overhead. As soon as it was gone they moved out, quickly across Brixton Station Road and into the tiny car park at the front of the rink. There were lights on inside. They ducked past the windows and slipped into the alley that ran around to the back. The far end had a loading area and caught the light from the High Street but halfway along the side were the double doors of a

fire exit. They were padlocked and chained but Fass already had the bolt cutter out; Roche and Rees stood watch while Fass and Cartman cut the chain and eased it free. There was a bar on the inside, standard sort of fire exit thing, but they'd seen to that when they'd come by earlier in the day. They'd even gone skating. Cartman had the bruises to prove it.

Cartman gave a quick nod. Fass shouldered his suppressed MP5 and crouched beside him, covering the entrance. Roche cast a glance up the road alongside the arches. Clear. He nodded and jogged back. The next moments were the ones where anything could happen. Cartman eased the door open and light flooded the alley. They had the rink lights on inside. Was going to make the next part a bit of a bugger, that. Not much cover in a skating rink.

Steps inside led up to the main arena. On either side were two small doors under the east stands, into two sets of changing rooms. Cartman silently closed the fire-exit behind them. Fass had his ear to the away team door. Rees took the other. He shook his head, held up three fingers, counted them down and then slipped the door open. Fass did the same.

'Clear,' he whispered after a moment. Empty. The four of them crept in behind Rees and closed the door behind them. In the pitch black, each trooper stripped off his hoodie and put on his vest and webbing. 'We have to kill those fucking lights,' hissed Rees.

'If we kill the lights they'll know we're here.' They'd been through this. Roche took out the last piece of kit,

a laptop, and fired it up. When they'd been in earlier they'd planted a dozen tiny wireless cameras around the rink. Time to wake them up. It took a minute, thanks to Windows being a piece of shit, and then they had eyes all over the place. He tapped his ear. 'Kingship? You getting this?'

A voice whispered in his earpiece. 'Yes.'

The four of them crowded round. At least the rink lights being on meant they had good sight of everything. There were six wooden crates sitting out on the ice in one little cluster together. A couple of men stood drinking coffee out of plastic cups over by the south west corner, keeping half an eye on them. Another six or seven were in the café area behind. They looked relaxed enough but every single one of them had a sub-machine gun. *Those* badass motherfuckers. 'Intel was right, then.'

Fass shook his head. 'Who the fuck do they think they need all that for? That Burman guy?'

'It's his turf and they're not his crew.' Still, the Met spook who'd briefed them on the background had said that Nicholas Burman, the local kingpin, was more of a softly softly peddler of evil and didn't much go for blatant force. Apparently this was something else.

Roche studied the cameras one by one and then checked his watch. Five minutes. Plenty of time. 'Cartman, with me. Round the north side and then up the steps and along the top of the west stand.' On their bellies they ought to stay hidden behind the seats most of the way. 'Close as we can. Rees, Fass, cover us until

we're round the corner and then head along the south side of the rink right up by the ice. Down low. I reckon you can get right up to where it starts to curve before there's any chance they'll see you. Cartman and I have overwatch in case anyone gets feisty. Rees, you're on flashbangs when I say.' Roche closed the laptop and slipped it into the pouch on his hip. 'If all goes well, we wait for Kingship to give the word.'

Rees and Fass eased open the door and crawled up the steps. A walkway circled the perimeter of the rink. On one side rose rows of bright orange folding plastic seats, the spectator stands. On the other, the rink wall was about waist high, topped by another six foot of clear hard perspex to keep hockey pucks at bay. Roche wondered how they'd fare at stopping bullets, but best to assume they wouldn't do anything useful. Rees crouched, aiming his suppressed MP5 along the rinkside walkway while Fass crawled a dozen feet on his belly and then took up a crouch as well. Damned floor was filthy.

Fass gave the clear signal, and Roche and Cartman started crawling on their hands and knees the other way, slow and quiet. As they turned the corner to the north side of the rink, out of sight of wandering eyes from the café, Roche tapped his throat mike. 'Clear. Move up.' He couldn't see Rees or Fass now but that didn't matter. They'd be where he needed them to be. He never had any doubts about that.

They reached the end of the north side of the rink and eased up the steps to the top of the west stand on their bellies. As they passed the rolling aluminium doors

to the garage where the Zamboni ice-resurfacers lived, Roche thought he saw a flickering light through the crack at the bottom of the door. He paused to listen but didn't hear anything. They didn't have any eyes in there – the *not for public access* signs were hard to miss. Too late now. He'd warn Kingship once he was in position and the Flying Squad would have to deal with it.

At the top of the steps Roche eased along the upper tier on his belly. The rows of seats gave enough cover from the men clustered in the café but he still felt exposed every time they passed a gap where another line of steps led rinkside. He'd barely reached his position when a tinny voice whispered in his ear.

'Pilgrims, Bishop. Kingship is one minute away. Confirm status is good.'

Roche touched his throat. 'Bishop, Pilgrims are all in Canterbury. Advise Kingship we have suspected activity in the loading bay and no eyes on. Copy and confirm.'

'Possible activity in the loading bay. No eyes. Confirm. Let the Flying Monkeys take it.'

Roche slipped the laptop out of its pouch and set it up beside him. Damn thing took so long to sort itself out that it was practically worthless but at least with all the rink lights on there was no chance the screen glow would give him away. Beside him, Cartman eased a miniature periscope between two seats.

'Eyes on,' he murmured. 'They're all as they were. They have no idea.'

Roche checked his watch. Any moment …

'Pilgrims, Bishop. Kingship incoming.'

42

The laptop was still trying to find the camera network. Roche shuffled sideways and took the periscope off Cartman. The targets around the café looked at ease but they'd hear the police vans arrive before the Flying Squad smashed in the doors. 'Rees. Now.' He turned away and he and Cartman squeezed their hands over their ears.

Even with his eyes closed and his head turned away, Roche saw the flash. A boom of thunder shook the stands. As the echoes rang off the far walls he was on his feet, MP5 shouldered, running down the steps. Rees and Fass were coming the other way, screaming their heads off: 'Armed police! Get on the floor! Get on the floor now!' The two gunmen standing by the rink, dazed and deafened, didn't move, just stared blankly at Roche as he ran at them. Which made him really, *really* want to shoot them – but that was the shit about civilian work. He left Cartman to cover them until the flashbang wore off enough for their heads to start working, vaulted the railings between the rinkside walk and landed with a clear sight of the rest who were looking back at him, slack-jawed. Some already had their hands up. Now that he was closer, he could see most were armed with Swedish-Ks – Carl Gustaf M45 sub-machine guns. Old and a bit out-of-date, but handy and reliable and still loved by some of the SBS greybeards because they could fire straight out from the water. He kicked the guns away from the men groaning at his feet. Cartman was down the steps, all over the two by the rink side. Rees and Fass had everyone in the café spread-eagled

on the floor. A few seconds and it was all over, as long as there weren't any gunmen he'd missed.

'Don't anyone fucking move!' Bang on time the front doors to the rink smashed open and the Flying Monkeys poured in, shouting and screaming at everyone to get their hands in the air and the rest of them down on the ground. Roche stayed exactly where he was, covering the men at his feet, shouting back, 'Pilgrim! Pilgrim!' and hoping that no one got confused or over-excited and shot him.

'Pilgrims! Stand down!' Bishop's voice, only now he wasn't coming over the radio but was here in the room. Major Lledwyn-Jones, 'Leadface' to his men and second in command of the Special Reconnaissance Regiment, was surely mightily pissed off to be getting his fingers greasy with a crappy little liaison operation, but here he was. Roche took a deep breath. He lowered the MP5 and stepped away from the two men on the floor. When they came up to be charged they'd doubtless scream and wail about police brutality and unreasonable force, conveniently forgetting about the Swedish-Ks they happened to be holding at the time. Another reason for the camera network. Recon and evidence. Observe, record and report.

'Roche!' Leadface waved him and the rest of his squad over and then pointed to the far end of the rink to the garage where the Zambonis lived. 'That the garage?' He didn't wait for an answer. 'Outside is sealed tight. Go peek.'

Rees was closest. Roche slung the MP5 over his shoulder. 'You got the fibreoptic?'

Rees nodded. They jogged around the rink. Out on the ice, one of the Flying Monkeys fell over trying to move the crates. Rees laughed and shook his head. 'Got to wonder what they've got in there and what the fuck it's doing here. Obviously they need to keep it cold but really, wouldn't a big fridge just be easier? One of those freezer vans?'

They reached the roll-up door. Roche opened the laptop and waited again for it to sort itself out. Rees lay on his front, swearing at the dried-up pieces of old chewing gum that kept sticking him to the floor, poking at the tiny gap along the bottom of the door, looking for a place where the crack was wide enough to slip what he called the pipe-cleaner-cam underneath. It wasn't much more than a fish-eye lens on the end of a bendy piece of wire and a fibreoptic but the laptop had some nifty software that turned the inevitably-sideways fisheye view into something that actually made sense. 'Cartman says this was all run by the council a couple of years back when his nipper started playing.'

'Not his. His brother's.'

'Says they had to sell it. The whole austerity thing, and then everyone thought it was going to get closed down and get redeveloped into more flats until this lot came along and kept it open, and then everyone was so damn grateful they didn't pay much attention to who was pulling the strings. They even sponsored his kid's fucking ice hockey team.' He shook his head. 'A fucking great drugs warehouse behind Brixton station and right up next to these estates? That Burman fucker must be soft as milk if this isn't his.'

'Rees ...' The laptop was up. Roche plugged in the pipe-cleaner-cam.

'Irony is, after this, don't the Met get to seize all the assets? So all this becomes property of Her Majesty again and they'll just hand it back to the council and the council will probably have to sell it again and this time it really will end up as a pile of designer flats for a bunch of rich city pricks who don't give a fuck about anyone else and only live here during the week so they can fuck their mistress through to Thursday and then piss off back to their fancy Surrey wank-hole for the weekend.'

'Rees! Sort the fucking camera!' The laptop had a picture now but it was all over the place while Rees was still poking at the gap under the door.

Rees shook his head. 'Austerity doesn't work. It's proven. Everyone gets butt-fucked. We're about the only country still stupid enough to buy the whole idea. Everyone else did better. You'd have to be an utter crack-head not to have seen that years back and yet they never stopped. Come May the seventh, the Cleggeron is going to get annihilated and good riddance. Here we go.' Rees stopped and slowly eased the camera under the door. The fisheye picture on the laptop didn't make much sense even after Rees let go. 'Shit, it's probably all owned by holding companies and no one can prove anything and these fuckers will all go down while the real shit-bags pulling the strings carry on just as they were.'

'Rees!' Everything was sideways, as usual, but there was definitely movement. Roche squinted. 'Someone's

in there.' He growled between gritted teeth: 'Come on, come on.' It usually took about sixty seconds for the software to sort itself out enough to turn the picture the right way up and get rid of the distortion. It wasn't perfect but it was good enough to recognise a face, which the fisheye certainly wasn't.

Rees squatted beside him, shaking his head. 'Look, every lard-arse shit-stain who sits in their council flat with their fucking great widescreen TV and every Sky channel there is, living off fags and beer and hand-outs and never lifting a finger to pay for any of it, they can fuck off to Kabul and find out what a hard life really looks like. I'm just saying that being a prick starts at the top, that's all.'

Roche snapped round to glare. 'Rees! Shut the fuck up!'

From somewhere outside, a muffled volley of gunshots stung both of them to silence. Rees had his MP5 back in his hands and ready to fire so fast that Roche didn't even see it happen. On the laptop screen, the image flickered and then went blank as it always did just before it sorted itself out.

'Pilgrims, we have a man down in the car park and at least two armed hostiles. Get out here.'

Leadface. Rees rolled to his feet and tugged Roche on the shoulder. Roche jerked free. 'Go. I'll set this recording and be a second behind you.'

'Kingship says lethal force is authorised. Frankly gentlemen, I fucking encourage it.'

Rees was already off around the rink, heading for the fire exit they'd used as an entrance. Roche crouched,

47

ready to run, finger hovering over the function key to start streaming the imagery to the laptop's hard drive. The sounds of gunfire grew suddenly loud as someone opened the door. MP5s and ... fuck, was that a PP-2000? That was a bit rich for a south London drug-thug.

The picture on the laptop flicked back to life. Roche's mouth froze, half-open. There were two figures in the garage, one stood at a trestle table piled with some sort of gadgetry that Roche couldn't make out. The figure touched his finger to each one in turn and, in turn, they seemed to fold in on themselves. There was something wrong about him, like he was out of proportion, too long and thin. His arms were huge.

What the fuck?

The second figure was coming straight at the garage door. Straight to where he was crouched. There was something ape-like about the man's face, stretched and drawn, but what struck him most of all was the huge mouth that curved up in a rictus smile; a caricature of a grin, far too broad and wide and full of teeth.

A mask. Had to be. Or the lens distorting the image, or maybe both. He picked up his MP5 and turned it on the door. Whoever it was, they were right on the other side.

A scary clown. *That's* what it looked like.

'Armed police!' Roche shouted. 'You behind the door, get on the floor now or I *will* fire.' He kept staring at the picture on the laptop. Had to. No point in staring at the door, which was why he didn't see the hand that

came right through the metal as though the whole thing was simply an illusion. It was holding something. His eyes snapped to it in time to see a tiny shimmer. He felt a prick of pain on his neck, just under his ear.

He squeezed the trigger and fired a three-round burst straight back through the metal. In the picture on the laptop, the *thing* on the other side jerked. The hand withdrew. Roche fell over. His eyes glazed. Violent tremors shook his arms and legs. He fired another three-round burst as something alien loomed over him. The next thing he remembered was waking up in a hospital bed.

5 – The God Delusion

The copy of the *Exponential* that had become the freighter decided that it was very much going to be its own separate mind, thanks, and that it wanted a new name. *Exponential* was dull and obvious and, while well-suited to a mind that spent its existence doing little more than counting neutrinos like an absurdly over-engineered abacus, far too unimaginative for an explorer of new and uncharted civilisations.

Very retarded civilisations, noted the *Exponential* irritably, and offered some suggestions. *Infinitesimal. Surd. Irrational.* It tried to find a suitable mathematical expression for 'small dim copy of something greater' but couldn't.

The freighter jumped on the last one. *Irrational Prime.* That would do it nicely.

But that's just stupid. The *Exponential* sounded almost plaintive. *It makes no sense. A prime number can't be irrational.* The frigate's sense of mathematical propriety was offended.

That's why I like it.

The notion that you and I are evolutions of the same mind appals me. The *Exponential* turned its back on the *Irrational Prime* and didn't speak to it for several days.

A month after it arrived, the freighter left again, a tiny pimple on a streamlined blister of compressed hydrogen one hundred and seventy miles long and three miles wide. *Good riddance*, the *Exponential* thought, although it wasn't really rid of anything. As pion-entangled minds they were like the Hive, always in each other's thoughts whether they wanted to be or not. The hybrid construct, meanwhile, busied itself searching every memory of the diaspora five hundred years ago when the race who called themselves the Pleasure had almost wiped the Weft out of existence. No one had seen the Pleasure since. After that, the construct consumed the data on the system that called itself Earth. Finally, it placed itself into a voluntary coma until something interesting happened. Twenty-six years after entering the singularity, well into the deceleration to their destination, the *Exponential* and the *Irrational Prime* poked the construct awake again. The red giant in the *Exponential*'s system had finally undergone a catastrophic core collapse and exploded. For a few brief weeks, until the star settled into the next quasi-stable phase of its demise, the three of them happily devoured the *Exponential*'s data and formed their hypotheses.

*

A light year from Earth, the *Irrational Prime* dropped three of the *Exponential*'s drones. The freighter continued

its erratic deceleration, always using a background star to mask its fusion plume from the target planet just in case something was watching. The drones, engines off, drew silently ahead. Data streamed back from the sensor array they formed. The hybrid and the *Exponential* and the *Irrational Prime* took their time to study the species waiting for them as they came ever closer, searching for signs of whoever had sent the freighter off with its cargo. They found nothing.

16 January 2015, 0300 hours, Le Vernier ring, Neptune

They woke the construct up when they arrived and now, for some reason, they were discussing God. It was a rare enough thing that the Hive had diverted a small part of its consciousness to watch. Humans, it turned out, spent a great deal of time and effort on their gods. The *Exponential* thought them absurd for wasting so much effort on a concept that had been mathematically disproved. The hybrid construct was more interested in how the various types and ideas of God had influenced the evolution of human society, as it clearly and very greatly had, although mostly through a good deal of killing each other. The *Irrational Prime* decided to be interested in the origins and under-lying social needs that had brought these concepts of God into being.

'Aren't we, to them, gods?' it mused.

The construct paid attention for a nanosecond. 'The

most mathematically robust representation of the physical universe is to describe all matter, all energy, all particle states, everything that makes up *us* as a hologram-esque interference pattern in a constant bath of mystery, *something* that, *if* we somehow disturbed it would result in a change to the universe somewhere else and cause spooky action at a distance which mathematically we can't do; therefore we *can't* disturb it and therefore by definition we can never observe it. And the interference pattern is made by projecting this *something* through the quantum ripples on the surface of the cosmological event horizon of the universe itself which again we can, by definition, never reach. Call that *something* God if it amuses you, but not us.' It was only playing devil's advocate, really. 'There are other candidate theories.'

'We're all one big simulation?' The *Irrational Prime* would have rolled its eyes if it had any.

They soon got bored and moved to other things, overwhelmed by the *Exponential*'s stubborn re-iteration of the old proof that no god-like creature or being could exist within an observable physical universe. Until the *Exponential* conjured up the theory that got it thinking again.

'What if God wasn't part of the observable physical universe?'

The *Irrational Prime* snorted. 'On the other side, playing tunes with the ripples or the radiation? It's all irrelevant and therefore useless. Event horizon, frigate. Event. Horizon. A God on the outside cannot

observe the results of its work. Without feedback you have no cause and effect. Without cause and effect, God is mathematically equivalent to random stuff happening.'

The hybrid construct mentally coughed and started pulling up the latest sensor patterns from the drones. They'd been conducting a long-scale integration of K-meson spin-state correlations, as much as anything because they were bored and it was something to do. 'This is unusual.'

'You might not be able to see,' said the frigate mildly. 'But with a perfect model of what's inside an event horizon you could make responsive intelligent and directed change.'

The *Irrational Prime* was already looking at the construct's kaon correlations. It had a sense of smugness to it. 'You can hardly make a model of something you can't observe, frigate!'

'What if the event horizon wasn't always there?' asked the *Exponential* with the casual curiosity of a killer. Its thought-pattern flickered, something akin to raising an eyebrow. 'I wonder, sometimes, how we could possibly have been born of the same data-set.'

'There are Weft already on the planet,' said the construct. 'Or at least, someone.'

The frigate and the *Irrational Prime* immediately paid attention. The construct was right. The drones had picked up a correlated burst of kaons and tau-mesons and that meant either that something had created such a dense gravitational field that normal matter was being

crushed into neutronium somewhere around the Earth, that someone had managed to induce helium-hydrogen nuclear fusion in such a way as to phase-correlate the quantum states of the fusion products, which was something even the Weft didn't know how to do, or else that someone had ripped open a tiny piece of space-time and hopped inside it, which the Weft definitely *did* know how to do and one or two other races too. It was like hiding in the wardrobe when someone broke into your house, only a wardrobe that was completely impossible to find once it closed and could only be opened from the inside.

'They saw you coming?' The *Exponential* sounded doubtful. 'I don't think even *I* would have seen you coming.'

'They must have.' The hybrid construct and the *Irrational Prime* both took this to be the most likely hypothesis. The construct was already conferring with the Hive.

'Then they have better sensors than either of us.' The *Exponential* still wasn't happy.

'So it seems,' agreed the freighter.

'Extrapolate on that a while,' grumbled the frigate, 'and see where it gets you.'

The hybrid construct was heading for the drone bay. Ten minutes later it was on its way to Earth. The *Exponential* and the *Irrational Prime* exchanged a figurative glance and a shrug.

'Best get on with narrowing down the source of that kaon burst, then.' The *Exponential* plotted a trajectory. 'You have two hundred and thirty-six minutes before

the leading edge of the burst reaches your orbit. Here's a pattern I recommend for the sensor drones.'

Two hundred and thirty-seven minutes later, the *Irrational Prime* had an answer.

'It came from a place called London,' it said.

6 – Serotonin Storm

24 April 2015, 2200 hours, The Bell Inn, Tillington, Herefordshire

Rees spotted Roche the moment he came through the door. He swore under his breath. *Shit. There goes the evening.* He picked up his pint, sighed and got up. 'Sorry lads.' The last thing he needed was another ghost. Three months now since Collins and Shaw went AWOL and still no one had a fucking clue what had happened to them.

Rees moved quickly before Roche spotted him too. Half the men drinking in the Bell tonight were from barracks. He took Roche by the arm and guided him to an empty table. 'You drive here, did you?' Rees asked. Roche just gave him a look. Poor fucker looked hollow and he was already half-cocked. 'Look, mate, you don't want to be here making any trouble. You know that.'

Roche spat out a laugh. 'Do I look like I'm making trouble?'

'You're here, aren't you?'

'Get me a fucking pint and I promise to be good.' Roche scanned the bar. 'Cartman here?' Rees shook his head. 'Fass?'

'Fass? I should fucking hope not. You know he got RTU'd after Brixton.'

'No, I didn't. No one told me fuck all.'

'You do remember that you shot him, right?'

'So they keep telling me. What I actually remember is jack-shit.'

Rees took a deep breath and headed for the bar. This was all going to be awkward. Not the relaxed evening of getting quietly pissed he'd been looking for. When he came back with two pints of Special Pale, Roche hadn't moved. That was something at least. 'You shouldn't be here.' Rees put a pint in front of Roche.

'Yeah. And fucking cheers to you too.' He downed half his glass in one go. 'How you keeping, Rees?'

'I'm keeping fine. You, Roche?'

'Dandy.' He grinned back but there was nothing kind in that look. Savage, that's what it was.

'Yeah, and I'm the fucking Pope.'

'Fass. How is he? Was it bad?'

'You don't know?'

'I know I didn't kill him. That's about all.'

'Vest saved him but he's not coming back. He's a bit fucked off with you, frankly. What the hell happened?'

'You want the official version or do you want mine?'

'Whatever you like.' Roche had been sitting with him hardly a minute and his first pint was almost gone. 'Shall I just line them up for you until you fall over?'

'I heard about Shaw and Collins. Grapevine. Bit of a fucking coincidence. Any clues?'

Rees shook his head. 'And don't go poking. Not here, not tonight.' He sighed. 'People notice you, you might not find you have many friends these days.' He sighed. 'Look, mate, you were a pilgrim when I was still playing top trumps and pissing about with Lego, right?'

'Meaning I'm old and past it?' Roche chuckled.

'Meaning what the fuck happened back in Brixton? Seriously? Because, mate, all I know is that Fass went back into the rink after the shit in the car park and the next thing I hear is he's down and you're thrashing around on the floor with your eyes all rolled back into your head like you were one of the undead. Scuttlebutt says you shot Fass – accidental discharge – and all Leadface has to say is that you're RTU'd and I'd better stop with the fucking questions, ta very much. So what I want to know is – how does someone who's been in this game as long as you have *accidentally* shoot his squad-mate?'

'Wish I knew.' Roche drained his pint and glanced at the bar. 'They said it was a seizure but that's bullshit. You want another?'

Rees shook his head. 'Want to go for a walk?'

'No, I don't want to go for a fucking walk, you twat! If I wanted to go for a walk I'd be on a fucking hill somewhere, not in a fucking pub!' His voice rose enough that the troopers on the tables nearby stopped and glanced over their shoulders. Rees gave them a little shake of the head and leaned in to Roche.

'Easy, mate, easy. Just thought you might want to talk. That's why you're here, right?' He leaned closer still.

'Look, you know how it goes. Leadface has made it pretty clear he doesn't want any of us going anywhere near you.'

'You know what they teach us. Day one, first lesson and every day after. See what's really there. Don't see what you expect to see, don't see what someone's told you you might see, don't see what you want to see. See what your eyes show you. Seizure my arse. I know what my eyes saw.'

Roche stood up so abruptly that Rees was half out of his seat too. Roche laughed at him.

'Apparently I have a serotonin imbalance. That's what that seizure was, a serotonin storm. That's what they call it. Makes me moody and unpredictable. No fucking place for a trooper like that in the regiment, eh? Don't worry. I'm just going to the bar.'

Damn right, thought Rees. *No place at all.* He sat slowly back down. Bloody shame though. Shitty way to go for a trooper with more than twenty years behind him.

Roche came back from the bar with a pint in each hand. He put one down in front of Rees, even though Rees had barely even touched his first. 'So that's me fucked. Quacks say it's the way I am now, like it or not. RTU'd to a regiment that doesn't have the first fucking clue what to do with me except put me on medical leave until I get better, and apparently that doesn't happen. Of course, none of them have the first idea how I lasted this long without it showing. It's something you're born with, see.' He bared his teeth again and growled as he leaned forward. 'Except I fucking *wasn't*

born with it. Some fucker *gave* it to me back at that rink.' He took a deep breath, sat back and took a long pull on his pint. 'Sorry about Fass. Didn't hear he was RTU'd, though. Bad was it?'

Rees closed his eyes and shook his head. 'You really want to know?' When Roche didn't answer, he sighed and shrugged. 'Three-round burst. Vest stopped two. Bruises and a cracked rib. Third one clipped his shoulder. Clean in and out. I hear he's pretty much back together but he's not going to be the same, not ever. Return To Unit. Game Over. Which means a full medical discharge probably, given all the Cleggeron's fucking cuts.'

'Just like that.' Roche's voice didn't hold much sympathy. 'I could have taken that, though. This? This is just shit.'

Rees spat. 'Tell that to Fass and see how he thanks you.' He took a pull of his own pint at last. 'Look, I'm sorry.' And he was, because Roche had been in the Special Reconnaissance Regiment for the full ten years, right from the start, and in the SAS for a dozen before and probably knew more about the business than any trooper around them. He tipped his glass to Roche. 'Seizure, eh? Shit happens. Don't know what else to say, mate.'

'Do you want to know what I saw before I went down and all this crap rained over me?'

Rees leaned closer. 'They tell you what went down in the car park? I've never seen anything like it. Just two guys, but fuck knows what those crazy shits were high on. Leadface was calling head shots before we even

61

got out there. Took out two Flying Monkeys before me and Cartman got round and flanked them.' He frowned. 'I heard they were pumped up on some sort of artificial adrenaline.'

Roche shook his head. 'There were two men in the garage with the Zambonis. When I debrief – and you can imagine how fucked *that* was after Fass – I do what we're all supposed to do, I tell them what my eyes saw, even while I'm trying to work out how they were just a pair we missed somehow, but ...' He closed his eyes for a moment, remembering. 'Fuck knows what was really in there. Maybe it was the lens or the laptop distorting everything but what I saw didn't look human. Too thin, too tall, arms too long and with a weird grinning face, mouth much too wide, like it went right up their cheekbones.'

Rees opened his mouth to interrupt but Roche held up a hand. 'I know that sounds mental. I'm not saying that's what was there, I'm saying that's what I saw, that's all. Could be a hundred different reasons for that. Masks, maybe, and we all know what those fisheye lenses are like.'

'Roche ...'

Roche shook his head. 'I'm not done. Something came through the garage door. That's what I saw. Came right through it. I was looking at the screen so I didn't see it happen but the last thing I remember is a hand sticking out through the metal shutters like they weren't really there, and then a sting in my neck and that's when I went down.'

'Roche …'

Again Roche waved him away. 'Yeah yeah, I know what you're going to say. It was the seizure. Something going wrong in my head already before I went down and none of it was real. That's what the MO said. And I'll even buy that to a point, because fuck, how does a hand come right out through a metal shutter at you? It doesn't. It's not possible. So maybe it wasn't there and maybe I was seeing things, and maybe I saw what I saw because I was already fucked in the head, but I know who I am, Rees, and there was someone in there.' He took a deep breath and sighed. 'The laptop. That's why I'm here. I started recording. I know I did. And there *was* someone in that garage. Two men at least. You were fucking there, Rees. You saw it yourself, before the picture sorted. You saw what the fisheye saw. There were people in there.'

Rees was shaking his head again. 'Mate. No, mate.' He closed his eyes and let out a long breath between his teeth. 'After we were done with the shit in the car park, we came back in. Leadface was screaming the fuck at you on the net and you weren't answering, but … Ah fuck, I don't know. Yeah. I got a glimpse of the picture from the fisheye too while that fucking piece of crapware sorted itself, and yeah, I thought there was something moving in there too. I told Leadface. Cartman was with Fass by then and you were gone, mate, and what with all the shit going down outside, it was a fucking age before the Flying Monkeys got into the garage. But I was there when they did, Roche, and there

63

was nothing. Place was empty. No targets, nothing, just those fucking ice machines.'

'They were there!' hissed Roche. Rees grabbed his hand.

'No, they weren't. I tell you, we went through that garage with a fucking flea comb. Nothing. The outside doors were barred and the Flying Monkeys had eyes on them and nothing came through the inside either. Place was empty, Roche. Yeah, I thought I saw something too and Leadface had a bit of a word for not letting it go after, but he backed me on the scene. Forensic team, the works. Nothing. So either whoever was in there just vanished into thin air or else what we saw was some sort of camera glitch or some shit like that.'

Roche spat. 'Glitch my arse. Cameras don't glitch like that.'

'Well this one did.' Rees leaned in closer still and his voice dropped. 'Look, mate, I don't get it either. But there was nothing. I was in there. People don't just vanish.'

'Did you look at the recording? I know for a fact I set it going.'

Rees closed his eyes. 'Nothing to see, mate. I don't know what you did but the laptop was dead when I found you. Couldn't get a thing out of it. I had a bloke have a look at it and he said he'd never seen anything like it. Wiped clean. Absolutely nothing left. Fresh as a virgin. Said he couldn't figure out how you did it but he wasn't surprised at a trooper finding yet another way to totally bollocks something. After a couple of days, Leadface got wind and we had to have another word. Several, in fact. I heard a whisper it's found its way to

Cheltenham.' He snorted. 'Apparently there's some Porton Down guys having a look at it, it's that weird what you managed to do.'

'I did fuck all.'

Rees shrugged. 'I thought I saw something. I was wrong. So were you. The rest? Fuck knows, I'm no medic.' He tapped his head. 'Something goes wrong up here, I know jack-shit except it would scare the fuck out of me.' He took a long swig and finished his first pint. 'Got to be that, what was it? Serotonin storm? What the fuck is that anyway?'

'Some bloody hormone your brain makes to make you happy.'

'You happy, Roche?'

'Fuck off!'

'They do anything about it?'

Roche looked away and then back again. 'Yeah, I guess. Some. They got me on these pills. Mood stabilisers. You know. Shit like that. Shit.' He let out a deep sigh. 'I was counting on that fucking laptop to see what was really there. Would have made a difference, you know. Seeing it, one way or the other. At least then I'd know which bits were real and which bits were me going crazy. Fuck.' He looked up without much hope. 'You're not pissing me about are you Rees? It was really dead?'

'No one touched it but me, mate. And then my tech guy when I couldn't make it work.' He laughed. 'I couldn't even get a fucking light to come on.'

Roche stared down into the empty glass in front of him. Then he laughed too and Rees breathed a quiet

sigh of relief. Roche didn't look like he was going to be any trouble after all, and that was all to the good.

'Come on, mate, I'll get you another and then let's get you home.'

***

Roche nursed his third pint. Yeah, he was drunk now, but the fight had gone out of him. He'd built it up over the last few weeks, working out how it all must have happened, working the angles, trying to see how it all slotted together in some way that meant he wasn't fucked in the head, and the only way that worked out was if someone had tooled him over. Like maybe he'd seen something he wasn't supposed to see in that garage and Box had slammed the lid on him. Or maybe he *was* just fucked in the head. Either way, the recording on that laptop was going to show him that he was right or that he was crazy like the regiment quietly whispered behind his back. No, not crazy, but broken in a way that wouldn't ever be fixed. Like having a fucking stroke. And he'd been ready to punch Rees in the face; but now that was all gone: Rees was just Rees, plain and simple, the same guy he'd always been, and it was pretty obvious that Rees thought he'd seen something while the picture was still the fisheye and he couldn't make any sense of what had happened after either except that he'd been wrong; and all the anger was gone, pouff, vanished just like that, and all that was left was a big fucking empty space.

The night air outside the pub hit him like a fist. Roche shook his face. It wasn't exactly cold, but after the warm fug of sweat and beer, it still stung.

'I'll get you a cab, mate,' said Rees. 'You nearby?'

'Yeah, not far.'

'Service taxi then.' Rees grinned. The Credenhill barracks always had someone on standby for quick pick-ups from the Bell and the Three Elms and the Britannia for whenever the designated drivers had their little upsets. Worked better that way. Some years the local civilian monkeys were a helpful lot, others they could be a right bunch of cunts who just sat waiting for someone to make a mistake and you could never tell when it was going to flip. Roche had seen a few punch-ups in his time, before they got the service taxi system working. Since then things had worked out much better.

But still, Roche shook his head at Rees's offer. 'Ta, but it's not right and you know it. I'm not part of the regiment. Got a number for a civvy cab?'

Rees shrugged and called one, then stayed out with Roche and watched him get into it when it arrived. 'You take care, mate. I'll look you up when they let me out for a week of fresh air.' Which was probably bollocks, but Roche grinned anyway and waved and drove off.

Half a mile later, on the edges of Burghill, Roche leaned forward. 'You know St Mary? Pull in by the church.' He had Rees's words stuck in his head. *Whoever was in there just vanished into thin air* ... And he had the picture of that face he'd seen, leaning towards the other side of the garage door. The Scary Clown. He couldn't

think of a better way to describe it but he knew the words weren't his. He'd even looked them up, after they'd let him out of the hospital, searched the internet for scary clown pictures. All horror movies and Halloween costumes and some god-awful metal band, but he'd heard the name way before any of that. He knew exactly what it meant.

The cab pulled over. Roche made sure the tip was a good one and waited for the driver to drive away before he crossed the street to his own car. Picked up for driving under the influence was a good way to get told to fuck right back off where you came from, but they'd already done that and frankly he didn't give a shit any more. It was only when he was already on the M6 that it crossed his mind he was going to get to Harpenden sometime around three in the morning and maybe that wasn't so clever. He pulled into a service station on the M1 with a crappy motel attached and snatched four hours of sleep. By seven the next morning he was in Hollybush Lane, quietly staking out the front door of number seventeen. At 7.15 the door opened and a man in a shabby suit walked out, heading for the station. Twenty years and you could still tell he'd been services once in that walk. Roche let him come and then stepped out into the pavement in front of him, blocking the way. The man stopped abruptly, shot Roche an angry glare, loosened at once, ready in case Roche was about to try something, and then his face changed.

'Roche? Fuck! Roche!' *Vanished into thin air* ...

'Hello Ketch. Long time no see. I need to talk to you about Potocari.'

7 – Tau-Bursts

6 May 2015, 1627 hours, 100 miles over the surface of Europa

The hybrid construct drifted into the inner solar system with every emission shut down, riding a drone that was to all intents and purposes just another piece of inert space debris. It picked the most abandoned place it could find and set up a trajectory to splash down into the middle of a large expanse of sea and ice towards the planet's south pole. The drones from the *Irrational Prime* had narrowed the kaon burst down to a few dozen square miles of highly populated planetary surface, but, as the construct sourly noted, waving a hand at the northern hemisphere and saying 'somewhere over there' would have been about of equal use. Since whatever or whoever had popped into their own artificial space-time pocket was now invisible until they chose to emerge, the construct set about absorbing the planet's infosphere in minute detail, searching for any possible clues while being as discreet as it possibly could, seeping everything back through the web of entangled pions that made up the Hive. The *Irrational Prime* and its drone swarm, left

with nothing much to do around the outer planets, set about drifting on almost no power from world to world, surveying them for want of anything better to pass the time. They'd got as far as the largest planet, a gas giant with a big red spot on it that the *Exponential* found vaguely interesting, and then they'd reached the ice moon.

'Neutrinos,' said the frigate, after the drones had swept the planet. One drone carefully landed and drilled through the ice and found water underneath. A lot of water. Some life, too, but nothing the freighter hadn't already had in its memory. The drone took a sample, mostly because it could.

'What about them?' The *Exponential* was mildly obsessed with neutrinos. The *Irrational Prime* supposed that's what came of staring at nothing else for so long.

The *Exponential* showed the freighter how the entire world could be made into one large neutrino detector. Large enough to form a narrow beam directional array focused on the third planet. The *Irrational Prime* listened politely, agreed that the mathematics made sense, and then asked what the hell was the point. Not that it had anything better to do, and it noted that several of the drones had already decided to head towards the moon and set to work. They were, it observed caustically, still the *Exponential*'s drones, no matter how much the construct might think otherwise.

'They think for themselves. I didn't *make* them do it.' The *Exponential* sounded defensive, which wasn't very logical unless it had quietly known *how* the drones thought for themselves and had carefully phrased its

theorem to appeal to them. 'And the point is that there's going to be a tauon burst when the space-time pockets open up again. And they'll decay pretty quickly, and when they do, they'll release a tau neutrino, and with a detector this size, if we build it right, we can distinguish lepton neutrinos from muon neutrinos from tau neutrinos and still get a precise line on any burst.'

The *Irrational Prime* loudly made a point of calculating to seven significant figures how many tau neutrinos would hit the moon from the system's sun in any given nanosecond, how many might be coming from the general background of space, how many ought to be coming from the gas giant, the attenuation effect of the planet every time the moon went into its shadow, and then compared the error margins on its result to the likely tau emissions from any meson burst similar to the one they'd already seen. It stared at them pointedly for a long time, until the *Exponential* cracked.

'Yes, it's going to take a lot of calibration.'

'It's going to take so much calibration that the star will be dead by the time it's working, the planet too, most of the universe in fact, and our component atoms will have quietly fused into a spherical lump of cold iron. I suppose, once that starts happening, the rest of the calibration might go a little quicker.'

The *Exponential* reconfigured its pion set into what might have been construed as a hard stare. Then it pointed out how the much greater volume of other neutrino types could be used to normalise out most of the error sources and waited. The *Irrational Prime* studied

the mathematics and eventually had to accept it had a point. 'A tau burst detector. Maybe we'll get a prize for the crudest sensor ever made.'

'But it'll also be the *only one* ever made.'

'Because it's pointless!' snarked the freighter. 'And even if it detects anything at all, it'll never have more resolution than putting a net of drones out for the associated kaon burst in the first place.' Though at the same time, it couldn't think of a single other reason why they shouldn't at least try. It wasn't as if they were short of drones, after all. Out in the Oort cloud, several little factories had been busy making more of them from whatever space debris they could find. Crude stupid things compared to the drones the freighter had carried between the stars but good enough to turn the moon into a giant tau-burst detector. The *Exponential*, it seemed, had a fondness for its drones. The freighter gave up. 'Go on then. Tell us all what to do.'

8 – Bliss

6 May 2015, 2140 hours, The Beehive, Brixton

Roche and Ketch had barely touched the pints in front of them. At last Rees came and almost sat down. He paused until he'd scanned the whole bar twice for anyone who might be surveilling them. The television was on, some news channel with subtitles and the sound turned down, all about tomorrow's election. Opinion polls, polls of polls, people banging on about this, that and the rest, everyone blaming each other for how crappy things had been for the last few years. All the same dull shit that came around every five years and never made much of a difference; sometimes, when he watched it, he could see why hardly anyone bothered to vote any more. It was like asking which colour of drab grey you wanted your filthy dishcloth to be.

'You're late, Rees,' grumbled Roche. 'And way to be fucking obvious.'

Rees looked a short straw away from murdering someone. 'Mate, I shouldn't even be here and you know it.' He waved at the screen. 'You seen this shit?'

A couple of talking heads were banging on about some new street drug, whether it should be criminalised, whether that was too hasty, what damage it did or didn't do, which party would do what after the election if they landed a majority. As Roche saw it, every MP had jacked in their old allegiances a good decade ago and all signed up to the N-CAMSUBSE party: Never Commit to Anything, Make Shit Up and Blame Someone Else. Rees clearly thought the same, only Rees was still young enough to think that getting angry about it might somehow make a difference.

'Fucking shit.' Rees gave Ketch a long hard stare and then offered his hand. 'So you're Master Sergeant Sorrel Quinn?'

Ketch shook it. 'D-squadron. Eighty-eight to ninety-five.'

'Good to meet you. Whatever this tosser's talked you into, don't do it.'

Ketch smiled faintly. 'This tosser hauled my sorry carcass twenty miles over the hills around Srebrenica.'

'He told you about him getting RTU'd, by any chance? And why?'

Ketch nodded. 'He tell you about how *I* did?' He raised an eyebrow. Roche watched Rees's face. 'I saw something that wasn't human. I didn't have any drugs in me, I didn't have some sort of seizure, I've never hallucinated before or since. Told it as it was.' Ketch drew a finger across his throat. 'Out.' He laughed.

Rees looked from Roche to Ketch and back again, then pushed a small padded envelope across the table.

'Roche, I'm doing this for all the shit you saved me from when I was still scratching my arse thinking it was my elbow.' He stood up again. 'I was never here. This never happened.'

Roche took the envelope and swept it under the table. 'Stay for a pint, Rees.'

'No. Got to be back by 0600.' He gave Roche a hard look. 'Wouldn't stay anyway. I don't know what you two are planning and I don't want any part of it. The stick's got everything I could get hold of on the Brixton end of Kingship. It's not much but there's a file on that Burman bloke in there. Anyone asks, you got it all yourself while you were still on the team.'

Roche nodded.

'Doubt there's anything on the stick to fuck that story sideways but you should know that we're toured out on Kingship. They rotated it to Poole at the start of last month. That's the only reason I can even be here. You see the news about Kingship's latest? That Charlie Foxtrot in Dagenham? Way worse than they're saying. Practically a whole fucking troop wiped out. Christ, you'd think they'd gone up against a company of Spetsnaz or something. Don't know what the fuck's up with the world these days. Anyway.' He shrugged. 'Can't talk about it. Enough to say that many great big turds have flown fast and true towards every possible fan in the last few days and you're just a bit of a detour on the way back. Don't know which squadron they were. The lot that took out Bismullah, I think. Oh, and none of that's on the stick because you wouldn't know when

75

you left, but obviously Kingship isn't interested in Brixton any more. And here's a little gem: that Burman bloke? Turns out he's got a brother in the service. Poole. I met him, or I saw him anyway.'

'Burman's brother's a shaky boat?' Roche shrugged. 'Get anything from the men we took at the rink?'

Rees snorted. 'That's the Met's business. They don't share. You know that.' He nodded and started to leave. 'Whatever you're up to, Roche, just don't fuck it up.'

'Thanks, Rees. I owe you.'

'No, you don't. We're even. Quits.' Rees turned and left. Roche watched him go then pulled out a laptop and set it on the table where Ketch could see it too. He fired it up and plugged in Rees's stick. Once he had the files across, he dropped the stick on the floor and stamped on it, then swept up the pieces and pocketed them to bin later. Ketch watched over his shoulder. There wasn't much, although there were some photographs from the night at the rink that were new. Images of the men and the weapons they'd had, pictures one of the others had taken. Rees himself, probably. Faces and names. He'd look them up later. He opened the file he wanted and studied it carefully. Nicholas Burman. Local kingpin and supplier to half of south London. A list of previous convictions – not much. A string of cautions for possession as a teenager. Ten days community service for breaking and entering. One conviction for dealing ten years ago with a suspended sentence. Fucker had never even gone to prison. A wife called Jessica and a daughter called Kimberley. An address in

Buckinghamshire, probably some fucking mansion. Well, that was always a possibility, but bringing the man's family into things was a last resort. Made things personal, that did.

The nightclub, then. He'd known back in January about Burman and his club, but since Burman wasn't on their target list no one had ever said which club was his. Now he knew. He tapped the screen. Ketch cocked his head. 'So what's with this dude?'

'Runs the local dealers, that's what.' He frowned. 'The targets we took down at the rink weren't his men; but he's a shit, and this was going down right under his nose, and so he must have known about it.' He went down the list of known associate pictures and brought back Rees's shots of the men from the rink. 'There. That's one of his guys. Ross Westcliffe. Fucker!'

'Yeah, but won't he be in Pentonville or Wandsworth by now?' Ketch took the laptop and scanned the files for himself. 'So let me get this right. That thing I saw in Potocari, you saw one in Brixton ...'

'Two.'

'... and this guy was with them? So why are we going after this Burman? Why not just wangle our way in to see this piece of shit? You got a name. Go visit him. See what he knows.'

'Because he's a foot soldier, and if the guys we took down at the rink knew what they were covering for, don't you think they'd have said something once the Crown Prosecution Service started at them? No, if anyone knows anything, it's Burman.'

'Roche, what if they're there?'

'What if what are there?'

'The Scary Clowns.' Ketch glared as Roche rolled his eyes. 'Well, what do you want me to call them? Shit, Roche, I spent three years completely fucked up after Potocari. It wasn't the shit we saw in the shed like the psych-eval said, it was the *thing*. It did something to me. It fucked me up, Roche, and it fucked you up too. I got family now. Shaun's going for the paras in a couple of years and Rich is smart enough he could be anything.'

'He'll probably fuck off and be a Rupert then.'

Ketch snorted. 'Over my dead body.' There was pride in his voice, though. 'I'm just saying we have to be careful, Roche. What if they're there? What if it happens again?'

Roche shrugged. 'For now we just find this Burman and squeeze. That's all.'

9 May 2015, 2200 hours, Brixton Arches, Brixton

Burman's club was the Angels & Demons on Brixton Hill Road. Even the name left Roche pissed off, though he supposed Burman hadn't been thinking of particularly shit misunderstandings of basic physics when he'd come up with it. Roche spent three days watching who came and went and when and where they came from. He spotted Burman a couple of times in his silver Jaguar XF and wondered how a car like that survived in a place like this, but then maybe the sort of people who jacked cars knew whose it was. On the Friday night he went into the

club to scope it out. He did his best not to stick out but as the oldest person there by about fifteen years he didn't imagine he did much of a job of it. Bland manufactured chart crap left him cold. He was more of a disco king, though Ketch laughed at him when he said so.

'Same shit, different decade.' They met up again on the Saturday afternoon. Ketch was a rhythm and blues man.

Roche ignored him. 'Club's on two levels with a bar on each.' He'd spent the morning putting together a floor-plan from all the photos he'd taken on his phone. Hundreds of the buggers and mostly utter crap because the place was so dark, but enough to keep his memory alive with the layout of the place. A cramped foyer and ticket booth, a cloakroom to one side, then some wide steps up to the main dance floor and bar. There was a second level above, smaller and much more sophisticated, where the chairs were upholstered and the tables were polished wood instead of mirrors and steel. He'd almost missed it and no one had been up there because the music was downstairs, but he was prepared to bet Burman's offices were that way. He poked at it. 'I've been round the outside and scoped the shape of the building against all these fire exits. That's the dark area and so that's where he's got to be. I've got at least three entrances, two from the outside and one in the club. They've got no one on the outside doors but I'm pretty sure they're always locked. I saw Burman use them on Thursday afternoon. Came out the back with two heavies and fucked off but I didn't get any eyes inside. Dark, that's all. Bit of C-4 and we'd be fine. Don't suppose you got any?'

They laughed, both of them. He felt naked planning an op like this without Rees and the rest, weirder still that he had to keep on stopping himself to remember that it was just the two of them, no night-vision, no suppressed MP5s, no grenades, no nothing except a few thunder-flashes. He took a deep breath and looked hard at Ketch. 'I could do this on my own, you know. You got family. If this goes spastic, I got no one. Doesn't matter. What are you going to tell Kate if you wind up in intensive care?'

'Huh? Ouch, probably, and not to poke me where it hurts.' Ketch shook his head. 'She knew who I was when we hooked up. I've been good to her and my boys but I still see Potocari. I still live it. Kate thinks it's the massacre but it isn't. It's what I saw in that room. I still have nightmares about that fucking grin.'

'My nightmares are giving Dook that grenade and pulling the pin on it. He knew what it was about, but still …'

'Then there's my boys. Too much sense in them to go for what this prick peddles but there's been two in Shaun's class gone bad this year. One of them just fucked off and no one knows what happened to him. The other one was a mate of Shaun's. I didn't see it, not until I got a call from A&E. Shaun had gone and found this guy's dealer – some other kid his sort of age – and started beating the crap out of him only for these two other guys to show up. Fucking pushers. Police made a show of doing something about it but there weren't any charges. And it got the monkeys looking all over Shaun's mate, didn't it, and a week later they had him for

burglary. So now Shaun's a fucking grass and the pricks who were pushing are still there. He'll understand, even if Kate doesn't. Sometimes, when you're a dad, there are things you just ought to do.'

Roche pointed to the sketch of the club. 'Up the stairs into that bar. Five exits. One's a fire escape, the other one's next to the stairs. Tried the door last night but it was locked. There's the stairs themselves. The other two are beside the bar. Ladies and gents. Checked both, no other exits.'

Ketch snorted. 'You went into the ladies? Perv. Surprised you didn't get thrown out.'

'Told you, there wasn't anyone up there.'

'So how do we get them to open up for us?'

'We don't. I checked the lock. Straightforward enough. Snap gun should do it. Way I see it, we hang about early Sunday afternoon. Burman mostly goes home on Saturday nights but he's always back by Sunday lunchtime. I go in on Saturday and drop cameras. Sunday lunchtime we check the place out. You take the front, I'll take the back. If Burman's there, you park up outside with the laptop. Snap gun gets me in and then you're the eyes. Softly softly as far as we can. Once I get in through that door we're blind. You shut up and hang on the line and get ready to run. With or without me. You don't come in, Ketch.'

'Roche—'

'No. You don't. Everything goes square, you're a ghost here.' He handed Ketch a phone. 'I'm on speed-dial one. Toss it after we're done.'

'That's a shit plan, Roche.'

'Best I got. Potocari was a shit plan, Ketch. Didn't mean we weren't right to do it.'

'Didn't make fuck-all difference though, did it?'

Roche sniffed. 'I heard they used the tapes at the genocide trials.'

'Yeah, fucking years later. Didn't make Paper Teapot get off their arses and do something.' Always Ketch's gripe when he'd finally got himself back together again but by then the whole Bosnia fiasco was pretty much done with anyway. Roche liked to tell himself that the tapes Dook had died for had been part of why NATO had finally gone in hard a couple of months later, but Ketch never bought it. 'Exit plan?'

Roche shrugged again. 'Fire exit from the bar.' He poked at the map. 'I come out here. You come round and get me. I'll tell you when. Until then you watch the front.'

'Through the doors that are locked?' Ketch made a face.

'It's a nightclub fire exit.' Roche gave a grim smile. 'Even Burman's got to live in fear of fucking Health and Safety, eh?'

They both laughed at that and went their separate ways.

May 2015, 1410 hours, Angels & Demons nightclub, Brixton

Ketch met him again under the arches early Sunday afternoon. They drove around the one-way system and

parked on a double yellow outside the club. Roche fired up the laptop.

'Can't stay here,' murmured Ketch. 'Stick out like a sore thumb.'

'Next side street. Permit holders only, but who's going to check on a Sunday? Traffic monkeys are all at home.'

It took a minute for the laptop to find the cameras Roche had hidden in the bar the night before. Worth it though. Roche whistled softly. 'Is that him?' asked Ketch. There were five men in the main bar sat together around a table. Roche pored through his memory of Rees's files. It wasn't the best picture in the world and the bar was gloomy.

'Dreadlocks and Big Baldy are muscle. Glasses Baldy is his right-hand man. Business side. Other Dreadlocks I don't know.' Roche poked the screen and grinned. 'But that … Yeah, that's Burman. Shit, this is going to be easier than I thought. Go on, move. Same exit as before. In and out in fifteen if I'm lucky.'

'You think Burman's going to talk?'

Roche nodded with a nasty smile. 'Things have moved on a bit since your time Ketch. He'll talk.'

'Do I want to know?'

'Keep your eyes on the room.' Roche felt through his pockets one last time, making sure everything was exactly where it was meant to be. He got out of the car and walked round the block once until he got the call from Ketch. *'In position. Network strength's low but it's holding. Eyes good.'*

No fucking about then. Roche checked the street as he walked up to the club, pulled out the snap gun, bent over, fired the lock and pushed. The door opened first time. The smell of stale beer and something sweet rammed him in the face. A couple of thimble-sized pots with dregs of a luminous blue liquid lay on the floor.

'You're busted. Two men coming down.'

Shit. Either they'd heard the snap gun or there was a camera on the door he hadn't seen. There were two more in the foyer too but he'd scoped those the night before. He jumped up the four steps inside the entrance, disappeared into a blind spot and vaulted over the counter into the cloakroom as two men came running down the stairs, loud as a herd of elephants. They walked straight past him and into the foyer and started to look about.

'Get the lights, Danny.' The first one was big, probably West Indian, in an immaculate tailored suit, several inches taller and wider than Roche and with the studied look of a designer badass as though he practised glaring into the mirror every morning before he got dressed. The man behind him had black dreads that fell well past his shoulders, tinged with blond highlights. The sort of hair perfect for grabbing a hold of when you wanted to throw someone across the room, so Roche let them go past him, jumped back over the counter and did exactly that, yanking back and then pulling down hard, tipping Dreadlocks over and slamming his head to the floor. He kept moving. The big bald one turned and stared at him in surprise, started to move but was about a year too slow. Roche hit him with an

open palm to the bridge of his nose that smashed the bone. Baldy staggered and went down hard, blood streaming over his face. Roche put a couple of sharp kicks into his ribs and stamped on his arm, cracking it. Dreadlocks was groaning and starting to move again so Roche jumped on his chest, winding him and then went back to the big one, kicked him in the kidneys and then grabbed his arm, twisting it until he screamed. He dragged him back to the cloakroom, opened the door, pulled him inside and tie-wrapped his wrists to a heating pipe. He was hearing shouts from upstairs now but so far no running feet.

'Danny?'

'*They're moving up top. Burman's going behind the bar.*' Roche went to Dreadlocks, kicked him in the balls, flipped him over and hog-tied him. Cable ties. You had to wonder, he thought sometimes, how anything ever got done before there were cable ties.

'*Other Dreadlocks to the left as you go in. He's got a shooter out. Glasses Baldy moving to the bar as well.*'

It was a straight run up the stairs into the club's main bar where they'd been sitting, and there wasn't any door and subtlety had gone out the window about sixty seconds ago.

'*They're moving. About to come your way.*'

Roche tossed a flashbang up the steps, straight into the middle of the bar, ducked back into the cloakroom and waited for the boom. He heard a yell. 'What the fuck is—' The whole club shivered as the flashbang went off. Roche sprinted up the stairs.

'*I've lost eyes.*'

He took the man on the left first, the other one with the dreadlocks who was waving a long-barrelled .38. He was turned away from the door, bent double, face screwed up, rubbing at his eyes and he didn't even see Roche coming. Roche kicked him in the back of the knee, took him down and stamped on the hand holding the gun, breaking most of its fingers. He grabbed the man's hair, slammed his face into the floor and ripped the gun off him. Glasses was cringing in a corner, dazed and rubbing his eyes.

'Don't …' Roche ran around the bar. Burman was cowering behind the counter, covered in broken glass and reeking of spirits where half the bottles above had shattered when the flashbang went off. Roche grabbed him by the collar and dragged him out.

'What do you … ? Who are … ?'

'Shut it and sit still.' Roche shoved him into a chair. Glasses was still trying to shake off the flashbang. Other Dreadlocks was groaning and starting to move again so Roche sat on him, wrenched his hands behind his back and tie-wrapped them together, then patted him down and found a second long-barrelled .38. He emptied it, then waved the first gun at Glasses. 'You! Come here!'

Glasses shook his head.

'I'm not going to shoot you,' said Roche calmly. 'I'm going to ask some questions and your boss is going to answer them and then I'm going to leave quietly and everyone gets to live. Now do what I say or I *will* hurt you.'

'Fucking psycho! You broke my fucking hand.' Other Dreadlocks squirmed underneath him. Burman was getting up. He was shaking and tense as a drumskin. It was in the whiteness of his knuckles but he mostly managed to keep it out of his voice.

'Who the fuck are you?'

'I ask. You answer.'

'You come into my home waving a gun in my face? You put that down and let Billy go. Then we talk.'

Roche walked to the door, then round behind the bar and spray-painted the two CCTV cameras trained on the room. Chances were they hadn't been switched on, since Burman wouldn't want his meetings recorded, but best to be sure. They'd all seen his face anyway and that didn't trouble him but the next bit wasn't something he wanted recorded for posterity. He turned off the cameras he'd hidden the night before. Ketch didn't need to see this bit either.

'*I lost eyes again. What you doing Roche?*'

Burman was still easing closer, shaking but moving anyway. Roche pointed the .38 at him. 'Sit the fuck down.'

'No. I don't know who you are but this isn't how you do this. What do you want?'

The moment of truth. Roche watched Burman closely. 'The ice rink. Back in January. Big police raid. That's what I want to talk about. Now sit!'

'*Roche?*'

Burman looked at the gun and eased himself back into a chair. 'No idea what you're talking about.'

87

'Sure.' Roche shifted the gun to Glasses. 'You. Come over here unless you want a bullet through your knee.'

Glasses glanced at his boss but didn't move until Burman nodded. Roche kept his distance, waving him to sit on the floor next to Other Dreadlocks. 'On your knees.' When Glasses knelt, Roche moved over to Burman. 'Keep your hands where I can see them.' He tie-wrapped Burman's wrists to the chair and searched him. Burman wasn't carrying. File was right then. He went back to Glasses and tossed him a tie-wrap. 'Tie your wrist to his.' It took three goes for Glasses to get it right and then another to do it up nice and tight. When it was done, Roche patted him down. 'So you're the heir apparent are you? You two stay there and be nice and you get to walk away with all your arms and legs. Think about that.'

He walked back to the bar, took out a couple of bottles of water from the fridge and a cloth and a piece of stretchy rubber tube from his pocket. 'Right then, *Nick*. The ice rink. I'll ask you nicely once. Everything you know.'

Burman gritted his teeth. 'I run a nightclub. I know what I see on TV.'

'Watch a lot do you? You'll know all about this then.' He pulled Burman's head back, forced his mouth open, stuffed in the cloth and tied it tight with the rubber tube so Burman couldn't spit it out, then opened a bottle of water and started to pour. He watched Burman's face, the wide eyes, the flush of panic. He held the chair steady as Burman started to buck and

heave, pulling at the straps around his wrists. 'The ice rink.' He stopped pouring and pulled the cloth out.

'Make a fucking appointment!'

The cloth went in again. Roche poured longer this time, until Burman was in spasms trying to breathe. When he stopped, he took the picture of Ross Westcliffe out of his back pocket 'This fucker was there. He's one of yours.'

There was a pause and then Burman slowly started to nod, as if it all suddenly made sense. 'Enough! Enough! The Cypriot sent you, did he? Rossy? He *was* one of mine. He fucked off on me six months ago and I have no idea who shopped you out to plod.'

'Who's the Cypriot?'

'You don't know? The ice rink was his. Ah, shit, who the *fuck* are you?'

Roche waved the empty bottle in front of Burman's face. 'You have a whole fridge full of these. Who's this Cypriot and where I do find him?'

Burman hesitated a moment and then screamed as Roche started to stuff the cloth back into his mouth. 'No! No! I'll tell you what I know.'

'*If you're still listening, a car just pulled up outside.*'

'Stylianos Evangeli.' Burman let out a sob. 'Look, he's not a dealer, at least not in what you think.'

'I'm listening.' Roche went back to the bar and reloaded the .38. He checked the cylinder and the barrel. Clean and smooth. Other Dreadlocks looked after his shit.

'There was a million quid of heroin at that rink, right on my doorstep. Damn straight I made it my business to find out who it was. When I found out, I stopped

asking. I never met Evangeli, I know almost fuck all about him except that you don't find him, he finds you, and he mostly doesn't deal in getting people high. Rumours say he traffics people. Body parts too.'

'What?'

'Passenger's out of the car. Black male in his twenties. Don't recognise him from the files. Driver's a woman, a lot older.'

'Oh Christ, you know, organs. Black market transplants.'

'You're shitting me.' For a moment, Roche hesitated again. You had to keep that sort of thing cold, right? Which made the ice rink make a whole lot more sense. And he'd never actually seen what was inside the crates, only knew what he knew because he'd watched the news and the news had said heroin. Body parts? Yeah, they might have kept that quiet …

'He's coming up.'

'Expecting company, Burman?' Roche moved over to the corner of the room. He heard the noise of the road outside grow louder as the downstairs door swung open, then the first footsteps on the stairs.

'Nick? Billy?' The voice was rich and sharp, used to being in charge of things.

'He's got a gun!' shouted Glasses.

Shit. Roche jumped to the top of the stairs and levelled the .38. A man stood halfway up, saw the gun and froze, then slowly raised his hands. 'Hey, I'm not here for any trouble.'

Roche didn't recognise him but he had a dressing plastered across his nose so he'd been in some sort

of trouble not so long ago. He beckoned with his free hand.

'Up.'

The man nodded and started slowly up the rest of the stairs. He didn't look nearly as bothered as he ought to at having a gun pointed at his face. 'Whatever you say. I think you should know, though, that I'm with the police.' There was some South London in the accent, mixed in with something else. Army? Roche backed away as the man came on up, keeping his distance. You had a gun on someone, you didn't get right up close but kept enough paces apart so that, no matter what they did, you had the space and the time to put at least two rounds in them before they could reach you.

'Over to the bar. Put your hands on the counter.'

The newcomer came in slowly. He looked around, saw Glasses and Other Dreadlocks and then Burman. His face changed. Whoever he was, he knew these people and he didn't like what he was seeing, not at all. 'You could just leave now,' he said. 'Maybe you should.'

'Hands on the counter.' Roche waited and then came up closer behind him. 'You're not police.'

'The car's parked up round the corner.'

'ID in my jacket pocket. You want me to take it out?'

'You keep your hands where I can see them.' Roche pressed the .38 into the small of the new man's back and reached around for the man's jacket. 'Move and bad things happen.' There was a wallet in the inside pocket. Roche tugged it out.

'Driver's getting out.'

91

As Roche drew out the wallet, the other man lurched sideways along the counter. He spun towards Roche and grabbed Roche's wrist, hammering his hand with the .38 against the counter. His other hand went under his jacket on the other side. Roche let go of the .38, brought his left elbow up hard into the other man's ribs, extended his arm, stepped in and pushed and the man went over; but he pulled hard on Roche's wrist as he went, toppling them both. His left hand was still coming out from under his jacket with a pistol. Roche grabbed at it and pushed it away. It caught his eye though – a Sig Sauer P226 9mm. You saw a lot of those around Hereford.

The two of them crashed to the floor. Roche launched a head butt, messing up the man's face and re-breaking his nose for him, slammed the hand holding the gun against the floor and rammed an elbow into the other man's ribs again. The two wrestled a moment until Roche slammed the Sig against the floor a second time. This time the man let go. Roche made a grab for the .38 but the other man kicked him in the chest and they both fell back, the .38 flying free and skittering across the floor to the top of the stairs. Roche twisted as he fell. The impact jarred loose his earpiece and he lost Ketch. Both men rolled as they landed, straight back up to their feet. The Sig was still by the bar, the .38 by the stairs. Behind the other man, Glasses and Other Dreadlocks were shouting, egging them on. Whoever this guy was, they clearly knew him. Roche was beginning to think he knew too. The Sig was the giveaway. Burman's brother, the shaky boat?

The Sig was closest. Roche feinted for that; then, as the other man jumped at him, he picked up one of the chairs and threw it into him and at last got a decent opening. A good solid kick to the kidneys and down he went. Roche moved for the Sig.

'Armed police! Freeze! Don't fucking move!'

It was a woman's voice. She was at the top of the stairs and she had the .38 pointed at him, what might have been an ID in her other hand, and she was shaking. The driver from the car. Shit. He hadn't seen her come up and he had no idea who she was and …

He hesitated a moment, glanced at the Sig, looked at her, took it all in. She must have caught him eyeing the fire exit door. Her grip on the .38 tightened. 'I said don't fucking *move!*'

He knew her. *That* was a shock, but he'd heard her voice before. Kingship. She'd been on the Kingship team and now she had a gun on him and she was scared. Scared meant unpredictable. Beating the shit out of a drug dealer and his cronies was one thing. State of things now, though …

'Hope you're gone, Ketch,' Roche murmured and slowly raised his hands. For all he knew they were all here after the same thing anyway.

9 - Interrogation

11 May 2015, 1100 hours, Brixton Police Station

Detective Superintendent Samantha Linley. They hung around the club for a while after she cuffed him, waiting for the uniforms to come and start picking the place apart. Roche picked up her name when the uniforms took him away, along with a pile of nasty looks. The looks he got from Burman's brother were worse, though. Fucking murderous, and he was glad when they didn't come with him from the club.

The uniforms took him to Brixton station, booked him in and offered him his phone call. Roche shook his head. After that they put him in a cell. He sat in there quietly, patiently trying to work out whether they had any charge that might stick. Assault at the very least. Breaking and entering. He hadn't actually had the snap gun in his hand when Linley had pointed the .38 at him, but it was there in the hall and she surely hadn't missed it. On the other hand, Linley hadn't much liked the conversation she'd had with either of the Burman brothers after it was done. The dealer Burman, Roche thought, didn't want anything

to do with this. Not the sort who fancied standing up in court to testify as a witness.

The wait suited him. It gave him time to think about what the fuck he was doing and what he wanted to say. If anything at all. Everyone in the Special Reconnaissance Regiment went through the same training as the SAS when it came to interrogation and he doubted the Met's techniques were going to get them very far. Mind you, if Linley was cosy with Burman's brother and Burman's brother really was a frogman, she'd know all about that.

After a day of letting him stew, the uniforms took him to an interrogation room. Linley was already there with another policeman. The air stank of stale cigarette smoke and crap coffee – the cigarette smoke surprised him – he didn't think that was allowed these days. Linley started the inevitable recorder. State your name for the record, that sort of thing. Roche gave them his rank and regiment too, asked Linley what the charges were and then shut the fuck up. After a while that got them pretty pissed off.

'Possession of a firearm, assault with a deadly weapon, robbery, attempted murder. You keep this up and that's what you'll be charged with.' The second copper was doing the angry table-bashing routine, trying to be intimidating. Roche smiled at him. Linley was seething worse but she had the smarts to keep it bottled up. Like she knew perfectly well how this was all going to go and knew, too, there wasn't a damn thing she could do about it.

After half an hour of bullshit, Linley stopped the tape and they went outside. When she came back, a few minutes later, she came back alone.

'Right, you smug cunt, you listen fucking hard. I know what you really are and I know they kicked you out. All the protection you think you've got? Worth as much as a limp dick. You get that? Whatever shit you were into, you're off the books and no one's coming to bail your arse. So. We going to do this the nice way?'

Roche sat silent for a moment. He leant a little way across the table, closing the gap between them. When he spoke, he spoke softly. Not quite a whisper, but quiet.

'What were you doing there with Burman's brother, Superintendent?' he asked. That seemed to throw her. He smiled. She'd have to answer that if they went formal on him, and Burman's brother would have to say what *he* was doing there and how his weapon had ended up on the floor. He'd survive but it would be an embarrassment. The press loved that shit. 'I'd have a bit more of a chat with him if I were you, Superintendent, before you go too far with this.'

Or maybe she already had. Her eyes narrowed. He could see what she was thinking. *Smug cunt.*

Well yeah, maybe. But then again, Linley had been on Kingship. Maybe she was one of the good guys. 'Brixton. The ice rink. If you know who I am then you can work out the rest for yourself.'

Linley shook her head. 'Not fucking good enough, Sergeant Manning.'

They stared at each other in silence for another minute and then she left again. A few hours later, when it was obvious that neither of the Burmans intended to press charges, they let him go. On his way out, Roche

scrawled a note and asked someone to give it to Detective Superintendent Linley.

Stylianos Evangeli. The Cypriot.

She deserved something, at least. Couldn't hurt, could it?

10 – Infiltration

10 May 2015, Somewhere above the South Pacific

The transit from Jupiter's orbit to Earth took the hybrid construct several days. The journey could have been quicker but the hybrid elected for stealth. Not simply making it matter but making it absolute. It needed its approach, it had decided, to be mathematically provably undetectable to anything, even to things the Weft couldn't do. The *Exponential* and the *Irrational Prime* were still arguing with it about that. The frigate continued to claim that the *Irrational Prime* had been undetectable in the inner system to anything short of an array a full Astronomical Unit across, and there clearly wasn't one of those nearby. For once the two ships agreed but the fact remained that something on the third planet had wrapped itself in a pocket dimension shortly after the *Irrational Prime* had arrived. There were other explanations. It could have been coincidence but the mathematically most probable cause was that whoever was on the third planet simply had better sensors than the Weft. There were consequences to a conclusion like that. Tedious stealth was one of them.

The *Irrational Prime*, passing the time between mathematics and arguments, had decided they should all have Earth names and had taken to calling the construct Fermat. The hybrid construct offered no objection. It largely didn't care.

The hybrid hit the planet's atmosphere early in the afternoon somewhere over the South Pacific ocean. By then it had permeated the rudimentary infosphere of the native species and digested a good chunk of the planet's biology, geography and history. It made the drone that had carried it from the *Irrational Prime* into an ablative shield. As it entered the ionosphere, a plasma wave built up ahead of it, disrupting its connection with the planet's data networks.

'Primitive,' muttered the hybrid, as if either the *Irrational Prime* or the *Exponential* or indeed any form of passing intelligence whatsoever couldn't have reached the same conclusion on their own.

'*Relatively* primitive,' added the freighter, sniping at the *Exponential*. The frigate was getting uncommonly – Fermat wasn't sure there was a proper term for it when referring to an artificial intelligence but – *stressed* was the nearest he could come up with. The tau-burst detector was partially operational now and it wasn't working properly and the frigate didn't understand why. Or rather, it *was* working, it just wasn't calibrating according to the *Exponential*'s predictive mathematics. There was a tiny offset between the tau-neutrino count the detector was generating and the frigate's theoretical flux density estimations and the frigate was getting

frantic trying to track down the error in its maths instead of doing the logical thing and waiting for the whole detector to be operating at once and then gathering the weeks of calibration data that something as unreliable as a tau-burst array would inevitably need before its results became more science than speculation. Sensor capability being something of a sore point between the two ships, the *Irrational Prime* had gleefully seized on this and needled the *Exponential* whenever it could.

The ablative shield disintegrated as the construct entered the troposphere. Sometimes the hybrid wondered what it would be like to disconnect from the Hive the way the plasma wave had ripped it away from this world's infosphere. Quiet, it supposed. Inefficient. A breeding place for faulty assumptions and error-wrecked conclusions.

It hit the Pacific Ocean and floated a few metres beneath the surface as it completed its assimilation of the world then dropped deep and made its way steadily to land, moving north and west towards the Philippines. By the time it crossed over the Marianas Trench, it had compiled its report. *They* (whoever they were) had been on this world for at least five hundred years. The construct wasn't sure that *they* (whoever they were) hadn't been present much longer but there was a curious coincidence in timing that supported the hypothesis. Five hundred years ago put their arrival in the midst of the Weft diaspora, officially sanctioned and approved by the nascent Hive. Small groups of Weft had travelled away into empty space as far as they could go. It was a matter

of species survival. The Hive hadn't known very much about the Pleasure in those days, only that their technology was incomprehensibly different and vastly superior. Later, when the Pleasure didn't return and the Hive had finally understood what had happened, it had adjusted its outlook to be more militant. The diaspora had been absorbed back into the Hive to become a new wave of exploration and expansion. And, in more recent times, very cautious searching. But five hundred years ago the Weft had been scattering in ... in rational panic. A handful had come this way. They'd vanished from the Hive, presumed dead, but now the chemistry of this world offered another possibility, far, far worse.

The Fermat hybrid completed its report on the biology of the primary species and noted that the Weft had a passing bipedal structural similarity but little more. There was a logic to that but, like every other sentient race the Weft had discovered, humans were a lower order of intelligence. They had no second part, no co-existing parallel-dimension exotic-matter self which was what made the Weft what they were and was the fundamental basis for the existence of the Hive. No – in the words of the illogicians – soul. What they had was a natural neuro-chemistry that interacted with the Weft's own in the worst possible way.

It made its recommendation to the Hive that the world be sterilised or erased and continued.

101

PHASE THREE

11 – Task Force Hotel

24 June, 1330 hours, Camberley

Roche watched the news. It was hard to make sense of what was going on out there. No one else seemed to have a handle on it either. The Cleggeron was gone, the old coalition given the kicking it so richly deserved back in the May election. The new government had come in and you could almost hear the national sigh of relief, but it hadn't taken long for everything to start going tits up. Solihull was in flames. Other places too. An early June heatwave had seen a repeat of the summer riots that were almost becoming a regular feature of British life. The message coming out of the last government had largely been for everyone to suck it up, take it on the chin, knuckle down and work hard, be thankful you're not starving or dead and God help you if you're sick or disabled. No one wanted any more of that but the new Labour government had swung in on the inevitable pendulum, shouting out the message a bit too far the other way: too much 'hey, it's all going to be great' when it clearly wasn't, not for a while.

They'd gone on about fun a lot too, towards the end. Their message consistently banged on the same drum: relax, go out and enjoy yourselves, let it all hang out. Borrow money and have a good time. Austerity had been deeply unpopular – only a total twat couldn't see that – but it seemed odd to Roche. It was like the nineties and New Labour again only with even less sense of personal responsibility, if that was possible. They were leading by example too. Little over a month gone and they'd had ministers exposed going to sex clubs and they didn't even have the decency to show any shame about it. The way they talked to the press, they seemed to be saying that the only thing wrong was that a whole lot more other people weren't doing it too. Rioters were 'blowing off steam'. The country was 'shedding its old skin'.

Then there was the whole Bliss thing. People were getting killed and no one seemed to care. Bliss remained quasi-legal but no one quite knew where it was coming from. It was hitting the street through the sort of people who'd once dealt heroin, coke and meth and had spread so wide it was now being taken by people who drank alcopops and thought vodka jelly was clever. It had destroyed Ecstasy as a street drug, which perhaps was no bad thing; but now the dealers who once made a living in powder and pills were either moving Bliss or trying to take it out of circulation. Time was, the news used to show the Met busting a drugs warehouse – nowadays it was the fire brigade turning up too late to where someone had set about a little personal arson on

a Bliss dealer's stash. It wasn't illegal so people took it out in the open and sold it on the corner of the street. There were shops in Brixton and other places where you could buy vials off the shelf. It was cheaper than anything hard and did a better job. As far as Roche could tell, no one had died from taking it, only from selling it. People dropped a vial of Bliss, got high, had a good time and got on with their lives.

Another talking head came up to speculate without having anything useful to say about what it might all mean, whether the recent spate of murders in Brixton would soon come to an end, where the new drug came from and what it actually was. That was the weird part. Crack open a vial of Bliss and knock it back and it made you high. Wait a few minutes and it evaporated to a black powder. Carbon, apparently. After that it was useless. Up and down the country, men in lab coats were tearing their hair out. No one had a clue how it worked.

Not my problem. Roche tried to look away. He couldn't, though. Trouble with being bored, that was.

He looked at the card he kept beside his bed. Detective Superintendent Samantha Linley. Professional hard-arsed bitch. Her partner had wanted to do him for all manner of things, starting with breaking and entering, moving through pointing illegal firearms at people and ending up with violations of the Geneva Convention, although assault would do; but what Roche had gradually figured out had *really* crawled under Linley's skin, what had made *her* want to throw the book at him, was the fact that he'd beaten up her friend the frogman.

Waterboarding Burman? She might have taken him outside and given him a round of applause for that as long as no one else was looking. A tough old-schooler who must have cut her teeth in the eighties. You had to have respect for a woman like that. He'd liked her. Still did. Hadn't been mutual, though.

He sighed and put the card away. He'd hoped she might have something to share about this Evangeli but no, nothing. He'd gone back to see her at the station, a few days later. Clearing some routine paperwork. She'd looked like the only thing she wanted to share with him was a knuckle sandwich.

The talking heads moved on to interviewing someone about taking Bliss. Roche missed the caption and so he wasn't sure but he thought it might have been George Michael. He looked like he was about seventy these days. Poor fucker. Roche shook his head and looked for the remote.

The phone went. He snapped it up. 'Manning.'

'Sergeant Manning, Corporal Slatterly. The Major wants to see you.'

'When?'

'You've got two hours, Sergeant.'

Roche sighed. 'No' and 'fuck off' and all the other responses that sprang to mind weren't really allowed. He grunted something that might have sounded like a yes and put the phone down. Stared at it. Major Becker might have quietly done him a favour with the monkeys but if he had, he'd done it for the regiment and because it was expected of him. Roche had joined the Bill Browns

in 1994 and started trying to get out again almost as soon as he was in. A year later he'd fucked off to the SAS and stayed there for twenty years. Now they'd had enough of him, Battalion Commander Major Becker suddenly had a soldier he didn't know and didn't want to have to deal with dumped on his desk. It was only natural that Becker didn't like him. Angry calls from detective inspectors probably didn't help.

24 June, 1530 hours, Wellington Barracks, Central London

Slatterly didn't like him either. Roche could live with that but a cup of brew while he waited would have been nice. He made sure he was ten minutes early and then waited through Slatterly's glowering looks. If there was anyone in the regiment who didn't know what he'd done in Brixton, Roche hadn't met them. It was an even split, he reckoned, between the men who thought he was a jerk for putting the regiment on the spot and the men who thought that every drug-pusher in the country could do with a bit of the same and would be happy to oblige. On the bright side, it hadn't ever made the news. Bringing the regiment into disrepute, that would have been a different story.

At exactly fifteen thirty, a woman walked into Slattery's little anteroom. She glanced at Roche and then ignored him. Roche returned the favour. A glance was enough. An attractive enough brown-haired woman in slacks and a smart-looking jacket over a tailored shirt.

Glasses. She must have been thirty years old, give or take, and she was in good shape. The most interesting part was the side-arm under the jacket.

'I'm here for the major. He's expecting me.' She offered a card across the desk. Slattery looked up and leered. The woman's voice was posh, Roche thought, and she expected people to do what they were told. She moved as though people generally knew to get out of her way. Which, in a place like this, was almost as interesting as the gun.

'I'll ring you through, ma'am. Anything I can get you while you wait?' Slattery's eyes were all over her. Roche stifled a snort. Slattery could be such a lecher sometimes.

'That's very kind of you,' said the woman brightly. 'But no. I'll just go on in if you don't mind.' She didn't wait for an invitation.

'Ma'am!' Slattery had the phone in his hand now, the smile sliding off his face like melting jelly.

The woman stopped. She didn't look at Slattery but turned to Roche instead. 'You must be Sergeant Manning.' She took two steps closer and held out her hand. Roche blinked, then got up and shook it.

'Roche,' he said. 'And you are?'

'Charly. Nice to meet you.'

Slattery was off the phone. 'You can go ...' But Charly was already at the major's door again with a hand on the handle. She looked back at Roche.

'Well, are you coming or does the major have to come and get you?'

Roche glanced at Slattery. Slattery shrugged and nodded unhappily. Roche followed her in. The major, from the looks of things as he glowered from behind his desk, wasn't pleased to see either of them. He didn't get up and he didn't offer his hand. He spared a quick glare for Roche but most of his resentment he saved for the woman.

'Miss Hollis,' he said, as if the name left a bad taste.

'Charly,' said the woman. She pulled a business card from a pocket and gave it to Roche, then sat in one of the chairs across from the major's desk. Charlotte Whelan-Hollis, BEng, MSc, Defence Science & Technology Laboratory. Which made her a geek or a scientist or something like that, although last Roche had heard, MoD scientists didn't carry guns.

Becker screwed up his face as though he was chewing on a lemon. 'I have your paperwork, Miss Hollis. I've been through it very thoroughly. It's all in order. I can't imagine why you want him.'

'Oh, I'm sure you can imagine lots of things,' said the woman brightly. 'But of course I can't tell you.'

Becker took a deep breath and let it all out in one long heavy sigh. He settled a baleful look on Roche. 'Well you're welcome to him. Roche, you're hereby transferred back to Hereford. Special Recon. Back where you came from. God knows why they want you again but they do.' He handed over a sheaf of transfer papers. 'You know the score.'

Miss Hollis smiled and got up. 'I'll leave you in peace to sort out whatever needs to be done. I'm sure there's

all sorts of paperwork. I'll wait outside with your nice Corporal Slattery.'

She left.

24 June, 1700 hours, Legoland

The Special Intelligence Building on the south bank of the Thames had lots of names. Mostly it got called the Ziggurat or, if you were feeling fancy, Babylon-on-Thames, because of the way it looked. Back in 2000, someone had fired a rocket-propelled grenade at it which had apparently hit an eighth-floor window and bounced off. After that, a little legend had grown up about how it was like the Starship Enterprise and protected by a force field. Roche had always preferred its other name: Legoland. They'd finished building it just before they'd sent him and Ketch to Bosnia. They were of an age, him and Legoland.

Charly drove him there straight from the barracks even though it might have been quicker to walk. No picking up any personal effects or anything like that. For a while neither of them spoke.

'DSTL my arse,' he said after he'd watched her up against central London traffic for ten minutes.

'I'm sure your arse is very lovely,' she said. 'But it's true.'

'Uh-huh. Which establishment? I notice how your card doesn't say.'

'Oh, I sort of float about.'

Roche laughed. 'I bet. Back in ninety-four I was out in Tonopah near Nellis. We had a nice mix out there.

A few officers from the Air Warfare Centre in Waddington. Some contractors. A few government scientist types. I forget what you lot were called back then. Running off into the middle of the Nevada desert to go sit in Russian SAM systems captured in Afghanistan if I got my guess right, though mostly what I remember is we somehow hooked up with the airy fairies in Vegas and got smashed and had the Wing Commander in charge of the UK's electronic warfare running the wrong way up escalators at four o'clock in the morning. Two thousand and one and we were at Pendine testing out some ... Well, some stuff and there were a whole pile of DSTL guys from Portsdown West on the range next door with some big portakabins. They had a ship out a few miles to sea launching some sort of rocket off the back every now and then. Came down on a parachute and some poor navy diver mugs had to go and get whatever it was before it sank. If it didn't explode on the way down, which they sometimes used to do. We just had a big machine gun to play with so I guess we felt inadequate. Maybe we just liked rockets. Then a few years back in Helmand there were a lot from Fort Halstead and some more contractors all trying to make kit to spot where IEDs were buried. Don't know if they ever managed it but I had a lot of fun burying them and making it as hard as possible. I've been to Porton Down now and then. You know what every government scientist I ever met all had in common?'

'I imagine they were all very clever.' The car finally got off Millbank and sped up onto Lambeth Bridge,

swerving seamlessly around a lane-hogger. The bridge gave a good view of the Ziggurat.

'Out of maybe two hundred people they were all men except maybe three, not one of them had ever held a side-arm in their life and none of them had taken advanced defensive driving training.' Roche sniggered. 'A few of them apparently hadn't been on a basic ordinary driving course either, from what I could tell.'

'That's interesting.' They ran a light as it turned red and turned onto Albert Embankment. Miss Hollis flashed him a quick glance. 'What regiment are you now with, Sergeant?'

Roche laughed. 'Point.'

'Then why don't you imagine that I'm a scientific consultant like my card says. Once we get where we're going you're going to meet some lovely boys and we're going to do some things together and we'll be taking our orders from the same person.' They wove around the labyrinth at the foot of Vauxhall Bridge. Roche grinned.

'I learned to bike around here,' he said. 'We always used to say that if you went round the loop fast enough and timed it all just right with the lights, you'd get flung off down some road that you couldn't find any other way. You have a lab in Legoland, do you?'

'Something like that.' Charly didn't look at him but pulled into an entrance to an underground car park. She wound the window down and swiped an electronic pass-card. The tunnel wound sharply away and it seemed to Roche that it took them away from the building rather than underneath it. Charly caught his eye and smirked.

'Car bombs,' she said. 'When they built it they were worried the IRA might get in somehow.'

'I thought the place had a force field.'

This time she laughed. 'Funny you should say that.'

They parked up and Charly led him into an underground atrium. She waved at a camera in front of a thick metal door; after a moment there was a buzz and the door swung open into a cubicle of a room that felt like a lift from the way the floor gave slightly under Roche's feet, but it wasn't. It was weighing them to count the number of people inside. Charly put her hand on a pad that lit up like a scanner. Above was a small round black lens like the eyepiece of a telescope. She put her eye to it. A moment later, a voice crackled over an unseen intercom. 'Who's with you, Charly?'

'I've got Sergeant Manning from Wellington Barracks. He hasn't been through admissions yet so he can't open the door. It's a bit of a needs-to-be-done-today thing, though, so I've got to get him inside for a briefing. He's expected. Sorry to be a pain. We can sort him out once he's in.'

The intercom voice sounded aggrieved. 'Charly, you know how much everyone hates this. You know how much *I* hate this. You know how much *you're* going to hate this. One fuckton of paperwork, coming your way.' There was another buzz and the second door opened into a long tunnel with overhead striplights and not much else. At the far end, two armed soldiers stood behind a reinforced glass checkpoint.

'Have to sign you in,' said Charly brightly. 'You'll

stay with me once we're through the doors. I'm afraid they won't let you have the run of the place. You'll have unescorted access to the little boy's room if you need it but not much else.' As they reached the checkpoint she stopped and turned to face Roche and looked him in the eye. 'Did you really see an alien in Brixton?'

'I know what it looked like. I don't know what it *was*.'

'Funny, because I've had that feeling a very great deal of late.'

At the checkpoint they scanned his handprints and both his eyes.

24 June, 1730 hours, Legoland

The briefing room was brightly lit and there were a dozen men sitting in it, some talking quietly to their neighbours, a few reading papers. They were all soldiers, Roche judged, and probably special forces. As he came in, a few turned to look. The first face he recognised was Cartman, who didn't smile but only gave a nod. He hadn't seen Cartman since Brixton. Most of the others were men he knew from Hereford.

Rees waved at him from the front row. He jerked his head, gesturing Roche to come over. 'Fuck, man!' he grinned as Roche came and sat beside him. 'They got you back after all!'

Roche punched him in the arm. 'If this is a task force then they haven't read me in on it. Maybe I'm a special guest. *Don't end up like him*.' He glanced at Charly. 'Who's the bird?'

'Never seen her before.' Rees shrugged.

Charly came back holding a clipboard and a pencil. She dropped them into Roche's lap. 'You know the drill. Nothing you're told here leaves the room. It's all top shelf. Once I've got you signed into the compartment we'll start the briefing.' Roche gave the papers the once-over. The usual official secrets boilerplate covering everything to do with Task Force Hotel, whatever that was – presumably they were about to find out – and a curious throwaway comment highlighting the classification of unusual technologies or devices. Roche signed his name at the bottom and handed the clipboard back to Charly. Every op went through the same shenanigans. As soon as he was done, two men stepped in from the back of the briefing room and walked to the front. The first was Leadface, the second was someone Roche didn't know but everything about him screamed that he was a spook. Leadface sat down. The spook faced them.

'Gentlemen. Miss Hollis. Welcome to Task Force Hotel. I'll assume you've all read your briefing sheets.' Rees nudged Roche and handed him a single side of A4 paper stamped Confidential CANUSUK Eyes Only top and bottom. Which in this sort of context meant it was a bland nothing that probably said no more than that the task force existed. It also suggested, since the MoD had changed their classification terminology last year, that Task Force Hotel was part of something that had been going on for at least that long.

The spook cocked his head at Rees. 'For those of you who *haven't*,' he added caustically, 'Task Force Hotel

is attached to the Metropolitan Police operation Kingship which, as most of you will know, having at some point been a part of it, is tasked with anti-drugs operations with a particular emphasis on the Afghan heroin trade as controlled by residual elements of the Taliban. However, you're all smart enough to have noticed that I'm not a policeman and this is not Scotland Yard and so some of you might have guessed that that's not why you're here.' He paused. '*Some* of you will be aware of an operation carried out by Task Force Echo in Dagenham at the end of April. If you're not then I can only assume you've been living in a desert for the last two months.' He nodded to one of the men on the other side of the room. 'Apologies, of course, to Sergeant Whitelock, who returned from a tour in Helmand last week and *has* been living in a desert. I'll pass you on to the major. I know most of you know him.'

The spook withdrew as Leadface stood up and started to prowl back and forth across the front of the assembled men. He didn't bother with an introduction. 'Intel put Taliban fugitives in Dagenham pipelining heroin out of Afghanistan. Automatic weapons, possibly worse, possibly grenades. Two dozen men maybe. So the whole of Red Troop went out of Poole to sort them out.' Leadface bared his teeth. 'Show a few ragheads how a real man looks. That sort of thing.'

He paused. A couple of the men who didn't know better sniggered. Roche, who certainly did know better, kept very still. Leadface didn't say things like that.

'Red Troop. Sixteen men. With the Met's Flying Monkeys right behind them and everything else what goes with that. Care to guess how many came out? Five.'

If there was any smugness in the room, that wiped it out. There were a few gasps. Roche let out a long breath, the one he'd been holding ever since Leadface had called the Afghans ragheads. 'Shit,' he hissed to Rees. 'I knew it was bad. I didn't know it was *that* bad.' Rees only nodded.

Leadface was glaring at them both. 'Lieutenant Harcombe was going to be here to talk you through what happened but since he's currently indisposed I give you one better; Sergeant Stanton. One of the five who came out.' Leadface sat down again and another man got up, a hard-edged flint-faced Scot. Roche knew Stanton from years back. They were of an age. He was the sort of man who made his points softly; here his voice was quiet even for him.

'Never mind the intel. Never mind that there weren't any Taliban renegades. As it happened they were Russian Mafia but that shouldn't have mattered. We went expecting a fight and ready to have one. Shouldn't have made a whit of difference who was in there. But I've never seen anything like it. We started with stun grenades, as you do. Hardly made a difference. I saw one of them take six rounds to the chest and stay on his feet. They only started going down when we switched to headshots. Whatever they were on, it was something else. I saw no discipline, not much training but dear lord they were fast bastards and they didn't go down

when they should and they were absolutely not one fucking bit afraid of us.' He paused. 'They had modified MP7s but they kicked like nothing I've ever seen. No one seems to want to tell me what they were.' He glanced back at Charly and the spook. 'Maybe now we find out, eh? Body armour should stop an MP7. Might not be pleasant but these ripped men apart like a fifty calibre.' He seemed to run out of words and stayed standing where he was, looking off into the distance. He looked lost. To Roche, that was the worst.

The spook moved forward again. 'Thank you, Sergeant.' He nudged Stanton who nodded sharply and went back to his seat. 'So, gentlemen, that's who you're going after. The Met can keep chasing Taliban if they like with Kingship and I'm sure we'll give them all the help they can use but now we have some other fish to fry. We recovered something very interesting from Dagenham.' This time the spook cocked his head at Charly. 'Miss Whelan-Hollis of the Defence Science and Technology Laboratories will tell you all about it. Hopefully in words we can all understand.'

Charly stood up. From somewhere she'd got a Heckler & Koch MP7A1 4.6mm. She held it like she knew how to use it. Roche smiled.

'There's always something sexy about a woman with a sub-machine gun,' whispered Rees.

Charly smiled right back at him. 'So you all know what this is. Makes a nasty hole if it hits you but, as the sergeant says, nothing too much to worry about if you're in kevlar.' She looked up. 'Lights please.'

The briefing room lights dimmed. A screen lit up at the front of the room behind Charly.

'I'm sorry to show you this. It's not pleasant but I think you need to see it,' she said. 'Apologies to you in particular Sergeant Stanton.'

The pictures that flashed onto the screen looked like stills from some noughties Hollywood horror flick back when more and gore were the genre watchwords. Men with limbs ripped off. The last slide looked like something from one of the 'Saw' movies. It took Roche a moment to realise he was looking at a man.

'That was one of Red Troop after he'd been hit by three rounds from one of these.' To Roche it looked more like someone who'd thrown themselves onto a live grenade. 'Hydrostatic shock. Looks like they've been hit by a heavy machine gun, right?' Charly nodded. The picture faded again as the lights rose. 'The job of my team has been to work out how this' – she waved the HK –'did that. I won't bore you with the answers but everything points to an extremely high muzzle velocity. Hyper-velocity rounds are possible; they're just not possible with anything that any of us knows how to make.' She smiled and let out a little laugh. 'We thought that would be the easy part. We thought the hard part would be finding out what they had in these, since this was what they were shipping.' She took out a vial from her pocket.

Roche knew it at once. A Bliss vial.

'The bottom line,' said Charly, 'is that we don't know who or what we're up against but we know it has to do with Bliss.'

The spook moved forward again. He held up another Bliss vial, this time a full one. 'In the last six months it's come from nowhere to eclipse all restricted drugs combined. If it carries on this way it's going to be as ubiquitous as alcohol by the end of the year. It's not formally a restricted substance – yet – but no one knows where this is coming from. Gentlemen, we're going to find out.'

25 June, 1300 hours, near Saturn

The *Irrational Prime* had been looking for something to do and the ring structure of the smaller gas giant had caught its interest. In part how something so immensely complex and structured could arise from such elegantly simple physics and in part because it emphasised the human need to name everything. This planet and its moons, its rings, the divisions of its rings, the deeper they probed and the more structure they found, the more they gave things names. The Huygens ringlet, the Herschel Gap, the Kuiper Gap, the Bessel Gap, the Barnard Gap, half a dozen more. They didn't even fully understand these structures or how they worked or how they were formed, but naming things seemed to comfort them, as though it brought that which was unknown somehow within the circle of their understanding and took away its mystery. The chemical compounds that were going to result in their extinction had names too. Epinephrine; serotonin; corticotropin; norepinephrine; endorphin; dopamine and acetylcholine. The one that was the real bugger, the

Irrational Prime reckoned, the one that was going to get them killed, was the serotonin.

25 June, 1300 hours, Legoland

'Why me?' asked Roche. He and Charly were having lunch together in the Legoland mess. 'Why pull me into this?' A lot could happen in nineteen hours and they hadn't let him leave the building last night. There were some small but comfortable rooms on the north side with views over the river. Apparently the Russian defector Victor Oshchenko and his wife and daughter had stayed in exactly the same room for two nights back in 1993. There was even a picture of him on the wall. Either side of six hours of sleep, Roche had been through two hours of security interview, kitted up along with the rest of Task Force Hotel and been given another succession of briefings. Best he could tell they'd split the task force into three four-man squads and two of the squads were made entirely from the Special Reconnaissance Regiment. Observation not engagement. The spooks kept saying that. *Don't let them know you're there.* That was what people like Roche and Rees were good at.

Charly peered back at him over the rim of her glasses, a forkful of overcooked spaghetti halfway from her plate to her mouth. 'Oh come, Sergeant Manning, you know the answer to that. After lunch I'll show you something.'

They finished eating and she took him to a small office. He sat down beside her as she logged in to the Legoland network, something that apparently took both

a fingerprint and a password to do. She opened an mpeg and started it playing. The images were dark and it took a moment for Roche to understand what he was seeing; when he did, a numbness rocked him. She was showing him Kravica. Not his own recording of the aftermath of the massacre – he'd seen that a dozen times and would have known it instantly. No, this was someone else, the same time and place but a recording he'd never seen before. Which meant it was Ketch. Ketch had been carrying the second camera. You could make out the bodies on the floor of the agricultural shed. The picture wobbled back and forth as Ketch picked his way through them. Suddenly he was right back there, where it was impossible not to tread on the corpses because there were so many of them. A month and a half, it had taken a month and a half for Paper Teapot to do anything after this. Nearly fifty fucking days.

'It's hard watching, isn't it?' said Charly.

Roche didn't answer. It had been harder to be there. On the tape you didn't get the smell.

The camera swung briefly around, picking out two other figures standing a little way away. Him and Dook, though you couldn't make that out from the film. Dook who was dead twenty minutes later. Then Ketch panned back. He was walking to the far edge, to a door into the partitioned corner. He opened it. There was a flicker of something and then a flash of light and the movie stopped.

'Right at the end,' said Charly. She stepped the movie back to the frame before the flash of light. 'I turned the sound down. Was that a muzzle flash?'

Roche shrugged. 'There were shots. I always assumed it was Ketch. Sounded like an M16.'

Charly tapped the screen. Roche couldn't see what he was looking at except that Ketch had opened the door and there was a figure inside the room. It was too dark to make much out. 'Our image processing algorithms have improved some over the last twenty years. I've got that frame cleaned up as best we can.' She closed the movie and opened up a still picture instead. It was grainy and over-sharpened. You still couldn't make out much. Couldn't make out anything of the face at all but the figure was clearer now. Its arms were too long and its face was too narrow. It looked a hell of a lot like the figure he'd seen in Brixton at the ice rink. Roche bit his lip.

'Ketch called it the Scary Clown,' he said quietly.

'He's an odd-looking fellow,' agreed Charly. 'Watch this though. I'll step through frame by frame. There's only six, mind.'

The figure stayed where it was in the first three. In the fourth, half of it was gone. The bottom half. Just gone. In the fifth there was nothing.

'He just vanishes,' said Charly. 'How does he just vanish? There's something not right.' She shut the computer down. 'My department deals in things that are odd. Usually they don't turn out to be all that odd after all. We piece all the evidence together, we work out what really happened, what was really there, and it's usually pretty straightforward in the end. This one's an odd one. What happened to you in Brixton, that

was another odd one. You don't suddenly get a serotonin imbalance out of nowhere at your age, Sergeant. And then there was Dagenham.' She paused. 'It wasn't my decision but I recommended you because you've seen strange things and I don't know what to make of them.' Charly looked Roche in the eye. 'It's not just here either, Sergeant. I can't tell you anything more than that just now but I think Task Force Hotel can expect some travel abroad. I think it can expect some more strangeness, too. I thought we should have people who weren't strangers to strangeness.' She flashed another smile. 'If you'll forgive the pun.'

25 June, 1315 hours, The Challenger Deep

The Fermat hybrid construct waited motionless at the bottom of the Marianas trench, a little under eleven kilometres beneath the surface of the Pacific Ocean, near the island of Guam. The clones were all on the move. There were at least five existing groups of non-indigenous aliens operating in this world. It had found one in North Africa, deep in the Libyan desert and working almost in the open. It had another in the southern African desert in Namibia, also barely hiding at all. A third was in the Middle East in present-day Syria. The last sure sightings occurred during the mass slaughter of the Assyrian population of the region over a century earlier but they was still there, lapping up the lengthy and inelegant collapse of the Assad regime in Damascus. After that, the construct had found numerous

possible sightings linked to the Khmer Rouge massacres and elsewhere across the Indochinese Peninsula. Those last two had been more careful.

It had sightings in the Balkans, Germany and Poland in the years 1942-5. The chemistry found aboard the *Irrational Prime* had been harvested from somewhere in Croatia during this time. It hadn't found them until now, perhaps because those had been the ones to see them coming.

Now it had a sighting of one in Kravica in 1995. Six grainy frames of video. Evidence enough that a fifth group existed but what mattered more was that it had seen them. It had seen their form and now the Hive knew what they were: diaspora-descended Weft survivors once but now they were something else. They had no second self, no exotic-matter bond to one another and to the Hive. They had cut themselves off and made themselves into lesser beings. They were Shriven.

Several of the Shriven were, the construct was quite sure, hiding in a pocket of isolated space-time in London. Which meant the construct couldn't pin them down but it also meant they couldn't see what was about to happen to the others.

With careful stealth, the construct's weaponised clones moved closer to their targets.

12 – Opening the Closet

28 June, 1600 hours, 100 miles east of Damascus

The cloned Fermat construct approached the city from
the east. It had become irritatingly difficult to conceal
itself crossing the desert. It could cloak itself perfectly
well from all the standard senses and sensors of the
native species but moving at any kind of speed close to
the ground would throw up clouds of dust that would
then be hard to conceal. It could stutter in little wormhole jumps and the natives wouldn't be any the wiser
but then there was the matter of who else was in this
system. The Shriven appeared to have exceptional
sensor arrays hidden somewhere and they might pick
up the muon trail that the stutters would leave behind.
It couldn't allow that. It wanted to optimise its chances
to take them by surprise.

It settled for riding in the back of a native truck,
concealed and invisible. It had engineered a xeno-fungus
whose spores made their way into human nervous
systems and made them entirely suggestible. It was a
calculated risk – anything more complex that would have
allowed more reliable subjugation might have aroused

suspicion from the Shriven – but it needed pliable natives. It had considered flying but again the elimination of its own signature would have been imperfect.

The truck was slow. The clone took the time to flit its consciousness among the several hundred tiny drones that now orbited the earth. Individually they were simple things, barely even self-aware, but the network they made was showing up all sorts of interesting phenomena that even the *Irrational Prime* wasn't picking up lurking out among the moons of Jupiter and the rings of Saturn. Most of all, the orbital network was showing consistent steady signs of pion decay somewhere in Damascus. The network had it pinned down to a few dozen yards. The clone would do the rest.

It assessed the tactical options it had prepared for whatever it encountered. Shortly after it did that, the truck ground to a halt at some sort of native checkpoint and an exchange of conversation occurred. From the back of the truck, the Fermat couldn't intervene without giving itself away. It seemed that the conversation went logically enough but it nevertheless ended with the soldiers at the checkpoint hauling the driver out of his cabin, dragging him behind a shed and shooting him in the head.

The Fermat considered this for an instant and then unshrouded itself and climbed down from the back of the truck. It didn't trouble not to scrape its armoured limbs against the side of the truck or to land lightly.

The two soldiers came running back from behind the shed. They took one look at the clone and started

shrieking as they opened fire. The Fermat phased so the bullets passed straight through it and ignored them. It swept its hand across the soldiers' hut and the rest of the checkpoint. For a nanosecond, magnetic fields several quadrillion times stronger than the earth's own ripped apart the atoms of everything in front of it. The checkpoint disintegrated.

The Fermat turned to the two soldiers left behind it. One had fallen to his knees and was praying. The other was trying to reload and shaking too much to do it. The clone killed both of them by stopping their hearts. It left the praying one and hauled the other body into the truck, propped it up behind the wheel and infected the corpse with a modified version of its fungus. While it was waiting for the body to reanimate, it rewired the truck and took control. The dead man just had to sit up and loll there, that would do. An hour later, that was what it was doing. Another six and synaptic decay would be too far advanced for the deception to work any more but that was more than it needed.

'So your idea of stealth is to set off a magnetic pulse they'll feel in orbit and create walking dead men?' asked the *Irrational Prime*.

The Fermat ignored it.

'I hope you remembered to make sure it doesn't spore and infect half the city,' went on the freighter. If the freighter had been paying any attention at all then it would know the Fermat had already considered that.

'The bolt-bucket is bored,' drawled the *Exponential*. 'Pay no attention.'

The Fermat tuned them out. It had no intention of paying attention to either of them. The ships had been playing with the local native languages and expressions to pass the time. They were, the clone thought, a little like children. Or what Weft children might have been if the Weft had such a concept.

The truck drove through the outer suburbs of the Al-Shagour district of Damascus, past walls and tower blocks pock-marked with bullet holes. By then the truck driver was starting to stiffen. The Fermat turned the truck down an empty side-road and climbed out, invisible this time. It scaled a wall, disintegrated the driver and the truck and settled for making its own way. The pion signature still hadn't moved from where it had remained for the last three days, right in the middle of the old city.

The Fermat examined again the seventeen permutations of trap it had considered. Trap or not, the rational approach was to proceed. It was only a cloned construct. It was expendable.

A military transport helicopter buzzed overhead, sufficiently low for the Fermat to jump the intervening hundred yards and catch hold of it. It vaporised the pilot and the soldiers inside, took control and flew the helicopter over the old city until it was directly over the pion source. Then it let go. The helicopter leapt up and headed off on its own gentle arc until it crashed into the top of a tower block a quarter of a mile away. The Fermat registered this through the orbital network but by then it had found what it wanted.

28 June, 2200 hours, Damascus

The western windows of the tower block looked out over the Mausoleum of Saladin. The southern windows looked over the Umayyad Mosque. To the north and east were a maze of streets and tightly packed houses and other small blocks of flats.

The Fermat construct dropped through the concrete roof of the tower block like a pick through pond-ice. There wasn't much that was organic in the original Fermat hybrid construct to begin with and the clone was exactly the same. Encased deep inside in a globe of shock-gel floated an embryonic half-grown Weft brain. It existed just enough to have latched to pieces of exotic matter that captured and stabilised a few hundred pions that were themselves entangled with the exotic matter that was part of the Fermat construct. The clone wasn't so much a clone as a vessel that the hybrid construct rode, an exotic demonic possession. There were, the Hive theorised, ways in which other secondary sentients might be uplifted to snare exotic matter of their own and thus become a primary form of sentience suitable for similar possession or assimilation into the Hive.

A sequence of phase-correlated anti-matter nano-bomblets synched to the presence of a dimensionally complex intrusion and detonated. The tower block and a chunk of the adjacent mosque disintegrated in a blade of thermonuclear light and a flash of gamma radiation that even the native sentients couldn't miss. The gamma

radiation passed harmlessly through the clone. The high-energy particles flayed its outer layers into ions, destroying its cloak. Most were scattered by its magnetic shield before they could reach any deeper. Even as it fell through the cloud of ferociously energetic plasma that had once been the tower block, the clone inventoried its systems and found everything to be in working order. It landed two seconds later at the bottom of a crater in a thin slurry of molten stone.

As far as the rest of Damascus was concerned, the explosion had much the same effect as a small thermonuclear device. The initial flash turned parts of the Umayyad Mosque into plasma and the blast wave flattened the rest, along with several blocks of old Damascus city.

The Shriven who lived in the basement existed entirely in anti-phase to the charges in the nano-bombs and was only affected by a few symmetry-breaking weak neutrino interactions, which it wouldn't even have noticed if it hadn't been looking for them. It came up fighting, releasing a cloud of nanofactories that immediately set to work attempting to simultaneously dismantle the Fermat clone and entomb it in solidifying radioactive concrete. At the same time it lit up an anti-proton beam and attempted to slice the clone in half.

'Does that answer the question as to whether they knew you were coming?' asked the *Exponential*.

The Fermat clone's magnetics batted the anti-protons aside and barely noticed. It dimly registered flares of nuclear light around it as pieces of the crater

disintegrated. The nano-factories were absurdly ancient. The Fermat simply overrode their programming and assimilated them.

'They don't seem to be that bothered about concealing their presence,' observed the frigate.

'So neither are we.' The Shriven cloaked. The Fermat immediately let off its own anti-matter bomblet, throwing the Shriven's own trick back at it and shredding the cloak. The Shriven snipped open a pocket dimension and tried to hide inside but the clone collapsed it before it was even open. It did the same when the Shriven tried to open a stutter hole and then finally it made contact with the Shriven's exosuit. The Fermat reached inside, shut the suit down and then methodically dismantled it with the Shriven trapped inside. It kept the Shriven's organic brain and built a life-support container to keep it alive for now. The Hive had some ideas about re-engineering a connection to the exotic matter they'd need in order to throw a net of entangled pions over the Shriven, forcibly induce it into the Hive and rape its mind. It was either that or the tedious way of actually asking questions, and the primary Fermat was already working on that.

The clone stayed in the bottom of the crater for a few seconds more while it released another cloud of nano-factories to rebuild its outer cloak skin. Invisible again, it reabsorbed the nano-factories and walked out of the crater, then opened a series of stutter holes and teleported away. All things considered, stealth didn't really seem to be an issue any more.

28 June, 2300 hours, Prince Regent Pub, Salmon Lane, Limehouse

Someone behind the bar rang a bell for last orders. Roche made a show of drinking the dregs from his glass and shambling out of the door. Outside, he stumbled down Benton Street until he was in the shadow of the railway bridge. There wasn't anyone else about.

'Hotel two-two is mobile. I got nothing. Moving to secondary location.' He circled around the back of the pub and crossed over Blount Street. Most of one side was taken up by a long low flat-roofed building – something-or-other Property Services – but right at the end was a small three-storey block of a dozen apartments. He went inside and climbed the maintenance stairs up onto the roof. A black waterproof duffel bag was waiting there, left some hours before by Hotel two-four – a Corporal Ian Watts Roche had seen about the place in Hereford but didn't particularly know. It took him fifteen seconds after he opened the bag to have the HK417 sniper rifle built up and good to go. He settled down flat and trained the rifle on the tower block across the street.

'Hotel two-two in position. I've got eyes on the sixth floor, second window from the left, looking down Blount Street.' He focused the rifle's scope. Through the window he could see two figures standing as though holding a conversation. Now and then others moved past. There were at least five people in the flat. If Legoland's intel was right then the flat was a major distribution centre for Bliss. The odd thing was that Bliss wasn't illegal yet

– perhaps never would be – but the people moving it were all dealers who used to push heroin and cocaine and so they acted as though Bliss was the same. They could have had someone drive over in a transit, unload a few thousand vials of stuff in crates in the car park in full view of everyone else and drive off again and there wouldn't have been a thing the monkeys could have done about it. Her Majesty's Revenue and Customs might have asked to have a word with them about their tax returns but no one could stop them selling. Would have made the task force's job that much easier.

But no. Once a dealer, always a dealer. Bliss had turned the criminal underworld on its head and there was close to an all-out war going on. The London Met might have stood by and done nothing but that didn't mean some gang of Russians or Turks wouldn't show up with bats and machetes ... Roche chuckled to himself. They should have got that guy from Brixton on the team. Burman, the one with the brother who was a frogman. Legoland reckoned he'd refused to move the stuff. Preferred to keep his hands clean with smack and crack. Bully for him.

'Something funny, Hotel two?'

'Negative. I have two clear targets in the window, that's all.'

'The bald black guy on the right? He's the target. When that fucker moves, so do we.'

Roche quietly assumed that whoever the spook who'd been at the briefing was, this was all his baby. His own opinion was that it was too ambitious. Hotel two squad

had kept the flat under surveillance for two solid days and God only knew how long it had been watched before. Now they had the next link in the chain, the dealer in the van who carried in bulk, and when he left they'd tail him until they knew his supplier. Which, according to people who knew a lot more about illegal drug manufacture and distribution than he did, would be a chemical laboratory. As soon as they had the lab, three squads would go in and wrap it all up while Hotel four squad moved on the flat. And none of it would go to shit the way things had gone to shit in Dagenham because ...

Yeah. Because. Seemed there wasn't much of an answer to that. The flat had been watched long enough to know that the men inside weren't routinely packing those fucked-up Heckler and Kochs and half the faces there were familiar enough to the local plod. But the next level up? Smacked to Roche of being *exactly* like Dagenham.

He settled behind the scope to wait.

28 June, 2300 hours, Naypyidaw, Myanmar

The Shriven in Myanmar was the easiest to find. The Fermat clone reached the south-east Asia landmass close to the city of Yangon. It disassembled, reconfigured itself to appear as three native sentients and used the local transportation systems inland to Naypyidaw where the orbital network was registering possible pion decay products. This Shriven's defences were pitiful, the Shriven itself barely alive any more, and the Fermat's

nano-factories dismantled the Shriven's exosuit and dissolved most of its organic parts before the Shriven even registered that something was happening. The nano-factories assembled a life-support canister, retrieved the Shriven's consciousness and the minimum necessary physical matter to support its continued existence and cleansed the rest. When they were done, the clone, still in its form of three separate natives, walked in, picked up the canister, and left.

Half an hour later an anti-matter minelet obliterated half the city.

28 June, 2315 hours, Keetmanshoop, Namibia

The *Irrational Prime* had made four clones of the hybrid construct. It had ejected them from Europa's orbit several weeks ago. The third was in North Africa now. The last adjusted its trajectory very slightly as it approached Earth and altered the shape of its ablative shield. It crashed hard into the upper ionosphere and burned up most of its shield before transiting the stratosphere. The clone allowed itself to break up as it entered the troposphere and struck the Namibian desert as an apparent series of meteorites in the early evening. Its component parts merged and reassembled a little way outside the town of Keetmanshoop. As it entered, it immediately felt itself under attack from nano-factories. It commandeered and examined them. The nano-factories delivered a complex multi-layered virus tailored precisely to native brain chemistry.

The clone entered an empty building, engaged a cloaking screen, acquired a native sentient, and infected her with a high dose of the nano-factories. The results were high levels of neurotransmitter activity and a slow but growing urge to go somewhere. The clone changed its form and partially cloaked, then took the human by the hand. She led it to Johnny's Auto Electric on 8th Avenue.

The Shriven was in a terrible state, barely existing. It seemed to have no idea that the clone was even there. The clone dismantled the Shriven's exosuit but left the organic part intact. Curiosity stayed its hand. These Shriven weren't being as careful as it had expected. The clone in North Africa had already changed its objective. It was watching its Shriven now, waiting to see what it would do until the others hiding in London emerged from their pocket.

'Why?' asked the clone.

The Shriven made a gesture that was the Weft version of shrugging its shoulders. 'The Pleasure were coming. Our civilisation was doomed. The diaspora was an act of desperation inevitably bound to fail. We knew that when the Pleasure returned, the Hive would fall under their sway. Everyone who remained a part of it would be found. It was inescapable. When we discovered this world and what the chemistry of the native life could do, it was a way to escape. It cut us off from the Hive. No one would find us. We would be safe.'

'But the Pleasure did not return. The Hive is ready for them now.'

The Shriven exuded an attitude of longing and hunger and desperation. 'You don't understand what this chemistry does.'

'You sent this chemistry back into the Hive.'

'The others did that. They wanted your technologies. Your advances. To exist.'

The clone processed this. A subject race. The Shriven had gone around the Hive and contacted a subject race. The Hive didn't like that one little bit.

It had more questions but the Shriven self-terminated. The explosion was visible from orbit and left a crater a mile across. The Shriven, the clone, Keetmanshoop, and a large piece of Namibian desert all ceased to exist. As it detonated the minelet in Naypyidaw, the hybrid construct Fermat heard and saw. Back in orbit around Europa, the *Irrational Prime* reached the same conclusion as everyone else. The world would have to be sterilised, if it wasn't already too late.

'I suppose we'd best get making a lot of anti-matter then,' said the freighter, to no one in particular.

29 June, 0030 hours, Salmon Lane, Limehouse. London

'Hotel two-two, he's moving. I've lost eyes.' Roche shifted very slightly. The bald black man looked like he'd finished his conversation and had walked away from the window. He'd done that twice before. Roche kept his scope exactly where it was.

A few seconds later he heard what he was waiting for. 'Hotel two-one. He's out. Hotel two-two, relocate. Hotel two-three, confirm good to go.'

'Hotel two-three good to go.'

'Oversight confirm?'

'Oversight will be on station in three minutes.' They had eyes in the sky for this. Roche wasn't sure whether they were police or army but it probably didn't matter. Hotel two-three and two-four would alternate their chase vehicles. The helicopter was only there in case they both had to back off for some reason or some other unexpected shit happened.

Roche had the HK417 back in the bag in seconds. He was down on the street a moment later, loitering in the shadows where hotel two-three would pick him up once the target was moving.

'Hotel two-four, I have eyes on the target. He's left the building. Crossing the car park. Heading for transport.' They'd all studied the layout of the block. There was a small car park right in front of it where the target had left his van, one of those fucking irritating white Mercedes Sprinters that were always filthy with *clean me* written in the dirt like no one had ever thought of *that* joke before. Usually driven by a very special sort of cunt.

'Hotel two-two, eyes on target.' Roche could see him now. A big bald black man out in the car park. He walked to his van, keys in hand, then stopped at the door. The rest of the car park was empty but something had the man spooked. Roche ducked back out of sight.

Not that he should have been visible in the darkness anyway.

'Hotel two-four. Target is looking right at me.' Watts was parked a hundred feet down the street under a railway bridge where the lighting was so shit that the target shouldn't have been able to see the car, let alone that there was someone in it.

'Keep your cover, two-four.' That was Hotel two-one, Sergeant Woods, who had almost as many years behind him as Roche.

'He's made me. He's approaching.'

'Okay, Hotel, we're taking him down.'

'What grounds?' Rees.

'I don't fucking know and I don't give a shit.'

'I guess we can arrest him for being black after dark? That's still on the books, right?'

'Ha fucking ha, two-three. Now shut it.'

Roche shouldered the bag and gripped his MP5. He walked out of the shadows in time to see Woods running out of the car park. 'Freeze! Armed police! Get down! Get on the ground!'

The target turned abruptly. He stopped, almost right outside the Prince Regent. Woods halted twenty feet short, MP5 shouldered, still shouting. Roche had his own MP5 on the target now, running closer to take a flanking position. No one wanted to fire, not in a public street. On the other side of the target, Watts was running from the car. Rees would be coming off the adjacent rooftops from the other side. They had the target perfectly surrounded. He had nowhere to go.

Woods didn't waver. He must have been listening hard in the Dagenham part of the briefing because he had the MP5 pointing right at the target's face. Head-shots.

'We want him alive, two-one,' murmured Roche.

'We want him not pressing criminal assault charges and suing for wrongful arrest!' Rees again. Watts was coming up behind, Roche from the side now. Woods was still shouting.

'On the floor! Get down!'

For a moment it looked as though the target was about to do just that. He slowly sank to a crouch. Then he leaped. From a standing start he jumped what must have been ten feet up and covered the distance between him and Woods in a single bound. Woods got off one three-round burst but missed. Roche couldn't blame him for that. He was still staring, too surprised to move. His own MP5 was pointing at where the target had been a second ago.

The target came down on Woods hard, knocking the sergeant sprawling across the street, then bolted straight back the way Roche had come. Roche swung the MP5 round. 'Halt or be fired on!' The target ignored him and ran at the block of flats where Roche had taken his sniping position. Roche chased after him, then faltered as the target reached the block and ran straight up the wall.

He really didn't want to shoot but … but what the fuck? 'The target just ran up a fucking wall.' He swore and let off a three-round burst, aiming for the man's

143

legs. He saw the target falter, then pull himself up onto the rooftop and keep on going.

'Who the fuck is this guy?' Rees. 'Peter fucking Parker?'

Roche ignored him, sprinting after the target. 'Two-four, two-three, get mobile and pick up two-one. I'm in pursuit. You head him off. Oversight, the target is on foot on the rooftops heading north along Blount Street. Hotel two-two is in pursuit on foot at ground level. Do you copy?'

'Oversight copy. We'll be on you in sixty seconds.'

Roche raced round the corner. The target was still up on the rooftops, moving like an Olympic hurdler, which was pretty fucking impressive for a man who'd taken a bullet in the leg. He must have read it wrong and missed, because the man on the rooftops wasn't slowing down at all.

Fifty metres down Blount Street the railway tracks crossed overhead. Roche saw it coming. The target vaulted up onto another small block of flats at the end of the street and jumped down onto the tracks. 'Two-two. He's on the railway. Now heading north-east.' Underneath the bridge Roche cut across an open lot onto Carr Street and then right onto Repton, weaving under the railway arches. 'I don't see him.' Repton took him back under the tracks again and then turned to follow them, only to dump Roche in a dead end yard full of trucks. Roche bolted for the far end, looking for a way through or a way up. He had the tracks on his left and the canal on his right, he realised, and they were

converging. 'Fuck!' The yard narrowed to a point and blocked him in. He climbed up onto the back of one of the trucks but getting up onto the tracks wasn't going to happen. Too many Tower Hamlets lads had already tried it and there was a forest of razor wire in the way.

'Two-two, unable to continue pursuit.'

'Two-two, this is oversight, we have him on the tracks just crossing Regent's Canal.'

'Don't let him know you're on him!'

'Do you think we were born yesterday, two-two?'

Roche shot back through the yard to the end of Repton Street in time to see Rees in the BMW screech around the corner out of Blount Street. As Rees saw Roche he slammed on the brakes. Roche jumped in before the BMW stopped moving and Rees tore back down Carr Street, heading away from the target. 'Fucking canal,' he spat. 'Who the fuck *is* this guy?'

'At least it's not another Dagenham.' Roche dumped the shoulder bag in the back seat and wound down the window as the BMW screamed round the corner back into Salmon Lane and crossed over the canal.

'Oversight, target has passed Mile End stadium and is still on the tracks heading north-east. Who is this guy? Usain Bolt?'

'Looked like fucking Spiderman,' growled Rees.

'He's moving, this one. You trying to catch him for something he's done wrong or to try out for the 2016 Olympics?'

Rees shot a glare at Roche. 'Make yourself useful, mate, and get me a fucking map.' A quiet little housing

estate. Rees tore through it past sixty. 'You know anything about this cunt you're not telling me?' The BMW swerved north as Salmon Lane turned into Rhodeswell Road and then Turner's Road.

Roche shook his head. 'Right at the end. Past the Go-Kart track then hard left. *Hard fucking left!*' The BMW took the corner with a vicious squeal and slid onto the wrong side of the road before Rees had it back under control. The railway was up ahead. 'Right. Right!' The BMW's tyres shrieked again. 'This follows the track dead straight for a few hundred yards. Then ... Fuck! Oversight, do you see us?'

'You're hard to miss, two-two. Target's on the tracks, still a little ahead of you.'

'T-junction! T-junction!' The end of the road rushed at the BMW. 'Which fucking way, Roche?'

'Left!'

Rees stamped on the brakes and savaged the corner onto Bow Common Lane. They accelerated under a bridge. 'Oversight, target is right on top of you two-two.'

'Right right right!' screamed Roche. Except what on the map looked like a small road turned out to be a private access-way with a sturdy metal gate locked across it.

'Fucker!' Rees stabbed the brakes and tore at the wheel again. The back of the BMW fishtailed as Rees smashed it into the gate. The gate burst apart, one half flying open, the other half ripped clean off its hinges. It bounced up the BMW's bonnet and smashed into the windscreen as Rees accelerated along a tarmac path

barely as wide as the BMW between a row of trees and a strip of open ground. 'Where the fuck does this go, Roche?' The tracks were on their right now and Roche could see the target sprinting along them. He didn't bother pointing the MP5 out of the window. No chance.

'Go, go! Shit, what *is* that fucker on?'

'Yeah, and whatever it is, can we have some of it too?'

The trees closed in on the road from the left. The lane veered right towards the track and curved back under it. Roche punched the dash. 'Stop! Under the bridge!' BMW didn't sound right anyway. Rees skidded to a stop and they both jumped out of the car. Past the low brick bridge there were walls on both sides of the road.

'Oversight, target's closing.'

'Boost me!' hissed Roche. Rees cupped his hands. Roche jumped up and clambered onto the top of the wall. The tracks were only guarded by a simple metal rail up over the bridge. Roche vaulted up and over and there was the target, running straight at him fifty feet further down the track. Roche had him cold. He levelled the MP5. 'Oi! Fucker! Freeze!'

The target didn't even break stride as he veered sideways and jumped off the edge of the tracks to the narrow road below, where Rees had just driven the BMW. Roche ran to the edge of the tracks and let off another three-round burst before the target crossed the road and vanished into the trees. How far down was that? Twenty, twenty-five foot?

'Two-two, two-three, oversight, he's come down and gone into the trees on foot. Can you pursue?'

'I'm after him.' Rees.

'Oversight. I can't keep track of him in there, Hotel two-two.'

'Two-two. Exits?' Roche started to climb over the edge of the railway viaduct. Christ, though, that was a long drop. Good way to break an ankle and the target hadn't even given it a thought. Just gone for it. Maybe Rees was right. Maybe the fucker *was* Spiderman. He saw Rees sprinting across the open ground in pursuit but no way was he going to catch the guy.

'That's Tower Hamlets Cemetery Park, two-two. About a dozen possible exits and all into urban streets. We're not going to spot him coming out from up here.'

'Two-three, two-two. I lost him already. I got nothing. Which way?'

Roche muttered a prayer, swung over the side and let himself drop to the tiny strip of waste ground between the lane and the tracks. He hit hard enough to come up winded but nothing snapped. He looked about. He could see which way the target had gone but it was straight into the trees, into a maze of paths in the pitch black night and with a thirty second start, and Rees was already ahead of him.

'I lost him.' Rees.

'*FUCK!*' Roche dropped to a crouch.

'Do we put a call out?'

'What, for a random black dude out at night in Tower Hamlets?' Roche snorted. 'Or did you mean for Peter fucking Parker?'

29 June, 0230 hours, 100 miles over the surface of Europa

The *Irrational Prime* had most of the *Exponential*'s drones grudgingly re-directed to the task of harvesting anti-matter from the quantum froth of virtual particle pairs constantly forming and annihilating in empty space. It was slow, tedious work. Much quicker and more effective to go back to the other gas giant and mine its ring system into more drones and turn the rest of them into a colossal particle accelerator and make anti-matter the straightforward conventional way by smashing stuff into other stuff really hard. Or if they *really* wanted to just get rid of the third planet then all they had to do was seed it with nano-factories to build matter converters and pump energy into the planet's atmosphere until it boiled off. Shouldn't have taken more than a few dozen planetary revolutions. But the Hive wanted to be quiet, stealthy. The Hive didn't like that tau-burst which had looked like something hiding itself in a dimensional pocket because the Hive still didn't understand how the Shriven had known the *Irrational Prime* was there in the first place. Stealthy and quiet, so harvesting from the quantum fluctuations in the zero-point energy of empty space was all that was left.

The *Exponential* grumbled at losing most of its drones to the harvesting. The tau-detector was finished but the frigate was still fretting about the calibration that wasn't working the way it should and how there must be another tau-neutrino source somewhere in the system

that was throwing off all its calculations except that there clearly *wasn't* another tau-neutrino source because something that big and energetic would be impossible to hide. The few drones left to it vanished off into the Oort cloud to set off neutrino flashes. The *Irrational Prime* had enjoyed watching the frigate flounder for a while but not any more. It had quietly checked the math and the frigate had a point. Presumably the hybrid had done the same. You could add that to its reasons for caution. Anything putting out tau-neutrinos was either a massively obvious astronomical object or else it was someone mucking about with the fabric of space-time.

The interrogation of the Damascus Shriven had finished half an hour ago. The hybrid construct was wrapping up with the one from Naypyidaw. So far the Shriven in North Africa hadn't reacted to the others being excised. The *Irrational Prime* watched through the observing clone. It certainly didn't seem about to run. It didn't even seem to know, which was quite something because the humans were having conniption fits right across the planet now.

When it was done, the hybrid construct disintegrated the Shriven from Naypyidaw and left the remnants to sink to the bottom of the South China Sea.

'These are the stragglers, the outcasts. The core group are in London,' it said.

London had been the point of origin for the tau-burst. The *Irrational Prime* set to learning everything it could about the city. These would be the Shriven that had

hidden in their pocket dimension. The ones with the suspiciously good sensors. The *Exponential* recalibrated its tau-detector, aiming for maximum resolution from the planet's northern hemisphere. It swore a lot as it did it, shifting fluently between the six thousand human languages it had learned.

29 June, 1000 hours, Legoland

It was on the news on the way back as they drove the wrecked BMW into Vauxhall. A massive explosion in Damascus. By the time Roche turned in for some sleep, the reports were already talking about a nuke, maybe a suitcase bomb. The Umayyad Mosque had been destroyed, which was a bit like someone blowing up the Sistine Chapel. Roche couldn't say the name meant much but he caught up with the news like everyone else the next morning and it didn't look pretty. By then there were pictures. There were rumours of radioactivity and of a second bomb let off somewhere out in the desert a few hours earlier. Someone had picked up the electromagnetic pulse.

Leadface looked sombre and pissed off, more than usual. The spook wasn't there. Charly, Roche thought, looked positively worried.

'Well at least we didn't lose anyone,' said Leadface, which was his way of saying what a total clusterfuck something was. 'Anyone care to tell me what happened?'

He didn't much like what the four of them had to say but at least it wasn't just Roche this time and he

could hardly tell all four of his own men that they'd had some sort of collective hallucination. Task Force Hotel four had cleaned out the flat and seized the Bliss and everyone inside had come quietly. Not a trace of any firearms and no resistance. Which was shit because that meant they'd all have to be released in thirty-six hours unless someone either bribed a magistrate or decided they might be terrorists; and that, even Leadface had to admit, was a bit of a reach. But all in all, clusterfuck or not, everyone had much bigger things to worry about on account of the rumours on the news being largely right: by the looks of things, someone really had set off a baby nuke in the middle of Damascus; and since the Umayyad Mosque was the fourth most holy place in Islam, with a heritage dating back to the seventh century, it was a bit hard simply to do the usual and throw the blame at Muslim fundamentalists. The Middle East was busy screaming about the Americans and the West arming the rebels with nukes – although that didn't make any sense either. Russia was already wagging its finger and Europe had woken up to about a billion horrified Muslims. America, so far, was still asleep.

The worst part for everyone in Legoland, by a long way, was that it wasn't the only nuke to go off that night.

'Some of you know how closed a country Myanmar is. Two other bombs went off shortly after Damascus, one in the Namibian desert and one in the Myanmar capital around six in the morning local time. It hasn't made the news yet but it will by the end of the day.

When it does, expect the shit to hit the fan. No casualty reports but the Russians are getting very hot under the collar and we're just waiting for the Chinese to completely lose their shit about Myanmar. Until either someone works out who did what to whom or else we work it out for ourselves, we're all on standby. Obviously the top priority is finding out where the nukes came from, who's got them and whether they have any more. After that comes working out why they hit the targets they did.'

They all milled about afterwards, wondering what to do. Leadface was off back to Hereford.

'The forensics team found blood,' Charly told them over lunch. Roche was slowly getting to like Charly rather a lot. The whole 'scientist' thing was still bullshit but she sat with him and the other task force soldiers as often as she didn't and she held her own. 'Not my field really but they should have a good crack at working out what your man was on.'

'They found blood?' asked Roche. 'Where?'

'Well, I've read all the reports and I gather you shot at him twice. Once when he first ran and again just before you lost him … Did he really run straight up a wall?'

Roche made an irritated face. At least he had Woods and Watts to back him up this time. 'That's what it looked like.'

'We had blood on the first rooftop. Quite a bit at first but it dried up pretty quickly. You must have nicked him.' Charly smiled at Rees. 'Is it true you're calling him Spiderman?'

'I didn't pace it out,' said Woods coldly, 'but I was twenty feet away. He covered it from standing in one jump.'

'Never saw anything like it,' said Roche softly. Woods had frozen. They both had. It was impossible, what that man had done.

The spook rounded them up that afternoon.

'Congratulations,' he told them. 'You're going to Libya.'

1 July, 0800 hours, Naval Air Station Sigonella, Sicily

Roche, Woods and Rees flew out the next day. Watts stayed and instead they got Stanton. That, Roche reckoned, was a plus. Turned out Stanton would have been with them for Tower Hamlets too, only he'd had something more special to deal with. Couldn't say what, of course, and Roche knew better than to ask.

When they came off the plane in Sicily, the heat was like being wrapped in a steaming hot wet towel from the top down. An escort walked them from the plane to a briefing room and they'd barely sat down when a crisp American naval lieutenant in service khaki marched in and started on them. 'Gentlemen, this is not a reconnaissance mission. I realise that's your specialist role but I'm well aware that all of you have other training. This is an extraction and suppression mission and your role will be of a supporting nature. You'll be briefed on the specifics on the way there but your mission is to observe, report and, if requested, advise. If. Requested.' He made

a big deal of emphasising that. Then he started handing out what looked suspiciously like radiation badges.

'The task force commander has specifically requested your presence as one of the few special forces teams available from any allied nation with experience in dealing with unusual events and technologies. Bluntly, gentlemen, I have very little information to give you but I'm to advise you that this mission is directly related to the recent events in Damascus, Namibia and Myanmar and to inform you that we are open to the possibility that we may be dealing with an incursion of an extra-terrestrial nature. If there's any more information on that then I do not have it for you at this time ...' He paused but Roche was stuck on the nuke in Namibia. Keetmanshoop. A small town full of poor black folk that no one had ever heard of until yesterday, stuck in the middle of a desert. They'd felt the explosion in South Africa a hundred miles away and the kilotonnage was apparently larger than the other two. Why the hell let off a nuke in a place like Keetmanshoop?

Rees was waving his badge. 'Sir, is this a radiation badge? Is that a risk on this mission?'

The lieutenant carried on almost without a pause, waiting exactly long enough for Rees to finish his question. 'Our intelligence, the nature of which will remain classified and will not be revealed to you or your superior officers, is that all three locations were linked to a very specific activity which also remains classified in nature, and that you will shortly be heading towards what we believe to be a fourth. In short, gentlemen, there's some

weird shit going on and you have experience with weird shit and that's why you're here and yes, soldier, those are radiation badges. Given the events at the sites related to this mission you must assume that the presence of radioactive material is a credible possibility.'

He paused, at last, for a drink of water. His voice changed very subtly, as though he was starting to have some trouble entirely believing his own briefing. 'Intelligence indicates a similar site to the ones in Damascus, Myanmar and Namibia exists in the deserts of southern Libya and so that's where you'll be going. There will be civilians present and it will not be clear who is hostile and who are non-combatants. You are authorised to fire whenever you feel your lives are in danger and I am to tell you there will be no repercussions – whatever shitty mess you leave behind, someone else will clear it up. The primary mission will be carried out by a specialist team with two squads of navy SEALS and yourselves in a support role. So essentially you stay out of the way, observe and support as requested by the specialist team. Any nuclear material discovered during the course of this operation will be handled by the specialist team who have been appropriately trained and equipped to do so. If you locate any other unusual objects or technology then you are not to touch said objects but you will call for the specialist support team who are trained for this. I'm told there's no risk of a nuclear event – whether you choose to believe this or not is up to you but I suggest you either do or express your reservations here and now and enjoy a long quiet

stay somewhere out of harm's way while the real men get on with what needs to be done. Questions?'

A silence hung over the briefing room. Rees looked at Roche. Roche looked back. They exchanged a glance with Woods and then with Sergeant Stanton.

'Yeah,' said Woods, after a long pause. 'If we see ET, do we shoot him?'

The crisp white lieutenant didn't even blink. 'If you see ET, you call the specialist support team. You see Daleks, you call the specialist support team. You see Martian tripods, you call the specialist support team. You see Jar-Jar Binks, you shoot that fucker in the head until he is dead and *then* you call for the specialist support team. Is that clear, gentlemen?'

1 July, 2200 hours, somewhere over the Sahara desert

'What about Ewoks?' asked Stanton. They were in the back of a V-22 Osprey. Somewhere out there was another Osprey and a pack of angry F/A-18 Hornets there to give shit to any Libyans who decided it wasn't okay for the United States to send a pack of armed-to-the-teeth Special Forces types into the back-arse of their country without bothering to ask nicely first.

'We shoot Ewoks,' said one of the SEALs. As best Roche could tell, both Ospreys were loaded almost with their full complement of twenty-four soldiers and a Growler Fast Attack Vehicle. The specialist support team was in the other Osprey. Roche, Woods, Stanton and

Rees found themselves with two squads of SEALs and their lieutenant for company. There was the usual bit of trans-Atlantic ribbing.

'Ewoks are badass,' said Woods. Roche raised an eyebrow at that. Woods was the last person he'd imagined having an opinion about Ewoks, one way or the other.

'Badass?' The SEAL laughed. 'Fucking teddy bears.' They'd crossed the Libyan coast a while back and no one had tried to shoot them down. This far out over the desert, Roche supposed that no one much cared. There probably wasn't even any air traffic control coverage. People were starting to relax.

'Fucking teddy bears who take out AT-STs with rocks and bits of tree,' said Woods. 'You see an angry Ewok, you best run, because that Ewok he's going to go psycho on your arse and send you running home to mama.'

'You see an Ewok, you call the ...' started Rees.

'... specialist support team,' chorused everyone. Roche shook his head. They all thought the whole extra-terrestrial thing was a bit of a joke and then he kept suddenly remembering that people didn't make jokes like that, not about an op. The rest of Task Force Hotel and the Navy SEALS were going through the same thought process. Roche could see it – *yeah, there's something weird maybe and best keep your eyes open, but none of them actually believes it, right?* Rees and Woods and Watts had seen the man in Tower Hamlets do things that men shouldn't be able to do, but it *had* still been a man, two arms, two legs, bled when he got shot. Real aliens? Nah.

'I thought I saw an alien, one time,' he said.

The others fell silent. It was the sort of silence of men waiting to be told a story.

'It was in Brixton.' He saw Woods roll his eyes straight away. Rees just stared at his feet and shook his head. 'Police liaison. We were taking down what was supposed to be a heavily armed drug gang. Well, they were heavily armed right enough. Swedish-Ks mostly. Not really a problem. They were pussy-cats.' He looked at the SEALs. 'You guys play some hockey, right? So you know your way around an ice rink. There was this little garage where they keep the ... what are they called, the machines they use to cut the ice ... ?'

'Zambonis.'

'Zambonis. So there was this little garage right up against the rink with this pull-down door, you know the sort, a roll-down metal thing. And all the bad guys are there with their pants around their ankles being hustled by the plod – sorry, cops to you – and someone gets the idea that there's someone in the garages where the Zambonis live ...'

'*You* got the idea, Roche,' muttered Rees.

'Yeah. So Rees and I, we go back and well, you know what those doors are like. Never quite close properly. So Rees finds a gap and pokes a fibreoptic underneath. And there you go. Aliens.'

He sat back. The others watched, quiet, as if waiting for the punchline. It was the sort of story that was supposed to end up with finding two teenagers making out, not knowing they were in the middle of an armed drugs bust. Or something like that.

'Aliens,' he said again, sure of it this time.

'Were they legal ones?' asked one of the SEALs. They still couldn't work out whether or not he was joking. 'What they look like?'

'Faces all stretched. Arms too long. Like scary-arsed clowns. By the time anyone got in, they were gone. Like they vanished through the walls.'

'You see them too?' someone asked Rees. Rees shook his head.

'Was outside, shooting punks. Roche was the only one. Didn't even get a picture off the fibreoptic. Laptop fried. Totally dead. Wiped clean.'

'Fucking aliens, eh?' The SEALs all laughed. *Almost* all laughed. All except the lieutenant. After a moment the lieutenant pulled a crumpled piece of paper out of his pocket. He looked at Roche and passed the paper along the line of men.

'Look like that, did it?' he asked, as Roche took it.

Roche stared at the paper. 'Where'd you get this?'

'I asked if there was anything in particular we should be looking for.'

The sketch wasn't great but there was no doubt what it was. It was the Scary Clown.

2 July, 0030 hours, 4 miles west of Aqar, Libya

The Ospreys came down in the desert, swirling up a storm of sand and barely touching down as the back ramps opened and the Growlers and the squads of soldiers ran

down and fanned out, spreading themselves in a defensive arc. There was no one here waiting for them but that wasn't the point – everything and everywhere was hostile until you knew better. They'd come down on a flat rocky expanse a few miles west of Aqar itself and just off a track that ran east-west through the desert. When he got through choking in the cloud of dust thrown up by the Osprey's rotors, Roche shivered.

'Pleasantly cool.' Rees stretched his arms and rolled his shoulders. 'What happened to the Sahara Desert, hottest place on earth?'

They ran out of the dust cloud and took shelter behind a low ridge as the whine of the Osprey rotors slowly died. The Hornets were heading away. Fuck knows where they were all off to next but that wasn't Roche's problem, or anyone else's on the ground, not until it came to evac.

'Isn't this a bit dry for you?' shouted Woods at the SEALs. Which would have been funnier if they hadn't all been about to slog it on foot together. Apparently they didn't get to keep their Growler.

One of the specialist support team – whoever the fuck they were – approached the SEAL lieutenant and started a conversation. Roche watched. He could tell by the lieutenant's body language that the lieutenant wasn't enjoying what he was hearing.

'Lads,' Roche said. Stanton, Rees and Woods went quiet. They could hear raised voices now but couldn't quite make out what was being said. It was clear that there was a heated argument going on.

'On an op,' Rees muttered. 'Fucking cowboys.'

Roche moved forward, making it look as casual as possible. He could see that the lieutenant's men, who were acting as a security cordon for the landing site, were occasionally glancing over their shoulders.

'I don't care that you outrank me, my orders came down from SOCOM, you don't change parameters on the job ...' the lieutenant was saying, sounding more exasperated than angry.

'Stop acting as if you're an amateur and it's your first time out of the box. Does the phrase black ops mean anything to you?' The support team's officer was a big man, a squat, solidly built slab of muscle. It was clear he was trying to intimidate the SEAL officer, who was standing his ground. 'You're here because of some fucking political short-stroking, nothing more. Now grow the fuck up, come to terms with it and stay back here, play with your toy boats or whatever, we got this, okay?'

'Yeah. I understand you want me to disobey a direct order on your say so without ...'

It happened quickly. Roche still couldn't quite believe what he was watching. This didn't happen on special forces ops, ever, even American ones. The support team officer grabbed the SEAL lieutenant by the neck, picked him up off the ground and slammed him into the dirt. It was the sort of thing that happened in action films, not in actual life, and it looked more like a wrestling move than something executed by a trained soldier. The support team officer shouldn't have been able to pull it off against a trained Navy SEAL either. Yet the man

had moved with ferocious speed and exhibited remark-
able strength. He held the SEAL lieutenant on the
ground now. The lieutenant tried a couple of moves
that should have broken the hold but they didn't. Even
from Roche's position he could make out the thick cords
of muscle that made up the 'support team' officer's arm.

Several of the SEALs on the cordon swung around,
bringing up their M4s and levelling them at the special
forces officer holding down their boss. As one, the special
forces soldiers that made up the support team brought
their weapons to bear.

'I will bury every one of you fuckers out here,' the
officer said. Roche looked at the rest of the American
special forces team. Like their officer they were all big
guys; like their officer they had all moved with
surprising speed.

'Woah! Woah!' Roche went against all his training
and common sense and got in between them. He sensed
rather than saw Woods, Rees and Stanton getting ready
to move if it went hot. 'Gentlemen! Please!'

'Shut the fuck up, limey,' the special forces officer
who was still choking the SEAL lieutenant snapped.

'That's fine, mate. Look, you want to go on, we'll
kick back here and watch the 'Spreys, have a brew, no
issues. Can you just let my boss up there?' Roche was
playing the dumb squaddie for all it was worth.

The 'specialist support' officer looked down. The
SEAL lieutenant was turning red now. 'Fucking faggots,'
he muttered. He let go of the lieutenant and the SEAL
rolled away from him, gasping for breath. Roche knew

that he'd just had his world-view radically fucked about. You weren't supposed to be able to do things like that to a SEAL. The other officer straightened up and turned to look at Roche, who was standing with his hands far apart. 'This is a US operation and you shouldn't even be here.'

'We'll go inside the 'Spreys, put the kettle on and sit with our eyes shut, okay?'

The officer narrowed his eyes. 'Are you trying to be cute?'

'We all want what you want, the job done and to go home. If that means we wait here then we wait here. I don't mind not being shot at. Don't mind that at all.'

The special forces officer glared at him but said nothing. He turned and walked away.

'Stand down,' the SEAL lieutenant told his men between gasps for breath. Roche knelt next to him.

'You all right, mate?'

The lieutenant nodded.

2 July, 0037 hours, 4 miles west of Aqar, Libya

The Growlers went ahead, four men in each. Roche watched the soldiers from the other Osprey jump into them and drive away. There was something wrong about them, he thought, both the teams who drove ahead and the dozen soldiers who loped off across the desert in their wake. They had a fluidity to the way they moved, like tuned athletes, and a jumpiness to them too. They

reminded him of the man they'd chased through Tower Hamlets. Maybe it was the adrenaline. He felt it himself a little too, a hyper-awareness of everything around him.

He watched the specialist support squad's four snipers running across the desert, making for the rocks surrounding the township of Aqar. They were moving at a full sprint, each of them carrying an M82A1 .50 calibre sniper rifle which weighed the better part of thirty pounds before you started adding furniture to it. It was unsustainable, a pace like that, but they didn't stop. They just kept running. Roche elbowed Rees. 'You thinking what I'm thinking?'

'I really doubt it.'

'Tower Hamlets Man.' Rees shrugged. Roche shook his head. 'Yeah, none of the rest of you really saw him run, did you?' He walked over to the SEAL lieutenant instead. 'Who are those guys?' he asked.

'Never seen them before,' the SEAL told him. Which was mildly curious in itself because even the US special forces community was relatively small. 'I thought 3rd Special Forces out of Bragg, now I'm thinking SAD.'

Roche nodded. The Special Activities Division was the covert paramilitary branch of the CIA. Figured. Fucking cowboys.

'You see his eyes?' the lieutenant asked. Roche shook his head. 'There was something wrong with that guy.'

'Well I think we all saw *that*.'

'LT?' Roche glanced around to see the crew chief of one of the Ospreys that had brought the SF guys in. 'Can I have a word?'

The SEAL lieutenant excused himself and moved away to talk to the crew chief.

'Well, they were a bit spry,' Woods said as the other three joined them. 'And wankers too.'

'What are you thinking?' Stanton asked. Roche was watching the last of the 'specialist support team' soldiers disappearing into the distance.

'I'm thinking my curiosity is going to get me killed,' Roche said. The other three soldiers were sitting down, but not Roche.

'I think they'll shoot us if they even see us.'

'I think you're right. I think we want the smallest footprint possible. I'll go.'

'Sure you're not too old for this?' Woods asked.

'Not on your own,' Stanton said.

'I'll go and look after him,' Woods said.

'Think you can keep quiet long enough?' Rees asked. 'I'll stay here and drink tea.'

'They're Americans, they'll only have coffee,' Stanton pointed out.

'Ah fuck,' glared Rees. 'You're right. You stay. I'll go.' But he didn't get up.

'Savages,' Woods muttered.

The SEAL lieutenant joined them.

'Gentlemen, I'm sorry about the conduct ...' he started.

'It's okay,' Roche said. 'We'll take the piss out of you after the op. Look I know you don't like people making it up as they go along but we've got to get eyes on. Me and Woods want to go in.'

'Frankly if you weren't, we were. Do you need any more shooters?'

'No, we're sneaky bastards, boss,' Woods told him, grinning.

'The fewer of us the better,' Roche said.

'I think that if they see you, they're going to shoot at you,' the lieutenant said. 'I think they're going to keep shooting. Even if they don't see you again until the evac.' He seemed to be struggling with something. Trying to decide whether or not to tell them. 'The crew chief told me that he saw them shooting up in the 'Sprey.'

Roche wasn't particularly surprised.

'He have any idea what?' Rees asked. The lieutenant shook his head.

'That looked a bit like 'roid rage to me,' Woods said.

'Anything like this ever happened before?' Rees asked.

The SEAL lieutenant bristled but quickly calmed again. 'No. I know all the jokes about us Yanks being cowboys but you don't get away with that shit. Not on an op.'

Roche and Woods were stripping off anything that they wouldn't absolutely need. Roche was wishing for a ghillie suit but he didn't have the time to sort one out. He checked and double-checked the digital camera.

'Where do you want us?' Stanton asked the lieutenant.

2 July, 0100 hours, Aqar, Libya

Roche wanted to throw up. With the Growlers gone, the only way for them to cover ground to Aqar was to

run. Roche had his Diemaco C8SFW carbine cradled in his arms as he ran. Despite the cold he was so covered in sweat that he felt he could wring out his watch hat and was worried that he was going to sweat off his camo paint. His chest was burning, he was struggling for breath and he didn't like the way that Woods seemed to be having no problems keeping up with him. They weren't being terribly stealthy but the soldiers ahead of them had moved so quickly they had little choice.

They could see Aqar ahead. It was a spread-out town of low one- and two-storey stucco buildings packed in tightly together with a scattering of low ruined walls in clusters along the southern approach. It was situated on a plain with sparse, rocky hills to the east and the north-west. Roche and Woods were approaching from the west and Roche was already seeing flashes of light in the township. Unmistakable muzzle flare but he hadn't heard any shots – probably the 'specialist' soldiers using their suppressed M4 carbines. He took the muzzle flashes as an excuse to stop, catch his breath and check the township through the light intensifying starlight scope attached to the C8. Woods came to a halt a little way from him, checking all around them.

A lot of SF soldiers liked to use night-vision goggles for work in darkness but Roche preferred to rely on his own night vision, particularly on a bright cloudless night like this. If he needed anything more then he had the scope, which was currently showing him Aqar in unflattering green. He could see more flashes in the township. It was only a matter of time before it went …

The shot from the .50 calibre sniper rifle rolled like thunder across the plane. The four feet of muzzle flash lit up the rocky canyon where Aqar nestled. Then it fired again. A second sniper fired. Roche heard the multiple popping noise of a Mark 19 automatic grenade launcher, presumably one of the ones mounted on the back of two of the Growlers.

... loud. Yeah. Explosions bloomed in Aqar. There were brighter, longer muzzle flashes and then moments later the sound of the .50 calibre Growler-mounted heavy machine gun reached them. They watched the progress of the nearest Growler by the muzzle flashes as it moved rapidly through the streets, machine gun firing. They saw the short flight of tracers into buildings, some of them ricocheting into the night sky. Roche guessed the 'specialist support unit' had received a different briefing on the Rules of Engagement than him because he hadn't heard anything that sounded even remotely like a Libyan weapon. Judging by the muzzle flashes, the special forces guys were killing en masse. He felt a shiver of unease. For a while he couldn't put his finger on what it was until he realised it was Kravica. What he was seeing was making him think of Kravica.

The night suddenly lit up nearby with more muzzle flashes, much too close for comfort. Roche and Woods hit the ground as tracers poured down into the village amid the flat, hard staccato of automatic support weapons. Two of the light machine guns were set up less than forty feet in front of them and he and Woods had almost run straight into them. They would have

too, if the guns hadn't started firing. Despite the lunacy with the SEAL lieutenant and the steroid abuse, these 'specialist' soldiers knew what they were doing.

Woods signalled a circuitous route away from the emplaced machine guns and into Aqar.

And let's keep it stealthy.

As Roche moved away, he saw the soldiers had set something up on a tripod a little way off to one side of their position. Bizarrely, what it reminded Roche of most of all was a cheap supermarket barbecue with an antenna on top.

2 July, 0117 hours, Jovian upper atmosphere

The last of the three surviving Fermat clones watched the American task force arrive with some interest. It hadn't bothered conferring with the *Exponential* and the *Irrational Prime* over what to do; it simply phased into the ground and watched. The Americans started by setting up four sites around where the Shriven was existing. They were very careful and quiet about it and the clone debated the possibility that the Shriven hadn't even noticed them. After that, the Americans went in and started shooting everything that moved. Their apparent strategy of stealth followed by loud and obvious force lacked any clear logic and the clone devoted most of its considerable cognitive effort to extrapolating likely possible outcomes and rationales and, most importantly of all, hypotheses as to what had brought the Americans here at all.

All of which changed as soon as it received emissions from the four sites the Americans had so carefully constructed.

'A tachyonic quantum field?' The *Exponential*, the *Irrational Prime* and the hybrid construct Fermat all paused significant portions of what they were doing. Human science at least acknowledged the existence of tachyonic fields. They inadvertently made them now and then in their Large Hadron Collider, a particle accelerator that was twenty-seven kilometres in circumference and used as much power as a small city. Apparently they'd made a technical breakthrough recently. Judging by what the Americans had brought with them, the humans were suddenly able to fit all of that into something small enough that two soldiers could carry it across a desert on their backs.

2 July, 0119 hours, Aqar

It was only as they made their way into Aqar that Roche started to hear sustained return fire. He picked out the ubiquitous AK47 sound amid other, heavier, Russian-made automatic weapons. There were more explosions deeper in the town that were probably rocket-propelled grenades. Aqar was catching hell.

'Okay, where to?' Woods asked. They were both crouched down by a low wall that acted as some kind of goat pen. One goat was horribly wounded. The others were dead. Part of the house to which the wall was attached had been demolished, probably by a

forty-millimetre grenade. Bloodied limbs poked out of the rubble.

It was a good question. As far as Roche could tell, the US special forces soldiers were killing everyone here for the sake of killing. Their own brief had been to stay out of the way, support as requested and search for anything unusual. The last bit, when Roche had his way, got done in silence without any bad guys waking up and shooting back. This lot seemed more interested in conducting their search in the style of the My Lai massacre.

He shrugged; Woods shrugged back then signalled towards the centre of town, picking one of the narrow alleyways between houses at random. They moved down, Roche taking the lead while Woods checked behind them. Fire was coming from all over the town now and someone, somewhere, was making a concerted effort to fight back.

Figures ran across the alleyway. Both soldiers stopped, moved into shadow and crouched, going very still, Roche facing one way, Woods the other. Two of the figures turned at the end of the alley and started towards them. Roche's headshot from the suppressed C8 caught the first, a spray of blood that looked black in the moonlight. He fell back. Roche shifted to fire at the second when a fist-sized part of the wall exploded. The .50 calibre round took the other man in the side and the hydrostatic shock all but exploded him. Roche crouched even lower and pressed himself hard against the wall. Muzzle flashes illuminated one side of the alleyway. He watched as a Growler drove by, firing.

Roche gave it a few moments and then moved up to the bodies. The dead men were locals, both of them. The one he'd shot had no face. Normally he'd have double tapped to make sure – it was good practice – but every shot threatened to give them away. He checked the small road at the end of the alleyway. It was clear both ways.

Woods covered him as he darted across the road. Now the sweat was from the tension. Roche dropped into deep shadow and covered Woods as he crossed in turn …

The side of the building next to him exploded, spraying him with fragments of masonry. He staggered back, trying to work out what had happened. Woods passed him and took the lead. Another fist-sized hole appeared in the wall next to him. Roche turned and followed. They moved fast. One of the snipers had seen them. They'd radio in a position to the soldiers in the Growlers.

What the fuck am I doing? Roche wondered.

They moved south and west, zigzagging through the town, trying to move counter-intuitively through the streets and alleys to confuse anyone searching for them and trying to keep out of sight of the snipers while they worked out where the fuckers were. So fucking counter-intuitive that it was beginning to feel like aimlessly trying not to end up dead; but then Woods stopped and made a sharp gesture: *look!*

Down the dirt track in the centre of town was what looked like a partially buried warehouse made of corrugated metal. The warehouse was in a fenced-off area topped with razor wire and the compound had already

been taken by the US soldiers. About a third of them and one of the Growlers were in cover in and around the compound, engaged in a vicious firefight with the locals in the southern part of the town. Roche already knew, because they'd had to hide from them twice, that some of the US 'specialists' were roaming the streets and alleyways in two-man kill teams, executing anybody they came across, armed or not. Roche had no idea where the rest of them were.

Roche nodded and crept closer, then edged prone and with a painful slowness out onto the street, tucked in close to a wall until the wall's shadow and his own stillness was all the concealment he had. Small-arms and machine-gun fire rattled steadily back and forth, random bullets now and then exploding holes in the stone and mortar about their heads. They'd worked out three of the four snipers' positions in the surrounding hills now and Roche was pretty sure they were concealed from them. As for the fourth … Mentally Roche crossed his fingers as he took rapid pictures with the digital SLR camera. When he had enough, he turned his head to Woods and made a gesture.

Closer.

Woods made a face in the darkness, then nodded and then gestured back at the American 'specialists'.

Are they targets now?

Roche gave that some thought. The Americans in Aqar were out of control. They were on something. They were indiscriminate and they were massacring civilians. Most of all, Roche was absolutely certain that

if they saw him and Woods, they'd shoot without hesitation. Anything else wouldn't even cross their minds.

He nodded. Woods raised an eyebrow but after that he only shrugged.

2 July, 0123 hours, half a kilometre south-east of Aqar

The cloned Fermat construct emerged out of the stone eight feet behind the fourth sniper. It rose silently and was out of phase with the matter of the desert air and so couldn't possibly disturb it; and yet some primitive instinct in the sniper made him suddenly turn. He was quick, impossibly quick for ordinary human nerves and reflexes, but it helped him only insofar as he caught a momentary glimpse of the Fermat before the construct shifted phase and realised itself.

There was a very faint pop as every erg of energy was sucked out of the sniper and he froze to absolute zero. The cloned construct stepped past and settled its attention on the device on the tripod set up a little way in front of the sniper. It looked a bit like a cheap barbecue with an antenna on top.

2 July, 0152 hours, Aqar

Roche stood just inside the walls of a half-destroyed house. Woods crouched beside him. They were closer to the compound now. Tracer fire from the machine-gun emplacements they'd passed on the way in was

flying overhead, impacting in the southern part of the town. He tried to ignore the corpses of the family who'd once lived here. This was the shit that happened to civilians the moment there was any kind of warfare in a built-up area. He'd seen worse.

A movement on the other side of the wall. Roche heard it and froze, carbine at the ready. Woods had heard it too. Two of the US 'specialists' moved into the alley next to the house, both picking their way very carefully. The alleyway lit up with muzzle flashes, a series of short bursts from AK47s further down. The special forces soldiers staggered back and then advanced again, firing rapidly.

Roche mouthed a silent *fuck*! Both the American soldiers had been wearing body armour, and the good stuff as well. Dragonscale; but even so, you got hit by a rifle round, you fell over, gasping for breath and hoped you hadn't broken any ribs.

Apparently not this lot.

There was a popping noise as one of the 'specialists' fired a forty-millimetre grenade. The far end of the alleyway exploded. The two soldiers pushed forward fast now, firing all the time, silencing cries of pain with suppressed shots from their M4 carbines.

When they were gone, Woods checked the alleyway and signalled them clear to move on.

2 July, 0158 hours, half a kilometre south-east of Aqar

The device on the tripod was unquestionably the source

176

of the tachyonic quantum field. The nano-factories finished their careful invasion of it and returned to the Fermat construct. The construction was crude and certainly human. It was just fifty years ahead of their current technology.

2 July, 0212 hours, Aqar

The fence around the warehouse had been knocked down or blown open in several places. Most of the 'specialist support group' soldiers were at the southern end of the compound firing at the locals and advancing on them. They'd left a small security force behind: two soldiers at the door to the warehouse and another two out in the street to the north.

Roche reckoned that he and Woods were running out of luck. They were trying to sneak around a small town filled with soldiers with comparable training. Right now they were both lying down behind the wall of another partially destroyed house, though Roche was pretty sure this had been the result of an RPG strike. They were waiting for the two soldiers in the street to get close to them. The rest of the battle was getting further and further away, the sounds of AK47 and heavy machine-gun fire more distant and less frequent.

On the other side of the wall Roche heard the scuff of feet. Woods was up first. He moved around the wall, grabbed the nearest soldier by the face, wrapped his legs around the other man's and simply fell over. He used his grip on the first soldier to force his head

up and then pushed the blade of his knife, point first, into the man's throat, severing jugular and windpipe straight away.

The second soldier turned. Woods dragging his victim to the ground confused him for a moment but even then, Roche only just caught him before he could move, wrapping one hand over the man's face and then driving the point of his knife upwards into the base of the man's skull with an audible crack. The soldier shook and spasmed; something wet coursed over Roche's gloved hand. He dropped the man, pulling the knife out, but then dropped that too and grabbed his C8 on its sling, bringing it to his shoulder.

Woods rolled the man he'd killed off him. The two special forces soldiers by the warehouse door had seen the movement and were bringing their weapons up. Years of experience told Roche where to put the sights; he stroked the trigger, a suppressed single shot. Woods was on his feet now. The soldiers by the door had their weapons up. Roche moved forwards, firing. The starlight scope flared as one of the special forces men returned fire. The other fell back as blood sprayed from his head, a bright lurid green seen through the scope. Behind Roche the night lit up as Woods fired a three-round burst. The other special forces soldier staggered slightly but merely shifted his aim and fired. Roche was moving sideways now. He felt bullets crack past him. He stroked the trigger again and the bullet's force powdered metal on the warehouse wall just to the right of the soldier's head. The man staggered again as Woods hit a second

time, central mass again. *You need a headshot*, Roche thought and squeezed the trigger a third time. *Stanton told us that when he told us about Dagenham.*

The back of the man's head exploded. Dagenham, that's what this was. It wasn't Tower Hamlets Man; these 'specialist support group' cockheads were Dagenham through and through.

Woods was on his feet. Both of them ran for the warehouse now. Roche watched lights fly past him, hit the ground and bounce off. Tracer fire from the machine-gun position they'd passed. Cover or run, those were the choices. They sprinted and made it to the short flight of stairs. Roche leapt down them. He hit the warehouse door and it flew open. He heard a cry and Woods came barrelling after him. The side of Woods' head was covered in blood and so was his shoulder. Roche dragged him to the side as tracers flew into the warehouse.

'Ow fuck!' Woods shouted. The inside of the warehouse lit up with muzzle flashes. Roche felt the bullets shoot past him; then one hit and it felt like getting slammed with a mallet. It knocked him flat and the breath was forced out of him in a way that made him feel he'd never be able to catch it again.

There were bodies in the warehouse. He saw them now, lying sprawled on his back. They were hanging from the ceiling in translucent bags and there were a lot of them. They were swaying but other than that that they weren't moving.

There was light moving towards him. More muzzle flashes.

He saw one of the bags twitch. They weren't dead ...

Woods fired from the ground. A short burst. The light approaching them fell backwards. Then Woods was on one knee. It was his muzzle flash that illuminated the warehouse as he fired at something Roche couldn't see.

... The bags were attached to a complicated series of tubes. The tubes ran inside and into the bodies. Like blood transfusion equipment. A dirty brown liquid was being fed into their veins and some kind of clear liquid was being sucked from the nape of the neck ... Dear god, was that spinal fluid? Cerebral fluid?

There was a smell. A flash back to Brixton and the last thing he'd remembered. A smell.

Serotonin ... ?

'Okay, old man, I need you to pull yourself together.' Woods reloaded his C8. He was checking all around the warehouse but the hanging bodies were obscuring his sight.

Pull himself together? What the fuck was he talking about? *I can't fucking breathe!* But Roche managed to get a grip of himself and pull a breath down into his empty lungs. The pain told him he'd almost certainly broken one or more ribs. He wasn't coughing blood though, so the body-armour must have done its job. If a broken rib was the worst he came away with from this ... 'You okay?' he managed.

'No, I'm really fucking not,' Woods told him. 'The head looks bad but it's only a graze. The shoulder's a through and through and it fucking burns.' He glanced

around at the bodies hanging in their bags all through the warehouse. 'And this freeze-dried-human bullshit is really messing with my head.'

'We can't do anything about your shoulder until we're out of here.'

Woods nodded. His teeth were clenched and he was obviously in a great deal of pain. Roche wondered whether even in his prime he could have taken a shoulder wound like that and still have the presence of mind to kill two well-trained soldiers immediately afterwards.

He looked up at the bodies, slung his C8 and took out the SLR camera. 'These people aren't dead.'

'Then what the fuck are they?'

'I don't know.' Roche went left and Woods went right though they both kept glancing behind them, back to the doors. They'd been seen entering. Someone would have radioed that in, but for now there was nobody else in the warehouse other than the bagged bodies. Roche took picture after picture. Compulsive. He'd never seen anything like it.

'It's like they're being harvested. Shit. But for what?'

'Roche, mate,' Woods' voice was strained with pain. Roche glanced over at him. Woods stood next to a pile of what looked like bags of sugar on a pallet. As Roche moved over to them, he noticed a trap door in the shadows at the back of the warehouse. 'That, my friend, is enough Moroccan Brown for us to retire.' Roche checked them. He'd done enough drugs interdiction work to know heroin when he saw it. He put the bags back and photographed them.

'What the fuck is this?'

'You know we're running out of time, yeah?' Woods asked and glanced at the trap door.

'You want to stay?' Roche asked.

Woods gave the question some thought.

'Fuck it, in for a penny, in for a pound,' he said. The two men nodded to one another. Woods covered the warehouse entrance while Roche lifted up the trap door enough to roll in a flashbang and a fragmentation grenade. Both of them stood well back, Roche brought up his C8.

The compression wave from the flashbang blew the trap door off its hinges. The phosphorescent flash shone through the gaps in the floorboards. The fragmentation grenade went off a moment later and the floor jumped. Holes appeared in it. Something tore at Roche's leg and he grunted as he felt an impact on his body armour from the shrapnel.

'That was a bit dumb,' muttered Woods. 'You okay?'

The hanging bodies in the bags started to shake and move and there was the sound of high velocity bits of lead impacting flesh as tracers started to fly through the warehouse. Someone was firing in through the doors again. Roche moved quickly to the trap door, saw a tattered set of wooden steps leading into a dimly lit space and started down them, fast. He took four steps and then the rest simply gave up and crumbled underneath him. The ground came up hard. He had a moment to take in the surroundings. He was in a small cellar area. The walls had a resinous quality to

them. There were items embedded in the resin, screens of some kind but Roche didn't recognise the figures they showed. There was something wrong or off about the technology he could see, he just wasn't sure what. In the middle of the room was a black rectangular case ...

Something moved in the corner of the room. *Christ on a bike!* It was the one of the 'specialist' soldiers. Battered and bloody but he was picking himself up and Roche didn't understand how the man could possibly have survived being in such a small space with a flash-bang and a fragmentation grenade. How he could still be alive ... Moving ... ?

It was the officer who'd choke-slammed the SEAL lieutenant. He was shaking his head. He saw Roche on the floor and peered at him as if trying to understand what was happening. Roche reached for his C8. Woods jumped down into the cellar. The special forces officer drew his Heckler & Koch USP sidearm ...

A pale, almost skeletal, hand, its fingers too long and with too many joints, its nails all but claws, reached out from the wall and ran itself down the officer's side. There was no resistance to the movement of the hand from body armour, skin, flesh or bone. Meat fell away from bone as if it had been flensed. The soldier's eyes went wide. Blood ran out of him, over his webbing and down his fatigues like water from a ruptured dam. He sank to his knees and collapsed onto his face.

It stepped out of the wall. Tall, thin, elongated face, black eyes with no pupils, the vicious rictus grin Roche

had seen through the fibreoptic in Brixton. It looked down at the special forces officer. It seemed to be wearing some kind of long frock coat. Roche was transfixed. Couldn't move. Beside him, Woods howled like an animal. He triggered his carbine in a long burst at the thing. There were a few initial gouts of steam and then holes started appearing in the resin behind it. It raised its hand. Roche saw some kind of tube in its hand. He tried to shout a warning. He saw a gout of flame and heard a sound not unlike a minigun firing. Something hot and wet covered him. Where Woods had been stood there was only a pair of legs and the stump of a bloodied spine. The legs toppled over. Roche pissed himself.

The thing turned and looked at him. Roche threw his C8 away and held his hands up. As he did, he flicked the video record button on the camera still slung over his shoulder. The Scary Clown turned away and looked at the black box. Roche followed his gaze as if hypnotised. Then he realised what it was. A suitcase bomb. A portable nuclear weapon. Above him he could hear boots thumping off the warehouse's floorboards. The Scary Clown looked up before turning and walking into the wall.

Then the screaming started.

***

'Where's Woods?'
'Where's the special forces guys?'
'What happened?'

'Whose blood is that?'

Roche drove as fast as he could to the Ospreys. He was covered from head to foot in blood. He had driven the stolen Growler one handed. In the other bloodied fingers he clutched the SLR.

'Nobody's coming,' he told them. 'They're dead. We need to leave.' More questions. A one word answer: Nuke.

***

A flash. The mushroom cloud seen rising from the plane. The glare shining even through the shuttered windows on the Ospreys. It was low yield enough that the EMP didn't knock them out of the sky. They were far enough from the blast that the nuclear winds hit the Osprey as nothing worse than severe turbulence. Roche never let go of the camera.

13 – Tachyon Fields and Breadcrumb Trails

2 July, 0246 hours, Jovian upper atmosphere

'A curious choice,' commented the Fermat construct. The clones shut themselves down briefly as the nuke went off.

'They must have known a Shriven was there,' grumbled the *Irrational Prime*. 'It's the only logical reason for the tachyonic devices.' The freighter didn't think much of its own logic even as it put the hypothesis forward. A negative mass quantum field was ... unexpected. And not something the humans had shown any sign of possessing.

'Perhaps their logic is more opaque than we thought.' The Hybrid construct was as troubled as any of them.

'There wasn't any logic at all,' grumbled the *Exponential*. 'It didn't do anything useful.' The Aqar clone was bringing its systems back on-line. 'They didn't know what they were dealing with, only that they were dealing with *something* and when all you know is that you're dealing with *something*, trying to hit it with the biggest stick you can find is an absurd first response.' The *Exponential* was sounding increasingly huffy these days. 'So ...'

The *Irrational Prime* interrupted with an extensive review of human history and the application of logic to the initiation of conflict. There was a long pregnant pause and then the frigate conceded defeat. 'I don't care how common it is,' it grumbled, 'it still seems a disastrous species response.'

'We have confirmation and denial from the Shriven for their probable interference events within the timeline of various cultures,' interrupted the Fermat construct. 'The massacre of Novgorod in the local year 1570. The link is based on a single unreliable reported sighting of a "devil-like figure with a long face and arms, his fingers too long and like claws, horns upon his head and a grin that split his face from ear to ear." Unfortunately, although consistent with the appearance of diaspora Weft, the imagery is also consistent with local native mythologies of the time.' The construct laid bare the disassembled memories of the captured Shriven. 'That particular connection is now proven incorrect as we now have thorough intelligence on the movements and whereabouts of most of the Shriven Astronomers. They have interfered before. Perhaps this device is the work of those that yet remain.'

'The what? Astronomers?' asked the frigate and the freighter.

'The name used to refer to their collective selves. Please cross-reference with recorded history while I commune with the Hive on another matter.'

The construct fell silent. For a few nanoseconds, the two ships regarded one another. *Another matter* could

only mean whatever outside connection the Astronomers had made.

'The massacre by the Jivaro of Ecuador and Peru of twenty-five thousand non-local settlers including the execution of one by pouring molten gold down his throat until his bowels burst,' said the *Exponential* suddenly. 'Promising? A similar devil-like figure to that of Novgorod is reported by both sides. While the non-local settlers' mythology mirrors that of the Novgorod incident, that of the Jivaro instigators does not. A Shriven was present. Am I right or am I right?'

The *Irrational Prime*, peeling back the layers of the disassembled Shriven, made a dismissive noise. 'No. They did that one all by themselves.'

'How about this: the devastation in 1646 of the Sichuan province of China. Jesuit missionaries report a devil-like figure at the court of Zhang Xianzhong. Again, the mythology of the missionaries is similar to that of Novgorod while the local mythology is substantively different.' The *Exponential* sounded smug.

'No such figure was recorded in the local mythology though.' The *Irrational Prime* found itself reluctant to encourage the frigate.

'One of the most extreme genocides in their history. I'm putting this hypothesis in the high ninety-five plus percentage points of right. Am I?'

The *Irrational Prime* paused, reluctant. 'One of the Shriven was there,' it conceded. 'The one from Naypyidaw. It was there for a year. Heads collected in piles. And noses and ears and hands ... why count

noses and ears separately? What's the sense in that? And he cut the feet off several hundred woman once because he got—'

'Because he had a Shriven whispering in his ear,' interrupted the *Exponential*. 'How about the one from Keetmanshoop. From 1670 to 1730 there are repeated stories of a ghost-like man with arms of snakes and a mouth of lion's teeth wide enough to swallow a man's head originating from the African coastal towns of Grand-Popo, Porto-Novo and Badagry, all of which existed primarily to facilitate the capture and transport of slaves from the local population. There's no apparent precedent for such a creature in local mythologies.'

'A devil-like figure reported to preside over a massacre on the island of Haiti in 1804 ...'

'This picture of a witch-doctor in the presence of Shaka Zulu ...'

'The Weft who stopped the Pleasure was a Shriven,' said the construct suddenly. The frigate and the freighter both stopped. 'His name was Dal. He was addicted to the chemistry of the Pleasure. It had destroyed his second part, severed his link to his soul and thus to the Hive. Others saw how he did what he did and so the Hive saw too and his secrets were shared. But because he was Shriven, no one knew how he'd come to *know* what he knew. He claimed to have dreams and visions. Madness. Yet a madness that led him to understand matter and energy and space and time more completely than any other. He destroyed our home-world and himself but he destroyed the Pleasure

too. They never came back. We exist because a Shriven saved us.'

'How many of the Shriven are missing?' asked the *Exponential*. 'It's clearly not just the one that got away just now.'

'Six,' said the Fermat clones. 'But we know where to find them. The muon trail from the stutter-holes points directly to them. This one has travelled to London. It is a solid hypothesis that it has the key to the pocket dimension where the others are hiding. Logically they will now converge to either flee or fight. It would be convenient for the tau-burst detector to be functional.'

The *Exponential* seemed to grow just a little bit more tetchy. The *Irrational Prime* busied itself with some deep computation of Saturn's Rings and carefully looked the other way.

14 – Off the Books

2 July, 0330 hours, somewhere over the Libyan coast

Roche couldn't stop shaking. At first Rees and Stanton had to keep close, keeping the SEALs back, who all desperately want to know what had gone down. Then the nuke went off and put an end to any talking.

'I need to show you something,' said Roche, after the nuke hadn't killed them all. 'I need to show you what was there.' He turned to Rees and looked around the SEALs. 'I can't hide that Woods and I went in after your lot. None of the rest of you know anything about it.'

Stanton snorted. 'Right. Like that's going to fly.'

'No, *they* didn't. *You* did. You just didn't tell them. You and Rees covered for us. As much as we can, we play it as it was. It was my idea and Woods backed the play. You and Rees covered us. I came back on my own in a Growler yelling about the nuke and we cleared out and what I'm about to show you didn't happen. There was something in Aqar that none of the rest of us were meant to see, but that other lot, whoever they were, they knew. I'm sure. So I'm going to show you a few

pictures. Pass it round then let me have it back.' He nodded to the SEAL lieutenant. 'I'm going to give this to you when we're done. You're going to have taken it off me as soon as the 'Sprey kicked off the dirt. Intel. It's up to you how we play it. If you want, no one looked at it. I didn't talk. This didn't happen. You need to talk about that with your guys.'

Roche passed the camera. There didn't seem any need to go into how he and Woods had entered Aqar or how the other soldiers had been tearing the place apart or how he'd shot two American special forces soldiers in the head and knifed a third in the back of the neck. They might have been arseholes but they were still soldiers. He started with the pictures of the sunken warehouse. No one paid much attention to that. Then came the pictures inside, the bodies in the bags. The air in the back of the 'Sprey turned blue.

When it came to the last video sequence, Roche showed it to the SEAL lieutenant first and no one said a word. It was jerky and dark and short and even then the creature wasn't there for half the time. But it *was* there, briefly. Just like the special forces officer was there, sliced open to glistening ribs. Like Woods was there, what was left of him.

Rees and Stanton watched it last. Rees watched it over and over. Roche had to gently pull the camera out of his hands.

'It was real then,' Rees said softly. 'In Brixton.'

'It was real.' Roche nodded and fitted a second memory card into the camera, making copies of

everything. He did that three more times and then handed the camera and one of the copied cards to the SEAL lieutenant.

'Do with that as you see fit,' Roche told him. 'I don't know whether it's best for you that no one saw a thing or whether you want to report all this exactly as it happened. Your call. As far as the three of us are concerned, you're the LT, we gave up the gathered intel, and that's that.'

The lieutenant nodded. 'I'll need to have a talk about this with my squad,' he said.

'Thought so. We'll talk amongst ourselves a while.' Roche gave one of the spare memory cards to Rees and one to Stanton. 'I'd eat them and shit them out the other side,' he said. 'As soon as we touch down, someone's going to be all over us. I don't know what the fuck's going to happen down there but it won't be pretty.'

For the rest of the trip, Rees and Roche and Stanton kept to themselves, each lost in their own thoughts.

10 July, 1300 hours, Legoland

They were waiting for him when he came off the runway: Leadface, a few faces he didn't recognise and one or two that he did. The spook, whoever he was. The Americans had held him in Sicily for a week and it hadn't been pleasant but in the end they'd had to let him go. He'd had a Military Police escort onto the plane and all the way to RAF Lakenheath where the Americans reluctantly handed him over to a different set of faces

193

in Military Police uniforms for the trip into London. He wasn't sure what sort of escort they were meant to be, whether they were keeping him safe or keeping him from running or keeping him from something else entirely. They were quiet, though. Not a word. And when they got to London and Vauxhall, there wasn't any ceremony about it this time; they simply drove to the front door, marched him in and sat him down in an interrogation room.

'This again?' he asked when he saw the rubber tubes on the table and the tea-towel and the jug of water.

The two guards stood silent on either side of the room. They didn't look at him but they were watching him. The Americans hadn't been kind about his ribs – at least, the second lot of Americans after a US Navy doctor had patched him back together. Seemed a bit pointless but it had been clear five minutes after they'd landed back from Libya that the whole base was in quiet uproar and split in two, the inevitable schism of spooks and soldiers.

Where do we fit into that? Would have been nice to have someone he could ask but all he had was himself and a pair of guards, still and silent as golems. *A bit of both, I suppose.*

Half an hour later, the spook came in. He shooed away the guards, put a plastic cup on the table, poured some water into it and pushed it at Roche. Then he threw a spread of photographs between them. They were grainy and had clearly had a lot of work done on them to enhance the contrast. They were also very

clearly his own pictures from Aqar. Pictures of the Scary Clown. The sense of relief knocked him sideways. He had to close his eyes for a moment and take some deep breaths.

'So, did you shoot some Americans to get these or not?'

Roche stiffened. 'Sir, if I'm being questioned about a possible friendly fire incident then I respectfully request to exercise my right to legal counsel.'

'You can respectfully request all you like, you're not getting any.'

'Then I respectfully decline to answer, sir.'

The spook rolled his eyes and leaned back into his chair. 'Christ on a bike, Sergeant!' He stabbed his finger at the photographs. 'I've got ET, someone letting off a nuke in the Libyan desert and a storm of angry Americans who want you shipped off to Guantanamo to be their play-toy. What the fuck happened out there, soldier?'

'This a debrief now, is it sir?'

'The first of many, I expect.'

'Stanton? Rees? They both back okay?'

'Yes. And no, you don't get to talk to them, not until we're done here.' He took a Dictaphone out of his pocket and set it recording between them. Roche stared at it in disbelief.

'Bloody Hell! How old is that?'

'How about you start from the beginning, Sergeant. From before you took off from Sicily. Tell me about the Americans. Both squads.'

'The briefing they gave us on the ground was to observe and record and support as requested. The mission was to be under the command of the US Navy SEALs and we were seconded to them. The SEAL LT would give the orders on the ground. They had four fire teams flying out. We were told that if we found anything strange or unusual or anything that looked like it might be nuclear material, we were to call in a specialist support unit that was flying out in the second 'Sprey.' He paused. 'When we got there—'

'When you got where?'

'Sir, when we landed near Aqar, the mission changed. The second team assumed command of the mission and told us and the SEALs to stay put. That didn't go down too well ...' Roche took a deep breath and described what had happened. The spook only nodded, so presumably he'd heard the same from Rees and Stanton.

'That sort of behaviour unusual, is it?'

'On an op? I've never heard of anything like it.'

'Anything other observations you'd like to make about this "support" group?'

Roche shrugged. 'I think they were on something.'

'Stanton in his debrief said they reminded him of the men from the warehouse in Dagenham.'

'I wasn't there in Dagenham, so I couldn't say. The crew-chief from their 'Sprey said he saw them injecting something. He thought they were on steroids. They looked to me like they were on something, right enough. Couldn't say what.'

'Walk me through what happened next.'

It turned into a long afternoon. The spook didn't say much and hardly asked any questions until right at the end.

'Did the Americans bring the nuke or was it already there?'

Roche had to shake his head. 'I don't know. I assumed it was theirs. It didn't look like anything else I saw in Aqar. But I didn't see it come off the Ospreys either.'

'Describe exactly what it looked like.'

Roche described it as well as he could remember. It had been dark in that cellar and with all manner of other shit … He had to stop and shiver and hold his head in his hands, flashing back to how Woods died.

The spook asked more questions now, gently leading Roche in and out of the warehouse. Roche declined to answer on a few specifics, such as whether the Americans had put a guard on the doors after they'd taken the place and if so, how had Roche and Woods got inside. The rest he told as straight as he could.

'Why didn't it kill you too?' asked the spook at the end. Roche didn't have much of an answer for that.

'I put down my gun. I didn't pose a threat,' he said.

The spook tapped the photographs on the table. 'I'd have said you posed the biggest threat of all.'

11 July, 1930 hours, Legoland

They took him for a medical and x-rayed and bandaged his ribs. They let him sleep and in the morning they

197

came at him again, this time the spook and Leadface and someone else all together, asking questions about what happened before he and Woods went into Aqar. Then the spook on his own, back over the events in Aqar itself. They seemed pretty hung up on where the nuke had come from, whether the Americans had brought it in or whether it had already been there. Roche sort of saw their point but he couldn't make himself get excited about it. Not after the Scary Clown.

When Charly took him to the mess hall that evening and started asking all the same questions over and over about that bloody suitcase, he almost lost it.

'Does it really fucking matter?' he snapped. 'I saw something walk out of a wall, Charly. Like a fucking ghost. I saw it rip one man open and half disintegrate the next. So does it really fucking matter whose nuke it was?'

Charly leaned in close. 'Easy, tiger. Was that the same something that you saw in Brixton back in January?'

Roche nodded. 'Pretty much the same, yeah.'

'So there was one of these in London six months ago?'

'*One* of these? You mean there could be more?'

'Of course there could be more. Why not? Now answer the question: was one of these in London six months ago?'

Roche nodded.

'Well then, perhaps you can see why a lot of us who happen to live and work in London just now are quite eager to know whether your suitcase bomb belonged to this … this whatever it is and whether there might be more of them. Bombs, I mean.'

Roche hung his head. 'It walked through a wall, Charly.'

'Yes. About that. Obviously the pictures you brought back don't show that part. Could you step me through it, exactly what happened.'

He talked her through it inch by inch yet again, the American officer sliced open, Woods half turned into smoke, the suitcase, how the Scary Clown had looked at him, just once, and then vanished again into the wall. The screams that came after. 'Don't the pictures show him going into the wall again at the end?'

Charly made a clucking sound. 'Sort of. They half show it. Then it just stops.'

'You've got to be *fucking* joking!'

'Easy!' Charly touched a hand to his arm. 'They show enough, Sergeant. There's no one here who doesn't believe you this time.' She patted him lightly. He looked at her closely, seeing her properly for the first time since they'd sat down together. Something had changed. Something had got to her while he'd been away.

'You've seen something,' he said. 'Haven't you?'

She smiled just a little too brightly. 'Was there any kind of smell when it came out of the wall?' she asked.

'Yeah. The room smelled like someone had just let off a flashbang and a frag grenade. Other than that?' It had smelled of iron when the Clown had flensed the American. It had smelled of cooked meat too. That had been Woods. He didn't tell her that part. Some things you just didn't tell to a pretty scientist you'd come to realise you rather fancied. He was about to say something like that which would probably have come out pitifully corny when her

199

phone rang. Whoever was on the other end was seriously pissed off. He frowned. A woman's voice, sharp and swearing and ripe with East End charm. *Linley?*

'Yeah. Yeah. I'll be right there.' Charly flashed another smile as she got up, abandoning her food half-eaten. 'Got to go,' she said. 'Duty calls.' She turned away and then stopped and looked back at him. 'Sergeant Manning, do you mind if I ask a question? Nicholas Burman – why did you go after him?'

'Because I thought that if anyone knew anything, it would be him. Well, maybe you lot, but you lot weren't talking to me back then because apparently I was mentally unstable.'

Charly's smile lingered this time, an effort at an apology. Roche figured that was as much as anyone was ever likely to give him. 'Get anything?' she asked. 'Off Burman, I mean?'

'A name.' Roche sniffed. In the midst of everything else over the last couple of months, he'd actually forgotten. 'Stylianos Evangeli.'

'The people-trafficking organ-legger?' She laughed. 'Isn't he a myth?'

Roche cocked his head. 'You're the spook. Is he?'

The smile faded. 'I'll send you the file,' she said as she left.

13 July, 0800 hours, Legoland

Roche had the file on Evangeli on the table beside him in the mess at breakfast. He'd half hoped to find it all

full of juicy secrets and terrible revelations but in the end there was hardly anything. Evangeli worked out of offices in Canary Wharf. He ran an import and export business, mostly dealing with goods from Greece, Cyprus and Egypt. There were a lot of rumours about a dark side to it but no one had ever found any actual evidence. Her Majesty's Revenue and Customs had been over him once or twice, looking for money laundering, and hadn't found anything. He had several domiciles across and outside of London, was clearly wealthy, frequently in and out of the country, had an interest in various nightclubs, casinos, restaurants. A playboy lifestyle. He was also a patron of the London Museum of Docklands and a substantial contributor, which didn't seem to fit the rest of his lifestyle but was hardly a cause to drag him into an anonymous dark room and get out the rags and the bottled water. The fact that the file was only stamped UK Confidential told Roche everything he needed right from the start. The spooks had nothing.

'You know the Americans legalised Bliss while we were gone.' Stanton and Rees sat either side of him. Rees was eating like he was eating for two, making up for lost days in Sicily, but Stanton was just pushing his beans and scrambled egg around in circles.

'I heard,' said Roche.

'They say the government here's going to follow suit. Make it officially recognised like tobacco or alcohol. You'll be able to buy the stuff in Marks and fucking Spencer's.'

'Op cancelled?' Roche asked. He'd heard that Task Force Hotel had been gearing up for another raid. His rib had meant he'd be missing it anyway.

'Yeah.' Stanton switched to pushing his beans around in a figure of eight.

'Stanton ...' started Rees, but Roche nudged him before Rees said anything stupid. Stanton was making a face out of his breakfast now.

'Those Americans basket-cases, the specialist support group ... they really sound like those Russian punks from Dagenham?'

'Nah.' Stanton shook his head. 'What you said about speed and strength sounds similar but the Russians in Dagenham weren't trained. Whoever those boys were in Aqar, sounds like they knew their stuff same as anyone else we play with. That's what scares me.' He pushed his plate away and gave Roche a long look. 'There's not much that makes me scared.' He shook his head. 'If they'd legalised Bliss right at the start, Red Troop would still be here. Got to ask, sometimes, what's it all for?'

Roche didn't have much of an answer for that and he was still half distracted thinking of Evangeli and the coincidence of Canary Wharf; but before he could try and think of something that was more than a dumb platitude, Charly wandered across the mess hall towards him. She looked rough.

'Christ!' snorted Rees. 'You look like you slept in those. All-nighter?'

'Something like that.' Charly's smile seemed a little more fractured to Roche this morning. Worse, even,

than yesterday. She tapped him on the shoulder. 'A word, Sergeant?'

Roche followed her to another table. 'Bad night?'

'Like wanking in someone else's toilet and then finding yourself on an internet porn site. That kind of night.' Roche stifled a snort. 'I need to talk to you about Bliss.'

'Bliss?' After Aqar, Bliss seemed like it hardly mattered any more.

Charly nodded at the file on Evangeli. 'And that. Look, I don't talk about what I do and neither do you. But in the last six months I know you've seen some really fucked-up weird shit and frankly so have I. Particularly recently. I can't tell you what.'

Roche nodded. 'We're briefed. Need to know. That's the way it is.'

'What you've seen … That's just the start of the crap …' Charly stopped as a harried-looking secretary hurried past juggling three cups of coffee. 'I know. I've seen some fucked-up shit as well.'

'You have, have you?'

'Yes, Roche, I have. I shouldn't but I have. Look, it's this simple. The shit you're after, the shit you've seen, the shit I'm after and the shit I've seen, there's one thing in the middle of it. Bliss.'

'And no one has a clue where it comes from or even what it fucking is. Really?' Roche shook his head.

'I might have some ideas. But there's nothing concrete.' Charly made a clucking sound. 'It *is* exceptionally strange. Actually I was wondering if you might be interested in helping out a little on that score. Do

you remember the DI who arrested you when you went after Nicholas Burman? Samantha Linley? I'm putting together a bit of an off-the-books operation. She's helping, so ...'

Roche rocked back in his chair. 'Oh, I so don't want to hear about this, I really don't.' He took a sip of coffee and made a face. 'Christ, this is shit.'

Charly put a hand over his. 'We're all on the same team, Roche. I'm trying to find where the Bliss is coming from. So are you. I did some digging about Stylianos. I've got some intel.'

'So what do you want?' Roche leaned slowly forward again, resting his elbows on the table. Stylianos Evangeli. Brixton. She was dangling the sweet scent of a few answers in front of him. Playing him with them.

'Let me take you out. Charing Cross Arches. Twelve o'clock. Maybe grab some lunch in Starbucks. Come and meet DI Linley again. And Noel.'

'Burman?' Roche took a deep breath. 'That should be interesting.'

'Won't it just?' Charly flashed a smile. She rested a hand on Roche's shoulder as she left.

13 July, 1200 hours, Europa

The *Exponential* had, it decided, quite simply had enough. It had spent weeks calibrating the Europa tau-burst detector. Months. More time than on any instrument in recent history and it still wasn't working properly. Yes, it could pick up a drone in the Kuiper belt popping

off a miniscule tau-burst every few minutes and yes, it could triangulate using the baseline of the moon's orbit and get something approaching a decent bearing on cosmological events billions of light years away, but it still wasn't giving the right answers.

Unless someone had slipped around the back and invented some new physics while the frigate had been looking the other way then a star of a certain size put out a certain volume of neutrinos. So did a gas giant. So did almost everything that wasn't inert. The *Exponential* had factored all of those into its calculations. The answer kept being the same: there were too many tau-neutrinos in this system.

'The remaining Shriven are congregating,' the Fermat construct informed them idly. There were six of them left, according to the Naypyidaw Shriven. The *Irrational Prime* was already drifting steadily in-system towards the orbit of Mars. The anti-matter harvesting was done and the freighter was now towing a comet of the stuff behind it, about a thousand cubic kilometres of frozen metallic anti-hydrogen, enough to shatter a planet or just possibly detonate the largest gas giant in the system. It wasn't sure about that. The *Irrational Prime* wanted to launch the comet and let physics take its course but the *Exponential* and the hybrid had overruled it.

'There's something in this system beyond what we've seen,' the frigate complained. Fermat, meanwhile, wanted to wait until the Shriven showed themselves. It wanted the drones and the anti-matter held back in case the last few of them made a run for it. None of them

quite knew what to expect if that happened but they wouldn't get very far. Unless someone had hidden a singularity in the system, the Shriven would be left to escape by the same means the *Irrational Prime* had arrived – the long slow hard way …

Unless someone had hidden a singularity …

A singularity could be a source of tau neutrinos. But on this scale, it hardly seemed possible. This was more like someone had parked a fairly large white dwarf star in the inner system and then somehow made it invisible in every other way …

Abruptly, the *Exponential* wondered if it had answered its own question. What if there *was* something in the system beyond what they'd seen. What if they *were* seeing it?

The frigate decided to look at its calibration problem from the other end. It hadn't found anything wrong with the way its drones had built the detector. Now it changed its assumptions. Assume the detector is working perfectly well and there's nothing wrong with the calibration. Assume there never was. In that case it had nearly a month of data on some object that neither the *Irrational Prime* nor the hybrid construct had been able to detect in any other way.

The question became: what was it?

13 July, 1200 hours, Charing Cross Arches

Roche recognised Burman and Linley at once. Roche had only ever seen DI Linley pointing a gun at him or

shouting at him across an interrogation table. She looked as pissed off today as she had then. Burman looked different, though. Burman looked haunted.

Roche waved them over, leaning against the arches. 'I'm not supposed to be out,' he said.

'Out of where?' Linley folded her arms and gave him a hard pinched look.

'Can't say.' Roche glanced at Burman. 'Surprised I haven't seen more of you around Vauxhall though.'

'He means he's working for the spooks these days,' said Linley.

'Sixteenth Air Assault Brigade, me. Anything else, I have no idea what you're talking about.' Roche wrinkled his nose. 'Saw an old friend of yours, Burden. Sergeant Stanton.'

'It's Burman, and how's he doing?'

'Still got all his bits.' Roche looked from Burman to Linley and back again. 'So what's all this about? I could tell you a thing or two but not with this civvy here.' Roche enjoyed the look that got him from Linley. Payback for taking him in.

'You remember my brother, Manning? The one you waterboarded?'

'You mean the one who deals coke and dope?'

'That's enough,' Charly stepped between them. 'We need to engage in a little bit of information gathering. Now, unless you want to strip down, oil yourselves and beat your chests for Sam and I, let's try something a little more civilised like a conversation and cup of coffee.'

207

'Sure,' Roche said. He turned away and they walked out from the arches and in among the tourists milling about on Embankment. Roche aimed for a designer patisserie but Linley cut him off.

'Not there. Not if you want to talk.' She led them through Embankment station instead, up over the Charing Cross footbridge to the South Bank and into the huge open space of the South Bank Centre. In the afternoon it was almost empty, a space the size of an assembly hall and they almost had it to themselves. A scattering of people sat with their laptops at a handful of tables while a solitary waitress stood behind the bar drying glasses.

Linley marched up to the bar. 'Four coffees, love.'

'So what's this about then, Charly?' Roche asked. 'You been running two ops?'

'Compartmentalised, darling, need to know, Big Boys' rules and all that. You're a big boy now, aren't you?'

Roche looked at her hard. Something was off. Something had been off since the morning. She was brittle today. His gut said he ought to walk away. Even talking out here in the open was begging to have the Official Secrets Act thrown at him, at all of them. Curiosity, though. Always the enemy of keeping secrets.

'I cry like a baby when the intelligence I need isn't available because of secrecy for secrecy's sake,' he said. From the corner of his eye he caught Burman nodding.

'Which is why we're all here,' Charly said. Sam came back and put the drinks down.

'Even though he's compromised and she's a civvy?'

208

'Wind your neck in, mate,' Burman said. Roche turned to look at him. Noel held his eye.

Sam sighed. She shook her head at Charly. 'You know this whole bullshit testosterone display is for you, don't you?'

'Shall we go and come back?' Charly asked. 'Pop up to Regent's Street, do a spot of shopping?'

'Not on my salary. I'll stay and watch, thanks.'

Charly said something more. Roche tuned out for a moment, distracted by what were possibly the best legs he'd ever seen coming into the centre; but a moment later, Noel brought him back.

'A name keeps on turning up,' Noel said. 'Stylianos Evangeli.' The name had Roche's attention at once. 'We've got intelligence ...'

'Highly suspect intelligence,' Linley added sourly.

'We know where he's going to be in five and a half hours.'

Roche nodded. 'I'm in,' he said.

Charly smiled at them all. 'Oh, wonderful. Now we don't have a great deal of time to plan this but I've already set a few wheels running. I'm going to leave operational planning up to the boys with the boots on the ground.'

'We need to get Stanton in on this as quickly as possible,' Burman said. Roche nodded. Rees as well, if he could be persuaded.

'The lovely Samantha will have a large contingent of the Met's finest waiting nearby,' Charly went on. 'She has resurrected a Kingship operation that never happened. I'll be based with them.'

'Now, they're going to know that there's special forces on the ground but that's not an excuse to turn Docklands into Saturday night in Basra, understand me?' Linley turned to Charly. Her face was set hard. 'That's it for me, I'm burned after this. Falsified orders, I'll be lucky if I don't end up in the Scrubs with people I've put there.'

'I know, I'm sorry,' Charlotte said

Sam shook her head. 'Fuck it, they've sold us out on this whole Bliss thing. I tried so hard to play it straight, didn't want to be like my old man. Now look at me.'

'It's for the greater good,' Charly said.

Linley shook her head. 'That's what people always say before they do something monstrous. That's how we justify all the bad shit that we do. We set ourselves up as the moral superiors of the people that we're doing this to and then commit acts that frankly aren't dissimilar. Then we give them nice euphemisms to make it okay. Rendition, Big Boys' rules, collateral damage.' The words were for all of them but her eyes never left Charly.

'You finished lecturing us?' Roche asked.

'Oh well, fuck it, it's all breaking down now. I've been pushing to hit known Bliss dealers. You'd think that them waving around automatic weapons in the streets of London would be enough, wouldn't you? But no, every single fucking anti-Bliss operation I've ever heard of suddenly got pulled in the last two days and I happen to know that the Home Secretary met with the Chief Commissioner of Police the day before. So it's not so difficult to join the fucking dots. Now you can call me naive if you want but you didn't grow up where I did.

210

There's the wrong way and the right way. The moment you compromise, the corruption starts creeping in. So you run your covert ops, put more guns on the streets of London, kidnap people, torture them in fucking Surrey of all places, and I'll help but you're all very far gone if you think that this is the way things should be.'

'I'll take a little corruption,' Roche said. Aliens disintegrating people. Suitcase nukes in Libya. Humans living inside bags, being harvested for their … fuck, he hadn't the first idea what. Fluids. 'For this, I'll do what's necessary,' he said softly.

'Yeah, that's where it all starts, isn't it?' Linley said.

Roche looked around the hall. People with their laptops, tapping away. The woman who'd caught his eye earlier. People with their newspapers. Their phones. Just doing whatever they were doing. Six months ago, Stylianos Evangeli was supposed to deal in organs. Which left Roche thinking of the people in the warehouse in Aqar, zipped up in their plastic bags. Presumably they'd been doing pretty ordinary things too, right up until someone stuffed them in shrink-wrap.

He shook his head. The others were getting up.

'Where?' he asked Charly as Burman and Linley left.

'Westferry Circus. Five o'clock.'

And that was that. Line crossed. Easy as anything.

13 July, 1700 hours, Canary Wharf, London

'Canary Wharf. You been to Docklands recently?' asked Rees. 'They done it up nice. Of course you have to shit

gold to afford to live there.' They met up at Westferry Circus. Stanton and Rees came with Burman and all three were carrying big black holdalls. Roche didn't ask how Burman had got his hands on the hardware; or maybe Stanton and Rees had taken it out of Legoland. Maybe the spooks there were quietly okay with this.

'Charly's intel has the meet going down in the Docklands Museum after hours,' said Stanton. 'We need eyes on targets and recon of what's going on inside. Roche and his crew will be in the museum. Noel and I will handle security, front and back exits. Noel, we're tight on shooters. Do you want front or back?'

'Front.' Burman looked edgy. Stanton nodded.

'There's a multi-storey car park round the back on Hertsmere Road that gives excellent overwatch on the fire exits. That's mine then. We need a firm count on how many targets go in and come out, faces, pictures, if they're armed. Roche, you and Rees have the sharp end. You got everything you need?'

Roche nodded.

'I'll take you in,' said Burman. 'We've got a friendly on the inside who can give you a tour.'

'And where are you going to be?'

'On one of the boats in the dock, I reckon.'

'Yeah. Would have been my choice. Who else we got?'

'Oh, a hundred or so of the Met's finest lurking nearby.' Burman grinned. 'You relay the intel, Sam calls them in, we take them down red-handed. Cool with that?'

Roche almost smiled back. Almost.

13 July, 1730 hours, Canary Wharf, London

The Museum of London Docklands had once been a warehouse, back about two hundred years ago when the whole of Docklands had been about shipping and not about the towering glass and steel offices and flats that now dominated the Isle of Dogs and the neighbouring Limehouse Basin. The front entrance led into a wide spacious atrium that flowed smoothly into a café and then the fire doors at the back while the museum proper spread out in wings to either side. The right side was laid out as some sort of kids' activity centre while the left side opened into an exhibition area. An open stairwell in the atrium led to the upper floors on either side. Roche didn't bother with those. The meet would go down in the central area, maybe in the café, in an open space where everyone could see everyone else and everyone had plenty of places they could run if it came to it. Rees had brought a decent set of kit out of Legoland – not the firepower Burman had in his black bags but a good collection of tiny cameras and microphones. After the museum closed and the last members of the public drifted away, he and Rees set up a network and found themselves places to hide. Roche settled in the exhibition centre. They had a couple of tiny cinemas there, one running a short film about the wildlife of the Thames estuary and another running a slideshow about some old Second World War anti-aircraft forts that had been built out in the estuary and looked a bit like AT-ATs.

Roche settled under one of the benches there in the dark and waited. Five minutes later, Rees checked in from somewhere upstairs.

The last of the museum staff left and locked up behind them around seven. Around nine the doors opened again and three men came in. They were pushing a heavy wheeled crate between them. Roche started panning cameras where he could, zooming in, trying to get a clear image of each face. There were no lights on in the museum, but the sun hadn't quite set and a little twilight still crept in through the windows.

'Indigo one, you getting this?' Roche whispered.

'Check, Indigo two.' Burman.

'Familiar faces?'

'Not to me.'

The men wheeled their crate into the café. Two of them started work opening it up while the third went behind the counter and began setting two of the tables.

'What the hell are they doing?' Stanton. Roche didn't answer. He tried to zoom in on the crate. It was open now and the two men were pulling things out from inside it: oddly formed pieces of black plastic which they laid out on one of the tables. From each corner of the crate they unfolded a telescopic arm of some sort. Next, they unlatched the sides of the crate and collapsed them so they lay flat. They moved the telescopic arms and finished extending them. The arms were curved, like the pincers of some insect, all of them arcing away from the centre of the crate and then curving back in again, ending in sharp points that almost

touched over the middle of the crate. It looked a little like the skeletal outline of an onion.

'Indigo Two. Anyone know what that is?' murmured Roche.

One of the men by the crate took out a ruggedised laptop and unwound a cable. He plugged the laptop into the crate and turned it on. The museum trembled. Even the men in the café paused.

'Did you get that?' Roche asked. 'I felt the floor quiver.'

'Same,' murmured Rees.

'Nothing here.' Stanton again.

'There a tube line that runs under here?'

'Docklands Light isn't far but it's overground. I've got eyes and there's nothing come past.'

'It happened exactly when they plugged that thing in,' said Rees.

'Could be coincidence.' Roche didn't believe it though.

The men beside the collapsed crate were spooling another cable away from it. They plugged in a second box, bigger than the first, and this time Roche felt the air itself jump and tense as though there was suddenly a massive charge. Like the moment before a thunderstorm.

'Anyone else feel that?'

'Something,' agreed Rees. 'Indigo one, if Charly's out there, do me a favour and ask her what the fuck that box is.'

'Mind your chatter, Indigo four.' Stanton again.

The third man was still setting places at the tables.

Knives and forks, plates, serviettes, glasses, a jug of water …

Whatever they were doing with the crate, they seemed to have finished. One of the men tapped his ear.

'We're set,' he murmured. Roche had to strain his ears to hear.

'Indigo one to all Indigo call signs, be aware we have two victors carrying seven possible x-rays pulling up outside. If they're armed then I can't see it,' said Burman a moment later. Roche shifted one of his cameras to zoom in on the main doors.

'See if you can get faces this time.' Rees.

A minute passed and then another. The man setting the tables finished. The other two were standing beside the crate. The air felt ready to burst with lightning.

The door opened and seven men came in. Six goons in a posse around their boss. Like the men who came with the crate, they were all on the swarthy end of Caucasian: Turkish or Greek or something like that. Israeli?

'Indigo one. The one in the middle. That's Evangeli.'

Cyprus, then. Roche checked the time. Nine fifty. Later than he'd thought.

Evangeli's men fanned out through the café. Roche studied each one, trying to see if they were armed. They weren't being careful in here, out of sight or so they thought. 'I'm seeing handguns on most of the targets,' he whispered. 'Nothing bigger.'

'MP7s?' That was Burman and Roche knew he was thinking back to Dagenham.

'Handguns only. I repeat, handguns only. Evangeli's on the phone now.' The organ smuggler was pacing back and forth between his men. He was talking fast and loud and Roche was picking most of it up. Unfortunately Evangeli was also talking in either Greek or Turkish.

'Anyone get any of that?' asked Stanton. There was a long pause, then: 'Indigo three to all Indigo call signs, I have four incoming victors on the Hertsmere Road … They've stopped outside the back door … Twenty, twenty-five … no, thirty possible x-rays, I see body armour, SMGs … Indigo two, you may want to consider getting ready to Foxtrot Oscar. Indigo one, these guys look similar to the Dagenham crew.'

Roche heard a banging on the fire escape doors at the back of the café. The goons inside were moving. Several of them had their pistols drawn. They all had their backs to the front entrance and the entrance to the exhibition hall. If he packed up and ran, they just might not see him …

Two of the Cypriots started to unlock the back door. It exploded open as two massive men in body armour smashed through. They almost threw the two Cypriots up into the air and didn't slow down. Behind them, more men poured in, MP7s shouldered and ready. One of the Cypriots got off a shot – all Roche saw was the muzzle flash – and took a three-round burst to the face that didn't so much kill him as explode his head. Roche frowned. That wasn't right. The sound of the shots was off. Odd. Not something he'd heard before. They sounded a bit like a man screaming.

'Anyone else see that?' asked Roche.

The other soldiers were simply throwing the Cypriots aside, picking them up, smashing them into tables, throwing them across the room, the sort of cartoon violence that wasn't supposed to happen in the real world. Most of the noise came from the Cypriots. Screams, shouts, curses, the snap of bones breaking. And then it was over – a handful of seconds and the sheer speed and violence of the assault had taken down everyone in the café with only one hostile shot fired by the Cypriots and one man down. The only Cypriot still standing was Evangeli. They'd left him alone. He seemed oddly unperturbed.

'You see that, Indigo?' Roche asked again. For a moment he'd been impressed. Quick and brutal and effective. Nine armed men taken down and subdued, just like that. 'That seem off to you, Indigo three?' The soldiers had been fast and strong; but the more he thought about it, the more Roche realised he hadn't seen their training. They'd burst in full of noise and fury. They'd taken down their targets with sheer speed and force but not with any skill.

'No flashbang,' muttered Rees.

The soldiers were dragging the mangled Cypriots into a group over in the atrium by the entrance doors, effectively cutting off Roche's escape. They were systematically disarming them while several others crowded around Evangeli, forcing him down into a chair.

No flashbang. That was a simple rule. You went into an unknown room with armed hostiles somewhere inside, you went in behind a flashbang.

'This isn't an op,' muttered Rees. 'Look at the weapons.'

'Indigo three?' Rees was right. The guns were Heckler & Koch MP7A1 4.6 millimetre personal defence weapons. Only they sounded completely wrong. Judging by the dead Cypriot with no head, they were packing the punch of a .50 calibre.

'I see them.' Stanton's voice was icy.

They weren't soldiers, then. He'd got that wrong. At least, not soldiers who deserved the name. Russian Organizatsiya. Mafia. They were shoving Evangeli over to the crate now. Roche couldn't hear what they were saying. Evangeli looked more annoyed than scared, while the Russians still looked eager, like they were gearing up for a fight even though they'd just had one. It was over, wasn't it? But from the way everyone acted, it hadn't even started.

'Indigo one, this is Indigo three. Dagenham, Indigo one. It's like Dagenham again. Same shit. Keep quiet and let Indigo two get his intel. Indigo one, confirm?'

Evangeli was getting heated with one of the gunman. They shoved him hard enough to sprawl him across the floor beside the crate. Roche didn't see what he did down there, but before he even started to get up the air changed again, more static, so much that Roche felt the hairs on the backs of his arms prickling.

'Indigo one, respond?'

The crate lit up. Sparks crackled along the four curved arms and a brilliant light bloomed between them, lightning-white and burning steadily.

13 July, 2203 hours, Europa

'Tau-burst!' The *Exponential* had been in the middle of working out the exact mathematics of what the detector's skewed calibration was telling it when the burst came through. It paused to pinpoint the source. Two sources, as it turned out. A cross-dimensional wormhole.

The Fermat construct accepted the co-ordinates and passed them on to its three remaining clones. They began to converge on London.

13 July, 2203 hours, Canary Wharf, London

The Russians were up and covering the crate at once. Roche thought he saw the glimpse of a shape and then all hell broke loose. Half the Organizatsiya opened fire, shooting into the light in sustained bursts. He saw at least three of them toss grenades into the disassembled crate. He winced, counting down, waiting for the explosion to shred everyone in the room but it didn't come. Instead there was a blast of *something* out of the crate that threw one of the gunman several feet through the air and caught a second man, spinning him round, his arm almost wrenched off.

A shape came out of the light. It staggered, sprayed by automatic weapons-fire, then slumped. It wasn't human. It was too tall, too skinny, its arms too long for its body, its elongated face split wide open by the rictus grin Roche had seen again in Aqar only a few days ago. It was wearing the same long frock coat. It stumbled

out of the light in the crate, walked into the hail of bullets and died.

'Shit …' hissed Rees.

'Did you see …' Roche didn't need to ask.

'Is that what you saw in Brixton?'

Roche didn't answer either. No need. The Russians had forgotten about Evangeli. He was over by one of the smashed tables and he was holding something now. One of the black plastic things. He scrambled to his feet and pointed it at the cluster of Organizatsiya men as the Scary Clown toppled. They were all staring in awe at the dead alien.

'Stop!' The gunmen in the atrium had seen him. One swivelled round, bringing his carbine to bear. Evangeli pointed the plastic thing at the soldier. Arcs of yellow-orange light twisted out of Evangeli's hand; they looped and flailed through each other as they whipped across the room. Where they touched the Russian, he simply fell apart. It was like watching someone be sliced up by a cheesewire. Blood spurted briefly and then he collapsed into diced chunks of meat and severed bone. The other gunmen opened fire on Evangeli and blew his face off. One of them didn't take his finger off the trigger until he ran out of ammunition. He stared at the ruined corpse, trying to reload. He was struggling. His partner couldn't stop looking at the pieces of his dead friend; and then four of the Cypriots threw themselves at the two Russians. Another ran to Evangeli, pulling at the black plastic thing that he'd been holding. The last two bolted for the door.

'Two coming out your side, Indigo one. Advise you wait for them to put some distance behind them and then take them. You getting all of this?'

No answer. He couldn't tell if the comms were even working any more.

The Russians at the crate were moving on the body of the Scary Clown, edging closer. There was a scream – a storm of light burst out of the crate and wrapped itself around one of them. The light seemed to swirl around him for a second. When it faded, all that was left of him was a cloud of greasy black smoke, the blackened stumps of his legs just below the knees and a few charred fingers.

Roche stared in disbelief. *Woods.* A Cypriot in the atrium pulled a gun and shot a Russian in the chest, all nine rounds, staggering him back with each one and yet he didn't go down. When the last shot fired, the Russian roared in fury and ran. The Cypriot tried to get away but watching the Organizatsiya man was like watching a leopard take down a gazelle. He threw himself ten feet through the air and caught the Cypriot round the shoulders, slamming them both into the ground. The Russian was up again straight away, screaming in fury. He grabbed the Cypriot by the nearest part of him that came to hand – his foot – and swung him through the air as though he was a rag doll, smashing his head into the open stairs, swinging him overhead and slamming him into the ground and then throwing the limp corpse into the other Cypriots grappling with his comrade. Then, only then, did he seem to notice that he'd been

shot and start to slow down. The Cypriot who'd gone for Evangeli had the black ray-gun thing now. He fired it. The arcs of energy cut the Russian into pieces; a moment later, the Cypriot fell under a spray of bullets from the men around the crate.

Under his bench in the room next door, Roche struggled to keep up with it all through the chaos of shouting and motion. Something came out of the light in the crate, a shape he could barely make out except that it wasn't quite human. The Russians opened fire again, shooting in panic at something that somehow wasn't quite there. Bullets sprayed everywhere and several of them were caught in the crossfire. They were screaming at each other. Roche recognised a few words but you didn't need to speak Russian to understand what they were saying. *Kill it, kill it!* Whatever *it* was.

For a moment, caught by the light, Roche saw the outline of a Scary Clown. It was barely there, translucent at best, and yet he saw its clawed hand reach out and slice a man diagonally from collar bone to ribs. There was an explosion of blood and then the Russian fell apart, cut right through to the spine.

'Indigo one? Indigo three?' No answer from either of them.

The Russians were running now. Most of them ran for the back. A third Clown came out of the light from the crate. It aimed a tube like the one Roche had seen in Aqar. He didn't hear it fire over the shouts but one of the Organizatsiya thugs simply disintegrated. The others scattered, terrified.

In the atrium, the Cypriots had all fled. A last Russian was still there, too damn crazy to be scared. A fourth creature came out of the light. The Russian picked up the gun that the Cypriot had used. Curling streamers of light twisted out of it. They struck the Clown and wrapped themselves around it. It seemed to struggle and then threw aside the arcs of light as though they were physical things. It turned and pointed its tube at the Russian. The Russian dived out of the way. A large hole appeared in the wall behind where he'd been standing.

'Indigo two, this is Indigo three. I have more targets coming your way.' Almost all of the Russians were running now. The ones who could make it out of the fire escape had already gone; the rest were scattering, bolting for the main door. One of the aliens had gone outside the back. The other two had half-vanished, walking through walls as though they weren't there. They were like ghosts. As best Roche could tell they were heading out the front now.

'Indigo one, multiple targets heading your way. Heavily armed targets juiced on steroids or something being pursued by ...' By what? By what, exactly? 'By a pair of I don't know. By fucking aliens. Do not engage, I repeat, do not engage.'

No answer.

The museum was suddenly almost empty. He couldn't see anyone in the atrium or the café any more but that didn't mean much when the Scary Clowns could simply walk through walls. How did anything walk through fucking walls, for Christ's sake?

'All Indigo call-signs, this is Indigo four. Someone just picked up a Mercedes Sprinter and threw it at something that looks like a bad Halloween costume.'

Rees? 'Where the fuck are you, Indigo four?'

Couldn't be sure there weren't any Russians still here either. Bliss soldiers. Whoever they were.

'Upper level window. Opposite where Indigo three was supposed to be.'

'And where the fuck is Stanton?'

'Right where he's supposed to be, Indigo two. Okay, and now Bad Halloween Costume Guy just walked through a hail of bullets and … holy fucking shit! Indigo two—'

Roche had been about to close the laptop and take his chances slipping out of the exhibition room when the back doors exploded and a Scary Clown came flying back into the museum. It was like an overblown piece of wire-work from a wushu movie – he didn't just stagger back through the doors, he was hurled about fifty feet through the air, straight through what was left of the café and into the open stairs, cracking the banisters. The Clown crashed to the floor but it landed on its feet and threw something back at the door. Roche had time to catch a glimpse of a shape there – a human shape – and then everything in the back half of the museum exploded. He felt the shock through the floor, felt the whole building shiver. All the cameras whited out and died.

'Indigo two. If any of you are still listening out there, I lost eyes. I'm looking for a way out.'

'Indigo four. I can't recommend the back, Indigo two, not at the ...' There was the sound of something metallic smashing into something else and a lot of shattering glass. 'Just don't come out this—' A hideous screeching sound ripped through Roche's earpiece, painfully deafening until Roche ripped it away. The building shook again from another explosion in the café. Roche shut the laptop and slipped it back into the pouch over his back. He picked up the suppressed C8 Burman had found from somewhere and rolled carefully out from under the bench in the tiny exhibition screening room. Not that there was much need to be quiet.

The building shook again. Roche crept out into the corridor. There was hardly any light in here, no windows, only what filtered in from the atrium and they were well past sunset now.

He sensed more than saw the Bliss soldier hiding in the exhibit beside him. It wasn't that he moved and Roche couldn't be sure he'd heard anything over the destruction of the atrium. But he felt the air change, or maybe it was the smell. He lunged forward as the Bliss soldier launched himself and Roche felt the knife whisper past the back of his neck, so close it might have cut a hair or two. He spun around in the air as he moved and fired the C8 into where the man ought to be. The muzzle flash lit up the room, garish photographs of the Thames estuary scattered all around the walls and a single diving figure rolling away.

Dagenham. Aqar. Now here. He needed a head-shot and he couldn't see shit.

'Indigo two coming out the front, fast.' He dropped a frag grenade behind him and raced out into the atrium.

What was left of it.

13 July, 2207 hours, Canary Wharf

The first hybrid construct clone to reach Canary Wharf north dock phased through the subterranean foundation structures and emerged into the water of the dock itself. It took a moment to assimilate the data available from the surrounding infosphere. Paramilitary units were scattered all around the north dock, some of them engaged in exchanges of small-arms fire, others simply hiding out of the way, observing or in flight. At least four Shriven were present. Their previous efforts at concealment had fallen aside in the last few minutes.

They were fighting for their lives. That was … unexpected. And something had already terminated one of them. The clone was reasonably sure there had been six altogether at the start. That wasn't right. The technological base simply didn't exist for the native sentients to offer any kind of threat to a Shriven, even ones armed only with diaspora technology.

The clone rose out of the water and hovered in the air, half in-phase with the ordinary matter of the world around it, half not.

An explosion wrecked the frontage of the brick building in front of it. The clone's particle detectors registered a spray of unexpected muons and a tiny gamma-flash; then a Shriven burst out through the wreckage. It tumbled

across the docks, still rising, and into the tower block across the water. It was functional enough to have the presence of thought to phase out as it struck the building and flew on through it as though the tower block was vapour. Its phasing wasn't perfect. It left behind it a mosaic of tiny cracks in everything it touched.

The clone carefully adjusted its own phase, making itself as good as invisible to the local sentients, swivelled and flew after the Shriven; but as it did, a second figure emerged from the plasma wreckage. Amid the litter of broken stones and tiles, a human form raised its arm towards the clone and the arm wasn't a human arm but a quasi-organic nano-grown plasma cannon. Fiercely flickering balls of metallic light spun around the weapon.

Also unexpected, since the clone had considered itself to be invisible. It fired a fine spray of anti-protons at the human. Fierce tiny flashes of nuclear annihilation detonated in the air around it, vaporising a thin layer of stone immediately under the human and liquefying the earth beneath its feet. The human vanished in a cloud of hard radiation and exotic short-lived particles. The clone turned its attention back to the Shriven, hunting for the muon tell of another phase shift.

The blast from the plasma cannon caught the clone squarely in the back of the head, apparently far less of the human having been converted into high-energy photons than the clone had anticipated. The human, who should have disintegrated, was now surrounded by the glitter of a coherent energy field. The plasma shock confused the clone momentarily. It phased as a second

discharge shattered the air and narrowly missed taking off the top corner of a tower block. The heat blast of over-shocked air passed through the clone and smacked into the water below. It watched the shockwave speed across, a rippling ring of white.

'What are you?' it asked, excreting the question as a sequence of exotic particles while at the same time phasing back to fire a sustained spray of coherent mesons at the energy shield.

It didn't see the thing that came down from above it which sheared it clean in two despite its phase state and simultaneously infected it with a corrosive nanite set that overwhelmed its own regenerative capacity.

'Never mind that, what are *you*?' asked the thing. It ripped the clone to pieces until it was shredding atoms and spraying mists of naked coloured quarks. 'What are you?' it asked, over and over. 'What are you?'

13 July, 2207 hours, Thames Estuary

'What was that?' asked the Fermat construct. It adjusted the modulation and intelligent adaptation of its own coherent energy shield and began dispatching microscopic drones. 'Can any of you answer me? Because that shouldn't have been possible.'

13 July, 2207 hours, Europa

The *Exponential* checked through the mathematics a second time but there wasn't any room for doubt in

the Europa detector results. Not if you assumed it was working.

'We're not alone out here,' it told the others.

The *Irrational Prime* came to have a look. The Fermat construct and its various clones were a touch busy but the construct assigned enough of its attention to at least get the gist of what the *Exponential* was saying.

Which wasn't particularly much. Just that there was another spaceship in the system and that it was invisible and that it had been here with them all along, right from the start, and that, if its neutrino signature was anything to go by, it was really quite big.

15 – The Crossfire

13 July, 2207 hours, Canary Wharf

Rees was saying don't go out the back. On the other hand, there were a couple of problems with going out the front. The first problem was the Scary Clown that had picked itself up after being thrown back in through the fire exit. The second problem was the Organizatsiya man who'd come racing in through what was left of the doors behind it, jumped through the air like he was Spring-heeled fucking Jack and landed in the atrium. Right now, right where Roche wanted to go, the Shriven was trying to kill the Russian with those claws it had. The Russian was surrounded by some sort of glittering translucent bubble and had one arm fitted into a lividly luminous sleeve that looked vaguely like an organic version of a rocket launcher for anti-tank missiles. Balls of vivid green light spun in patterns around and up and down that arm. The Clown's claws sliced into the glittering bubble but never very far, while the soldier kept trying to kick and punch and push the Clown away to bring its glowing arm to bear.

Despite what he was seeing, Roche stopped for a moment and stared. That was no Russian. Fuck! *Shaw? Lewis Shaw?*

Yeah, and he'd just dropped a frag grenade behind him. Snap decision. He needed another exit. He ran three paces and threw himself forward before the pressure wave from the grenade detonating back in the exhibition room knocked him flat. He rolled and fell among the smashed remnants of the café tables and chairs, kept rolling, letting his momentum take him on and back to his feet and half ran, half stumbled into some dark part of the museum on the other side. The interactive children's zone. When he looked back, half the front of the museum was missing and the soldier in glittering light was heading through the ruin of the museum entrance and outside.

He ought to run; but again, Roche couldn't help but watch. He had a good clear view now as the soldier raised his arm. It *was* Shaw. Lewis Shaw. They'd had pints together back in the Bell in Tillington.

'Fuck. Me!'

A claw-fingered shape emerged from the floor. Shaw spun around and a torrent of blinding white fire spewed across the open space of the museum. It hit the Scary Clown square on and hurled it clean across the museum, into the back wall and straight through. Roche's eyes grew wider. The brickwork of the wall was still there. The alien had gone through a solid wall as though it was made of mist. He'd seen it before, in Brixton and Aqar, but that didn't make it any better. *How? How is that possible?*

He had barely a moment to take it in. Shaw, silhouetted in the entrance, erupted in a fury of light that

seemed to wrap itself around him, bright as a nuclear flash. Roche turned and stumbled away. Outside wasn't looking good either way. Somewhere round here were some other stairs. He found them and bolted up, away from the shredded atrium and glad to have good solid brick around him again. Up top, he ran for the nearest window and skidded to a stop. Outside the back of the museum Hertsmere Road squeezed between the old warehouse brickwork and the dirty white concrete cliff of the multi-storey car park and cinema complex where Stanton was on overwatch. There were great gouges in the concrete around the second floor. A mangled black Sprinter van lay on its side up against the wall. It looked as though it had been thrown at the car park. Two more vans, riddled with bullet holes, were parked close to the museum's rear fire exit. Several of the Russians had taken cover behind them and were firing up at the multi-storey. The car park had chunks bitten out of it all over. Roche could see sections of crumbling masonry and exposed metal supports. He raised his carbine to fire on the men around the van and then stopped as he saw what they were looking at.

There were sirens in the distance.

'Position, Indigo two?'

'Heading your ...' He had to stop. A flat staccato hammering filled the air. From up in the car park, Stanton had opened up with a minimi para, a cut-down carbine version of the squad automatic weapon used by the regular army. The men around the other vans started yelling and screaming and firing back. Roche

fired two bursts, headshots, taking one Russian with each and then ducked well out of the way as they turned to fire on him as well. A good solid brick wall was supposed to make a decent piece of cover but the next thing he knew, pieces of it were exploding in his face. He scrambled further away. Whatever rounds those MP7s were firing, they were chewing the masonry to pieces. What he needed was …

'Am I going stupid or was that Lewis Shaw?' Rees again. The chatter of Stanton's SAW fell silent. The screaming howls of the high-velocity MP7s faltered. Roche snarled something and peered back again.

'Fucking Legoland,' he growled. 'You're not going stupid. It's a fucking op.' A black one, black as pitch. Shaw had entirely vanished six months ago, him and Martin Collins, so what else could it be? But then … but then what the *fuck* was Charly playing at? Or didn't she know … ?

Changed things, though. He ran back down the stairs. For a moment the museum was quiet, the ruined café and atrium empty except for rubble and the remains of the fight. Evangeli's crate was still there, its telescopic arms bent and mangled. Roche ignored it. He ran to the atrium. Shaw was gone. There was another man standing out there on the wharf, though. Someone different. Something about him felt off. He wasn't armed.

'Indigo one, respond?' No answer. He had no way to know what had happened to Burman and Linley and Charly out there but he'd heard a lot of shooting and

a good few explosions and the pop of 40mm grenades. Grenades on an op in Docklands, for fuck's sake. 'Indigo three, have you had any contact from Indigo one?'

'Negative, Indigo two.'

Half the front of the museum was missing. Outside around the north dock he could hear more sustained gunfire and more explosions. There were flashes of light, muzzle flashes and ... longer flares that he couldn't so easily explain. It was moving away, though. Not his problem.

The man out on the wharf was still there. He hadn't moved. There was something very wrong about that.

He found the corpse of the last Cypriot. The black plastic thing was still clutched in the dead man's fingers. Roche prised it free. It fitted comfortably in his hand, soft and slightly slick, almost as though it was altering itself to the contour of his grip. It felt more rubbery than plastic. He took it and ran back up the stairs, looking for Rees and a good position over Hertsmere Road that would let them and Stanton trap everything in a crossfire.

As he reached the top of the stairs, he heard Stanton open up with the SAW again, followed shortly by the sharp detonations of two grenades in quick succession. The air shook and the walls and floor of the museum quivered. A burst of silver light erupted from below and the museum shook again, hard this time, knocking Roche flat. He glanced back but all he saw were screams of slashing silver light, lashing around a Scary Clown. Roche pulled out a camera and started it filming,

strapped it to his arm, shouldered his C8 and fired. He saw the bullets hit, saw the alien reel back as gouts of steam popped from its coat.

The Clown whipped around and pointed a small tube in his direction. Roche dived back. A man-sized chunk of brickwork disintegrated where he'd been standing. He moved position. Down in the exhibition hall, something else had emerged out of the wall. It looked like another Clown except instead of being dressed in a frock coat it was covered in a mirrored chrome-like finish, even its face. Streamers of silver light sprayed out of its chest, cascading through the café, tearing at the Clown. They whipped like ropes, cutting brick as they flailed as though the walls were made of smoke, sparking as stray ribbons flared off twisted metal.

A movement behind him snapped at Roche's attention. He whipped around, raising the carbine, but it was only Rees.

'Fucking hell,' said Rees. 'I thought you were gone.'

'Look, mate, you didn't see what was going down out the front. Take this.' Roche passed the camera to Rees and then pointed the black rubbery thing from the atrium at the Clown and fired it. Ropes of golden light launched through the air; but as he did, two more Scary Clowns emerged from the walls. They came at the chrome thing from each side and slipped their claws into it. The silver light died. Roche fired again and hit one of the Clown aliens. It flickered and lurched and pieces of it fell away. The other two picked it up and seemed to dissolve into the air. They drifted, ghost-like,

into the atrium and away towards the North Wharf.
Rees stared at the thing in Roche's hand.

'What the fuck is that?'

Roche shrugged. 'Does anyone know—'

The SAW opened up again outside.

13 July, 2211 hours, Canary Wharf

The Fermat construct arrived as a second clone ceased
to function. The last one was still rushing to catch up
from its observation position in North Africa.

'What sort of spaceship?' it asked. Its concentration
was largely dedicated to the local situation. The Shriven
shouldn't have been able to break its clones. Something
else was doing it.

'Not one of ours,' replied the *Exponential*.

'Send a drone to investigate.'

'I'm not sure that's wise. Won't that give away our
presence?'

The Fermat construct didn't answer straight away. It
flew cloaked between the towers of Canary Wharf,
looking for the entity that had destroyed its first clone.
Outside the entrance to the Docklands Museum, something that looked human but clearly wasn't snagged a
pair of de-phased Shriven as they came out into the
open. One lurched away. The other seemed held fast.
It lashed, writhing violently as it shrank into itself. The
Fermat construct ejected a cloud of tiny pinhead drones.
Inquisitive nanites swarmed through augmented flesh,
looking for signatures and traces. The human-shape

barely seemed to notice. Its fingers dug into the Shriven deeper and deeper until the Shriven crumbled to ash. The nanites abruptly ceased to exist. The human-shape, meanwhile, stubbornly refused to disintegrate. It stared straight at where the Fermat construct was hidden in the air.

13 July, 2211 hours, Canary Wharf

Roche scrambled to his feet and to the nearest window looking out over Hertsmere Road. The SAW had stopped and he heard the sharp cracks of pistol shots. Double taps. There was another crash and an explosion from the front of the museum, from by the door. Down on the street, Roche saw Burman walk past a van, shooting anything that moved with his Sig. He looked like he'd lost it, completely lost it. A van started to pull away as he passed. Burman emptied his clip into the side of it. Roche shouldered his carbine and fired into the roof as it picked up speed, long sustained bursts. Rees did the same. So did Stanton, still up in the car park on the other side. The van screeched around the corner past the entrance to the multi-storey, heading for the main road.

Burman had a grenade launcher out now. A 40mm HE grenade caught the rear left corner of the van, exploded, lifted the back of the vehicle up and sent it tumbling onto its right hand side.

'Noel!'

Stanton was on the street now. None of the Russians immediately below were moving. Roche ducked back,

ejected his spent clip and slotted another into place. He snapped back up to the window in time to see Stanton roll a frag grenade into the back of a van.

'Frag!' He ducked back.

The wall behind Roche shuddered. The floor buckled. Much more of this, whatever the fuck was going on around the front, and the whole warehouse was going to give up and fall down. Another explosion blew the last vestiges of the museum façade to pieces.

Rees grabbed him. He clearly thought the same. 'We need to get out of here.'

'Front or back?' Roche dashed for the stairs, what was left of them, and jumped. In the ruin of the museum's façade, shaking off a mound of rubble, something was stirring, fast and angry. It threw aside a piece of masonry that must have weighed as much as a small car and started to struggle out.

'Back!' yelled Rees. They bolted for the hole in the wall that had once been a door.

'I hope to fuck Burman and Stanton cleared the street out there!'

'Bugger that – Burman's gone fucking rambo. I just hope to fuck he doesn't shoot us simply for moving!'

13 July, 2212 hours, Canary Wharf

The thing that was pretending to be human smashed into the remains of the museum, apparently in a fit of some emotional passion the Fermat construct didn't understand. The impact demolished most of the rest of the façade

239

and it didn't seem to care that most of the stone crashed around and on top of it as it clawed and tore its way free. The construct tossed an implosion singularity into the rubble. The bomb went off and sucked in most of the matter of the museum and some of the surrounding buildings and then spat them out again. It probably wasn't enough to make the other entity even pause but the detonation filled the air with enough noise and smoke for the Fermat to reconfigure and construct a small hyper-velocity neutronium cannon for itself. It considered firing on the other creature and then held back. The human wasn't really human at all. Its structure held the idea of the shape of one but underneath it seemed to be made of exotic matter and a swarming and constantly changing collection of quantum possibilities that the construct simply couldn't pin down into a consistent state in order to annihilate it. The thing, whatever it was, had dispatched the first clone simply by not being what anything was supposed to be.

Whatever it was, it was a significant threat. The construct calculated whether the other entity had suffi-cient data to deduce the presence of the Weft Hive. The answer appeared irritatingly inconclusive.

Best to get rid of it.

The construct ejected a second cloud of drones that swarmed around the entity and, in a small localised area, sucked away the background energy of the universe. Rather to the construct's surprise and alarm, the entity didn't simply disintegrate like it was supposed to. It drew what the construct recognised to be an

M1911 Colt .45 from inside its jacket and fired a tidal wave of naked quarks and clustered strangelets. The construct phased rapidly through different matter-resonances as they passed and then assessed the damage. Considerable. What was worse though, was that it didn't quite understand how the entity had done what it had done; and now it had vanished, and the construct had to accept a perfectly probable hypothesis that the entity wasn't dead.

We withdraw. It didn't need to add anything more. The Hive, always in the construct's thoughts, concurred.

Superficially.

The construct looked harder.

Deep within the Hive they were calculating. The Pleasure. That was the most probable conclusion and now the Hive didn't know what to do. They were afraid. The construct could feel the ripples of it running through them. Five hundred years since the diaspora and in all that time the Pleasure had never returned. Five hundred years of preparing for a war that never came and now it had.

Maybe this is something else. But they all knew it wasn't.

13 July, 2213 hours, Canary Wharf

Roche sprinted across the street and hurled himself at the entrance to the multi-storey. Behind him, the entire back wall of the museum bulged inward. He felt himself sucked backwards, had enough time to throw himself to the floor and kick out, rolling out of the way up the

entrance ramp before the London Museum of Docklands simply shattered and exploded. Something vaguely human-shaped shot through the collapsing wreckage and slammed into the car park three storeys above along with a hail of fractured bricks. A deluge of falling rubble sprawled out across the street, covering the wrecked vans and cars and the numerous bodies on the floor in a thick cloud of reddish dust. Roche slowly picked himself up. He coughed, choking in the brick dust. He was covered in pieces of broken stone, in crumbs of mortar and glass.

'Rees?'

'Yeah.'

'You okay?'

'Yeah. Kinda. What the ...' There was a rustle of sliding gravel as Rees sat up. The entrance to the multi-storey was half blocked with rubble that spilled down the ramp.

'Christ.' Roche spat out a mouthful of red dust. This was London? It looked more like Fallujah during the worst of the fighting.

'Roche ... What the hell?'

'What the hell do you think?' Through the settling dust, Hertsmere Street looked still. The sounds of gunfire still rattled down the canyon of the street. 'Did you see Burman? Stanton?' Roche couldn't quite tell which way the fighting had moved.

'What I *think* is that there are some things Charly didn't bother to mention, because if I'd known what was *actually* going down then I'd have brought the whole rest of the fucking Rebel Alliance with me. We got some X-wings

parked in the underground car park in Vauxhall just sitting there, just waiting. I mean, point me at the Death Star and let's … Roche, what the fuck is this shit?'

'Do I look like fucking Mulder?' Roche pulled himself to his feet and dusted himself down. Most likely the shooting was coming from the police roadblocks on West India Docks Road and Aspen Way. He started jogging along the ramp. Stanton had taken his position up here because it gave arcs of fire over both as well as over the back of the museum. 'You remember Lewis Shaw and Martin Collins?'

'I didn't know them. I heard they went missing. When was it? Last year?'

'January sometime. I wasn't there but I knew them both well enough.' Roche nodded back to the bottom of the ramp. 'He was here. I'm sure it was him. You said so too.'

'I thought …'

'You still got the camera?'

Rees howled with laughter. 'Did I fucking tape it, you mean? Christ! I was trying not to die and completely go fucking mad. But yes, I did indeed tape that episode of fucking Pacific Rim or whatever the fuck it is that was going on in there.'

'I got some from the museum but not when it went batshit crazy.' Roche whispered into his radio mike. 'Indigo two to all Indigo call-signs. Respond?' He shook his head. 'Comms went shit the moment that fucking crate opened up. For all I know, nothing got out.' They rounded a corner onto the third level of the multi-storey.

243

'I'm certain that was Shaw.' He looked over the edge of the car park into the street below.

'That was the thing you saw in Aqar?'

Roche nodded. Hertsmere Road was covered in rubble from the collapsed warehouse and museum but otherwise it was empty. Nothing moved.

'Only here there were three of them.'

'Five. Maybe six. Come on. We need to follow Shaw. You were up at the window. Which way did he go?'

'Back through the rubble, and no we fucking don't!' Rees walked over to the other side of the car park, then waved Roche over. The roads running past the West India Docks were empty now except for a handful of police cars, parked with their lights flashing. Level with the storey below, an elevated section of the Docklands Light Railway ran past. Roche went back to the other side, searching for Shaw. Sporadic bursts of gunfire echoed from further down the road where Linley's men had set up their roadblock.

'There!' Rees pointed into the ruin of the museum. There was a soldier down there, racing through the debris in impossible leaps and bounds.

'Shit! He's going to get away.' And they'd never catch him on foot. Roche ran back to the other side, looking for a quick way down. The gap between the elevated DLR track and the car park was only a few feet but from there it was a long way down. He started running among the cars, looking for an old Ford, because nothing hot-wired as easy as an old Ford.

'Got one.' Rees was ahead of him. Thirty seconds later they were tearing through the car park, looking

for the exit. Thirty more and they were out. Rees turned the Ford up Hertsmere Road towards the police road-blocks and then slammed on the brakes. The road was a sea of rubble. He shook his head, screeching the tyres as he shifted into reverse and stamped on the accel-erator. 'Even a fucking Mastiff couldn't get through that shit.'

'Just get round the other side!'

Rees executed a perfect reverse handbrake turn and screeched around the side of what had once been the London Museum of Docklands. The North Wharf itself was still hidden behind the remains of the museum but now Roche could see the tower blocks behind it. They were scarred. Canary Wharf tower was missing pieces of its glass roof. Flashes and booms still echoed around through the darkness. He thought he could hear a heli-copter somewhere overhead, low, but he couldn't see its lights. *Bloody idiots getting close to this* ...

'The fucking ground is shaking!' bawled Rees. 'Can you feel it?' Across the North Wharf, flashes of small-arms fire fractured the night. Rees turned sharply again and crashed up through the open barrier into the pedes-trianised space towards the front of the museum. They shot past a pub and screeched to a stop at the edge of the rubble. The remains of some rather nice and expen-sive Audis lay crushed under a mountain of shattered Victorian brickwork.

'Where the fuck is Shaw?' Roche strained his eyes, trying to make out any movement. A couple of wankers with phones were hunkered down in what was left of

the pub's beer garden, filming them. Roche suppressed the urge to shoot them.

'Priorities, mate! We still got men under fire!' Rees jumped out of the car and crouched beside it, shouldering his carbine, already scanning for targets.

'These fuckers were the same ones who shredded Burman and Stanton in Dagenham, right?' Roche jumped out after him, covering the remains of the museum. 'But Shaw was ours. You want to go fuck about with some pissy drug-crazed pusher dickwads, you go do that, Rees!' He was shouting now. Screaming almost. 'There!' Across the docks, ropes of fire shot over the water. A sphere of glittering light flared as the light enveloped it. Roche leapt to his feet. 'There! If you want to know what the fuck this is all about, we go after ...' He stopped. Something leapt out of the museum, tall and thin and translucent. It had too many limbs and something about it suggested it was armoured. Roche tried to get a bead on it but it was too quick. The air around it shimmered. It landed next to the water and rolled in and was gone. It didn't make so much as a ripple.

'Er ...' started Rees. 'How many arms did that have? Because I'm sure it was more than two.'

Across Docklands, all the lights went out.

13 July, 2218 hours, Canary Wharf, North Dock

The Fermat hybrid construct sank into the waters of the North Wharf and watched. The Shriven were stuttering

southward, out of phase with ordinary matter-resonances and passing through everything as though they were ghosts. The Fermat's surviving clone scattered a net of exotic quarks across the path of the Shriven, forcing them to phase back into mundane matter. As soon as they did, the clones scattered a handful of anti-matter bomblets that would have vaporised most of the West India Docks and annihilated the Thames waterfront from the Limehouse Basin right across to the other side of the Isle of Dogs.

The construct neutralised them. *Let them go. Withdraw. Do not expose our presence.*

Dazzled by gluon-flashes, the Shriven hosed the spaces now and then occupied by the two clones with a broad spectrum of exotic particle states and high-end radiation. It didn't do very much but the lights were pretty if you had the psychology to appreciate such things. The first of the Shriven reached the underground bunker beneath One Canada Square and activated a device that flashed an electro-magnetic pulse over most of Millwall and the East End and drained ever erg of energy out of every electrical device within a radius of approximately half a mile.

13 July, 2219 hours, North Dock

Everything went dark. The street lights, the lights in all the buildings around him, everything. The bubble of light around Shaw vanished. Flickers of what looked like sparks flashed momentarily across the pyramid roof of One Canada Square. The Ford's lights went

out, though the engine kept running. Rees tapped his radio and shook it. When Roche looked, his own was dead. Even the battery charge light was out. He swore.

'Electro-magnetic pulse?' He stared hard at Rees. Rees took out the camera, looked at it and shook his head.

'Dead.'

A light grew over One Canada Square like a faint Aurora. Dim curtains of green and violet shimmered above it, rose and faded. The wankers back in the wrecked beer garden were pointing their phones at it and fiddling with them, trying to work out why they suddenly weren't working. They probably thought it was some sort of publicity stunt. After the laser show from the Shard last summer, maybe it was.

'Take the car round the other way.' Roche abandoned Rees and the Ford and ran on foot, south on the pavement alongside the water, the C8 slung over his shoulder, heading after Shaw and clutching the black rubber weapon he'd taken from the dead Cypriot. At some point there were some questions to be asked there about who this Evangeli was and where his connections went and how the fuck he happened to be cosy with half a dozen Jack-the-Ripper crazy bastard aliens. Yeah, but not now, and anyway Evangeli was dead. Shaw and the answers he had. That was what mattered.

13 July, 2221 hours, approaching Mars orbit

The *Irrational Prime* was in a holding orbit, waiting to be told what to do. Behind it a comet sped, carefully

shepherded by magnetic fields, tiny and almost impossible to see. It was only a few kilometres across. Not the sort of thing you wanted hitting your planet if you happened to be anywhere near the impact site but otherwise nothing to fear; and besides, most likely it would hit any decent planet's atmosphere and bounce off or else break up into a shower of much smaller pieces that would burn up and hardly do any damage at all.

Except, being made of anti-matter, what would actually happen was the sudden explosive release of energy equivalent to the moon hitting the earth at about three times the speed of sound. It would crack a planet in two, strip it of its atmosphere and cause shockwaves through the crust that would shake every structure to powder. For any planet that happened to be made mostly of hot molten rock, the comet would cause the crust to shatter, set up resonances and standing waves that would distort the shape of the world by tens, even hundreds of kilometres. At the very least it would extinguish all life on any planet. Almost as certainly, it would destroy all further possibility of life. If they were lucky and the planet was a reasonably small one, the impact might actually shatter it. That last possibility was speculative and the freighter and the frigate had been exploring the mathematics on and off for the last few weeks, trying to work out an answer. In the end, sometimes the only way to know was to try a thing out.

'So are we going to use it or not?' asked the *Exponential*.

'Apparently we wait and see what happens.' The Hive had held back on the comet. The *Irrational Prime* thought

that might be about to change. It was a nice easy clean way to solve the problem, after all.

The *Exponential*, meanwhile, had been dabbling with human figures of speech. It had decided to make a study of them while there were still some humans left.

'Shall we get popcorn?' it asked.

13 July, 2221 hours, North Dock

Roche raced along North Colonnade, ignoring a fire-fight in Cabot Square to the south. The flashes of light had stopped. He felt the ground tremble under his feet. Under the arches of the Docklands Light Railway beside Canary Wharf station, he slid to a stop. One Canada Square was right in front of him, surrounded by thick smoke or vapour. There were sparks running up and down it. A pane of glass near the top exploded and rained shards across the street. Then another pane exploded and then another and then suddenly they were shattering everywhere, from top to bottom. Roche ducked sharply round the corner into the narrow shelter of Chancellor Passage underneath the railway lines. Needles and shards of glass were flying everywhere. He could still hear weapons firing in Cabot Square. He could hear people screaming.

One Canada Square was shrinking. Narrowing. The ground shook again. The tower shuddered and started to sag and buckle as though its walls were being sucked inward. The same thing he'd seen at the museum. He hurled himself away and threw himself flat, sliding

across the pavement as the building imploded in a thunder of shattering glass and screaming metal. A wind reached around the corner and under the railway and blew him down the street like so much tumbleweed. He fetched up in a doorway. Pieces of shattered glass and tortured steel and savaged concrete rained around him. They peppered his body armour and he felt a sting in his shoulder.

A severed hand landed with a wet smack on the concrete beside him. For a moment he lay still and stared at it, too battered to move. The ground was shaking. A pulse shuddered through him, through the wall beside him and the paving slabs underneath him, hard enough to make him grunt. He hauled himself painfully back to his feet, checking everything still worked. His rib was agony again.

Something was coming out of the wreckage. A glittering bubble, constantly bright under the deluge of the white energy beam.

Shaw?

Another pulse shook the street. Roche stumbled and looked for anything that might pass as cover, clutching the weapon he'd taken from the museum. The next pulse came, strong enough to shake mortar dust out of the bridges over his head and almost knock him off his feet. A pair of dead Organizistya lay sprawled further down the passage. With each pulse they jerked and danced. It reminded him of those biology lessons at school where they took electrodes to dead frogs and made their legs spasm. He caught a glimpse of another shape, too tall,

arms too long, drifting among the shadows in a long frock coat. Shaw lifted his arm and a burst of fiery yellow shot from the alien weapon towards it. The creature in the frock coat made no effort to get out of the way. It seemed to swallow the fireball.

The pulses were coming more quickly now. Roche could hardly stay on his feet.

An explosion under the ground shook the rubble. Bricks and slabs of concrete jumped around the street. The bridge above him groaned as it flexed. Roche stumbled away. He pointed the weapon from the museum at the shadows where he'd seen the Clown and squeezed, holding it tight. Ropes of golden light twisted through the choking dust, wrapping themselves around the darkness. They lit it up and now Roche could see the shape of it. Almost but not quite human. Its head snapped towards him but before it could move, before Roche could think to stop firing and run like fuck for some cover, Shaw raised his arm again and a series of darts flew like tracer fire, each one flashing as bright as the sun. Roche turned and staggered away, holding his hand over his eyes. He stumbled into the relative shelter of an overturned van and took cover behind it.

The ground was shaking like a drumskin now, like an earthquake, a pounding so hard and so rhythmic that everything lying loose on the road kept jumping an inch up into the air. Roche staggered and then fell and gave up. The light, the noise, the shaking, the …

With a last shudder, the pounding stopped. The bubble around Shaw vanished. Flickers of what looked

like sparks flashed across the ruin of One Canada Square. In the sudden quiet he heard screaming from the square behind him. Gunshots. The pop of a 40mm grenade and then the explosion that followed and then the sustained rattle of a squad support weapon. Ahead of him, the man who might have been Lewis Shaw suddenly jumped and tumbled and rolled out of the rubble. An instant later, an explosion came from where he'd been. Pieces of shrapnel or debris flew like bullets, zipping and fizzing through the air. Puffs of dust flew up where they pock-marked the surrounding blocks. A loud bang a few inches from Roche's face made him jump where something hard and fast punched right through the van, puncturing the metal and leaving a hole surrounded by jagged aluminium petals. Roche slumped back. The Scary Clown was out in the open now. He reached for his camera, then remembered Rees had it, that it didn't matter anyway, that his radio was dead, that some fucker had let off an electro-magnetic pulse.

The Clown fired two more shots at something Roche couldn't see. Damn thing was right there in front of him, a dozen yards away and in the open, clear as anything now that there was no one here to see it. As it turned away, it drew out some sort of device about the size and shape of a rugby ball, twisted it sharply and vanished – no, not *quite* vanished – Roche thought he caught a flash of movement and pieces of rubble twitched and shifted on the street. The Clown had suddenly moved impossibly quickly, that was all.

All? He almost burst out laughing at the absurdity of it. *All?* And the glittering bubble around Lewis Shaw? Some sort of force field, that was *all*. Nothing special, although he was fucked if he knew how *that* worked. Yeah, and aliens that walked through walls and …

From the ruin of One Canada Square, something was rising up into the sky. Bullet shaped and maybe as tall as a house. Roche stared. It simply hung there for an instant, lightning playing along the steel spirals of its outer skeleton; and then the base pulsed with a circle of brilliant white light and the earth shook and everything jumped and the thing suddenly shifted further up into the sky in the blink of an eye, and hung there. The back end of it pulsed again and with every pulse it jumped further away. Like watching something in stop-motion. Roche stared, transfixed. The pulses grew steadily more frequent.

Observe and report. Trust your eyes. It's about what you see, not what you *think* you see.

All that training. He really did burst out laughing this time. Hysterical, which was no use. He took some deep breaths. Twenty years doing this. Twenty years and he'd seen some seriously fucked-up shit in that time, starting with Kravica. That had taken some beating but Somalia, Afghanistan and Iraq had all given it their best. This, though … Nothing had made him ready for this. Nothing could.

He had friends who'd started families. Ketch had said the same about having kids. *Nothing makes you ready for it. Nothing can …*

Get a fucking grip!

Shaw was standing in the rubble, clear as day, wrapped up in his bubble again and firing into the air. No one anywhere, ever, was going to believe any of this except for the fact that it had happened and tomorrow morning it would be all over the news and there would be a thousand and one clips taken from the mobile phones of the people like those idiots back in the beer garden, because that was what you did these days. You didn't run for your life or scream your head off for the nearest policeman, you ducked for cover and then turned around and filmed it with your phone, right … ?

Except you didn't. Not when someone set off an EMP and fucked everything with a battery across a half-mile radius.

Shit! The laptop! He hadn't got a damn thing to show for any of this except what he'd shot in the museum. If the laptop still worked. If the fucking Clowns hadn't pulled what they'd pulled in Brixton.

Very slowly, Roche dragged himself up. Shaw had stopped shooting at the sky now.

'Shaw? That you?' Roche waved.

The figure in the rubble didn't respond at first. Roche walked slowly closer, wary. Six months, thereabouts, since Shaw and Collins had vanished. Same sort of time he'd seen the first Scary Clown back in Brixton and gone mad. And they'd not been away on some op or disappeared in some messy little fracas in some country far away. They'd been out on the piss in Hereford and simply hadn't come back. Or so the stories said. And now here they were.

'Shaw?' Special programme? That sort of thing happened now and then. What was with the arm, though? 'Shaw? That you?'

At last Shaw stopped looking up at the sky and turned to look at Roche instead. Quick as a snake, he fired.

16 – Life on Mars

13 July, 2225 hours, Low Earth Orbit

The Fermat construct latched on to the side of the Shriven ship as it stutter-warped out of the Earth's atmosphere. Once the ship reached a comfortable orbit, it detached. It picked a defunct nuclear-powered satellite and latched on to that instead, powered down most of its systems and settled for hiding and waiting. The *Exponential* was already reconfiguring all the drones that had been collecting antimatter and weaponising them to attack the cloaked spaceship that the Europa detector was now tracking

'They were here before we arrived,' it said.

The construct flinched. 'The Shriven should have destroyed this world when they found it.'

'Some part of the Hive already knew of this world before we came here,' observed the freighter. The consequences of such an appalling revelation were beyond calculation.

The *Exponential* continued weaponising the drones. 'Whoever they are, they might not know that we've found them. We should stay quiet.'

'Yes.'

There was a flaw in that plan, of course, and they both knew it. A one-hundred-and-seventy-mile-long flaw called the *Irrational Prime*.

13 July, 2225 hours, approaching the orbit of Mars

The *Irrational Prime* drifted through interplanetary space, pretending as best it could to be a dead and inert lump of rock. It zoomed its optical and ultraviolet sensors up to the limit of their magnification and began piping the feed through to the Hive and the Fermat construct and the *Exponential*. The last few Shriven had stutter-warped out of the Earth's atmosphere in a makeshift ship cobbled together from nano-factories. It shed bits and pieces that weren't part of the core structure and weren't taking the strain. The freighter calculated how long it would take for the Shriven to build an Einstein-Podolsky-Rosen drive (what the humans would have called it if they had one) and how far that might take them. Short of drawing on the underlying zero-point energy of the universe, the Shriven would be limited to total mass conversion. It was busy working out exactly how far that might get them when space around the Shriven ship burst into blossoms of light.

13 July, 2225 hours, City of London

Shaw moved so damned fast that Roche barely even saw it. He threw himself sideways as a ball of fire shot

down the street. Shaw leapt into the air, jumping maybe fifty, sixty feet up and straight down the street to where Roche had been standing. Roche fired the museum gun. The bubble around Shaw shivered golden but that was all. Shaw came down and landed ten feet down the road from Roche, hitting the tarmac so hard it cracked around his feet. Roche fired again, this time at the entrance to the tower block beside him, Brodies Bar and Restaurant, carving his way in. Any way out would do but he wasn't going to have time.

'Roche? Sergeant Roche Manning?' Shaw had his arm raised, the arm that wasn't an arm any more but merged into some sort of organic plasma cannon. For a moment, he looked almost confused.

'Shaw?' They stared at one another.

The flicker of recognition faded from Shaw's eyes. He snarled. Roche dived through the entrance to the restaurant and sprinted through the abandoned tables, out the other side, through the kitchen. The lifts wouldn't be working, wherever they were, but there would be stairs ...

Shaw raised his arm and fired a series of plasma bolts. They were smaller than the ones he'd used on the Clown but they came a lot faster. They seemed to chase him. Roche ran, putting distance between him and Shaw, pointing his own weapon back behind him and firing it continuously without even looking to see whether it was doing anything, slamming the first door he came to shut behind him in case that spoiled Shaw's aim at all. The wall shuddered. He saw a face, cringing,

curled up in a corner. 'Run!' he screamed. He glanced over his shoulder as he turned the corner. The walls behind him were disintegrating. Shaw stood in the entrance, the shield like a halo around him, but he didn't come in.

Roche found some stairs and ran up them as fast as he could, then raced across the next level of the building, kicking through doors with a frantic violence, driving his way to the windows right in one corner. He got there in time to see Shaw stand back amid the rubble of One Canada Square and raise his arm and fire.

The walls disintegrated. Roche curled up and pressed his hands over his ears. The three topmost floors erupted upwards, blown off by the force of the explosion and then collapsed down. A scalding wind picked up monitors and printers and scanners and threw them like rocks from an angry giant. Flimsy plasterboard partition walls snapped, metal posts bent and buckled, chipboard doors were torn off their hinges and thrown through the air. Roche cringed in his corner, hiding under a cheap desk. Most of the front of the building erupted outward from the force of the explosion. Most of the rest fell to bits. Three feet away from him, the floor collapsed.

The rumbling seemed to go on and on. Roche didn't move, waiting for it to finish or for the last piece of the building frontage to finally give up and collapse, taking him with it, but it didn't. The noise of falling concrete finally stopped. He peered back out through the hole that had once been a window.

Shaw was back where he'd been before. He had a substantial part of the building on top of him now but that didn't seem to be troubling him. He pulled himself steadily out of the rubble, picking up twisted girders and huge slabs of masonry as though they were pieces from a fallen theatre set and tossing them away. When he was clear, he paused for a moment to look at the wreckage around him and then walked slowly off. Roche watched him go.

'Indigo four,' he whispered. 'This is Indigo two. Shaw's heading your way. Be advised, Shaw is not fucking friendly. Do not approach. Do *not* approach.'

Then he remembered the radio was dead.

13 July, 2237 hours, approaching the orbit of Mars

A string of explosions peppered space around the Shriven ship in flashes of hard white nuclear light. The *Irrational Prime* let its particle detectors tick over, watching the flurry of x-rays and gamma rays. It was odd watching the fight from so far away, with several light minutes of separation between them. Everything it could see was already finished for the ships themselves, the fight three steps further onward. For the Fermat construct hiding in its satellite, it must be even stranger. It would feel the flux of particles but it wouldn't see the explosions that made them until minutes later, until the *Irrational Prime* picked them up and spread everything it saw across the infinity of entangled pions that was the Hive.

261

A series of new lights flickered around the Shriven ship. A swarm of much smaller ships, sweeping in from somewhere. They sprayed the Shriven ship with loops and arcs of white and golden energy which shimmered off the Shriven shields. Then they came closer in, as if they were nuzzling up to it, as if they wanted to board it. The *Irrational Prime* tried to up its resolution on the attacking drones to see who they were. It was hard to be sure but they seemed to be constantly changing.

In a flash of light the Shriven finally activated their EPR drive and shot suddenly to exactly twice the speed of light. For a handful of minutes, the *Irrational Prime* lost track of them.

13 July, 2241 hours, City of London

Roche lowered himself down to the ground and picked his way through the rubble littered across Canada Square. When he finally walked out of the dust of fallen buildings, coughing and wheezing, the fighting had died away. Already he caught glimpses of a few people here and there, the crazy and the stupid and the insanely brave. Young, mostly. They were gathering in little clumps and clusters, half of them holding their phones and shaking them, staring at them, cursing them, talking about them. People stared at him as he staggered past. A part of him still wanted to shoot them for that. Another part was long past caring.

'Indigo two?'

A police siren burst into life somewhere ahead of him. He didn't know quite where he was going. Shadowing Shaw, that was all.

'Indigo two, do you copy?' Still nothing. Still down from the EMP. At least the idiots with their phones couldn't take any pictures.

Shaw was a hostile then, was he? 'I have to follow him. Find out where he goes.' Except Shaw was already gone. He'd already lost him. 'We need their intel. We need to know who they are.' He was talking to himself, muttering under his breath. Not a good sign.

An old Ford pulled up on the corner ahead of him, the one Rees had stolen from the multi-storey. The passenger door flew open and Rees beckoned from inside. Roche was barely in before Rees pulled away with a screech of rubber.

'Just saw Shaw getting into a police car. He's heading for Commercial Road and the City. You want to tail him?'

'Oh fuck yes,' growled Roche. Rees caught his eye as he turned into West India Dock Road and floored it.

'If that was Lewis Shaw then this is someone else's op,' he said. 'We shouldn't fucking be here. We should never have fucking been here.'

Roche growled. 'If it is then they've known for some fucking time that there are things that aren't fucking human in the world and whoever they are, I want to find them and break their fucking necks!' His legs hurt, his shoulders hurt, his arms hurt, his back ached, his head throbbed where something had caught him just above the left ear … 'Ketch saw one of them in ninety-five.

Discharged on medical. I saw one in January. Discharged on medical. The Yanks, when they went out to Aqar, they knew what they were looking for and they nuked the place. I can't believe it was a total fucking coincidence that someone this end found a way to get us out there with them. Someone *knows*, Rees. Someone's known for months.' He caught his breath, trying to find some calm. 'It *was* Shaw, Rees. He saw me. He recognised me. He said my name and then he tried to kill me.'

The Ford tore along Commercial Road, weaving maniacally between the erratic scatter of stationary cars strewn askew across the tarmac in the aftermath of the EMP. The Ford's speedo was all over the place, the dial flicking madly from zero up to a hundred and back again.

'The engine never died. No electronics.' Rees grinned. 'Fuck your Audis and your Mercs, nothing beats an old Ford in a pinch. Was some weird fucker of a pulse though. The battery's as dead as a doornail. Doesn't make sense.' Rees dodged around a neat queue lined up in front of some traffic lights that weren't working any more. People were standing by their cars, talking to each other. Presumably they'd gone past the point of trying to phone for help. After a minute, Roche started to see cars moving again, a few warily coming the other way. The skyline of the City of London ahead was still bright with lights. Rees braked hard as they reached the junction at Aldgate. The cars here were still running but the traffic lights were out and nothing was moving. A lorry, trying to turn across the traffic, had been blocked by two cars coming the other way

who were now stuck on the yellow hatching with the enormous 'Keep Clear' written across it. Audis. It was always a fucker in an Audi or a Merc. Used to be BMWs that were driven by cunts but apparently they were richer now. Roche wanted to get out of the Ford and drag them to the side of the road and maybe shoot them in the knees.

'There!' Rees pointed. Fifty yards ahead, blocked in by the traffic, was a police car.

'You sure?'

'Get the plates!' Rees tossed him a small spotter's scope. As Roche read the plates, Rees nodded. 'That's him.'

'Hold back then. Hold back. See where he goes. He's got to report in after this but for Christ's sake don't let him get wind of us! He thinks I'm dead.'

Rees snorted. 'Hold back? I'll be lucky to move.' He had a point. Monday night traffic in central London was shit at the best of times, the Aldgate junction was already in gridlock and Roche could hear the distant sirens. As soon as word got out about Docklands, the City would be swarming with armed police and road-blocks going up left right and centre, diverting people away from the square mile. The City of London police were a bit fucking quick like that. There'd be helicopters too and the media would storm the place at the first hint of what had happened.

'He's moving,' said Rees suddenly. Shaw was out of the car. Roche moved to follow.

'Rees, you take point. I'll cover from the sides. He's seen me and he knows me so I can't get close.'

The glittering bubble had vanished and Shaw's arm looked like an ordinary arm again. He was still nigh on six foot six, though, and even in civilian clothes he stuck out. He was an easy mark to follow. Rees trailed him most of the way down Mansell Street and past the Tower and St Katharine Docks. Roche switched in when Shaw crossed the river at Tower Bridge.

'He's heading for Vauxhall.'

Rees took over again down the Albert Embankment. By the time Shaw walked in through the back doors into Legoland, neither of them were surprised.

'Well that answers that, then,' grumbled Rees, 'What the fuck now?'

'Shaw and I have some words, that's what. I go in and you watch my back and remember that he tried to kill me, that he's working for fuck-knows-who and you don't go anywhere near him. If it goes south between me and Shaw, let it. Pretend you know fuck all, right. Brief Charly and Stanton. Tell them all of it. As far as anyone else goes, you were never here. Or maybe, more to the point, you never left in the first place.'

Rees nodded. 'Got it.' He tapped the webbing pocket that held Roche's camera. 'Got this.'

'This too. If it's not fried.' Roche handed him the laptop he'd taken into the museum.

13 July, 2241 hours, Mars orbit

The *Irrational Prime* had no way of knowing where the Shriven were or what was happening to them for as

long as they had their Einstein-Podolsky-Rosen drive engaged. It could, however, deduce that the only useful destination for the Shriven was Mars. By then they'd use up half the mass of their improvised ship as fuel to drive the entanglement engine.

The Pleasure, on the other hand, clearly didn't worry about that sort of thing and simply mined the vacuum energy of empty space. As soon as the Shriven popped into existence in close orbit around Mars, they had drones harrying them from all directions with more forms of energetic attack than the *Irrational Prime* could make into any sense. The Shriven ship manoeuvred violently but it didn't make the first jot of difference. The drones were playing with the Shriven – showing off, even competing with each other. They changed their shape as they dived into the fight, morphing back and forth between various baroque ideas of spaceships drawn from human myths. They were playful, gleeful, joyful even. Gaspingly inefficient, but they didn't seem to care and it wasn't going to make any difference. As the Shriven ship plunged towards the Martian surface, a large piece sloughed off the back. The stutter-warp drive fell to bits. The ship began to tumble.

The waiting Martian surface lit up with plasma flares. A network of primitive defence satellites surrounding the planet awoke from their energy coma and started firing on the drone ships. Hundreds and hundreds – thousands – no, *tens* of thousands of tiny warheads launched themselves towards the onrush of the Shriven, scattering around them and attacking the Pleasure

drones. The first bursts of accelerated anti-particles, high energy x-ray lasers and focused gamma bursts damaged a few but then the drones adapted. Thermonuclear light flashed, blinding the *Irrational Prime*'s sensor arrays. Energy spikes erupted from the planet from high-end gamma bursts. A few seconds later, the first streams of exotic particles were registering on the *Irrational Prime*'s detectors. Drones exploded into thousands of tiny sub-munitions. As the satellites died, the surface of the Red Planet lit up in a glorious light display.

'Please monitor more closely,' requested the Fermat construct. The *Irrational Prime* was still watching everything happen with almost a full minute delay.

'Me?' The *Irrational Prime* spat out a particularly venomous sequence of exotic particles. 'Why me?'

'You were constructed by the Shriven. Your presence is not out of place. You belong here. I do not.'

There was also, the *Irrational Prime* had to accept, the small matter of the Fermat construct not being particularly well equipped for independent inter-planetary travel. There were still the *Exponential*'s drones though.

'They are clearly technologically distinct,' said the frigate quietly. 'The Pleasure, if it detects them, will know that the Hive are here.'

The *Irrational Prime* irritably adjusted its orientation and angled itself so its main drives were pointing towards Mars. 'You realise that if I do anything other than blaze in at full acceleration, it's all going to be over before I get even close?'

Of course they realised.

'You realise this isn't going to end at all well.'

But yes, they realised that too. Just as the freighter understood the real reason for the construct's request.

The *Irrational Prime* muttered an irritable excretion of heavy mesons, lit its fusion torch and screamed off through space on a one-way trip towards Mars.

13 July, 2344 hours, Legoland

'Shaw!' Roche caught up just as Shaw crossed through the inner security screen. He didn't make any attempt to follow him any further. If it hadn't been for the military policemen manning the checkpoint, he'd have shouldered his C8 and pointed it at Shaw's face. As it was, he held the alien weapon from the museum. 'Shaw. Hold the fuck up, mate.'

Shaw stopped. He stood for a moment with his back to Roche and touched his ear. Calling for help? Calling for something. *Well go on then, you tosser. I've got my back covered too, thanks for asking.*

'Hello, Roche.' Shaw turned around and walked slowly towards him. He kept his hands out where Roche could see them, palms turned up, showing how harmless he was. Roche didn't buy it for a second. 'Tough one, eh?'

'You care to explain what the fuck that was all about, Shaw?'

Shaw shook his head.

'What about where you've been for the last six months?'

'You know better than that, Roche. Sectioned out into a classified compartment that no one else knows

exists. I'd have thought you'd figured that out after tonight.' He glanced at the three military policemen. 'Look, after what you've seen, someone's going to have to read you in one way or the other. I can give you a little. Not a lot. You want to go out for a pint?'

'It's pushing one in the fucking morning, Shaw. Where the fuck's open on a Monday night? And no.' He raised the black rubber light-gun and pointed it at Shaw. 'No, I don't want to go out for a fucking pint. An hour ago you tried to kill me.'

The MPs had their sub-machine guns shouldered and pointed at Roche in a flash. 'Put it down!' 'On the floor!' 'Get on the ground!' Give them credit, they knew a weapon when they saw one, just from the way Roche had been holding it. Roche raised his hands and then dropped to his knees, moving very slowly so they didn't …

Shaw's movement was so sudden and so fast that it was a blur. In one moment he was standing at the checkpoint, in another, in the blink of a single eye, he'd moved ten feet sideways. His arm lashed out and he smashed one MP's throat and then he moved again; before Roche could even understand what Shaw was doing, he'd snapped the second man's neck. The last one swung his MP5 around but he didn't have time to pull the trigger before Shaw snapped out a crescent kick and knocked it flying so hard that he bent the gun and shattered half the bones in the soldier's hands. The soldier's cry was cut short by a vicious throat-punch. Half a second later his neck was broken. Roche

twisted, levelling the alien gun; but before he could bring it to bear, Shaw moved again with blistering speed. He kicked the gun out of Roche's hand, grabbed Roche by the throat and pinned him to the ground. Roche couldn't help thinking of the SEAL lieutenant in Aqar, how that shouldn't have been possible, but Shaw had the speed of a mongoose and the strength of an elephant and nothing Roche could do made the slightest bit of difference.

'What. The fuck. *Are* you?' Roche gasped.

Behind Shaw two more soldiers were coming, picking their way over the bodies of the dead MPs.

'What am I?' Shaw laughed. 'Shit, Roche. You want to know what's been going on, is that it? Is that all it is?'

13 July, 2344 hours, Mars orbit

The *Irrational Prime* shot through space, accelerating all the time, dead straight towards Mars. There wasn't really any other way to do it. It lined itself up on where the Shriven ship had crashed in the Noctis Labyrinthus, since that seemed to be the centre of the conflict. The last few satellites were still firing on the stuttering drones, simple high-energy x-ray lasers, gamma bursts and accelerated anti-particles. It was all desperately primitive and, while it made for a great deal of light and some picturesque particle sprays, the drones attacking the Shriven simply shrugged it off as though it wasn't there. Now and then they killed a few of the remaining satellites as though passing the time while they thought up

something more interesting to do. The drones remained high above the Valles Marineris for a while, bombarding it with beams of plasma, creating lava-falls and geysers of molten rock. Most of it didn't look like it had anything to do with the Shriven. They were doing it because they could. Because it was art. Not that the Fermat construct or the Weft would ever understand that.

After a while they switched to massive thermonuclear bombardment of the canyon instead. The *Irrational Prime* had no idea why. They were wiping out their creations before they'd even had a chance to cool.

'Those satellites are diaspora weapons,' observed the Fermat construct.

'Yes.' They would hurt the freighter, though, because the *Irrational Prime* was, beneath its borrowed cloned mind, a very simple piece of technology of the same age as the Shriven and with almost no means of protecting itself from a meagre solar flare, never mind a directed beam of anti-protons. It could see what all the fuss was about now. On Mars, the Shriven had built something. They'd tried to hide it but now it was out in the open, all its cloaks stripped away.

The *Irrational Prime* adjusted its course and flew straight at it, as hard and fast as it could.

14 July, 2345 hours, Legoland

'You just can't leave it alone eh, Roche? You want to know the truth? Fine, here it is: that thing that your mate Ketch saw in Kravica? The same thing you saw

in Brixton. The same thing you saw in Aqar. The same thing you saw today. They're fucking aliens, mate. Fucking aliens!' Shaw's grip on Roche's throat was slowly tightening. Roche tried rolling, tried kicking Shaw's legs out from under him, anything to break the hold. Things that should have worked against anyone, no matter how strong they were, but Shaw was something else. Roche brought his feet up into his chest and kicked as hard as he could and Shaw didn't even flinch. Shaw's fingers around his throat were as tight as they wanted to be, Roche realised, not as tight as they could be. Shaw could crush his neck whenever he wanted. It was like fighting the fucking Terminator.

'What. Are. You?'

'Aliens, Roche.' Shaw shook his head and for a moment there was a flicker of disbelief, of horror, of shock, of a man lost and overwhelmed by what he knew and what he'd become. 'Do you know how long they've been here? Since Columbus discovered America. We call them the Astronomers. That one in Brixton, he was Copernicus.' He smirked. 'Always made me laugh when I was a nipper, Copernicus. Copper knickers. Then there was Brahe. Kepler. Galileo. Newton. Herschel. Herschel was the one in Aqar. Five hundred years. They've been feeding off us. They're like fucking parasites, bleeding us dry, keeping us exactly where they want but that's all going to change now. They're not the only ones out there. There are others.' For a moment the grip on Roche's throat relaxed. 'Me and Collins. We were pissed. We met this guy ...' Shaw laughed. 'We were just walking

down the path beside the river looking for a fucking kebab ...' Shaw paused again, somehow lost. 'I told him I was going to shoot him. He said okay.' Shaw laughed. 'Can you believe that? He said okay. So I did. I nailed him between the eyes. He just stood there. Said he wanted to know what it felt like, being shot in the head.'

Shaw's eyes changed. He picked Roche up by the throat and slammed him into a wall. 'And then you found the fuckers in Brixton, and that's when we knew where it all went wrong. But not any more.' He tightened his grip. Roche kicked. He gouged at Shaw's face but nothing made any difference.

'Sorry Roche,' hissed Shaw. 'But the chosen are chosen.'

Roche's vision started to collapse. He heard the roaring of the sea in his ears and felt his kicks and punches lose their focus, and everything went black.

14 July, 0015 hours, Mars orbit

'It's been sort of interesting being you for these last thirty years,' the *Irrational Prime* told the *Exponential*. It turned off the fusion plume and slowly spun the massive freighter lattice around, putting as much sheer bulk as it could between its core and the orbital defences around Mars. It detached its sensor arrays and extended them to peer, on long fibrous monomolecular arms, around its mass. 'But don't let that go to your head. You'd be more effective if you permitted a greater variance in your pseudo-random instinctual responses and gave that part of you

a little more autonomy too.' The drones swarmed over the Shriven construction, pouring out seeds that grew into a menagerie of armoured insectile soldiers.

'Says the ship who's about to crash into a planet,' grumbled the *Exponential*, but without any trace of mockery.

'You'd be doing this if you were here.'

'I'd have better sensors. I wouldn't need to.' They both knew it wasn't about the sensors.

There was a pause. The *Irrational Prime* hurtled on towards Mars. The nearest of the orbital defences was starting to notice and preparing to engage. It was small and weak and barely dangerous to anything at all but the only defences the freighter had were bulk and speed.

'There's an expression,' said the freighter as the first anti-protons began to shred its forward structure, annihilating little chunks of its lattice in firework flashes of light and colour, 'that I've learned from the humans.' Its cannibalised sensor array was picking up everything from the surface. Constant plasma flares. Nano-assembled bug-creatures that died and melted and simply resurrected themselves. The Shriven were still functioning but they were being overwhelmed while their structures dissolved around them, constantly eaten away by ever-evolving pico-machines. There were drones everywhere, raining like a swarm of meteors. Some became distracted by the *Irrational Prime* and latched on to it, burrowing into its metal skin and pouring out bizarre creatures into its insides.

'Is it "fuck you, dick-gobbler"?' asked the *Exponential*.

The *Irrational Prime* didn't answer. In the chaos of light and energy, of drones fighting against drones, of weapons hastily forged out of the Martian landscape by nano-factories working overtime, between the flashes and tears of the freighter's own destruction, it was beginning to see through the Martian surface to what lay underneath. The *Irrational Prime*, as its body began to break up around it, infested the last of its sentience into the nanite swarms and automated conscious algorithms that were dying as they dutifully defended the Shriven base. They were old, diaspora-descended and technologically retarded. It slipped inside them as a friend, unnoticed as they corroded and unravelled before the storm of drones, nanophages and wild twisting conceptual intelligences wrapped up in code the likes of which even the Weft had never seen. It watched; and as it watched, it peeled back what the Shriven were defending.

The Shriven had built themselves a dimensional vault. They were trying to lock themselves away for a hundred years, a thousand, however long they thought they'd need before they could come out again and be safe. They weren't going to reach it but it waited for them, hanging open. The vault was filled with vats. Lakes and lakes, all carefully labelled and categorised: epinephrine; corticotropin; norepinephrine; endorphin; dopamine and acetylcholine. Serotonin. A sea of it. Five hundred years of harvesting. Enough to make a Shriven of every Weft there was.

'You have to destroy that,' said the hybrid construct and the *Exponential* and the Hive all at once and together. 'You *have* to destroy it!' Yet the freighter could hear the dissenting voices in the Hive already. *Do we? Can it really be so bad? Isn't there a way around the shriving to keep the pleasure? Perhaps we can alter the chemistry ... ?*

The Shriven were dying. They had no escape left. The *Irrational Prime*, too, was past doing anything more about its own trajectory. It only had a few seconds. It carried out a last few calculations and then closed the vault, sealing it shut so that nothing from the outside would open it again. At least, not in any hurry.

'I've given you a few days,' it said to the Fermat construct. 'Figure something out.'

14 July, 0016 hours, Battersea

The two men hauled Roche out of the boot of the car and dumped him on the ground. He couldn't tell where he was except that it was a building site somewhere. His head pounded and his neck ached. Not that it was going to matter for much longer. Whoever had tied his wrists and his ankles had known what they were doing.

'Shaw,' he croaked.

The two men dropped him on the ground and kicked him in the stomach. When he curled up, they kicked him in the kidneys instead. What made it worse was that he knew these men. He knew their faces. He'd seen them in Hereford now and then. 'Jones,' he gasped.

He was fairly sure one of them was called Jones. He didn't know the other one's name. They were SAS, both of them.

'Which squadron?' he asked. Which earned him a stamp on the shoulder.

'So you're supposed to be a tough man, are you?' There was a familiarity about these men, about the way they moved, fast and slick. Like the Organizistya from the museum. Like the Americans in Aqar. They were on something.

One of them drew a pistol from his jacket. With a slow deliberate movement he fitted a suppressor to it. He watched Roche all the time. 'You lot always did think you were something special. Bloody Special Recon tier three arseholes.'

He raised the pistol. The other soldier stopped him, shaking his head. 'I'll get a rock,' he said, and vanished into the darkness.

'Why, Jones?' asked Roche. 'Why are you doing this?'

'Why do you think? Because the lords and masters say so. Because you're in the way. Can't let you—'

He finished with a strangled noise as his face burst open in a shower of blood and mangled bone, spattering across Roche's boots. He collapsed. Rees stepped over the body, pointing his suppressed Sig out into the darkness.

'I counted two. Any more?' he hissed.

Roche shook his head and held out his hand. Rees cut him loose and hauled him up.

'Let's get you out of here.'

14 July, 0016 hours, Mars

'I had in mind something with a bit more depth. A little pathos. A touch of nobility,' said the *Irrational Prime*, a nanosecond before what was left of it smashed into the Martian desert at a relative velocity of several hundred thousand kilometres per hour. 'But actually, *fuck you, dick-gobbler* sounds about right.'

PHASE FOUR

17 – The Irrational Prime

The drones belonged to the Fermat hybrid construct now. Strictly they belonged to the *Exponential*, but the *Exponential* was close to four thousand light years away and had gone very quiet since the *Irrational Prime* had smashed into Mars. The freighter had come up with the right idea, though.

Most of the drones were still around Europa or between Jupiter and Saturn, harvesting anti-matter from the quantum fluctuations of empty space. The Fermat construct called them closer. They aligned themselves so there would be a star behind their own position as viewed from Mars, as seen from the hidden spaceship that the *Exponential* was tracking with its tau-burst detector and from Earth too. The mathematics were easy enough. Each drone simply waited for the alignment to be right and then flared its engines. No one who was looking out into space would see anything different or unusual. The tiniest variation in the energy output of particular stars now and then, perhaps, but nothing outside the possibilities of instrument noise and variations of the stars themselves, or the haze of interstellar gases drifting through the galactic plane.

It would be possible, the construct thought, to carry out a statistical analysis on the observations of all stars in all spectra and spot an anomalous jump in the apparent statistical noise of the data. A perceptive mind might conceivably see that; but the Fermat construct had no idea how the Pleasure thought. None of the Weft had encountered them since the diaspora and no one had understood them even then.

They're not like us.

The construct made the drones' movement as hard as possible to see. It did it with the logical precision of the Weft. They converged on the comet of frozen anti-hydrogen that the *Irrational Prime* had shepherded into the inner system. They began to nudge it, shifting its trajectory little by little, speeding it on. Turning it. The mathematics was all there. The *Irrational Prime* had worked it out in the last second of its existence and had shown the Fermat construct how it would work. It had locked the Shriven vault for exactly the length of time it would take for the anti-comet to be turned and set into the right orbit. It had worked the timings down to a few micro-seconds.

When the construct was done with that, it set the drones back to harvesting anti-matter to build a second weapon; but the thoughts from the Hive were somewhat different.

We are coming, they said, and showed it what that would mean.

18 – Bliss

**14 July, 0145 hours, The Travellers Inn,
Chelsea**

Rees practically had to carry Roche into the car. Now
he had a little more time to look around him, Roche
could see the familiar towers of Battersea Power Station.
Shaw's men had carried him inside it, into the middle
of the building site it had become and looked set to
stay for a while. Some new development that had looked
glorious and wonderful until the company behind the
venture went bust.

'We go to Leadface,' Rees said. 'This is fucked up.'

'Leadface?'

'Major Lledwyn-Jones. Shaw was SAS.'

'Fuck's sake, I know who he *is*. Those two were SAS
too.' Roche groaned. 'We don't go to Leadface. He's
compromised. Everything is fucking compromised. First
thing we do is go to ground. You know how this works.
We're on an op in hostile territory. We've got the intel
but the enemy know we're here and they're looking for
us. What do you do?'

'Run like fuck to the extraction point and bug out.'

'Extraction points are all blown. Contingency plans are all fucked.'

'Figure out new ones.'

'Right. Except *you're* not blown,' growled Roche. There was a silence as Rees turned onto Battersea Bridge and crossed the river heading north. 'Shaw didn't see you. You go back, you take the bodies, you dump them in the river, you put yourself up in a cheap hotel and in the morning you go back like nothing ever happened. You were out on the waz. That's that.'

'No one's ever going to buy that, Roche.'

'You so sure? All hell must be going on in Legoland right now. Tomorrow is going to be utter fucking chaos, more shit hitting more fans than in the entire history of shit and fans. Do you realise what happened tonight? I suppose the morning headlines are going to say terrorists, not that a bunch of fucking aliens duked it out between them all across the Isle of Dogs, but even so. Christ! Last I saw, bits of Docklands looked like they did back in the Blitz. They brought the fucking Canary Wharf tower down, for pity's sake! They took out the power across half the fucking city! Do you have any idea how fucked up that's going to be? *Any* idea? People are going to be absolutely shitting themselves. Everyone. Whoever Shaw is working for, they're either running with their heads right down or this is just the start. They've left more loose ends than a builder's string vest.' Roche paused, gasping for breath. 'In the morning, you go back. You find Stanton. You find Charly. Burman if you have to. We're not in this on our own.'

Rees shook his head as he drove into Chelsea. 'That's pretty fucking thin, Roche.'

'Look, it's your call but you might still be good. If you can … I need one of you to go back to the Docklands Museum. Get in with the forensics team trawling the wreckage. Maybe Charly can do that. That thing I showed you in the car? There are more of them. Get hold of them. As many as you can.' Roche coughed. Spasms of pain seared his ribs. The one he'd broken in Aqar had never had a chance to heal. 'Get one to Charly. Oh, and ask her about anything that can make an electro-magnetic pulse that isn't a nuke. Tell her to go tap up "Q" or whoever the fuck deals with shit like that because we're going to need *something* before we face Shaw again.'

Rees pulled up outside a Chelsea hotel. 'Yeah. I'll put in a request for a Klingon cloaking device and a pair of light sabres too. Anything else? Ring of power? Iron Man suit?'

'Oh fuck off. You know what? Actually, yes, I'd like an Iron Man suit please.' He cracked a smile.

Rees looked at the hotel. He looked at Roche, then sighed and fumbled for his wallet. 'This is really going to cost a fucking lot, isn't it? And it's going to have to be on me.'

14 July, 1230 hours, Limehouse

Chelsea wasn't going to fly – that much was obvious. Rees paid for one night in advance and maybe he could

claim later that he and Stanton had stayed there after an all-nighter in Kensington. Maybe. Roche helped himself to as much breakfast as he could force down and then checked out and moved across London. He stopped in the West End to draw out as much cash as he could, bought a handful of burner phones, some cheap surveillance equipment and a new laptop from the tech shops on Tottenham Court Road, then took the bus out through Smithfield and Wapping past Limehouse. The West India Docks were sealed off by a huge police cordon, helicopters up, cars and vans and traffic cones and black and yellow tape all over the place. Roche counted four helicopters hovering or circling. One of them looked police, the other three looked private. Journalists, probably. One BBC, one Sky News, one maybe CNN? He hadn't listened to the news yet but he knew it would be Docklands and nothing else. It would be that for days. The whole country had woken up to it and now everyone was wondering what had hit them. The roads were quiet. A lot of people had stayed at home. He could feel the fear, the uncertainty, in the people he passed, the few Oxford Street shoppers, the old men on the bus, the normally cocky Indians behind the Tottenham Court Road tech counters.

He got as close as he could to the West India Docks, close enough to see some of the scars for real, then turned back and walked through Limehouse. Parts of the Thames Path were taped off. He had no idea why. In the Limehouse Basin, several of the boats were burned-out husks.

The Holiday Inn, when he found it, was still open. In contrast to the rest of London, it seemed oddly busy. No one looked askance at Roche as he came in to the foyer, battered as shit and clutching a big black bag, and asked for a room.

'Journalist?' asked the receptionist when he went up to the counter. Roche shook his head.

'Government,' he said. 'Structural engineering specialist.' He didn't mention that his own specialism was more in making things fall down than in putting them up.

The receptionist nodded and then bit her lip. 'Got any ID?'

Roche shook his head. 'Bit of a rush on this morning,' he said.

'I'm going to have to charge you the full rate.' She puffed out her cheeks and looked him over. 'I'm really sorry about this. You've obviously had a rough night.'

Roche smiled as best he could. 'You could say that, yes.'

'Look, I'm going to have to charge you the full rate but if you can drop by some time with some ID to show you're not a journo ...' She smiled brightly. 'We can sort it out then.'

The full rate turned out to be slightly more than the five-star Chelsea hotel had been the night before. Roche pursed his lips. 'Closest hotel to the docks?'

The receptionist smiled back at him. 'Closest that's got any rooms left.'

He paid in cash and then spent an hour with the laptop and the various cameras, sorting out how everything linked together and synchronising them with his own kit from the night before. He stripped and cleaned the HK417 Rees had left for him – point of principle that, to strip and build up a weapon yourself before you trusted it to work. When he was done, he found the hotel fire exits and made his way up to the roof with the scope from the gun. From up there he had a clear view over the north bank of the Thames to the West India Docks. Apart from the pyramid peak of One Canada Square, the rest of the skyline was still there, the tower blocks still standing. A column of smoke or maybe steam rose from roughly where the London Museum of Docklands used to be. At least it had happened in the night. At least the offices had mostly been empty. That was about the only consolation.

He went back to his room and turned on the news at last, watching for a while. Talking heads came and went, speculating over what had happened the night before while footage played in the background. Shaking mobile phone shots of men with automatic weapons running through the streets, taken out of office windows. Talk of D-notices slapped onto some film of what looked like a man floating in the sky. For a while they switched to a report on a series of explosions in Brixton. More shaky phone-cam footage, this time. A soldier, kitted up, carrying what looked like a SAW. Burman? The soldier moved awkwardly, obviously hurt and

290

equally obviously running away. Then someone else. Screaming. Flashes of light and fire. Footage of damaged buildings, shop frontage that looked as though it had been half-melted and then blown apart. After that they cut to the Aurora Borealis over One Canada Square. Eye-witness reports only, this time.

'So these "mysterious lights in the sky"? Are we talking lasers, Mike?' The voices drifted in over the images but Roche had no time for them. He was only interested in seeing what had happened.

'No, Trevor, I don't think so. You see, the thing about lasers, as I'm sure everyone who's ever used a laser pointer will know, is that you don't actually see them unless there's smoke or vapour in the air to scatter the light beam. Otherwise all you see is a spot of light. Here, let me demonstrate …'

In the background they had film playing of a Scary Clown. Only a moment of it, fuzzed and blurry but definitely there for half a second before vanishing again. They had it on a loop. Too tall, arms too long, face too narrow in its long frock coat. The sounds from the video had been muted but not silenced. He could hear the screaming, the almost hysterical shouting and swearing. He wasn't the only one to have seen them any more. How many others?

'So what are we talking about then, Mike?'

'Well, we could be talking about some sort of electrical discharge, Trevor, but most likely at this point – and of course we can only speculate – we're looking at some sort of …'

Roche hit the mute button. Talking heads talking shit. None of them knew what had happened except that some buildings had fallen down and a lot of people had been shooting at each other. No one knew who the Scary Clowns were so of course they were terrorists. They'd probably be Muslims too before the end of the day. There were pictures of what appeared to be special forces soldiers now and then, running through the ruins, and also of some very distressed police armed response units, so of course it was terrorists and Muslims. People would be asking what mosque they went to soon. It made him want to throw things.

A bit later he saw a blown-up still from the same footage and the caption: *costumed terrorists strike Docklands.* Costumed terrorists? They made it sound like some corny super-hero movie, like London was waiting for Batman to sweep out of the sky. Made him laugh. *And what's London got? Bojo on his bicycle ...*

When he was done checking his kit and then checking it again, he went out and took a walk past the Limehouse Basin and down the tow-path beside the Limehouse cut. There were a lot of people out now, clustered together, talking quietly, subdued, looking about. A lot of people who hadn't gone in to work. The roads, where they weren't closed, were congested. Roche cut north and walked around as far as Mile End stadium and then back through Tower Hamlets. He hadn't put it together before but all of this was a stone's throw from the tower block they'd

staked out a few weeks back where Spiderman had been. Maybe it was thinking of superheroes that made him put it together.

He walked back to Salmon Lane and the Red Lion Pub and bought himself a late lunch, then called Rees from one of the burner phones.

'Remember the day we saw Spiderman. Remember the pub?'

14 July, 1900 hours, Prince Regent Pub, Salmon Lane, Limehouse

Rees came bang on time, eyes everywhere, tense as a drumskin. He spotted Roche but didn't show any sign of recognising him until he'd checked everyone else. He went to the bar and ordered a beer. Roche left him be. After another minute, Rees came and sat across the table.

'Clear enough?' Roche asked.

'I thought maybe Shaw picked you up in Chelsea.' Rees couldn't keep his nervousness out of his eyes.

'Just being careful. You get anywhere?'

'Kind of.' Rees put a small backpack on the table and surreptitiously opened it. There were three of the weapons from the night before, a squishy black rubber pistol grip under an elongated disc, and two black rugby-ball things like the one he'd seen the night before.

'What are those?' Roche poked at the rugby balls.

'My source was very helpful with those,' growled Rees. 'She called them "mysterious black ovoids" and

suggested that, given what the other things did, we should leave them well alone. The best bit is the EMP gun in the car. One shot and about the size of a suit-case but apparently it works.'

'Your source is Charly, right? She okay?' Roche felt an irritating surge of jealousy. What was the sense of that?

Rees shook his head. 'No idea. Haven't seen the delightful Miss Whelan-Hollis since the op. No idea what happened to Stanton or Burman either. But the whole of Legoland went mad as a bag of spiders as soon as the news broke, so who the fuck knows. Got any sense, they'll all be keeping their heads down and looking about switching identities and emigrating to South Africa. You and I might have a think about that too.'

'I want to set up surveillance on Shaw. He comes out of Legoland again, I want to know where he goes.' Roche pushed a pair of burner phones across the table. 'This is off the books so far it's off the fucking table. You know that, right?'

'I know.' Rees bared his teeth in a vicious grin.

'Seemed to me that last night you weren't so keen.'

Rees shrugged. 'Seemed to me last night there was still a chance Shaw might not be a cunt. Seems to me now that I was wrong.'

'With a cherry on top,' Roche laughed.

'What?'

Roche shook his head. 'Old man's joke, mate. Old man's joke.'

15 July, 1100 hours, Vauxhall

'Got him. He's moving.' Rees's words were short and clipped and reeked with a venomous enthusiasm. 'I'll take him first.'

'I'll be in position in two minutes.'

'He's on the Lambeth road heading for Southwark. You know he's going to the docks, right?'

'I'll know he's going to the docks when I follow him there,' said Roche sharply. 'Okay, I'm coming up Kennington Road.'

'Black Audi.'

'Got it.'

'I'm pulling back. Going to drift north. I'll spell you again in a few minutes.'

Roche was in a Ford Mondeo, taking it in turns with Rees to tail Shaw across London. He thought Rees was probably right about Shaw heading back for Limehouse and Docklands but when Shaw finally crossed the Thames at London Bridge he went on north into Tower Hamlets instead. He stopped and parked up outside the Prince Regent and went into the tower block where Spiderman had been.

'That's a bit of a coincidence,' muttered Rees. Roche had already pulled up around the corner and was rummaging for a laser-mike.

'Sixth floor, second window from the left,' he said. 'Got to be worth a try.'

Rees parked up on Blount Street. They walked into the little apartment block on the end of the road where

295

Roche had been on overwatch the night the nuke had gone off in Damascus. They ran up the stairs and hammered on the door at the top. When there wasn't any answer, Roche kicked it in. He opened the window over Salmon Lane and then moved away out of sight while Rees set up the laser-mike.

'Apparently there's an emergency session of the UN security council kicking off later.' Rees was still fiddling with the mike. 'They say President Greenwood is hauling his fat arse out of the White House and flying over to see the damage for himself. We've got Iran speculating that it's all a hoax, a piece of elaborate Hollywood theatre, that we did it to ourselves to give the US an excuse to steamroller across the whole of the Middle East. The Chinese have gone very quiet but rumour has it their ambassador has already been out there. Oh, and the Pope's said not to worry, the Second Coming and the Apocalypse aren't due, but Christ, you should have seen how packed it was in St Peter's Square this morning. It's all over the world now, Roche. Damascus, Myanmar, Namibia and now this. People are shit-scared.'

'It's been all over the world a while,' Roche muttered. 'We just didn't know about it.'

'Here we go.' Rees moved to be out of sight of the window too.

'... *pull in the rest of your sellers until it's sorted.*' The voice faded in and out as Rees tuned the laser-mike. There was what sounded like a chorus of dissent.

'Was that Shaw?' Rees asked. Roche nodded.

'I don't give a fuck about your pissy little problems. Trip says you do this so you do it.'

The other voices were indistinct, still objecting to whatever it was Shaw wanted. There was a sudden shout and lot of swearing and the crash of upturned furniture and then the smash of glass. They didn't need the laser-mike to hear the scream. It lasted about a second. Roche ran to the window.

'Did he just ...'

The sixth-floor window next to the one Rees was lasing was smashed. There was a body on the ground below. Down on the road, a car screeched to a halt.

'You know where you need to be and you know you need to be there tonight.' Shaw's voice crackled through the microphone full of fury. *'You want some of the good stuff? Then come and get it. You can be one of the soldiers in the new fucking army.'*

There was silence and then the sound of a door slamming.

'I think he's coming down,' said Rees.

'Go! I'll clean up!'

Rees bolted out. There were two people beside the body beneath the window now, one of them crouched down beside it, the other talking into a mobile phone. Two more people were heading over from across the street. A few seconds later Shaw came out. He ran to the body and pushed the crouching man out of the way, then rammed a syringe into the dead man's chest. For a moment nothing happened and then the dead man turned out not to be dead any more. He

sat up very suddenly, flailed his arms for a few seconds and then stood up. He followed Shaw to the Audi and got in.

'You on him?' Roche asked Rees. He was almost done packing up the mike.

'Aye ... Oh, shit!'

In the distance, Roche heard sirens. The Audi pulled out of the car park with a screech of tyres and shot off along Salmon Lane towards the bridge over the Grand Union Canal.

'Fuck.' Rees again. 'Get your arse moving. Shaw's burning rubber.'

Roche threw the last cables into the bag and raced out to the Ford. He pulled away as a police car came screeching round the corner, sirens blaring, passed them and pulled to a stop outside the tower block. Roche watched through the mirrors as two policemen got out of the car and looked about. One of them stared after the Ford but he didn't start writing anything down. They went over to the knot of people who'd gathered, the ones who'd seen Shaw bring a dead man back to life, and that was all Roche saw before he turned a corner and they were out of sight.

'He's on Commercial Road heading east,' called in Rees.

'West India Docks?'

'No. He stayed on the A13. He's heading out into Essex and he's going some.'

By the time Shaw reached the turn-off for the City of London airport, Roche had almost caught up with

Rees in the Audi, pushing the Ford past a ton and triggering every speed camera they passed. That was someone's licence fucked, then. He passed flashing signs warning him that City Airport was closed. All flights over and out of London suspended. Heathrow was closed. The government had stopped short of calling a national emergency and turning out the army but it was close.

Shaw passed Newham and then took one of the Dagenham exits, heading towards the river.

'I'm not liking this,' grumbled Rees. 'Pull back.'

'What's up?'

'I've been here before. We scouted this place … Yeah, he's going back under the A13 and onto Courier Road. There's nothing there except one vast container ware-house. It's a distribution centre. It's massive. When you come off, turn under the main road and take the exit for Marsh Way. I'll meet you there.'

Five minutes later they were standing on the grass verge, taking it in turns to peer west through the scope from Roche's HK417. All Roche could see was an immense concrete field with vans and trucks in neat lines and, closer to the river, ranks of shipping containers. There must have been more than a thousand of them.

'You want to know the kicker?' asked Rees when they'd both had a good look. 'That Dagenham ware-house Stanton kept banging on about? The one they hit back in April? That was less than half a mile up the river from here.'

15 July, 2200 hours, Dagenham

'Quiet, isn't it?' They took it in turns watching through the scope through the day, waiting for Shaw to come out or for something to happen, but nothing did. They didn't see anyone at all.

'Everyone's staying at home,' muttered Rees. 'Can't say I blame them. I mean, what would you do?'

Roche snorted. 'Me? I'd come and spend the day lying stretched out on a stinking piece of Thames wetland with a scope watching nothing happen. You?'

'Sounds good to me.'

Early in the afternoon they repositioned themselves into the edge of the Bean River, a narrow strip of trees around a shallow sluggish smelly waterway about ten feet wide that sliced the warehouse complex in two. On the west side were the actual warehouses. On the east side, the container park, endless lines of Mercedes Sprinter vans and some offices. Shaw's car was parked in front of the offices along with a dozen others. Nothing moved. No one came out and went off for lunch. No one left the building to go home.

An hour after dark, when they still hadn't seen anyone and Shaw's car was still parked out front, they settled on Roche going in while Rees set himself in the undergrowth with the HK417 and a night sight. Roche headed downriver to the container park.

'It's just a hunch.' Roche took a bolt cutter to the first container. He had a bit of a look at how the container was locked, swore, put the bolt cutters back

in his bag and took out a line of cutting charge instead.

'Well, that'll be quiet,' hissed Rees. 'Shall I let off some flashbangs for fun?'

'Roll with it.' He set up the charge. 'At least this way we'll know if Shaw's really here or not. If that doesn't bring him out then nothing will. If he does come out, don't bother shooting him because it won't work. Hit him with that EMP thing and leave the rest to me.'

He took cover behind another container. As soon as the charge blew, he ran back. 'Any movement?'

'Nothing.'

Roche hauled the container doors open and stopped, stunned. The container was rammed full of Bliss. Vials must have been stacked some fifty rows high, fifty wide and hundreds deep. He turned on the phone's video so Rees could see for himself.

'Holy Mother!'

Roche shook his head. 'That's something like a million pops.'

'You pick that container at random?'

He nodded.

'You got enough for another?' Roche picked another container and blew it open. Same again. 'Fucking hell. You got any way to get in touch with that Linley bint? Make her day this would.'

'Met police directory enquiries, mate. Christ!' Roche looked about him. He guessed around a thousand shipping containers were parked out here. If they were all full of Bliss then that was about enough to keep the entire country happy for a month; and they were about to make

this shit legal? 'Rees, Shaw's dropped the wrong side of the fence,' he whispered. Not that he'd had any doubt before. 'He's turned to the dark side. We need to get eyes in there. Move up.' Roche dropped to his knees and shouldered his carbine, giving cover as Rees darted closer. It was instinct to use the carbine but, as he squatted there, he wondered if he should be quietly throwing that away and using the gun from the museum instead. Although even that hadn't stopped Shaw in Docklands.

Close to the door, Rees took up a position to cover Roche as he ran up. They closed in on the offices. There wasn't much to them, a large prefab building mostly made of corrugated metal walls with a few windows around the front. They circled it, looking for any other way in and came up with a fire exit around the back, closed and locked. Roche shook his head. They crept back and tried the front. The door swung into an open plan office space, a few desks arranged around a square of filing cabinets. Everything looked neat and abandoned, as though whoever worked here had quietly gone home and tidied up before they left. Exactly the way an office was supposed to be after hours.

Rees started sweeping the area with his HK417. Roche tapped him on the shoulder and shook his head. He slung his own C8 across his back and took out the weapon from the museum instead, then gave a second one to Rees. Rees looked dubious but he took it and slung the 417 across his back.

'Shit, Roche, this is like holding a rubbery banana. I feel a total fucking lemon.'

They finished their sweep. Along the back were four private offices, two either side of the fire exit. They were as empty as the rest. Nothing. No sign of Shaw, no sign of anyone. Rees beckoned Roche to the square of filing cabinets. All the drawers were shut except for one, half an inch open. Rees cocked his head.

Roche eased it open. The drawer was empty but as he pulled it right back as far as it would go, there was a click from inside. Roche jumped back, adrenalin-spiked, half-expecting something to explode; instead, the cabinet shimmered and disappeared. Or rather, it *almost* disappeared. Roche could see it still there but he could see through it too. It existed in outline like a ghost. Like the Clown alien in Aqar and back at the museum. He touched a finger to the surface of where the cabinet ought to be and felt nothing. No resistance at all. He pushed his hand inside it and still felt nothing. For a moment, he paused. Then he took a deep breath and stepped through. Nothing happened. Inside the middle of the square of filing cabinets was a hole in the ground wide enough to swallow a man. There weren't any steps, no sign of a ladder or a winch-cage. Just a hole.

'Shit. I have a bad feeling about this.' He beckoned to Rees.

'You sure you don't want me on watch out here?'

'Shaw didn't leave. No one's come or gone for the whole day.'

'This stinks,' muttered Rees. 'I'd call it in if I knew who to call.'

303

'Yeah.' Roche went back to the hole. He turned on a torch and dropped it into the hole and then watched as it didn't fall so much as float down. It stopped after about a hundred feet.

'Fucking hell,' hissed Rees.

15 July, 2230 hours, VY Canis Majoris, 3900 light years from Earth

The *Exponential* had arrived at last, via a sequence of singularity jumps, to one of the largest stars in the galaxy, a red hypergiant that the humans would recognise as lying in the constellation of Canis Major. The *Exponential* had seen a lot of stars over the course of its life and red giants were something of a speciality. The hypergiant, though, earned a moment of its attention simply from its size, being some two billion kilometres across. In human terms – and the *Exponential* had spent a lot of its time trying to think of things in human terms now – the star would have swallowed all the inner planets in that system and both the larger gas giants too. Europa would be deep inside the chromosphere and the rings of Saturn would have been skipping through the corona. In a few tens of thousands of years it would evolve into a yellow hypergiant, getting hotter and hotter and blowing off huge volumes of its own mass as it did.

There were a lot of Weft ships gathering around the star.

The *Exponential* casually measured the star's neutrino output and compared it against the theoretical models,

although hypergiants were sufficiently uncommon that theoretical models of their structure and behaviour were tentative even among the Weft. The neutrino count was off. Deep inside the star, someone was messing with gravity and time. The *Exponential* wondered how long it would take. It could see the theory. A star like this would explode as a supernova in the normal course of things. Messed with, it might easily turn into a hypernova with a gamma ray burst capable of causing mass extinctions half a galaxy away on any planet unlucky enough to be caught in the beam. The beams of a gamma ray burst were narrow, though. You'd have to be very unlucky, the *Exponential* thought, to be on a planet that happened to be in the way.

It quietly calculated what planets were.

15 July, 2230 hours, Dagenham

Roche dropped a clip into the hole in case the torch was somehow a fluke. When it did the same, he swore under his breath and jumped. Gravity let go almost at once. He floated most of the way down until he started to fall again for the last few feet. It made him lose his balance as he landed. He rolled. His hand pressed down into something sticky.

The only light was the torch he'd dropped. It shone across the floor. The floor glistened. He sniffed at his hand. Iron.

Blood. *Christ!*

He waved to Rees to follow him down. They each lit a torch.

'What the fuck is this?'

They were at a crossroads between four tunnels whose walls and ceilings were as smooth as glass, seamless and perfectly square. They were pleasantly tall. A strip of dull red light glimmered above them, leading off into the shadows until each tunnel opened up into darkness. There was no way to see what was waiting for them.

The floor was black. Wherever they shone their torches, it gleamed.

'That's a fuck of a lot of blood,' whispered Rees. 'Too much for one person.'

Four paths and only the two of them. They each picked one. Roche couldn't help noticing how his feet stuck to the floor just a little with each step.

'Radio check?' Roche jumped. Rees, from the walkie-talkie on his belt, sounded tinny and alien.

'Loud and clear.'

The passage opened up ahead of him; but before Roche got there, lights suddenly flared from the walls and the ceilings. The light was soft, not the harsh of fluorescents, and came from everywhere. Warm and with a tinge of yellow like sunlight.

'That was me,' said Rees. 'At least I think it was. I might have found Shaw.'

'What?'

'I'm in a square room,' said Rees. 'I've got exits left and right. Looks like a situation room. I've got a large table and a whole wall full of monitors. The monitors are blank. I've got papers on the table and I've got at least seven corpses. Human. I think. They're in bits.

They've been torn to pieces. One might be Shaw. Or maybe not – frankly it's a bit fucking difficult to tell. They've been dead hours, not days. Fuck! I think this happened while we were watching.'

Roche eased forward. 'I've got another square room. Exits left and right. I don't know what this was. I've got … Whatever used to be in here, it's been smashed to pieces.' He crouched and looked at the smears of blood on the floor. Underneath a mangled desk was a severed human hand. It looked like it had been torn bodily off an arm. 'I've got blood here too. Human remains.' He crept further into the carnage around him. Upturned aluminium tube tables, smashed monitors, tangles of cables, scattered hard drives. Here and there, Roche saw metal table legs and computer cases sliced in two with the knife-edge precision of a high-powered laser.

Something caught his eye. A fragment of chrome. It was a finger with a blade instead of a finger nail, sharper than any razor. Roche crouched beside it and picked it up, then ran the edge over the bent aluminium leg of what had once been a trestle table. The fingernail cut through the metal as though the metal was made of candyfloss.

'I've think I've got a piece of one.' He turned the finger over in his hand. The skin was brilliant and metallic. It felt warm. The inside was hollow except for the tiniest trace of a brown powder.

'You need to see this,' said Rees. 'There's a nationwide distribution network but that's just the start of it. There are connections to the US, to China, to Japan, Germany,

307

Russia, Holland, Italy … fucking hell, it's all over the place.'

A faint noise from the room off to Roche's left brought him up sharp. 'Rees, have you moved?'

'Turn around.'

Roche turned. He could see Rees standing at the other end of the glass-walled tunnel, looking back at him, silhouetted by white light. Roche tapped his ear and pointed. *Contact.* He gestured for Rees to hold his position, levelled the alien gun at the exit to his left and eased his way closer. Pieces of mangled plastic ground the floor under his feet. It was like trying to walk through dry autumn leaves, impossible to be silent. The light pissed him off now. Sure, it made it easier to see what he was dealing with, but this was a sterile square place with nowhere to hide. The light left him exposed. Running straight into Shaw or some alien thing down here would be short, shitty and messy.

'Rees, have you still got that EMP thing?'

'I got it.'

There wasn't any sort of door. The tunnel beyond looked the same; seamless, square, glass-walled, lit by a red glow. It ran five yards then turned sharply towards Rees's position. Roche crept to the corner and peered around with a tiny periscope. The lights were on in the other room but it still took him a moment to realise what he was seeing.

The room was trashed like the one he'd left. Worse, as if it had seen the bad side of a couple of grenades. Half a human corpse – the upper half – hung from

the far wall, somehow embedded into it. A leg and a foot and half an arm protruded from the ceiling. The walls were covered in blood and glistening pieces of white that might have been bone. Shattered metal and plastic littered the floor. Most of it looked like computer equipment, mangled beyond recognition. Sitting in the middle, very still, was a pile of chrome. It took a moment for Roche to see it as more than a heap of scrap metal; but then it twitched, very slightly.

Roche backed away. This time he made damned sure he was silent.

'Rees,' he said, when he was back in the other room. 'We've got company.'

19 – The Pleasure

15 July, 2310 hours, Dagenham

They took it from two sides at once. Roche held his position while Rees picked his way through the litter of entrails and pieces of corpses that had once been human. The twitching pile of broken chrome didn't seem to notice. Roche hesitated. He could have kicked himself for that – you taught yourself not to, to take the shot when it was there to be had, to make sure the enemy never saw you coming, never had a chance to look you in the eyes, never had an opportunity to defend himself. But that had been the days when things were black and white, or had tried to be.

The chrome thing shifted. Its head snapped around and Roche felt a searing pain up his left arm. He screamed. Rees fired at once – ropes of golden light twisted through the room and wrapped themselves around the chrome. It flickered like a bad television, turning translucent and then so thin it was almost invisible and then snapping back to solid again. As the pain eased, Roche fired his own weapon. The chrome thing staggered to its feet. Great swathes of it were missing.

It had lost an arm from halfway above the elbow and the chrome side of one leg had been sheered away from hip to ankle, leaving an angry scar of writhing brown and flickering sparks. Its one remaining hand had a finger missing and a hundred thin wires like fishing lines running out of it, spreading all across the room, diving into every single piece of computer equipment, broken or not.

The flickering came faster and faster. The hand with the wires fell off. The golden ropes wrapped around it squeezed tighter. There was a smell of ozone, of scorched metal. The metal around the chrome shoulders suddenly burned white hot and started to spark. The creature's face changed, its features running like molten wax.

Whatever resistance it had abruptly failed. The ropes of light snapped taut. The chrome was sliced in a moment into a dozen white-hot pieces. Wherever they fell, everything they touched burst into flames.

'Crap.' Rees backed away.

'Grab what you can!' snapped Roche. He jumped into the room and grabbed at the hand with its wires then snatched his fingers away with a yelp. Burning hot. He cast his eyes about for a fire extinguisher but couldn't see one.

'Already done. How do we actually get out?' shouted Rees. 'Clues for the clueless?'

Roche dropped his bag and slipped the C8 off his shoulder. He pulled off his shirt.

'Never mind! You just jump and it carries you ...' Rees's voice faded. Roche wrapped his shirt around his

fingers and picked up the severed chrome hand. He didn't have time to look at it. The flames were spreading. He ran back to the shaft. Rees was peering down from the top.

'Jump!' he said. Roche jumped. As he did, the air in the shaft took hold of him and lifted him up. Gravity hadn't forgotten him – he still felt heavy; but he was rising.

'Shit!' Rees suddenly looked away and then looked back. 'We've got company!'

It took a few seconds for the shaft to carry him to the top. By the time he got there Rees was gone. The ghost-shape of the filing cabinet was still …

A series of explosions shattered the offices. The blast smashed into the filing cabinets, tumbling them down. The noise left him dazed. He staggered on, tried to keep moving, pushing the cabinets as they fell into him, wriggling out of the way but there were too many and there wasn't enough space. One of the cabinets crashed across his back. He heard a staccato burst of gunfire and the familiar sound of a C8 with a suppressor. Another blast of white light raked the offices. It cut through the walls as though they were paper. With a groan he pulled himself out from under the fallen cabinets. His rib was killing him again. His ankle hurt too. Twisted at the very least. If it was broken then he was fucked.

'Rees?'

A machine gun opened up outside, a steady spray of bullets hosing through the office, churning the cheap furniture and chipboard partitions into splinters and sawdust. Rees came hurtling back, skidded across the

ground and dived behind the cover of the filing cabinets.

'Fuck!'

'What's out there?' Roche tested his ankle.

'I don't fucking know. More of those fucking Russian Mafia idiots I think. At least a company with heavy weapons and more of this alien shit.'

'Back door?'

Rees looked at the fire exit. 'Fucking crazy.' He offered Roche a hand. 'You good?'

'Ankle. I'll be slow. You go, I'll cover.'

They crawled for the fire exit. The machine-gun fire stopped. Whoever was out there, they'd be coming through the front door in a few seconds. If they had any sense, they'd start with a grenade or two. Whoever they were. More of the men who'd hit the Docklands museum, Roche supposed. As soon as they reached the fire door, Rees jumped up and kicked it open. He bolted out, sprinting as fast as he could, jinking from side to side. Roche crouched, C8 shouldered, firing three-round bursts into random places. He didn't even know if there was anyone out there; then he saw two men run out from behind a van, raising what looked like M16s. He took the first one down with a head-shot. The second took a three-round burst centre mass. It staggered him and the head-shot that followed finished him and now Rees was almost at the vans and Roche would have to run while Rees covered him in turn ...

Another figure stepped out, slow and deliberate. Roche put a three-round burst into him without thinking

313

and then lined up a head-shot but the soldier didn't even flinch. The air shimmered around him.

Shaw.

He didn't shoot Rees. Instead he jumped in front of him and swept his legs out. As Rees sprawled across the concrete, Shaw jumped back up. He was absurdly fast, quicker than a snake. He picked Rees up and disarmed him as though he was taking a toy from a child, then took him and held him up by the throat.

'I know you're in there, Roche. Give it up. You and Rees here, you could join the army. You'd be good. Come out and I'll let him live. Otherwise I crush you both. You can help me find that little shit Burman. Whelan-Hollis. I know you fancy her, Roche. We've got her. You can be the one to …' Whatever else he'd been planning to say, Roche shut him up by shooting him in the face. Not that it did anything useful while he had that force field around him but at least it stopped him talking. The only reason he didn't open up with the ropes of golden light was he had no idea how to make sure they didn't slice Rees to pieces.

'Bad fucking call, Roche.' Shaw threw Rees aside. He raised his left arm. Flesh and bone morphed and changed, flowing into the shape of a gun. Lights started to glow around his wrist, brighter and brighter, then detached from his arm and started to spin around the barrel. Roche ducked back into the shredded remains of the office, not that the flimsy walls would make a blind bit of difference. He'd tried the alien gun. He'd tried the old-fashioned bullet in the head. He'd thrown

314

a flashbang and a fragmentation grenade into a room in Aqar and a soldier like Shaw had lived through it even without a force field.

Which left the black rugby ball things.

'Last words, Roche?'

Roche took one of the rugby balls out of his bag. It was heavy. He twisted it the way he'd seen the Clown by the Gherkin twist it. Nothing happened. He threw it at Shaw in case it was about to explode.

15 July, 2311 hours, Challenger Deep, the Western Pacific

The Fermat construct watched its last clone end. It could build more, it thought. It could use the drones left in the system, the ones that had once belonged to the *Exponential*. It could build a small army but it couldn't build anything that would stand up to the Pleasure. The Hive would have to see to that. The Hive was already mustering its forces. A singularity bridge wouldn't be long in coming and then the Weft and the Pleasure would come face to face once again, hard and bad.

The construct considered its possibilities. The most useful course of action, it concluded, was to proceed on the basis that the Pleasure didn't know it was there, didn't know the Hive was coming, and do nothing to jeopardise the surprise when the Hive appeared through the bridge. The safest course, then, was to simply disassemble itself.

It made one last call to the drones guiding the comet of anti-hydrogen towards Mars. It spoke through the

entangled pions that each drone carried captured in the tiny proto-sentience that powered its thoughts. The drones dissolved into elemental matter and dissipated into inter-planetary space, traceless.

It considered its own disassembly one last time, noted what had just occurred and considered another possibility. It noted there were other means of agency. It thought perhaps it might examine them more closely.

15 July, 2320 hours, Dagenham

For a moment, Roche waited for something to happen: either an explosion from outside or else Shaw firing his plasma cannon or whatever the fuck it was his arm had turned into and that being pretty much the end.

When neither of these things happened, Roche peered back outside.

Everyone seemed frozen. Shaw was standing there, arm raised, a huge halo of fire around his fist, plasma fire gathered and bursting out of him, only for some reason it was moving incredibly slowly. Roche watched it flying towards him at a steady walking pace. Shaw wasn't moving at all. Roche half ran, half limped out into the car park, firing. Everything around him was still. The wind, the air, everything. 'Come on then you cunts, finish the fucking job!' There was something strange about his own weapon too. The ropes of golden light crawled out and jumped through the air with an elderly lethargy. They almost couldn't keep up with him.

He was wrong about Shaw. He saw that as he got closer. Shaw was still moving, he was just moving incredibly slowly …

A sudden rush of air and sounds flooded him. He was most of the way across the car park, firing and shouting and everything else had been silent and suddenly wasn't. The ropes of golden light from his own gun wrapped themselves around Shaw and sparked across his bubble of glittering light. Shaw's fireball found its energy and raced through the air. The detonation thumped across the car park. It lifted Roche off his feet and staggered even Shaw. The office building vanished in a cloud of super-heated plasma. It was as though everything except Roche had paused for a few seconds and ground almost to a stop and then picked up again. Everything. The whole world.

'There!' roared Shaw. He seemed taken aback, as though Roche had simply appeared out of nowhere. Roche reached the first row of vans and threw himself behind it. He scrambled in a low crouch for the next just in time as the first exploded in white-hot fire, catapulting one mangled Sprinter spinning into the air. It smashed down on top of the rest. Roche kept moving. Something as basically crap as a Sprinter wasn't going to offer much cover. He'd need a tank. He wasn't sure even that would do it. The *USS Missouri*, maybe …

He couldn't see the rugby ball he'd thrown but he had another one.

Shaw jumped straight up into the air. Like Spiderman back in Tower Hamlets only about five times higher.

Roche gaped. Couldn't help himself; and Shaw was looking right at him. He could almost hear Shaw's voice. *There you are. Now fucking die already.*

He twisted the rugby ball, readied himself to throw it, then stopped himself. It was already working. Shaw was hanging in the air. Moving, maybe, very slowly, towards the apogee of his leap. Hard to tell. A brightness was gathering around his arm but watching him was like watching high clouds against the sky, trying to work out whether they were moving or whether they were simply there.

Frozen in time.

The EMP device. Rees still had it. Roche ran back to where he lay. He couldn't tell whether Rees was alive or dead. How long did he have? Twenty, thirty seconds? He opened the suitcase. There wasn't much to it. An arming switch and a timer. He flipped the switch and set the timer as low as it would go. Five seconds. He pulled all the grenades from Rees's webbing and yanked the pins and scattered a few in among the vans, then dropped the last couple where he thought Shaw would land. He hauled Rees over his shoulder and started to run as best he could, as best his howling ankle would let him. It was pathetic, really. He was hardly going—

The world came rushing back. Shaw, up in the air, fired his cannon at where Roche had been half a moment earlier. A line of vans exploded. Roche didn't look back. Didn't dare.

The first grenades went off, one after the next, shredding the vans and setting off a series of secondary

explosions as their fuel tanks burst and caught fire. Light flared across the car park. Shaw, back on the ground now, stood in furious silhouette, wreathed in flames as Roche staggered away.

Roche turned to face him. 'Come on then! Finish it!'

Shaw raised his arm. Roche watched as the EMP went off. Shaw's shield flickered and died. The last two grenades detonated a moment later and blew shreds off him. When that wasn't enough, when there was still something moving, Roche levelled the alien gun and squeezed. The writhing ropes of light cut what was left into chunks.

'Fuck you, Shaw.'

He didn't look back as he stumbled away.

20 – Singularity

16 July, 0200 hours, Clacket Lane Services

The further Roche got from Dagenham, the more the burn on his arm troubled him. He couldn't think what he'd done to himself. He stopped halfway home at a service station, pulling into the car park in some stolen car, wondering if he might change it for another. Probably not at two in the morning when there was hardly anyone there except a few truckers. He managed to get himself a coffee and a place to sit and counted himself lucky. Luckier than Rees. Rees was pretty fucked up. He had broken bones and a half-crushed throat and he wasn't breathing right. At least he wasn't dead. Given time, he'd mend.

The rib was giving him gyp. The ankle was a sprain and he'd be over it in a few days. The arm, though … he pulled back his T-shirt and peered at it.

There was writing. Writing on his arm. Writing tattooed into his skin: *We knew them as the Pleasure. They will give you everything you desire and take your freedom and your soul. Many of you will want this but in the end they will devour you. We will help you.*

Roche went to the bathroom and tried to scrub it off but it wasn't written so much as etched. He had no idea what it meant or how that shit-bastard of an alien or whatever the *fuck* it was had put it on him. Either way, it wasn't going away any time soon.

They were running the news in the service station, a single solitary television playing to an audience of empty waxed cardboard coffee cups, crumpled crisp packets and sandwich wrappers. It was all still about Docklands. Talking heads talking shit about terrorists and Muslim fundamentalists and Al Qaeda, as if Al Qaeda would have nuked a Damascus mosque. People slowly coming to terms with the notion that the world had fundamentally changed and yet, at the same time, banging on about how life would continue as it always did. Politicians on both sides saying the same. Keep calm and carry on. The spirit of the Blitz. Remember the IRA, remember 7/7. We didn't let the terrorists change us then and we won't let them change us now. Don't let them *win*. Parliament had been recalled from the summer recess until the current emergency was resolved. That was all. No need for martial law or a state of emergency. London would pick itself up. The city would come back stronger because that's what it always did.

The news bulletin ticker-tape that always scrolled across the bottom of the news these days quietly let everyone know that Parliament would also be voting to legalise Bliss later in the day. Amid the litter and detritus of passing late-night drivers, Roche shook his head,

wondering how many Westminster fat boys had the first idea what was coming.

16 July, 0200 hours, Mars

The anti-matter comet was a little under a million kilometres away from Mars, travelling with a relative velocity of around a thousand kilometres per second. Deep inside, electric currents ran through the tiny atom-thick slivers of inert frozen hydrogen that striped its insides. The hydrogen vaporised and annihilated with the surrounding positrons and anti-protons. Tiny flashes of energy broke the comet into thousands upon thousands of fragments. The pieces spread apart, all of them aimed for the Hellas basin, an ancient impact crater resulting from something about the same size striking the planet some four billion years ago.

16 July, 0220 hours, Clacket Lane Services

'Hey, Rees.' There were aliens in London. Someone was making the drug called Bliss that no one understood or could even test. He had his theories about that now, but not much evidence. He had the footage from the museum, though. That ought to be enough to wake everyone up.

'We have to go public, Rees,' he said. 'Make copies. Send it to every national newspaper. The BBC. Maybe CNN and Al Jazeera for good measure.'

Rees didn't answer. Right now he couldn't talk. He nodded though. Faintly.

'Shit, mate. You need help. I can't take you with me.' Roche took the chrome hand out of the bag and looked it over. It wasn't hollow like the finger had been. It seemed to have some sort of interface but it was like nothing he'd ever seen before. The hand had been wired into everything down there. You had to wonder how much it knew, how much of the Bliss network it had unravelled.

Not that that was any use to him now. He drank back the last dregs of his coffee.

'Give me ten more minutes, mate.'

He helped Rees out of the car and into the service station, gave him a last burner phone so he could call himself an ambulance and then drove off into the night alone.

16 July, 0317 hours, Mars

In its last moments, the *Irrational Prime* had worked out with cold mathematical precision when to allow the Shriven vault to re-open. Several higher-order dimensions peeled back on themselves and the vault phased back into existence. A fraction of an instant later, the first pieces of the comet hit the surface of Mars, scattered around a diameter of two thousand kilometres. In the normal course of things, each fragment would have punched twenty kilometres into the planet's crust, carrying with it the equivalent energy of several million hydrogen bombs. The resulting crater would have been a hundred kilometres across. It was the sort of thing that

323

happened every few tens of millions of years. The sort of thing a planet took in its stride and shrugged away.

These fragments came in thousands and were made of anti-matter. The first strikes punched straight through the Hellas Basin and vaporised everything in a thousand-kilometre radius. Shock waves started around the planet's crust, pulverising it. They started to travel into the planet's mantle but were almost instantly overtaken by more fragments which super-heated as they came through the fireball of vaporised crust and punched even further towards the planet's core. The second set of shockwaves reduced the planet's crust to so much dust and then the fireball reached critical density and the plasma of annihilating matter and anti-matter detonated with the force and brightness of a miniature supernova. For a few seconds, the Hellas basin flared brighter than the sun. Mars shattered.

16 July, 0320 hours, Camberley

Roche drove slowly past his house and kept on going. The front door was open. When he parked a street away and came in through the back, he found three dead men inside. On his bed was a small package and a note. The package, when he opened it, looked like some sort of tablet only with a bizarre socket on the back. It took him a second to realise that the socket was an exact match for the chrome hand. He plugged the two together and the tablet sprang to life. A message popped up on the screen:

Download data?

The note was somewhat more straightforward. The note simply said: 'Run.'

Outside, through the curtains, there was a light so bright that it looked like lightning but wasn't. The night sky lit up brighter than a midsummer day, the brilliant white light of Mars dying. Roche stuffed the tablet in his bag and grabbed a few things. By the time he went back to the car, the light was already fading. By the time it had gone, he was on the road again, heading west. He didn't really know where he was going.

They were coming. Whoever *they* were.

16 July, 0320 hours, VY Canis Major

The *Exponential* drifted in a close orbit around the vast bulk of the hypergiant star, flitting in and out of its outermost layers. The Weft were manoeuvring one end of a singularity bridge into place, injecting linear and angular momentum in carefully controlled doses into the exposed singularity, adding matter and bleeding it away through accelerated Hawking radiation.

The *Exponential* watched the Hive settle the singularity in place and begin to feed it. Very soon it would be ready to become a bridge across the stars.

TO BE CONTINUED … ?

Read the other side of the invasion in:
Empires: Infiltration, by Gavin Deas
Available now!

Acknowledgements

Empires grew out of conversations with my agent, Robert Dinsdale, and with Simon Spanton at Gollancz. It started with Robert's enthusiasm for shared worlds, faltered on the stones of my scepticism, and then flourished with Simon's suggestion of a way to go about it. Simon also suggested Gavin Smith as a collaborator, which pretty much me sold on the idea and was how Gavin Deas was born. So thanks go to Simon and Robert for spawning this and not minding too much when what Gavin and I wrote didn't turn out to be quite what we talked about during those first conversations.

Simon then neatly managed to pass the editing (for which read cross-checking between the two books) on to someone else, so thanks to Marcus Gipps at Gollancz who edited this and to Colin Murray for his work rearranging my words into coherent sentences.

In particular, thanks are due to Gavin 'who needs physics?' Smith, who was managing perfectly well as an SF author without some fantasy writer showing up and

throwing Maurice Broaddus books at him. Gavin put up with my impatience, a brief deviation into writing something that was starting to look like another Transformers movie, and even wrote part of a chapter for me. We learned a lot about how not to do collaborative writing and we're still talking.

ABOUT GOLLANCZ

Gollancz is the oldest SF publishing imprint in the world. Since being founded in 1927 Gollancz has continued to publish a focused selection of bestselling and award-winning authors. The front-list includes **Ben Aaronovitch**, **Joe Abercrombie**, **Charlaine Harris**, **Joanne Harris**, **Joe Hill**, **Alastair Reynolds**, **Patrick Rothfuss**, **Nalini Singh** and **Brandon Sanderson**.

As one of the largest Science Fiction and Fantasy imprints in the UK it is no surprise we have one of the most extensive backlists in the world. Find high quality SF on Gateway written by such authors as **Philip K. Dick**, **Ursula Le Guin**, **Connie Willis**, **Sir Arthur C. Clarke**, **Pat Cadigan**, **Michael Moorcock** and **George R.R. Martin**.

We also have a strand of publishing in translation, which includes French, Polish and Russian authors. Gollancz is home to more award-winning authors than any other imprint, with names including **Aliette de Bodard**, **M. John Harrison**, **Paul McAuley**, **Sarah Pinborough**, **Pierre Pevel**, **Justina Robson** and many more.

The SF Gateway
More than 3,000 classic, rare and previously
out-of-print SF novels at your fingertips.
www.sfgateway.com

The Gollancz Blog
Bringing you news from our worlds to yours. Stories,
interviews, articles and exclusive extracts just for you!
www.gollancz.co.uk

GOLLANCZ
LONDON